Contents

Introduction i

In Olden Times 1

The Eighteenth Century 5

The Nineteenth Century 16

The Twentieth Century 85

The Time In Between 165

References 183

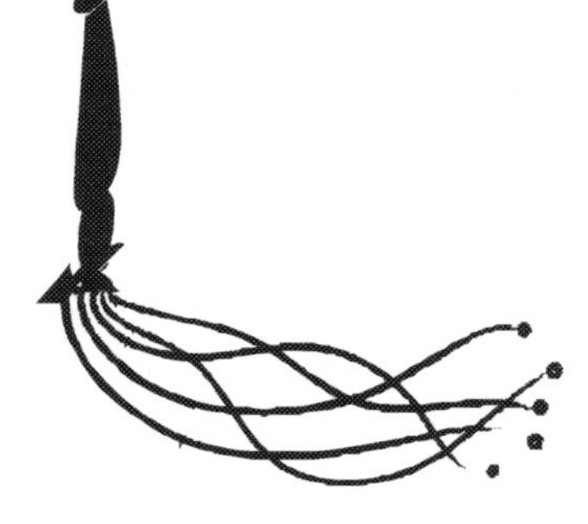

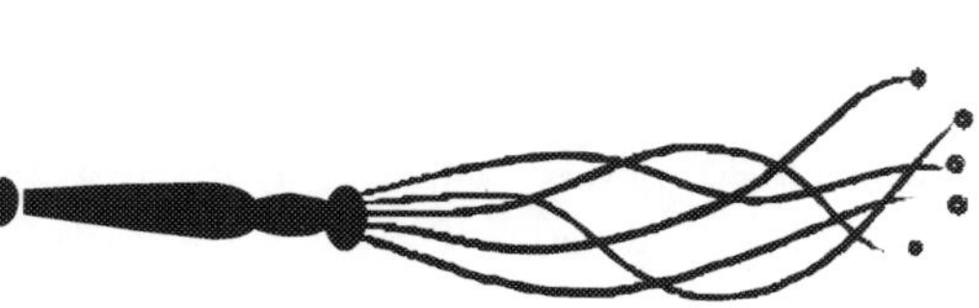

Introduction

IT IS A COMMON if slightly paranoid conception amongst some amateurs of erotic literature that if a book or other publication is obscure and hard to get hold of, then it must be good. For this reason, and no other, many works which would otherwise be consigned to the dustbin of history have been resurrected and re-published. So often has this happened, especially in recent years, that the word "Victorian" now sends a thrill of dread down the spine of true cognoscenti, for labels such as this have too often been employed to mask the otherwise unwelcome fact that a great deal of erotic literature, past as well as present, Victorian or merely cod-Victorian, or from any other period at all, is obscure and hitherto hard to get hold of simply because it is irredeemably bad. Sometimes obscurity is a well-deserved fate—one might even say a merciful one.

Erotica is a genre of fiction. Like True Romance, Westerns, Detective Novels or Science Fiction it forms a sub-species of its own: and like those other genres it has both good and bad in it. Rather more bad, perhaps, than good, since so much of erotic writing is, or was, clandestine that standards were, and are, inevitably lower—too often critical feedback or "market forces" play little or no part in the decision to publish.

Disciplinary writing is generally perceived as a sub-set of Erotica. In intent and form of presentation, it varies sharply, from factual (or apparently factual) first-person accounts with little or no obvious erotic content—sometimes decidedly unerotic, which does not prevent them having genuine disciplinary interest all the same—to obvious and deliberately sensual writing, which can appeal even to those who have no penchant for Discipline. In between are a host of variants on these two extremes. Like all other forms of erotica, and indeed all other genres of fiction, some of these works are good, a few are very good indeed, and the vast majority are either not really very good at all or downright bad.

We are sure that there are no examples of the latter groups in this book and moreover we have done our very best to ensure that the earlier categories are as well represented as we can contrive. The Alice Kerr-Sutherland Library is, as we have shown in the past, a rich archive of material of this type and over the years we have tended to concentrate on acquiring the good and the very good. That is not to say that some of the quoted passages which follow are not "better literature" than others. But, important though that is, it is not the only criterion to apply. A passage of writing that describes or otherwise illuminates an act of physical discipline may not, objectively speaking, be "well written" yet may still possess some quality that makes it notable, even meritorious. In this particular field of the human imagination all of us disagree—even if only slightly—in what we consider notable or meritorious. Our heartstrings resonate to frequencies that differ at least as often than they coincide. Nevertheless, harmonies do occur and the majority of the quoted passages will, we feel, appeal in some way to nearly all of those who are likely to read this book.

In organising the material we opted to arrange it according to "apparent period", the authentic date of publication notwithstanding. The reason is as follows. One particular curiosity of this particular sub-genre is the longstanding tradition whereby plots are very often set back in time by several generations (at least). For example, *Venus School-mistress*, published in the mid-19th century, purported to have been written towards the end of the previous century and was both written and typeset in a cunningly archaic style to reinforce the "legend". *The Rodiad* poem was not in fact written, as it is supposed to have been, by George Colman the Younger (an early nineteenth century bucolic poet), but dates from at least thirty years after his time—while the even longer poem *Squire Hardman*, also supposedly by Colman, was actually composed in the 1960s by a very clever Canadian gentleman, perhaps the greatest pasticheur of all time in this field. The body of disciplinary literature as a whole is permeated with strange twists and false attributions, pen-names, spurious sources and deliberate archaisms—nothing is quite what it seems, or at least it is best to assume that it is not. The tradition continues and today there are dozens of published works of disciplinary fiction set in earlier periods—with success directly proportionate to the author's grasp of the writing styles, idioms and everyday detail of the period he or she is attempting to recapture.

To arrange the book by author would therefore have necessitated jumping back and forth from the eighteenth century, or the sixteenth, to the twentieth, and then perhaps back again to the nineteenth by way of the twenty-first! It seemed to us that this would be irritating in the extreme, so we chose the alternative and arranged the quoted passages and poems by the era, or period, in which they are set, regardless of when they were written.

There are five of these chapters, each corresponding to an era: *In Olden Times* (From mythical times to the Age of Reason); *The Eighteenth*, *Nineteenth*, and *Twentieth Centuries*, and a final chapter called *The Time in Between* where we have placed those stories that do not belong in any particular period, or are for some reason timeless, or so phantastical that they might fairly be called futuristic. We have also supplied a General *Reference*.

The extracts are of all lengths, from single paragraphs to several pages, and of all types: every possible disciplinary configuration is represented with no overall gender preference. Many passages are moving, others humorous or at least mordant; a few are shocking, a great many are exciting and nearly all of them are stirring in some way to the amateur of disciplinary writing. Period exerts a strong influence. The Birch, for example, enjoys almost universal employment throughout the first half of the book—extract after extract features it—but by the dawn of the Twentieth Century it is fast falling into eclipse and being replaced by the cane and strap. Most of the earlier passages purport to describe real experiences—this was above all the era of the "Readers' Letters" to popular journals such as *Town Talk*, *Society* and *The Englishwoman's Domestic Magazine*, and a great deal of the letters were "true confessions" whose veracity can only be guessed at. (Some certainly ring truer than others but the reader will have to decide for him- or herself which these are.) Only after the Great War does the openly erotic theming (which all but vanishes after the Regency) make a reappearance: but as we said earlier, for many who read this book, erotic interest will have been there all the time.

We have sourced the extracts as widely as possible and would not be human if we had not included a (very) few works already published at some time by AKS Books, many of which are now out of print (if this sounds specious so be it!) At the same time many of the quoted passages are, we can vouchsafe, making their very first appearance in the English language, having been translated from both French and German specifically for this book; while many others are at least making their contextual débuts.

We have also provided a number of illustrations. One or two of these have been published in the companion volume to this, *The Art of Discipline;* and a very few more have been seen elsewhere in our publications: but the vast majority have never been published by us at any time before, so even if they are familiar to you (as some of the quoted passages will undoubtedly be), that is simply the result of the premium on quality that we described earlier.

Please enjoy the book.

THE EDITORS

July 1999

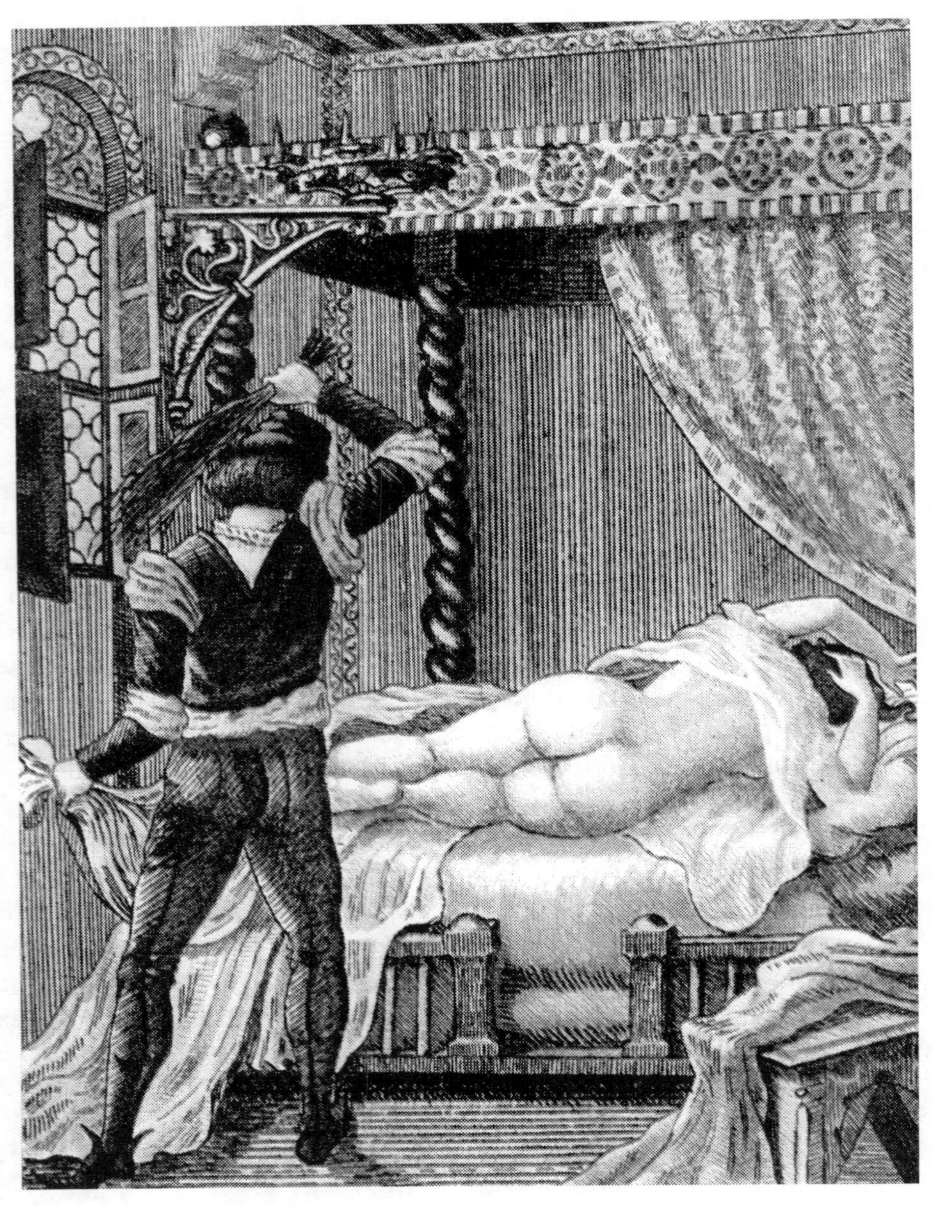

In Olden Times

1. A Legend of Venus and the Birch

Clyso, an adorable priestess of Venus, first caused the passion of flagellation to arise at Athens. She was one of the most entrancing and renowned courtesans at the epoch when the divine sculptor Praxiteles gave to the world his ideal types of marble beauty.

The story goes that an inhabitant of Creos, a village adjoining the fair city of Athens, had come into the town to sell the produce of his fields, when he chanced to meet Clyso, the delicious wanton. Straightway, he fell in love with her, and so mad was his yearning that he offered her the half of his worldly possessions for one hour in her arms. Clyso consented. He was the happiest of men.

Clyso was not only endowed with rare, surpassing beauty, but she was intellectually gifted. Being of an inquiring mind, she asked the peasant, as he shared her couch, a thousand questions relating to his homestead.

She gleaned from his frank and honest answers that the cult of Venus was completely forgotten and neglected. Few sacrifices were made on the altar of love, although Creos was inhabited by robust, healthy males; and many women, as comely as Aphrodite incarnate.

Despite their bodily vigour, these men were stirred by no violent desires when they looked upon the scarcely-veiled nudity of their wives or girlish companions. Never did the frigid village lads seek to pluck the half-open rosebuds ready to their hands.

The senses of the maidens were also dulled by this indifference and the quadruple pink petals of their secret love-blossoms slowly faded and withered, deprived as they were of the divine dew of passionate ecstasy.

Such dreadful news saddened soft-hearted Clyso. Her sole aim in life was the radiant embrace in which her soul mounted to realms of indescribable bliss. She had sworn to Venus to devote her existence to the propagation of the religion of love among mankind, so that the bodies of mortals should quiver in the giddy vortex of deep sensual joy.

She was inexpressibly grieved to learn that at Creos, men as well-proportioned as Apollo, and women equalling Aphrodite in grace and allurement could pass their time on earth without seeking to fathom the mysteries of love.

With heavy heart, away went saddened Clyso, tripping to the temple of her goddess. The fair priestess carried two trembling doves closely clasped to the tepid twin glories of her young bosom, as she prayed for help and inspiration. While the blood of the poor, white, feathered things gushed forth beneath the knife of the sacrificer, a branch fell from one of the trees of the sacred grove. As it dropped, the twig rebounded from Clyso's tiny, naked foot. It struck her white, firm flesh like a blow from the lash of a whip, but far from hurting her, seemed to vivify the whole frame of the gentle courtesan, causing her young blood to course through her veins with new and powerful ardour.

Recognising an omen of the gracious goddess, Clyso picked up the branch, and taking it with her, was absorbed in deep meditation as she wended her way homewards. Gathering all her handmaidens round her, she returned with them to Creos. But before entering the hamlet, she ordered her devoted servant lasses to cut a great quantity of branches resembling the one consecrated to Venus, furthermore telling the girls to tie them into bundles, thus forming rods. She next summoned all the inhabitants of the village to the market-place and whipped them—one after the other. The effect of this birching was magical; and new life-blood, as fierce and fiery as boiling lava, flowed in the veins of the lazy males. Their senses broke through all barriers. They threw themselves madly on their lovely wives, covering them with burning kisses; overwhelming them with the most intoxicating caresses; forcing their surprised and delighted companions to experience the most profound, sweet spasms of lustful felicity.

Clyso was happy at last, and when she went back to Athens, offered up another pair of white doves, immolating them in devout thankfulness to the beneficent goddess.

Athens was soon astir with the tidings of the miracle of Creos. There was not a Greek but who desired to taste the sweets of the love philtre sent on earth by Venus. Young or old, all men rushed to throw themselves at Clyso's feet, offering their muscular bodies to be flagellated, so that they might be strengthened and rejoiced by the divine nectar instilled through her stinging, magic rods.

The whole of Athens revelled in a splendid love-feast beneath the fire of the miraculous talisman—birchen twigs awakening desire, increasing manly vigour and causing the flame of lubricity to burn brightly in the veins. Clyso had not rods enough to lash all the writhing bodies prostrate before her, quivering impatiently to be fortified by the strokes of her bewitching birch. So her sister courtesans of Athens furnished themselves likewise with an ample store of supple green twigs. Under the aphrodisiacal influence of divine flagellation, old men acquired rejuvenescence and youths and middle-aged males found their amorous fury increased tenfold. Thus was voluptuous flagellation discovered by Clyso, and taking firm root at Athens, it gradually spread through the entire kingdom of Greece. Flourishing mightily, the worship of the rod passed into the Roman Empire, where young courtesans and harridan harlots were never without a bundle of whistling birch wherewith to invigorate their lovers and cause them to increase the force and number of their caresses, clippings, and intertwinings of soft sexual conjunction.

2. The Flagellants

When all Italy was sullied with crimes of every kind, a certain sudden superstition, hitherto unknown to the world, first seized the inhabitants of Perusa, afterwards the Romans, and then almost all the nations of Italy. To such a degree were they affected with the fear of God, that noble as well as ignoble persons, young and old, even children five years of age, would go naked about the streets without any sense of shame, walking in public two and two, in the manner of a solemn procession. Every one of them held in his hand a scourge, made of leather thongs, and with tears and groans they lashed themselves on their backs till the blood ran: all the while weeping and giving tokens of the same bitter affliction, as if they had really been spectators of the passion of our Saviour, imploring the forgiveness of God and His Mother, and praying that He, who had been appeased by the repentance of so many sinners, would not disdain theirs. And not only in the day time, but likewise during the nights, hundreds, thousands, and ten thousands of these penitents ran, notwithstanding the rigour of winter, about the streets, and in churches, with lighted wax candles in their hands, and preceded by priests, who carried crosses and banners along with them, and with humility prostrated themselves before the altars: the same scenes were to be seen in small towns and villages; so that the mountains and the fields seemed to resound alike the voice of men who were crying to God. All musical instruments and love songs ceased to be heard. The only music that prevailed both in town and country was that of the lugubrious voice of the penitent, whose mournful accents might have moved hearts of flint: and even the eyes of the obdurate sinner could not refrain from tears. Nor were women exempt from the general spirit of devotion we mention: for not only those among the common people, but also matrons and young ladies of noble families, would perform the same mortifications with modesty in their own rooms. Then those who were at enmity with one another became again friends. Usurers and robbers hastened to restore their ill-gotten riches to their right owners. Others, who were contaminated with different crimes, confessed them with humility, and renounced their vanities. Gaols were opened; prisoners were delivered; and banished persons permitted to return to their native habitations. So many and so great works of sanctity and Christian charity, in short, were then performed by both men and women, that it seemed as if an universal apprehension had seized mankind, that the divine power was preparing, either to consume them by fire, or destroy them by shaking the earth, or some other of those means which divine justice knows how to employ for avenging crimes. Such a sudden repentance, which had thus diffused itself all over Italy, and had even reached

Sir Ingoldsby's Penance

Thrice three times upon Candlemas-day,
Between Vespers and Compline, Sir Ingoldsby Bray
Shall run round the Abbey, as best he may
  Subjecting his back
  to thump and to thwack
Well and truly laid on by a bare-footed friar,
With a stout cat-o-nine tails of whipcord and wire

other countries, not only the unlearned, but wise persons also admired. They wondered whence such a vehement fervour of piety could have proceeded: especially since such public penances and ceremonies had been unheard of in former times, had not been approved by the sovereign pontiff, nor recommended by any preacher or person of eminence; but had taken their origin among simple persons, whose example both learned and unlearned had alike followed.

3. A Tudor Schoolroom

Master Stockwood opened the register and drew a deliberate line through Adam's name: at that moment it had the finality of a death sentence. Then he turned to Nicholas and commenced the homily which invariably preceded a flogging given outside Corrections, and as invariably contained promises of eternal damnation if the culprit did not mend his ways. In church, similar comminations, being spread over the whole congregation, could be disregarded: in the schoolroom, addressed to him personally, they alarmed Nicholas considerably. He tried to shut his ears and his mind; and was so far successful that he was half-taken by surprise when the birch-rod was presented for him to kiss: almost with relief he pulled himself together, knelt, and touched his lips to it.

"Untruss," said Master Stockwood, and stood up.

4. The Mistress and the Page

Frank: I have bled for your sake some twenty times a month, Some twenty drops each time; are these no services?

Imperia: I tell you, if you use me lovingly, I shall have you whipt again, most pitifully whipt, you little piece of love.

Frank: God knows I care not. So I may stand and play to you, and you kiss me as you used to kiss me, tender little side-touches of your lip's edge i' the neck.

Imperia: By my hand's hope, Which is the neck of my Lord Galeas, I'll love your beard one day; get you a beard, Frank; With such child's cheeks.

Frank: Madam, you have pleasant hands, What sweet and kissing colour goes in them, running like blood!

Imperia: Ay, child, last year in Rome I held the Pope six minutes kissing them before his eyes had grown up to my lips. Alas!

Frank: What makes you sigh still? You are now so kind; the sweetness in you stabs mine eyes with sharp tears through. I would so fain be hurt But really hurt, hurt deadly, to do good to your most sudden fancy.

Imperia: Nay, live safe, poor little red mouth. Does it love so much? I think when schooltime's off then thou wilt be no such good lover. Dost thou know, fool Frank, Thou art a sort of pleasant thing to me I would not lose for ten kings more to kiss? Poor child! I doubt I do too shamefully to make thy years my spoil thus: I am

The Schoolmistress

Ah! Luckless he, and born beneath the beam
Of evil star! it irks me whilst I write;
as erst the bard by Mulla's silver stream,
Oft, as he told of deadly dolorous plight,
sighed as he sung, and did in tears indite;
For brandishing the rod, she doth begin
To Loose the brogues, the stripling's late delight;
And down they drop; appears his dainty skin,
Fair as the furry coat of whitest ermilin…

But ah! what pen his piteous plight may trace?
Or what device his loud laments explain—
The form uncouth of his disguised face—
The pallid hue that dyes his looks amain—
The plenteous shower that doth his cheek distain?
When he, in abject wise, implores the dame,
Ne hopeth aught of sweet reprieve to gain;
Or when from high she levels well her aim,
And, through the thatch, his cries each
falling stroke proclaim.

ashamed. Would not thy mother weep, Frank, cry and curse that an Italian harlot and dyed face made out of sin should keep thee for a page, to be kissed and beaten, made so much Her humour's jesting-stock, so taught and used As I do here.

5. ANOTHER TUDOR SCHOOLROOM

"AND WHAT IS the meaning of this acting, pray, young man?" said the master in a voice that broke on Will somewhat harshly.

"I'm presenting Apollo, so please you, sir, embracing the laurel tree that the river god turned his fleeing daughter Daphne into," Will turned to him calmly and said simply, "for the boys, sir, would learn something of bright Apollo and his ways."

"Your business, young man, is to instruct them in Latin grammar, not to waste the time telling them these stories in this idle fashion," replied Pluto. "There is *nihil ad rem*—nothing to the point—young man, in these story actings of yours—"

"Nay, good sir, permit me to argue that there is *omnia ad rem*—everything to the point—in acquainting the scholars with these famous stories," Will returned roundly. "Better in sooth, is it not, to know a little of the ancients and their gods than to know but a parcel of their grammar?"

"There is a time for all things, young man," retorted Pluto curtly. "*Troja fuit*—Troy was."

"*Roma etiam fuit*—Rome also was," rallied Will sweetly. But the master ignored this sally, and after requesting Will's services to assist in a breeching that was to take place at the end of morning school at eleven, returned to his end of the room.

As for young Will, he dutifully filled in the intervening time, of some twenty minutes, by soberly leading his form back, much to their regret, to the formation of diminutives, and then on being summoned by a higher scholar (or senior boy), he walked firmly, though with wide-awake eyes, to the master's end of the room, where he found the culprit, a sturdy boy of fifteen or more with a deal of coarse, curly hair and bold but coarsish features, whose offence was the gross one of persisting in making uncouth noises in school, already standing out by a short form that had been placed in front of the master's class, and in the process of being untrussed by a couple more higher scholars.

On the process being completed, and the said boy being laid over the form with his buttocks bare, Will astonished everybody, including the master himself, by bursting with gusto into an uncommon queer speech after this fashion.

"I herewith pronounce a sweet union between the noble House of Breech and the noble House of Birch," he began, pointing prettily, first at the boy's robust bottom, and then at the heavy birch that the master already held in his hand, "and may much lasting good spring therefrom. May this erring scholar, through the ensuing blows to be inflicted upon his good breech, be made more wise in his behaviour, henceforward, and more diligent in his studies, and may the good birch be blessed for the zealous work that it is now called upon to perform, for in sooth the double benefit of school and scholar. Long truly may King Rod remain the bulwark of this blessed realm!"

The boys of the master's class had sat quite open-mouthed in surprise, some of them at least, at this jesting little speech, and one or two of course had been unable to suppress a titter, and Pluto himself had stood there frowning and looking decidedly perplexed, but he now signed to Will, who the while had been standing in a somewhat theatrical attitude over the untrussed boy, to catch hold of the boy's hands, and himself prepared to proceed to business, the two higher scholars who had untrussed the boy having hold of him by his feet, and the one who had summoned Will to this having hold of the boy by his hair.

The birch, let it be said, was a really formidable weapon, being quite twice the size of the average birch of our day, and made up of the savagest-looking twigs, and the punishment was quite ruthless, the master standing right over his victim in a most thorough fashion and laying it on with proper zeal. As for the boy, he writhed and struggled away in the grip of his holders, and gave a frantic bellow at every stroke, it apparently being no point of pride with Elizabethan schoolboys to take their whippings without giving vent to their feelings. But Pluto, presumably used to these noisy displays, showed no sign of relenting and beat on with dutiful vigour, and Will, not moved either by the boy's outcries, kept a firm hold of the bellower's sweating hands, and as for the main body of boys, who could all plainly hear if they could not all see the birching in progress, they greeted the victim's bellows with a buzz of mocking merriment. ❋

The Eighteenth Century

1. CATHERINE THE GREAT

CATHERINE II WAS an adept in the use of the Rod, and once had one of her maids of honour punished with the birch for telling a secret. This maid of honour had been her mistress' confidante in one of those numerous love intrigues with which Catherine amused her royal fancy. The maid was at the time engaged to be married, and could not keep a certain secret from her lover. Accordingly she communicated to him the particulars of her royal mistress' *affaire du cœur*, but unfortunately neglected to caution him not to tell it; and, as a matter of course, it was a secret no longer—indeed, it very soon came to the ears of the Empress. Catherine knew very well that the scandal could only have one source, and affecting to take no notice of it, helped on most zealously the marriage of the lady. On the day the young couple were united, and after they had retired to the nuptial chamber, the Empress sent six women (or rather, as is said, six men dressed as women) to the room, and having demanded admittance in the name of the Queen, "hoisted "the bride, and inflicted upon her a very severe flagellation with rods, the husband being compelled to witness the ceremony on his knees. At the conclusion of the chastisement, the culprit was politely informed that a repetition of the offence would send her to Siberia.

This royal lady did not disdain personally to handle the Rod—in fact, whipping was a pastime, or rather a passion, with her. She whipped her housemaids, dressers, and footmen, when she was ennuyée, with the greatest possible gusto: the maids being horsed on the backs of the footmen, and the footmen in their turn being hoisted on the backs of the maids. The Empress used also, by way of pastime, to bestow elegant flagellation on her ladies of honour. She compelled some of them, it is said, to dress themselves as children, and to act as if they were children; and then, pretending to be their mamma, she chastised them in truly maternal fashion! At times she acted as governess, and ordering her maids of honour to learn impossible lessons, she whipt them for not being perfect. It is related that she carried this craze so far, that the ladies had to come to school in one of the grand saloons of the Winter Palace ready for the Rod—that is with their dresses so adjusted that the Empress could whip them at once. Her Majesty would sometimes personate a Roman lady surrounded with slaves, whom she either whipt herself or caused to whip each other—

THE BIRCH TREE

A TREE there is, such was Apollo's will,
That grows uncultured on the Muses' Hill,
Its type in heaven the blest immortals know,
There called the Tree of Science, birch below.
These characters observed, thy guide shall be,
Unerring guide to the mysterious tree.
Smooth like its kindred poplar, to the skies
The trunk ascends, and quivering branches rise:
By teeming seeds it propagates its kind,
And with the year renew'd it casts the rind;
Pierc'd by the matron's hand, her bowl it fills,
Scarce yielding to the vine's nectareous rills.
Of this select, full in the moon's eclipse,
Of equal size thrice three coeval slips,
Around the osier's flexile band entwine,
And all their force in strictest union join.
Each muse shall o'er her favourite twig preside;
Sacred to Phoebus let their band be tied:
With this, when sloth and negligence provoke,
Thrice let thy vengeful arm impress the stroke,
Then shalt thou hear loud clamours rend the breast
—Attentive hear, and let the sound be blest:
So when the priestess at the Delphic shrine
Roar'd loud, the listening votary hail'd the sign.

indeed, there was no end to her eccentricities. She would visit incognito certain noble families, and insist upon the grown-up young ladies being severely birched for some real or fancied misdemeanour, and would not disdain at times to administer a chastisement with her own royal hand.

2. AN 18TH CENTURY GIRLS' SEMINARY

THERESE: I CAN'T get over my astonishment. Who could imagine in a house like this one, such follies, such debauchery?

AUGUSTE: Debauchery, perhaps, but… what harm is there in it? Not the slightest. On the contrary. This way we love one another and we have a lot of fun without anyone knowing anything about it, moreover, these frolics keep us in good humour and prevent us from feeling bored and under restraint.

THERESE: Doesn't it also prevent your feeling ashamed to show your posterior and being afraid of a real whipping?

AUGUSTE: A real whipping… from our convert Sisters?

THERESE: Yes.

AUGUSTE: They use real birch rods. But we send them all our money beforehand, so that la Giron lifts our skirts only half way up. A corner of the skirt always hangs down, and as we bend our backs we draw back our behinds and shake and shake and shake the cloth so that la Taupin whips the skirts and the Mother really imagines we are being whipped on the buttocks. I did not have that opportunity last Sunday when the Mother herself was holding me and lifted my skirt as she pleased. That little rascal Monique will tell you about it for she was peeping through the keyhole. I shall get back at her. At any rate the Mother did not hurt me greatly, and if she had hurt me, I would continue to love her just the same.

3. MADAME DODO

LAST WEEK A stranger called upon me at about nine in the evening and demanded, "Madame Dodo, are you a woman of rituals?" "At your service," I said, not quite understanding him. "You must," he then continued, "permit me to bandage your eyes and come with me in all confidence. You shall be handsomely rewarded." I agreed to everything and taking along my paraphernalia, we got into a carriage which was waiting for us. He closed the wooden shutters and we rode round and round until I lost all sense of direction. Finally we arrived at a little door which was obviously a rear entrance, went through a courtyard, climbed some steps, and then walked over parquet floors through several rooms in which I heard not a sound.

Suddenly, my bandages were removed and I found myself in the middle of a beautiful, gilded and well lighted room. I must admit I was astonished at what I saw there. A man and a woman, apparently his mistress, were sitting at one end of the room near each other. What made it so odd was the man, none too young, was dressed in a child's coat of a pinkish colour and a bonnet of the same style. The woman was tall with large, dark and fiery eyes. Her hair was the colour of ink with pearl strands and flowers running through it. She wore a foreign dress of cerise taffeta with golden spangles. From her exotic beauty and the weirdness of her head dress, one might almost have imagined her to be the Sultana of Constantinople. I sat down quietly without saying a word, for a moment not having the slightest idea of how to address them. Both got up. The man spoke first, assuming a childish and lisping voice. "Good day," he said. "Good day, nurse, good day!" I saw my part at once. "Yes, my children," I replied. "Here I am. And how are you today." "Really, nurse," he exclaimed, "you did well to come and keep Rosette quiet." "Nurse," cut in the lady, quickly, "Johnny is at fault, not I." "Nurse," he continued, "because she is taller than I she steals all the cookies and the jam tarts from me." "Nurse," denied Rosette, "he always wants me to tickle his little peter and to take hold of my pussy. He says it will give us milk with which to stick our lessons together." I listened to all this as serious as a bishop; it is fatal to laugh. I made the little boy approach me in the centre of the room. "Little rascal," I said, "come nearer. What have you done with all your money and who has eaten up my jam?" "He, nurse," exclaimed Rosette. "He ate the nut jam." "Over here," I said, "in this little corner." He followed me as though ready to weep, into the space between the bed and the wall. I made him kneel and took off his breeches. Under my apron I had two stout birch rods, one of which I laid on the bed. With the other, after I had lifted his coat and listened to him say the most amusing things, I gave him a dozen strong blows. "Nurse, oh nurse," exclaimed the lady who was on the other side and could not see very well, "if you do not spank Johnny before everyone in the middle of the room, it won't do." I guessed what she wanted, made him get up and after placing him in the middle of the room I said to the lady, "Come on, now!" She came over at once. "Little girl," I demanded, "why did you not mind the shop when I went to market? A jug of cream I left has disappeared." "She drank it up!" said the would-be boy. "Yes, I did it," she answered with an air of spite. "Oh, so it was you," I answered, Then I seized her and pushed her against the bed where she fell prone. I lifted her underskirt and chemise and uncovered her solid and dark buttocks. I gathered from her wriggling movements as well as from her exclamations what she wanted and gave her the most vigorous whipping imaginable. Then I placed the gentleman in the same posture near her and gave it to him with all my strength. This done, they both went into the bed, pulling the curtains. I left them, but returned presently and was paid handsomely. The retainer drove me home with the same precautions and I have not seen them since nor discovered in which quarter they lived.

4. A Charity School

The great event of the day was what we called "punishment hour," which was from four till five in the afternoon, when the ladies attended in person when they were at Saltire, bringing their friends with them to inspect the school. We used to regard that hour with very

Enigma

YE doughty physicalls attend to my lure,
For I'm grown famous for many a cure,
And in reason and justice deserve more regard
Than the greatest performance of Taylor or Ward.
I'm as old a prescription as any on earth,
And Solomon often does speak of my worth;
And still I continue with the greatest success,
If with skill and discretion I'm used, you'll confess.
I'm known for dispelling the fumes in the head,
For correcting the humours,
and sweet'ning the blood;
For refining the intellect, clearing the brain,
With a long roll of maladies all in a train.
I'm an excellent cure, and a remedy tried
But observe, I must always be outward applied.
I sometimes by sweating my virtues impart,
But bleeding's the top and the chief of my art.
Nay, once on a time I have bled a great prince,
And he—I much thank him—has
remembered me since.
I could name you a doctor—in peace
may he rest—
Stands famous on record for service confest,
Who by my assistance did more good I know,
Than all the physicians for ages ago—
Whose skill in his art was never disputed
And neither a quack nor an upstart reputed.
There are constitutions and tempers I own,
That are to be modelled or mended by none;
Those soon I give over, because 'tis in vain
To strive where the cure will not answer the pain.
But to make all your labours to prosper and thrive,
Apply me betimes, is the caution I give,
And then in all likelihood you'll find some relief
Against the most stubborn and obstinate grief.

mingled feelings. Sometimes—especially when they had gentleman visitors living with them—they would come in good temper, and with pleasant faces; sometimes they would be very cross, and ready to vent upon us all the annoyances they might have met with at home.

There was a great contrast between the two ladies. The Lady Marjory was fat and sleepy-looking, like her father, with fair hair and blue eyes, that seemed as though they could not flash; and the Lady Maria was slight and dark, with eyes like a hawk, the picture of her mother in features as well as temper. Both ladies had copied the French mode of dressing from their cousin, and used to come to the school daily in toilets that were to our eyes like the draperies in a fairy tale. Their feathers and flowers, their sparkling jewellery, and the huge scented fans they carried, were subjects of daily and hourly admiration amongst us.

All the bad marks against any girl or boy were laid before their ladyships, who would appoint the punishments and see them carried out—the Lady Maria and her cousin, Mdlle. Burgoyne from Paris, who was staying at the castle, wielding the rod with much grace and dignity. Lady Marjory used to bring her mother's maid with her to do the whipping, taking her to task severely for the awkward manner in which she sometimes managed the business. I remember, one afternoon, very well her giving the girl two or three sharp cuts with the rod before us all for not administering punishment in a sufficiently smart manner.

We were all mustered in school, and among the long list of black marks against many of us there were three to one girl who was a great trouble to the teachers. There was a laundry mark, a talking mark, and a mark for "want of respect to my lady": any omission of the ceremonies of duly curtseying to, or saluting, our teachers was called by that name: the school belonging to her, we were considered to have insulted her personally. For the laundry mark, she was to have six stripes of the rod, and stand with the spoiled caps pinned about her on the stool; for the second offence she was not to speak or be spoken to, except in school hours, for a week; and, for the third, she was to be "well whipped." Lady Marjory wrote these down on a piece of paper, for it was her day, and gave them to the governess, who read them aloud; and Lady Maria and her cousin smiled, and said it was only proper punishment.

Mdlle. Burgoyne would like to have taken some of the whipping into her own hands, being just fresh from a French school, with the full remembrance of her own experiences in her mind, but the ladies would not give up their privileges, and she had to be content with offering some suggestions, for which we did not thank her.

It was at her prompting that a slender whalebone rod was substituted for the old-fashioned birch, which, though it looked more formidable, did not hurt half so much, nor leave such weals upon one's skin. She was the pink of fashion, this young lady, and used perfectly to bewilder us with the elegance of her attire. She would come to the school in the most elegant brocade sacques over satin petticoats, with beautiful high-heeled satin shoes and clogs, and her hair dressed so that her head looked as large as a peck measure.

But I am digressing from my story of how Lady Marjory whipped Joan in the school. Betty Brown, the girl to be whipped, was ordered to stand out, which she did, looking very shamefaced. She was a big, tall girl in appearance, far more robust than either the Lady Maria or her cousin. She was going to be still-room maid at Lord Royston's, a fine house in the next county, for she was a clever girl, though careless and troublesome at times.

Betty stood before the party, till Miss Thomas, the schoolmistress, rose, and curtseying, read out the punishment. "Betty Brown will fetch the rod," my lady said; and the girl went, colouring crimson, and ready to cry. When she came back, she knelt, and presented it, as was the fashion, and then Mademoiselle said sharply—"Kiss it." That was one of the new notions she had brought from France, and we didn't like it—we never had to do it before she came.

Betty kissed it, looking dreadfully terrified while she was prepared for flogging. Joan stripped her, and she was made to fold up her clothes, one by one, as though she were going to bed, while we all sat in our places looking on, not allowed to move or speak. When she stood ready for the rod, the bell was rung for the dairy-woman—a great, stout person, who had the enviable task of horsing us when we were birched.

Joan tucked up her sleeves and receiving the rod from the Lady Marjory with a profound curtsey, prepared for business. But Betty was not going to be flogged without opposition: she was a big, strong girl, and it took a good many pairs of hands to get her fairly established on Dorothy's back, who did not like her office at all.

Once there, and the girl's hands pinioned by her brawny arms, there was little chance of the culprit escaping, however she might kick, for Dorothy was as strong as a man, and it was currently reported that she smacked her liege lord in the privacy of her own home.

"Hold that girl's feet," was Lady Marjory's next order, "or Joan will never be able to get at her."

So Miss Thomas made the feet fast, and then Joan began. The dreaded rod fell swiftly and surely on the white flesh, raising red weals in all directions. If Joan was clumsy, she was energetic, and Betty Brown roared and wrestled under the operation most lustily; but, for all that, the performance did not please the three ladies.

"What a clumsy creature!" said Mademoiselle; "she hasn't an atom of grace."

"Marjory should do it herself," said Lady Maria. "One can't expect everything from servants."

"I hate such violent exercise," said her sister; and then, turning to Joan, "You clumsy, awkward creature, you! Have I not shewn you how to use the rod a hundred times? Has not my mother shewn you?"

"Yes, and made me feel it, too," said the girl, sulkily; "the brat kicks so, there's no doing anything properly."

Lady Marjory had risen from her seat, and come nearer to the girl and her punisher as she spoke; and whether by accident or design did not appear, but Joan, in raising her arm to give an effective blow, happened to touch her ladyship's face. My lady forgot that she didn't like exercise then; she snatched the rod from her servant's hand, and posing herself in an attitude, commenced heartily lashing the astonished girl on her arms and neck, and wherever she could get an opportunity to hit her. For a minute Joan was too astonished to resist; but when she recovered her scattered wits, she rushed round the room, with the lady in full pursuit, leaving Betty Brown shivering and smarting on her uncomfortable elevation.

The ladies not only whipped us, but they whipped the boys too, at least the Lady Maria and her French cousin did. Lady Marjory had scruples of modesty about it, and declined.

Mademoiselle Burgoyne introduced a good many new customs into our school. Before she came, the whipping used to be entirely optional, and the ladies used to whip with short, sharp blows, without any method; but she recommended the French fashion of long, regular, sharp blows, counted and applied in a measured manner; so that, when we were sentenced to a whipping, we knelt and said, "May it please your ladyship to give me so many blows on account of my great fault;" and when we returned the rod, the formula was—"I thank your ladyship humbly for the whipping I have received;" and we had to say it without any sobbing or stuttering either.

Another Birch Tree

Though the Oak be the prince and the pride
of the grove,
The emblem of power, and the fav'rite of Jove:
Though Phoebus her temples with Laurel has
bound,
And with chaplets of Poplar Alcides is crowned:
Though Pallas the Argive has graced with her
choice,
And old mother Cybel in Hades may rejoice:
Yet the Muses declare—after diligent search—
That no tree can be found to compare with the
Birch.
The Birch, they affirm, is the true tree of knowledge:
Revered at each school, and remembered at college.
Though Virgil's famed tree might produce, as its
fruit,
A crop of vain dreams and strange whims
on each shoot,
Yet the Birch, on each bough, on the top
of each switch,
Bears the essence of grammar and the eight
parts of speech.
'Mongst the leaves are concealed more than memory
can mention—
Full cases, all genders, all forms of declension.
Nine branches, when cropp'd by the hands of the
nine,
And duly arranged in a parallel line;
Tied up in nine folds of a mystical string,
And soak'd for nine days in cold Helicon spring
Form a sceptre composed for a pedagogue's hand,
Like the Fasces of Rome, a true badge of command.
The sceptre thus finish'd, like Moses's rod,
From flints could draw tears, and give life to a clod.
Should darkness Egyptian, or ignorance, spread
Their clouds o'er the mind or envelope the head,
The Rod, thrice applied, puts the darkness to flight,
disperses the clouds, and restores us to light:
Like the Virga Divinita 'twill find out the vein
Where lurks the rich metal, the ore of the brain.
Should Genius, a captive in sloth, be confined,
Or the witchcraft of pleasure prevail o'er the mind,
The magical wand but apply—with a stroke
The spell is dissolved, the enchantment is broke.
Like Hermes's Caduceus, these switches inspire
Rhetorical thunder, poetical fire:
And if Morpheus our temples in Lethe should steep,
Their touch will untie all the fetters of sleep.
Here dwells strong conviction—of logic the glory,
When applied with precision a posteriori.
I've known a short lecture most strangely prevail
When duly conveyed to the head through the tail:
Like an electrical shock in an instant 'tis spread,
And flies with a jerk, from the tail to the head:
Promotes circulation, and thrills through each vein,
The faculties quicken, and purges the brain.
By sympathy thus, and consent of the parts,
We are taught, fundamentally, classics and arts,
The Birch, á priori, applied to the palm,
Can settle disputes and a passion becalm.
Whatever disorders prevail in the blood
The Birch can correct them, like guaiacum wood:
It sweetens the juices, corrects our ill humours,
Bad habits removes, and disperses foul tumours.
When applied to the hand, it can cure with a switch,
Like the salve of old Molyneux, used in the itch!
As the famed rod of Circe to brutes could turn men
So the twigs of the Birch can unbrute them again.
Like the wand of the Sybil, that branch of pure gold
These sprays can the gates of Elysium unfold—
The Elysium of learning, where pleasures abound,
Those sweets that still flourish on classical ground.
Prometheus's rod, which mythologists say
Fetched fire from the sun to give life to his clay,
Was a rod well applied, his men to inspire
With a taste for the arts and the genius to fire.
This bundle of rods may suggest one reflection—
That the arts with each other maintain a connexion.
Another good moral this bundle of switches
Points out to our notice, and silently teaches—
Of peace and good fellowship these are a token,
For the twigs, well united, can scarcely be broken.
Then if such are its virtues, we bow to the tree,
And The Birch, like the Muses, immortal shall be.

She was a regular Tartar, that young French lady; any one fonder of using the rod I never did see. After a whipping at school, we had to carry the rod fastened upright on our backs the most of the day, no matter who came to see the school, or where we went, and I have been sent with a message to my lady with the rod at my back before now.

5. MRS EDEN

MRS. EDEN WAS brought up in a convent. Her parents were Roman Catholics, and having no daughter but her, they were desirous of bestowing upon her every accomplishment, and foolishly imagined a convent education far superior to any this country could boast of. There she lived till she had attained her five-and-twentieth year, at which time her father died, and she found herself in possession of twenty-five thousand pounds.

At the importunities of a fond mother, who went to see her once every year, she visited England, and being a girl of good fortune it is not to be wondered at that she had a crowd of admirers. In her visits, she was very much taken with that part of a widower's family, that in general is found most disagreeable, at least to young ladies—I mean his children. She observed they were indulged by a weak father in everything, and were consequently very disobedient and unruly. Upon this gentleman she fixed her affections, and being a woman of ungovernable spirit, she was happy to find him an easy pusillanimous creature.

The match was scarcely mentioned when it was concluded, and in a few days after, she found herself in the seat of empire in his house. She had six little subjects to govern, three of whom were then at school in Herefordshire, who were instantly ordered home, as she said she would undertake to finish their education, which indeed was in her power, for she was a very sensible woman; but that was not her intent altogether. It was the boys that were ordered from school, who seemed very happy in leaving a place so irksome to youth in general; but they had only exchanged a male for a female flagellator.

As soon as she was married she discharged all the servants, and hired a set of her own choosing, and she took care to engage a French lady as her own woman, whose disposition she knew would just suit her. Mrs. Eden was of the first order of beauty, had a noble person, fine-turned limbs, good skin, fine blue eyes, and when not ruffled by passion, was certainly very captivating. If she had stepped across the room she discovered uncommon dignity and elegance, and every motion expressed that *Je ne sais quoi* an elegant French woman is so idolised for.

Though this whipping passion was inextinguishable within her, yet she was never observed to take the rod in hand without some offence to occasion it. She was convinced where there was such a number of children, and they ungovernable, many bickerings would arise, which would give her an opportunity to amuse herself with the rod. The first that gave her occasion to handle the rod was a boy of seventeen years old, who was so stupid at a lesson she gave him, that she was resolved to try the effects of birching. Her French woman was ordered to bring an excellent rod, which she had no sooner done, than she proceeded to exercise it; but she found the boy too strong for her.

The maid, with the assistance of her mistress, tied his hands behind him, and then they found him manageable enough, and the woman holding his legs, his step-mother whipped him till the twigs flew about the room. This was the first sample of her severity with the rod, and it made such an impression on the rest of the children that they trembled in her presence. A few hours after the boy was complaining of her treatment, to his elder sister, who advised him to burn the rod the first opportunity. This was overheard by the maid, who warned her lady of the affair. The young lady was summoned to the parlour, where she denied the fact, was confronted by the maid and well whipped.

6. THEATRE OF DECADENCE

THE THEATRE DES Deux Mains was a bijou little playhouse which breathed an elegance altogether Regency. Not more than ninety feet by sixty, its proportions were exquisite. The walls were spaced out by panels picturing the gilded shapes of amorous cupidons and caryatides, between which hung portières of dusty-yellow Utrecht velvet embellished with loops, tassels, fleurons and formalised heraldic figures; the ceiling, softly domed and figured with wreaths and curlicues of creamy plaster, was a little low.

Everything was arranged in the most intimate way, for the pit had been suppressed altogether. and behind the single row of stalls began the boxes and loges, each able to hold four or five persons.

Although the floor sloped down to a minuscule orchestra pit maintaining the classical separation of audience and actors, the stage was so close as to give you the impression of being a part of what was going on; and in fact, when Venus and her party slipped in during the entr'acte, the audience was still deeply moved. The lights were only half up, and everywhere was a buzz of comment and criticism, expressions of appreciation, ejaculations from behind masks, smiling retorts and suggestive grimaces. The occupants of some of the boxes had even drawn the curtains, from behind which came the sound of slaps and smothered laughter.

Tannhauser was delighted with everything, especially with the box-openers; for here, instead of the grumpy old women to whom the playgoer has become used—though not, I dare say, reconciled—were a dozen or so beautiful young creatures in plum-coloured jackets and yellow tapering trousers that strapped under the instep and fitted smoothly across their behinds; their build, their delicate features, and the short ringlets that played around their shoulders left their sex a matter of doubt; but this ambiguity, de la Pine explained in a whisper, was matched by their readiness to sustain the role of either.

Then the lights went down, the music began, and the curtains rose on the second of the two acts, discovering the interior of an orphanage where a dozen or more ravishing children, dressed in an old-fashioned and modest manner, were performing a graceful gavotte. Circling, dividing, forming and re-forming in intricate patterns and arabesques, they engrossed the stage with a charming collective movement, making quaint erotic gestures and accompanying their dance with the sweet treble of a cheerful little song. Soon the fun became more lively and more risqué, the couples detaching themselves for a few minutes in the centre of the stage to execute some really naughty pantomime, while the others clapped their hands in time, beat their little slippers on the floor, and laughed in a simple, wordless cascade of melody which was tossed to and fro, from the boys to the girls and back again, with infinite varieties of expression and cadence.

But all at once there was a roll of drums, the lights on the stage changed to a deep rose, and a drop-curtain swept aside, revealing two statuesque female figures in long white gowns, who had been watching. A wild arpeggio from the harp, like the susurrus of an autumn wind, succeeded, and the chorus of children, wailing, shrank back in a calculated disarray towards the wings; then the Matrons advanced slowly, to a solemn, throbbing pizzicato of bass viols.

Their appearance was truly wonderful. With faces painted dead white, mounting false chins and noses which almost met over tiny mouths, their foreheads graced with rows of curls like inverted question marks, and wearing enormous mob-caps which quivered and swayed on their heads, they moved slowly upstage, nodding portentously and making gestures of outrage. A round of applause greeted them, for these were Mrs. Bowyer and Mrs. Barker.

And now the former took a striking attitude, the harp sounded a few notes, and she delivered a glorious recitative, her majestic contralto filling the theatre as she expressed her indignation and horror, her well-nigh disbelief in the testimony of her eyes, while she clasped her hands, raised them in the air and dropped them to her sides, rolling her eyes and shaking her head; an occasional interpolation from Mrs. Barker's golden soprano cut across her words, and then the two voices joined in a sombre and stirring duet in which execrations were mingled with promises of punishment and invocations of the spirit of birch.

The duet ended with three long notes in alt, uttered by the Matrons in unison. This was the call to the servants, and as the applause of the audience reached its climax four strapping girls carrying rods rushed on the stage. Now, the orchestra struck up a jolly bourrée, to whose accented rhythm was executed a short and lively bacchanale, the orphans retreating and fleeing, the servant girls pursuing, grasping, and losing; cries of alarm, triumph, and vexation mingled with the invigorating music, the dance became a wild rout of flying forms, a whirling kaleidoscope of smock and sash, of bare limb and lacy pantalette, from which at last two of the serving wenches emerged, each with an orphan securely horsed on her back, and the music ceased with a plangent crash of cymbals.

To the sounds of an exquisite solo by the premier violin, the two captives, a boy and a girl, were now lovingly and ceremoniously untrussed. Ah, what a delightful operation this was! What ravishing contours were exposed, what quiverings, what tremblings and trepidations, what rosy reluctancies, as the plump fesses emerged and the two dear children were prepared for the neat birch rods in the hands of Bowyer and Barker!

Then all was quiet; the tableau arranged itself, each captive flanked by Matron and domestic, the remaining children creeping close as at the bidding of fear and fascination, and Mrs. Barker, her rod upraised, began to deliver a thrilling lecture full of the old-fashioned phrases of nursery eloquence. By degrees her emotion mounted, as if like a Homeric hero she were exciting herself by her own threats and vauntings; her voice rose, throbbing and fulminating in sombre crescendi, her arm gesturing with motions ever more purposeful, until at last, as a superb and stately period rolled to its close, the twigs descended with a rich and urgent hiss, and the flagellation commenced to a softly resumed music.

Tannhauser, already blushing with pleasure, followed everything eagerly, loving the strokes that fell so roundly, admiring the art with which the voices of fesseuse and fessé blended, this one rising, that falling, in a chromatic progression that decorated in obbligato the gentle but insistent beat of the bolero whispered by drums and muted strings. Now, the birch seemed to dominate all the sounds and movements, as if it, and not the conductor's baton were leading the music, evoking the cries of distress and satisfaction, and directing the reedlike swaying of the chorus from side to side and the leaps and bounds of the disciplined urchin. The Chevalier found himself beating time with the toe of his slipper.

Then the music and cries increased in volume as flutes and oboes joined in, echoing and mingling and competing with the singers, and all at once two other voices added themselves, as Mrs. Bowyer began to thrash the other culprit; and now the rhythms multiplied themselves in ingenious counterbeats and syncopations, notes short and long were exchanged like the repartees of a fugue, and at last, as agonised trills, roulades and fiorituri poured from the two children, the stirring quartet came to an end its final strains engulfed by roars and bravos from the audience of deboshed cognoscenti. Fresh melodies and fresh victims succeeded rapidly. The plot became confused, the story lost itself, the incidents grew more outrageous, as birch rods were supplanted by long, supple canes, these by limber straps, and these in turn by many-tongued martinets. At length, when matters had apparently reached some kind of crisis, there were only the Matrons, the four servants, and a beautiful youth, quite nude, occupying the stage. Forming a circle around him, they drove him to and fro between them with blows of their martinets, laughing silverly, until after a minute or two the boy sank down in an exquisite pose, quite motionless. The lights began to dim, Mrs. Bowyer made a sign with her hand, and in the hush the domestics let down a scale from the proscenium, fastened the youth's wrists to it, and drew him up on tiptoe. The stage was utterly dark for a moment; then a clear rosy light illuminated the three principals, and one saw the two Matrons were armed with long, supple whips.

The audience was tense and silent; Tannhauser himself felt his breath quickening as the blows began to fall. For now make-believe had turned to reality! He reached for the hand of Venus, which squeezed his in moist sympathy, as they both stared at the stage, hearing now the veritable sounds of punishment and the true accents of pain. The youth's body shook, twisted and trembled, his feet danced and kicked, the two whips sang in alternation, and piercing cries filled the little theatre, pleas for mercy, prayers for forgiveness, promises of amendment, all alike met by the Matrons' measured replies, calm and judicial, full of ironical sympathy and encouragement, a suave, antiphonal rhetoric made deliciously paradoxical by the steady accompaniment running beneath it, the repeated whistle and report of whipcord on flesh. "Oddsfish," said Cosme in a whisper, "'tis artistry with a vengeance, that throws art to the winds." De la Pine nodded, smiling and rubbing his hands. There was wild applause as the representation came to an end and the fainting youth hung limply in his bonds. Then, as the lights went up and the two Flagellantes advanced to the footlights, hand in hand, bowing, they were greeted by cries of "Unmask, unmask!"—and the next moment, when they twitched off their comic vizards, Tannhauser saw the two old frights replaced by a pair of handsome, smiling women who at once began to ogle the unattached gentlemen in the side-boxes. Bouquets were thrown from several directions; they were received with bows and courtesies by the divas, who held them to their breasts and then, smiling archly, held up the little notes concealed in them, blowing kisses and flourishing their whips playfully at the admirers they had made. ●

The Nineteenth Century

1. BLUECOAT BOYS

WHEN A BOY I was educated at Christ's Hospital, and I assure you the birch was not neglected there, and generally with beneficial effects. The punishment was sometimes inflicted privately, but when the offence was serious, due publicity was given it. The offender after supper was made to stand opposite the Warden's desk, and hold the instrument of torture in his hand (it being customary for punishments to be doled out after that meal). When the boys had retired (with the exception of the ward to which the delinquent belonged, who were ordered to remain in their seats), two of the school porters were summoned, and the offender was told to prepare himself. He was then hoisted on the back of one of the porters, when the other with great deliberation proceeded to remove all unnecessary clothing by tucking the inner garment beneath the back of his coat, and after having measured his distance, commenced the punishment, always allowing a little time between each stroke, so as to give them due effect. The offender having received the allotted number was let down, and after finishing his toilet was allowed to retire with his schoolfellows, who generally condoled with him if he bore it well. After once receiving a punishment of this kind it seldom required to be repeated. But it would be a good thing if schoolmasters, guardians, and parents, would study the characters of the children committed to their charge, as they would soon ascertain what punishments would be most effectual. I am convinced that flogging does not suit every case, though it might be effectual in extreme ones; but I think it is a great mistake to suppose that that is the only punishment that ought to be inflicted, as in some cases a word would be more effectual, especially with sensitive children. I am surprised that girls should require such correction, but I am acquainted with one or two to whom a good wholesome flogging would indeed be a great boon both to themselves and their parents.

2. A REGENCY SCHOOLGIRL LEARNS NEW SKILLS

THE UNHAPPY CHRISTABEL passed that evening away from the public eye, in the large, rather cold room that doubled as a sanatorium (when girls were ill), and as an isolation wing for girls awaiting or undergoing punishment. Her diet during this miserable few hours was simple bread and water—what else should we expect?—and she spent most of the time putting together two birch-rods from the vast pile of green twigs she had gathered that afternoon. Miss Newton was again on hand, to instruct in the manner in which rods ought to be made, and to chill the blood in other ways. Unlike Suzette Mansonard, who had thought that ten withes was the correct number, Agnes Crawfurd considered that the ideal total of contributory switches lay somewhere between seven and nine, inclusively, and that the final choice should be made on purely æsthetic grounds, though this was not quite how she had put it when explaining her philosophy to Miss Newton, who of course passed the substance of her requirements on to Miss De Vere.

"Start by assembling the correct number of birch twigs, then arrange them so that the tips can be pulled together into a single mass," she instructed the shivering Christabel. This operation left the thick ends of the withes—which were naturally of unequal length—in an untidy condition, but Miss Newton was equal to this and produced, from her capacious apron pocket, a pair of sharp secateurs with which to trim the base ends of the rod so that each twig was now of precisely equal length, with the fine tips unspoiled by lopping and cutting.

"Now turn the twigs so that any curvature of

the stems is inwards," she advised. "Otherwise you may leave a loose end which will be the worse for you, and will spoil the rod besides." Sitting on her cold white bed, Miss De Vere spoke no word but did as she was bid; in due course she had manipulated the trimmed twigs so that the curved tips pointed inwards, and the birch presented a compact appearance.

Having approved the finished design, Miss Newton then produced a roll of thick white silk ribbon, and instructed Miss De Vere to bind the handle of the birch with this elegant material, to be finished with a neat broad bow with trailing ends, which would then be sewn in place—by Miss De Vere, naturally—using needle and thread. All birches should be properly bound (white ribbon is not mandatory, merely tasteful) but as Miss Newton knew well, the mistake many novices make is to commence the binding one-third of the way up from the base and then to wind downwards. The pressure of the binding material is greatest where the binding starts, and by being bound in this way the finished rod presents an unpleasing, corseted appearance; also it furnishes less play for the twigs, and so is less efficient. But by starting from the bottom and working upwards, the binder of a good birch-rod preserves the generally conical shape. Of course, from the punisher's point of view, the ideal configuration is when the fanlike head of the birch, in full flight—and thus at the instant of impact—presents a spreading width nominally equal to the diameter of the bottom it is punishing. The broader the beam, the wider the fan, the more twigs necessary in the rod, and the longer most of them ought to be, since this spreading characteristic of the birch also depends on the way the switches lie together, and how loosely they are bound. Over-tightness and an over-supply of rods produces something akin to a besom broom, or even a sort of club; too few and too long, and you have, not a birch, but a whip. The fine adjustment of this refined instrument—which ought to made afresh each time occasion calls—is a matter of some expertise, and Miss De Vere learned much of this the hard way, since over and over again the perfectionist Miss Newton pulled her humble efforts apart and bade her try again.

LYDIA'S WOE

My charming lady, tell me why
That blubbered face, that wat'ry eye?
Whom lately, like a lambkin gay,
I saw so wanton skip and play.

Is little Beau, thy goldfinch, flown?
Or playsome kitten sulky grown?
Has frolic squirrel broke his chain,
And been sad author of thy pain?

Has saucy Tommy snatched a kiss,
Or done still something more amiss?
Has he through keyhole dared to spy
Thy taper leg or wat'ry eye?

These would not make my fair one grieve,
Nor her of wonted smile bereave:
Far sharper evils cause her gloom,
A Rod has been poor Lydia's doom!

In vain at mamma's feet she knelt,
Not less the tingling birch she felt;
How hard, mamma, must be thy heart
To make that lovely skin to smart!

Hence, baleful twigs! from hence depart,
Curst birch, that cause my Lydia smart,
May'st thou prove food for honest fire,
And there, though late, thy stings expire!

3. THE SCHOOLMASTER'S LITTLE DINNER

AT THE TIME I kept a school in the North Riding of Yorkshire, I was once invited to a "little dinner," at the house of a neighbouring schoolmaster, with whom I had hitherto had little acquaintance. He had the reputation of a clever man, of amiable disposition, but with a decided taste for the birch and a fancy for using it in the strangest ways. He was a widower, and his home was kept by a housekeeper who went by the name of Mother Birch, from her supposed ability in the fabrication of rods that had a fine sting in them.

When I arrived, I found the party consisted of two other pedagogues and myself. The one, whom I will designate as Dr. S., was the Master of the large Grammar School in the town of B–t, which he conducted with great ability and severity, and which had the peculiarity that all the assistants had licence to flog as well as the head-master, and were encouraged by his example to indulge that licence as far as possible. But the result was generally good, and as the boys were, many of them, successful at the Universities, nobody cared for the dunces whose posteriors passed from usher to usher on to the final arm of the Doctor himself, which he proudly asserted to be still the most vigorous in the school. The other guest, whom I will call Mr. T., was a younger man than myself, of a most agreeable exterior, but, from the shortness of his figure, the clearness of his complexion, and the curliness of his light hair, wearing an almost boyish appearance. He had been tutor in a noble family, who had enabled him to set up a small genteel school, and had entrusted their own children to his care.

After the usual salutations, talk about the weather, and an enquiry of the Doctor, whether he had had sufficient exercise in school this damp day; to which the sage replied, "only fifteen, and two of them babies", we entered the dining-room.

It was a spacious apartment, and, looking round, I saw that, besides the lights on the table, there were four candelabras in the corners of the room, which appeared to be held up by four boys, with their faces to the wall, their trousers down to their heels, and their shirts pinned up to their shoulders. I never saw four chubbier or whiter bottoms. On a nearer inspection it was seen that their hands were so fastened as to give them the appearance of holding up the candles. As the master of the house made no remark on these singular pieces of furniture, and the servants took no notice except pricking them with a fork as they passed, we guests said nothing, though I observed the Doctor casting ogreish eyes on one lad who turned his head round with an expression of manifest terror.

The conversation turned on ancient sculpture, and when the first course was removed, our host said, "I am desirous to colour those statues of mine bright red, if these gentlemen will help me," and the servant presented each of us with a long springy rod, decked with a

SQUIRE HARDMAN

BY GEORGE COLMAN THE YOUNGER

HAIL, GODDESS of the stern and bended brow,
Revered and worshipped, yet unnam'd till now
Ev'n in this land where Thou hast most acclaim,
And where the rites conducive to Thy fame
Have grown to be a kind of national game—
Hail, dear Domestic Discipline, the nurse
Of Albion's fame (for better or for worse)
And cast a fav'ring spell upon my verse!

And Ye, the votaries of her Deity,
Her lovely priestesses, where'er ye be,
Whether in castle, cottage, boarding school,
Nursery or workhouse, Ye that bear the rule
O'er British youth and British backsides: hail,
You strait-laced Tyrants of the head and tail!
To you I dedicate these tingling rhimes
Made for the delectation of the times,
So that they may, as other Farces do,
Amuse the public for a month or two—
Though if perchance posterity allows
Such merit in them that they still arouse
In future minds (congenial to the theme)
An int'rest in the Flagellant regime,
Pray let me pay their debt of gratitude
To One pre-eminent in the multitude
Of members of your whipping Sisterhood.
Aye, Mary Anne! ev'n Thee let me invoke,
With whom I've shared the matrimonial yoke
For nigh ten years, nor ever ceas'd to find
Fresh cause for jubilation since we join'd
Our hands and fortunes, and our tastes combin'd:
To Thee, then, if these lines should live indeed
To warm the future's blood, and fill a need
For all subscribers to the Flogging Creed,
I consecrate the song; and may it find
A lasting place among those works design'd
T'erect the carnal spirits of mankind.

Now Gentle Reader, lend me first of all
Your fancy's vision—what the "Lakers" call
"The inward eye," "the bliss of solitude,"
Or what else dignifies a moonstruck mood—
At any rate, pray lend me it, and gaze
On the two pictures which my poem lays
Before you (as 'twere in the Playhouse): so,
Turn down the lights, the curtain raise, and now—
See the Good Governess at close of day,
The supper eaten, the toys put away,
The ev'ning lesson heard, the prayers said,
And her young charges all sent up to bed,

Continues p. 21

hundred buds. The Doctor rushed at his choice, who reasonably shrieked at his approach. For some time no sound was heard but the swishing of the twigs, and the roaring of the twigged. The backsides consigned to Mr. F. and myself were only prettily striped; that of our host was well reddened; but the Doctor's was a mass of gore, and we tore him off from it with some difficulty.

When the lads were let down, their schoolmaster sent them to bed, saluting the sore bums with a vigorous kick, telling those which had come off best that he would make all even to-morrow morning. We certainly sat down to our partridges with monstrous appetites, and Dr. S. crunched the bones with his teeth as if they had been those of the boy he had been flogging.

Nothing remarkable occurred till dessert, when four small plates were placed at the corners of the table, which were occupied by four charming boys of twelve or thirteen, dressed in light-blue jackets trimmed with silver-braid and very tight white trousers. These Acolytes or Ganymedes, or whatever you please, handed round the fruit, cake, and wine, and cheerfully partook of the portions given to them. I saw them, however, eye with anxiety a long pasteboard box at the end of the table, which our host now opened, saying, "These are the sweetmeats for which my housekeeper is justly famous," and took out four most beautiful small rods, tied-up with blue riband. He then made over the biggest lad, his eldest nephew, to the Doctor's tender mercies, took the younger nephew to himself, and gave the other two, his own children, to Mr. T. and myself.

They were across our knees in a trice: we smacked the tight white trousers for some time in an Epicurean way, before we untrussed them, while the salacious Doctor could not stand the covering for a moment, but got to the nakedness at once, and, setting to with the rod, had worked it to a stump, while we were still enjoying the urchins' struggles. The housekeeper now came to carry off the little fellows, sobbing and puling, and was highly commended by the Doctor: He had never used a nicer rod; he should never be tired, if he could always get such rods; and so on, till she offered him a present of a dozen, which he accepted with gratitude, adding that he should reserve them for his own children in the holydays.

The conversation then naturally turned upon whipping: our host, an old Etonian, taking off the grotesque manner of Dr. Keate, and Mr. T. imitating the absurd contortions of a school-fellow at Winchester, which had the effect of making the master laugh so much, he could not go on flogging. "Ah! no wriggling would have stopped old Keate," said Dr. S., but said it would be great fun, to act what Keate would have done in such a case. "I've no objection," said T., and helped our host to bring out a horse from behind the curtain. "I should like you to try that horse," said he, "a boy is as comfortable on it as in bed." T. was tied on, his breeches taken down, and the drama begun. His gestures and grimaces were most ludicrous; but it was soon evident from the marks on his skin that there was no fiction in the strokes of Dr. Keate. T. took a few cuts as part of the play, but as they became severer and showed no symptoms of cessation, he took a serious tone and desired to be let down. "Dr. Keate", however, took all this remonstrance as part of the performance, and Dr. S. and I., with great laughter, affected to do the same. "Let me try," said Dr. S.,

A Polemic on the Birch

Curst as the meanest wretch is she,
The unlucky girl just whipt by thee,
Who sees and feels thy stinging rage
Which nought but time can e'er assuage.

'Tis thou that plagu'st us ev'ry day,
To shame and smart mak'st us a prey;
Is ought misdone—straight on the knee,
Poor culprits, we are twigged by thee.

Thy shattered ends and shabby plight
Shew e'en thou sufferest by thy spite;
Judge then, thou ugly shaggy thing,
How my poor flesh can bear thy sting.

Guardian powers protect me then,
Let me ne'er taste fell birch again;
To naughty boys confine thy rage,
and not with tender chits engage.

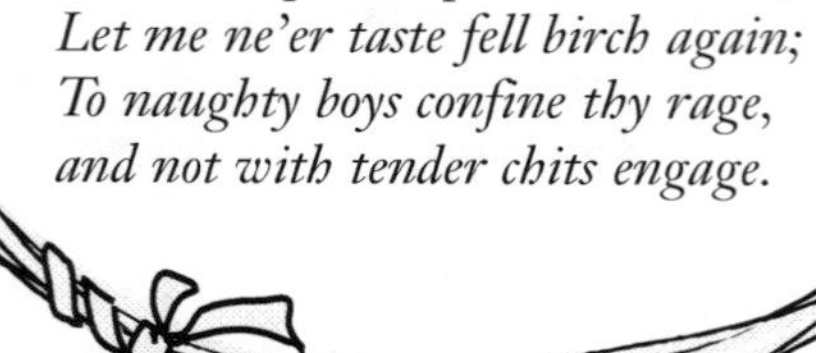

"whether I can't stop this fellow's impudence—let him down indeed! A pretty notion! won't stand it—won't he? we'll see that." And, taking a fresh rod, he laid four or five dozen into him, without a comma.

I now saw that the thing had gone too far. T. was furious at the pain and the trick: I therefore pushed the Doctor aside, and, with a new birch in hand, cried out: "It is my turn now. What say you, Master T., is this a joke or are you fool enough to be angry?" "It's no joke," said he, "as you all shall find to your cost." "Well, then", said I, "if it's no joke, do your worst, and I'll cut your arse off." He looked in my face, and saw I meant what I said. "It is a joke, but a very bad one; untie me and I will say nothing about it." I unfastened his right hand, made him shake hands with all of us, wiped his buttocks, pulled up his trousers, and set him on his legs again. As, after this incident, the talk did not flow very easily, we sat down to whist, and it was very ludicrous to see poor T. every now and then putting his hand behind him and then playing the wrong card. After a rubber or two, the party broke up, Dr. S. declaring he had never spent a more charming evening; but said he still hoped to whip a boy he had left to sit up to do an exercise, and who boarded in his house, before he betook himself to his conjugal duties. I told T. I hoped his fundamental experiences would make him merciful in his inflictions on others, and that I only regretted we had not had the Doctor in his place to complete the diversions of our "little dinner."

4. A REGENCY SEMINARY FOR YOUNG LADIES

THE MISSES POMEROY, who kept the school, were two maiden ladies of the greatest fashion, who enjoyed the reputation of sending out their pupils in a most finished style, and perfected in every grace of manner and deportment.

SQUIRE HARDMAN

from page 19

And she now reading from the little book
Wherein their daily crimes are summ'd: who took
That liberty, and who that extra jam;
Who lost his temper and let fall a d—n;
Who pull'd his little sister's hair, and lied
When tax'd with it—and so much more beside,
You see how well her patience has been tried.
Yet mark the pensive smile that steals apace
Over the features of that modest face,
That face so stern and sombre that you'd vow
'Twas downright plain, unless you saw it now!

Ah see, indeed, how the becoming blood
Tinges her neck and rises in a flood
To nurture in each cheek a lovely Rose,
See how her breath more swiftly comes and goes,
How her mouth softens and her glowing eyes
Have gain'd in brilliance and increas'd in size;
And when she rises, how her form has grown
In majesty, and in that motion shown
A very Juno rising from her throne!
She walks, 'tis Music, and she stands, 'tis Art;
But what is this which strikes you to the heart
In yond fine pose, so graceful and so grand?
Is it the cane that quivers in her hand?
At any rate, see how the dear girl's beauty
Wakes at the prospect of her painful duty:
Smiling she turns, and softly trips upstairs;
And let that Reader follow her who dares.

I, for my part, am loath to play the spy
On the good woman, and I'll tell you why.
There are some scenes, as ev'ry Author knows,
Whose power is multiplied, whose pathos grows
Through presentation by some means oblique:
E.g., Iphigeneia's dying shriek
Heard off the stage th' effect is full of power;
Or take the little Princes in the Tower,
mother'd by hearsay: how that moves the heart!
And Sophocles' Medea shews the art
Of moving sympathy's profoundest springs
By knocking off her children—in the wings.

Imagine to yourself a Guest, therefore,
in the same house, and one dividing door
Betwixt his chamber and the children's room—
A Bachelor of fortune, one to whom Such sounds
as from th' adjoining chamber come
Are music sweeter than the heavenly spheres'.
He stops, enraptured by the cries he hears,
His heart in's mouth, his whole soul in his ears:

Continues p. 23

My wardrobe was thoroughly inspected, and, for the most part, approved of, except my stays, which were immediately sent away to be made much stiffer, so that when they came back I could scarcely move; but Miss Pomeroy said that young ladies did not require to swing their bodies about like milkmaids. She never did, and we were trained to be as stiff and as upright as she was. Every morning when we had walked into the schoolroom, and saluted our governess with the latest dancing master's courtesy, we were placed with our feet in the stocks, the backboard at our shoulders, and a large darning needle, point uppermost, stuck in our bodice, so that if we stooped in the least we scratched our chins. We were punished if we did prick ourselves: ah, many a severe whipping have I had for that and other offences as trivial.

Whipping was at that time decreasing as a punishment in girls' schools, but the Misses

Pomeroy believed in its efficacy, and practised it largely. When a culprit had committed an offence (and it would astonish you very much to hear what slight things were offences then), and was adjudged worthy of being whipped, she had to march up to the governess's desk, and courtesying very low, request permission to fetch the rod. The permission granted—and it was given with much ceremony—she retired and returned, without her gloves, bearing the rod on a cushion. Then she knelt down and presented it, and the governess, bidding her rise, administered a few cuts upon her bare arms and shoulders.

The rods were of two kinds, one made of birchen twigs and the other of fine pieces of whalebone, wound round with waxed thread to keep them together. Either of them would give a stinging stroke, but the whalebone one, which we called "Soko" amongst ourselves, was especially dreaded. Its fangs were like a cat-o'-nine-tails, spreading over our unfortunate flesh. "Soko" was reserved for grave offences, amongst which any sort of disrespect to our governesses (and the Misses Pomeroy were regular martinets in these matters) was reckoned.

It was a very select school, not more than thirty young ladies being received, and these all of the first fashion. It was not at all an uncommon thing for a girl in those days to remain at school till she was nineteen or twenty years of age, only going from school when an eligible parti appeared for her to marry, or when the settling in life of an elder sister made way for her presentation to the gay world. But young or old, rich or noble though many of them were, none could 'scape whipping when it was the Misses Pomeroys' pleasure to whip. Enough castigation went on at Regent House to have satisfied the most strenuous upholders of the oft-quoted proverb, "Spare the Rod and spoil the child."

There were two or three degrees of severe whipping: one was in private,

SQUIRE HARDMAN *from page 21*

Each whistling stroke, each howl and plea and sob,
Make his blood boil, his very being throb;
For he, by taste and moral judgment both,
Favours the drastic governance of youth:
The study of the whip was, to his mind,
The "properest study" of all womankind,
And woman's proper sphere—a boy's behind.

Greedier than courtier for the Royal smile
Was he for flogging in the good old style;
Welcomer than to bride her wedding bells
To him the sounds of discipline, the yells
And shrieks of a well flagellated boy.
This was his Hobby, this is greatest joy.
So, little wonder that you see him stand
Mute-motionless, his chin within his hand,
His ears upon the stretch, and in his eyes
A vision of domestic paradise;
And when you understand this tranced guest
Was still unshav'd, and only partly dress'd,
'Tis still less wonder that the jolly sinner
Should be, that ev'ning, rather late for dinner.
And there, dear Reader, are the pictures twain
I promis'd you. Ah not (I hope) in vain
My efforts to arouse and entertain;
And if you ask me how I came to draw 'em,
This Governess and Guest, as if I saw 'em,
And think the portraits too high colour'd—well,
That Guest was I, and that cane-bearing belle
Was she who—but perhaps I'd best relate
The tale in proper form, at any rate.

So down to dinner did I take my way
To join the company, and tho' distrait
With all my mind still fixed on fustigation,
Manag'd to take part in the conversation;
And when it flagg'd, as talk is bound to do
In country houses all the country through,
I cunningly contriv'd to interject
That topic to which Mothers ne'er object:
"Your La'ship, and the children? Are they well?"
"Aye, Mr. Hardman, thank ye; but to tell
"The truth, I'm far from being satisfied
"With their Miss Lashley." Here she
paus'd and sighed.
"The pretty Governess, you mean?" I ask.
(My real int'rest I think best to mask)
"Well, plain or pretty, she must leave us soon—"
"How's that, my love?" his Lordship asks, the spoon
Arrested half way from the serving platter:
"Miss Lashley leaving us? Why, what's the matter?"

Continues p. 25

with only the Misses Pomeroy and a servant present; another was being publicly prepared for the punishment before the whole school and then being forgiven; and lastly there was the public whipping fully carried out. The only time I was privately whipped I remember, old woman though I am, as well as though it were only yesterday. I was formally bidden by the teacher in charge of the schoolroom at the time to fetch the rod, and carry it into a room which the lady principals called their study. There I found the two ladies, before whom I knelt and presented the rod, which the elder took and drew through her fingers, caressingly, as it seemed to me. Then she rang a hand bell which stood upon the table beside her, and one of the maids entered and was bidden to prepare me. This was done by simply turning my clothes up and holding my hands, though in the public performances the preparatory ceremony was much more elaborate. I was terribly frightened; the shame of the proceeding—I had never been whipped in my life before—completely overcame me, and a violent fit of hysterics was the result of my first school flogging.

Alas! I got used both to seeing and feeling them before I left Regent House. I have seen marriageable girls flogged for breaches of discipline, before all their schoolfellows, the necessary portion of their dress being removed. There was a dress put on for a public flogging, something like a nightgown, and in this the culprit was exhibited before all her school-mates, to receive her punishment. She was made to stoop forward over one of the desks, her hands being firmly held by an attendant, and her feet secured in the stocks on the floor. I remember well a young lady being chastised in this way only a few weeks before she left school to be married. I will call her Miss Darwin here. She was a bad girl—naturally bad, I do believe—and she was always pilfering; nothing was safe from her fingers. We lost all sorts of things—money, trinkets, and even clothes. It was what they call kleptomania now, but we had no grand names for crimes when I was young: stealing was stealing, and there was an end of it. I forget what particular theft caused the whipping I am going to tell you about, but I remember it very well. In the midst of the afternoon school Miss Pomeroy said—

"Young ladies, you will dress half-an-hour earlier than usual to-day, and be in the class-room at halfpast four instead of five o'clock."

We looked at one another, and Miss Darwin

THE STEPMOTHER

To look at her majestic figure
Would make you caper with more vigour!
The lightning flashing from each eye
Would lift your soul to ecstasy!
Her milk-white fleshy hand and arm,
That ev'n an Anchorite would charm,
Now tucking in your shirt-tail high,
Now smacking hard each plunging thigh,
And those twin orbs that near'em lie!
They to behold her di'mond rings,
Ev'n them you'd find delightful things!
But above all, you'd love that other
That told you she was your Step-mother!
Then handing you the rod to kiss,
She'd make you thank her for the bliss!
No female Busby then you'd find
E'r whipt you half so well behind!
Her lovely face, where beauty smiled,
Now frowning, and now seeming wild!
Her bubbies o'er their bound'ry broke,
Quick palpitating at each stroke!
With vigour o'er the bouncing bum
She'd tell ungovern'd boys who rul'd at home!

coloured a little, but made no other sign that she knew anything about the alteration, and we went to our rooms. Upstairs we found out what it meant, for the maid who dressed my hair had to make the rods, and a new one had been tied up that day, expressly for the coming ceremony. At the appointed time we were all in the class-room, and Miss Pomeroy took her place. Miss Darwin was ordered to stand in the middle of the room, and then our governess proceeded to tell us what she had done, and what she was going to suffer. She was a very handsome girl, quite a woman in appearance and size; yet she stood there to take her whipping as a matter of course. She was very handsomely dressed in a gown of green brocade, with a frilled under-petticoat of white silk, silk stockings, and embroidered shoes to match her dress. Her hair, which was only confined by a red ribbon, was frizzed and curled, and she wore a handsome necklace and earrings. Miss Pomeroy rang for an attendant, who came and stood beside her with a deep courtesy.

"Prepare her," was the mandate, and the girl courtesied again, and requested permission to remove the gloves. Miss Darwin bowed (that was the formula), and the process of disrobing went on. Then the punishment blouse was put on—it used to remind us of a shroud—and then the young lady, taking the rod, presented it, kneeling, to Miss Pomeroy.

The governess took it and came down from the dais, where her chair was placed, while Miss Darwin, between two teachers, was led to the desk, and fastened over it in the manner I have described. Then the governess, with right good will, whipped her till red weals rose in all directions on her white flesh. The castigation over, she now, trembling in every limb, and with blazing cheeks and sparkling eyes, returned the rod to the governess kneeling, and retired to make her toilet, a servant bearing her clothes in a basket.

Another curious punishment was practised in our school, to subdue our

SQUIRE HARDMAN *from page 23*

"The matter? Why, if you must know, my dear,
"'Tis that I find her—well, much too severe."
"Severe a fiddlestick!" my Lord exclaims:
"Whate'er her methods, I approve her aims.
"Hardman, d'ye know my Billy has the names
"Of all the Kings from Norman William down,
"And Bob can tell an adverb from a noun!"
"And at what cost, my Lord?" his wife puts in:
"The boys are black and blue from discipline!"
"No matter. Faith, Miss Lashley's in the right.
"I never knew the boys half so polite:
"Even little Oliver, who's only three"
"—She takes him every night across her knee!"
"But John, the French and Latin that
she's taught him—"
"—Granted, my dear, but have you seen his b—m?"

Amidst a gen'ral laugh the subject dies;
But it was plain who carried off the prize:
In this, as in all manner of retort,
My Lord was silenc'd; and I saw, in short,
This governess so apt at flagellation
Was soon to be without a situation;
And as the meal and conversation sped,
A wondrous plan was hatching in my head.
Up rose the sun next day, and so did I,
And hasten'd downstairs hoping to espy
The fair adept whose image all that night
Had filled my dreams with motions of delight;
And, whether by some leading from Above
(Or elsewhere, if the pious disapprove),
I' th' garden, all alone, I found my love.
—I greet her with my most majestic bow;
She answers with a curtsey, fine and low:
I break the ice by mentioning the weather,
And in no time we're walking on together.
O blessed hour when first I knew my Dear!
The image of that morning, cool and clear,
Is at this moment present to my sight;
I see once more, with all the old delight,
The dewy garden in the light of dawn,
The pale sky and the little clouds thereon,
The slanting sunlight pouring in a flood,
Gilding the grass and silvering the wood;
And clearer still than all, I see once more
The dark blue capuchin my darling wore,
Within whose hood her face peep'd like a flower.
Again I feel the dear disturbing charm
Of that first walk together, arm in arm;
And once again, transpos'd in time, I hear
The low, sweet voice which then enthrall'd my ear,

Continues p. 27

pride, our teachers said. Any girl transgressing against the rules respecting cleanliness or order—and it was no easy task to remember them all—was stripped of her clothes and dressed up in the costume of a charity girl! The slightest deviation from the regulations, the most trivial neglect of our toilet duties, sentenced us to this most provoking degradation. The dress used at Regent House was the facsimile of that worn by the "Red Girls," a large charity school in Bristol, whose attire was composed entirely of scarlet serge with a white apron. Anything more unbecoming or more uncomfortable could scarcely be imagined, and there was hardly one of us that would not have preferred a flogging. The same ceremony was observed as in the whippings: the culprit requested permission to fetch the clothes, and carried them in on a salver neatly folded, with the coarse shoes and stockings laid on the top. Then a servant was summoned, and her dress and ornaments were taken off, and she was attired in the gown, tippet, and cap. Then her fashionable shoes were removed, and the coarse leather ones put on, and in that dress she had to remain for the time prescribed. No matter who she was, or who came to see her, the garb must be worn: she attended the dancing-master, the different classes, and the drill-master in it, and stood upon a high stool during school hours, a mark for all our eyes.

5. A Village School Birching

A RUSH FROM all the desks ensued, and amidst shouting, yelling, and leaping, every soul disappeared except myself, who remained fixed to my form. The Domine rose from his pulpit and descended, the usher did the same, and both approached me on their way to their respective apartments. "Jacob Faithful, why still porest thou over thy book—didst thou not understand that the hours of recreation had arrived? Why risest thou not upon thy feet like the others?" "'Cause I've got no shoes." "And where are thy shoes, Jacob?" "One's in your pocket," replied I, "and t'other's in his'n." Each party placed their hands behind, and felt the truth of the assertion. "Expound, Jacob," said the Domine, "who hath done this?" "The big boy with the red hair, and a face picked all over with holes like the strainers in master's kitchen," replied I. "Mr. Knapps, it would be infra dig on my part, and also on yours, to suffer this disrespect to pass unnoticed. Ring in the boys." The boys were rung in, and I was desired to point out the offender, which I immediately did, and who as stoutly denied the offence; but he had abstracted my shoe-strings, and put them into his own shoes. I recognised them, and it was sufficient. "Barnaby Bracegirdle," said the Domine, "thou art convicted, not only of disrespect towards me and Mr. Knapps, but further, of the grievous sin of Lying. Simon Swapps, let him be hoisted." He was hoisted: his nether garments descended, and then the birch descended with all the vigour of the Domine's muscular arm. Barnaby Bracegirdle showed every symptom of his disapproval of the measures taken; but Simon Swapps held fast, and the Domine flogged fast. After a minute's flagellation, Barnaby was let down, his yellow tights pulled up, and the boys dismissed. Barnaby's face was red, but the antipodes were redder. The Domine departed, leaving us together—he adjusting his inexpressibles, I putting in my shoe-strings.

6. Whipping the Pageboy

IT WAS A Sunday morning. Mdlle. Fosse would go to Moorfields to her father confessor, and attend an afternoon lecture; so as soon as I had done luncheon I told Jane and the other two servants they might go out for the afternoon, and return by half-past six or seven, as I would dispense with dinner if Margaret the cook would have something nice for supper, and Charlie could answer my bell if anything was wanted.

As soon as the house was clear, and I knew the cook liked the society of her pots and pans too much to think of leaving the precincts of the kitchen, I rang for my page, and ordered him to bring a lemon, some iced water, sugar, &c., and seeing that he had dressed himself with scrupulous care in case I summoned him, I said, "Charlie, I'm glad to see you are particular about your appearance, although there is no one at home."

CHARLIE, with great modesty—"But you, Miss, are my mistress, and I always wish to show you the greatest possible respect even when you are not quite alone."

ROSA. —"Indeed, sir, you profess great respect for me, and seem afraid hardly to lift your eyes, as if I was too awful to look at, but I have my doubts about your goodness; will you please fetch me a rather long packet you will find wrapped in paper on the library table."

He soon returned with the parcel, and I proceeded to open it as he stood before me, awaiting his dismissal or further orders. The paper was removed, and I flourished before his face (which rather flushed at the sight) a good long rod of fresh green birch, tied up with scarlet ribbons. "Do you know what this is for, sir?" I asked the astonished boy.

CHARLIE, in some little confusion—"Ah! Oh! I don't know—unless it's what's used for whipping young ladies at school"

ROSA—"And why not boys, you stupid?"

CHARLIE—"Ah! Miss Rosa, you're making fun of me, they use canes and straps to boys—but—but—"

ROSA—"Out with what you are going to say, I'm the only one that can hear it."

CHARLIE—"Why… why…" (turning quite scarlet) "the thought came into my head that you might be going to whip me."

ROSA, with a smile—"Well, that shows that at least you must know you have been doing something very bad; what is it?"

CHARLIE, in confusion—"Oh! it was only a silly thought, and I didn't mean I knew I deserved it."

ROSA. —"That's a clever answer, Master Charlie. Now, answer me, am I your only mistress?"

He cast down his eyes at this poser, but managed to stammer out, "Why, of course you are, Miss, as I am in your service alone."

ROSA. —"Now you bad boy, I prepared this rod on purpose for you; can't you guess what I saw early this morning in Jane's room?"

Charlie seemed as if shot; he fell on his knees before me, in the deepest shame and distress, covering his face with his hands, as he exclaimed, "Oh, God! how wicked of me, I ought to have known I should be sure to be caught. Oh! be merciful, Miss Rosa, don't

SQUIRE HARDMAN

from page 25

As we paced slowly o'er the dewy sod,
Discoursing on the Virtues of the Rod.
Tho' I already knew my "cruel fair"
Was no fond, visionary Doctrinaire
In matters of correction, soon I found
Her theory was, like her practice, sound,
Full of good reasons back'd by ancient saws
And moral apothegms and natural laws.
She preach'd most eloquently on the text
Of "proper measures;" and on this pretext
Seem'd to find full occasion to reveal
The fleshly taste behind the moral zeal;
But then, just when her accents made me feel
She look'd on whipping as an amorous bout,
She alter'd, and to plunge me into doubt,
Like Dante to his sinners parcelling out
The various, nice intensities of fire,

She speaks of boys. —"Look ye, Sir, they require
"At different ages different instruments:
"I give good measure in my punishments,
"But would not task an infant with the weight
"Of cutting whipcord: 'tis beyond his state.
"No, no, indeed: although I do not shun
"The strictest methods, when all's said and done
"The naked palm is best for baby's skin;
"Not till the boy is four should we begin
"To use the leathern strap; and for the cane,
"He must be eight ere he can stand the pain.
"Tho' charm'd, I cast down a dissembling eye,
"Aye, aye, you're in the right," I make reply,
"But, Ma'am, you spoke of whipcord: tell me, pray,
"What is the age when that should come in play?"

She smil'd at that. O what a heavenly smile,
How well combin'd its gaiety and guile!
And in her eyes what sparkles of delight
Strove with the glow of wanton appetite!
Yet when she spoke, most circumspect and quiet
Her tone, as if the theme were dress or diet
Or other humdrum matter of debate:
"Why, Sir, the circumstances will dictate
"The wisest course of action. Much depends
"On the degree to which the boy offends;
"His growth, his health and habits, too, control
"The choice of instruments; but on the whole,
"'Tis my opinion, and has always been,
"A boy should have the horsewhip at thirteen."
And thus we talk'd. Ah, how my Heart did swell!
Her discourse charm'd me more than I can tell.

Continues p. 29

expose us, it shall never happen again. Punish us anyhow rather than let anyone know of it."

ROSA—"It's awful, but I'm inclined to keep your secret, and be merciful. Do you know that you are guilty of incest, and liable to be hung for it, both of you?"

CHARLIE, sobbing and crying—"What, for that? I only went to kiss her last night, and then laid down by her side somehow our kisses and the heat of our bodies led from one liberty to another, till—till—I stopped all night, and you found me there this morning."

ROSA—"You shall both smart for this. I will whip you well myself to cure such obscenity, and if ever it happens again, remember you shall swing for it. Now, sir, off with your coat and vest, and let down your breeches with your behind toward me."

He was terribly shame-faced over doing as I ordered him, but too frightened of the consequences to remonstrate, and turning his back to me, he soon stood in his shirt, with his breeches well pulled down.

"Now, sir," I said, "draw up that chair and kneel upon it, with your face over the back, then just pull up your shirt so as to properly offer your uncovered rump to the rod. Mind you bear it like a man, and keep as I order you, or I will yet send for a constable to take you to gaol."

CHARLIE, in a broken voice—"Oh! Miss, I won't even call out, if I can help it; punish me as much as you like, only don't betray us."

ROSA—"Well, sir, you'll find my hand rather heavy, but you must smart well for your awful crime," giving a couple of good stinging strokes which made their red marks, and suffused the white flesh of his pretty bum with a rosy tint all over.

"Will you? Will you? you bad boy, commit such incestuous wickedness with your sister again? There—there, I can't cut half hard enough to express my horror of the thing!" exclaimed I, striking every blow with great deliberation and force, till his skin was covered with bleeding weals, and I managed, as I walked round his posteriors in the exercise of the rod, to see that his face was a deep scarlet, but his lips were firmly closed; the sight of his bottom just beginning to trickle with blood so excited me that my arms seemed to be strengthened at every cut, to give a heavier stroke next time.

"Ah! Oh! Oh! I will never do it again. Ah—r—r—re! I can't keep my mouth shut any longer. It's awful! Oh! Oh! How it burns into my flesh!" as he was compelled to writhe and wriggle under my fearful cuts.

This went on for about twenty minutes; now and then I had to slacken a little for want of breath, but his sighs and suppressed cries urged me on; it was a most delicious sensation to me; the idea of flogging a pretty youth fired my blood so much more than if the victim had been a girl; the rod seemed to bind me in voluptuous sympathy with the boy, although I was in perfect ecstasy at the sight of his sufferings. At last I sank back on a sofa quite exhausted with my exertions, and presently found him kneeling in front of me, kissing my hand, which still had the birch...

7. A Prison Birching in Germany

THE EXECUTION TOOK place in our workroom. At ten o'clock the Governor appeared, accompanied by the Surgeon and the three "whippers", carrying their birch-rods still steeped in the dishes, while an overseer brought in the whipping-bench. Bitterly weeping, with clasped hands and bended knees did the unfortunate Catherine seek to move the Governor, casting herself in despair to the ground—but in vain; and now the foolish wench endeavoured to resist and had to be violently seized hold of and stretched upon the bench, where in a trice she was fastened and stripped of her frock and shift. By the rapidity with which this was done, the turns distributed, and the first birch-rod to be used steeped again deeply and thoroughly in the brine, it was easy to guess how much sharper would be the punishment inflicted upon her after the foolish attempt of hers to resist.

8. Daydreams

MY PARTICULAR HORROR of others knowing I had been punished led me to imagine the whipping, with which the day-dream always began, as taking place before the whole school. I was either leaning on a desk or bent forward in the middle of the room. Sometimes the whipping took place in tight drawers which pressed on the bladder or sex parts. Sometimes the drawers were unbuttoned and I was exposed to view with great chagrin and shame. I read in a book that at some girls' boarding-schools in the olden time, it was the custom to undress the victim and put on her a chemise reaching only to the waist; thus attired and mounted on a servant's back she was whipped before the whole school. This was a new idea for my day-dream and included much extra shame.

9. SLIPPERING TOM

LADY LYDIA WAS in a silent passion: she, to do her justice, believed in this instance that Tom was guilty. When did she not believe him guilty of anything he might be accused of? Had Jarvis brought her a story that Tom had drunk the Severn dry she would have given ear to it.

Baby though he was, or only little removed from one, she hated him with a bitter hatred. The fear of Sir Dene had not let her entirely crush him; but she was doing her best towards it in a quiet way, always working for it safely and silently.

"Wicked, crafty reptile!" cried Lady Lydia, her eyes blazing with light. "Poor dear Otto, poor inoffensive boy, riding without thought of treachery, must have his pony startled and his life endangered by you! Take him, Dovet, and whip him. Whip him well." Dovet seized Tom by the hand to bear him off to punishment. It came pretty often, this chastisement, and Tom neither might nor dared resist. On trying to resist once, the whipping had been redoubled: in Dovet's hands, a strong woman, Tom was not only powerless but conscious that he was so...

Tom took his punishment with tears and sobs; not loud but deep: if he had made much noise Dovet would have treated him to a double portion. She kept an old thin leather slipper for the purpose, and whipped him soundly... he was put to stand, by Dovet, in the corner of the room, his face to the wall. Leaning his head against it, he cried away the smarting pain, and finally cried himself to sleep.

SQUIRE HARDMAN

from page 27

And still I took occasion oft to view
Her animated face, approv'd the hue
Of her complection, brown but clear and warm,
Nor fail'd to note the beauties of her Form:
The length of limb, the slenderness of waist,
The amplitude of thigh—naught went untrac'd
By each inquiring and enraptur'd glance
I turn'd upon this queen of flagellants.
And, Reader, 'twas not long before I knew
My destiny, and what I had to do;
And tho' at first I found me rather queasy,
Once I had spoken, all the rest was easy.
My fortune and estate I did present,
So much in Consols and so much in rent;
My way of living, quiet and retir'd,
And how a wife was all that I desir'd
—"No fond conceited girl whose feather head
"Runs upon fashions and such ginger-bread,
"No pert, well-dowered, London-loving Miss,
"With dreams of naught save the metropolis,
"Of Op'ra boxes, balls and carriages;
"But some mature and sober votaress
"Of home-grown pleasures in a homely dress—
"And here, observing how the brown and red
Blent in her cheek, "Some woman grown," I said,
"Some woman clear of head and firm of hand,
"Whose natural disposition to command
"Should find its scope and exercise within
"Domestic rule and family discipline."

At these last words (insidiously stress'd)
I mark'd the sudden swelling of her breast,
The half-surpris'd unveiling of a glance
That met my own, like lance encountering lance;
And so I leapt into my peroration:
"In short, Miss Lashley, all my admiration
"Is, as I find, directed to those spheres
"Wherein the educative bent appears;
"There have I sought my Bride, my happiness,
"Have ask'd, 'Who better than a Governess?'
"And where a better governess than She
"Whom I behold," (here going on one knee)
"Before me now, and for whose hand I sue
"Thus formally?—I leave my fate to you."

She blush'd, and pal'd, then drawing breath replies,
"Ah, Mr. Hardman, let me beg you rise!
"Kneel not to one whose only merit lies"
In her awareness of your qualities
"And of the condescension that you shew
"In honouring a poor Instructress so.

Continues p. 31

BETSY FRY

"The Muses smiled, and gave consent,
When, whisk, at once away I went!
And, what was still more odd and risible,
I found myself become invisible,
And slily seated on a stool,
Among a pack of girls at school!—
All tongues! as fast as they could chatter—
Sure never was there such a clatter
But one, much louder than the rest,
Amused them with a mighty jest—
A word!—she had picked up in the street!
A word!—the bard will not repeat.
Now, hushed at once the little band,
Behold! the governess, so grand,
The schoolroom enters!—not a word,
Where all was riot, now is heard!
Each head, by her majestic look,
Bent down on sampler, or on book!
When, Lo! the gloomy, glowering eye
Prognosticates a storm is nigh:
Too sure a presage! Says the dame,
'What girl, as down the stairs I came,
Dared utter that vile naughty word
Which never in my school was heard?
If now this instant you won't own
Who 'twas—I'll whip you every one. '
All—all—were ready then to cry,
'Twas not me, ma'am—'twas Betsy Fry. '
'Who! Betsy Fry?—I'm quite ashamed—
Such a great girl!—to hear her named;
But for this crime, a whipping ample
Shall be to others an example.
Indecent wretch!—you, Sally Treacher,
Go run up stairs and tell the teacher
To bring that rod she made, just new,
And tied up with a ribbon blue:
Then such a punishment I'll give
As you'll remember while you live.
No begging, miss, will be of use,
For such a crime there's no excuse
—No further parley!' Here Miss Glynn
With the grand instrument came in:
So smartly tied up with a bow,
It might be deemed a rod for show:
Yet though thus elegant the plan,
And wide expanded like a fan,
When well applied, each twig apart
Would tend to multiply the smart.
'You know, Miss Glynn, it is my rule,
When wicked words invade my school,
T' employ this instrument of pain
To whip and drive them out again:
So down with that vile hussy Fry,
That I may flog her instantly. '
The ready teacher then, Miss Glynn
(A thorough friend to discipline),
Proceeds the culprit straight to seize,
Crying, and begging, on her knees:
But vain her tears, and vain her prayer!—
She laid her down across a chair.
The governess now takes her stand,
The birchen sceptre in her hand:
With lofty air, inspiring awe,
And upraised arm to inforce the law,
She shakes the whistling twigs, and then,
Whip—whip—whip—whip—inflicts the pain:
Now pauses—while miss roars aloud,
Sad warnings for the little crowd—
Crying, 'Oh! dear ma'am, pray give o'er,
I never will do so no more. '
In vain: the rod's reiterations
Produce fresh pauses, fresh orations.
'These stripes I'm sorry to impart;
But 'tis for your own good you smart.
Who spares the rod will spoil the child
By me the proverb shan't be spoiled. '
This brought the conflict to a close;
When quick the smarting culprit rose.
The governess, with awful state,
And head erect, resumed her seat:
Then calling up her victim, Fry
(Sobbing and wiping either eye),
Descanted, with all due reflection,
On crimes provoking such correction:
But, still to heighten the impression
Of punishment for this transgression,
On a high stool she made her perch,
And in her bosom stuck the birch:
Warning the school 'gainst crimes and errors
By the grand triumph of its terrors."

10. INDECENT DISCIPLINE

THE PUNISHMENT OF whipping is not in itself indecent (provided, of course that girls are only whipped by ladies, and that boys of the age of puberty are not whipped by women), It is the way the thing is done that sometimes constitutes impropriety.

At one of our best watering places there is a boys' school kept by ladies. The boys, some eighty in number, are divided into the "infant class" for very young children; the "lower school" for boys from five to eight years; the "middle school" for boys from eight to eleven; the "senior school" for boys from eleven to fourteen; and the "backward lass" for very bad or intractable boys from twelve to fifteen.

A lady friend of mine having a very backward nephew of fourteen, sent the boy to the school, hearing that the head mistress, although a severe disciplinarian, was very successful, but the first time the youth saw his aunt, he complained of the whipping, and my friend, after examining his person, found him very much wealed, but thought he had probably deserved it. However, when the lad went into details, the aunt made enquiries which led to the nephew being

SQUIRE HARDMAN *from page 29*

"Yet ere I answer—ah, I must refer
"To your ambition of a family, Sir:
"Did I not so, I should be false indeed
"Both to your trust and my own simple creed;
"For let me tell you, Sir, I cannot breed—
"Nay, Sir, I will continue! You must know
"I had a fever several years ago;
"It came, and pass'd, and tho' I rose ere long,
"My health as sound and my desires as strong,
"Since then, alas, I am a barren stock."
Her words went thro' me with a gentle shock
Of mild surprise, that swiftly turn'd to joy:
My bliss, indeed, was now without alloy,
And seizing on her trembling hand, I cried,
"My dear Miss Lashley—soon to be my Bride!—
"Nay, nay, lift up your head, incline your ear:
"Know, your misfortune makes you twice as dear!
"Ah listen, while I make my meaning clear:
"To breed was never part of my intent,
"And when I spoke of family cares, I meant
"No more than that our household should be grac'd
"By a few boys beneath your guidance plac'd:
"Let them be workhouse foundlings—two or three
"Tight youngsters pick'd for bloom and bonhomie,
"Whose wholesome discipline and due correction
"Should be entirely under your direction."

And now her eye takes fire, her lovely cheek
Mantles with crimson; but ere she could speak,
I drew her to me and pursued my theme
With limbs a-tremble and with eyes a-gleam:
"Oh say, (I cried) that you will realise
"My dreams of matrimonial paradise,
"Of seeing that divine phenomenon,
"A wife and governess roll'd into one!
"Speak, best of teachers, loveliest of wives,
"Say that henceforth we shall devote our lives
"To married happiness and mutual blisses,
"To love, and interspers'd between our kisses,
"To the more sober, self-rewarding joys
"Of wreaking Spartan discipline on boys."

She gathers breath, and meets my enraptur'd glance,
Her looks no longer modest or askance:
"Oh Sir," she whisper'd, "useless to conceal
"The sentiments of pleasure that I feel:
"Both Wife and Governess—ah, blessed dream
"Of double rapture in a single scheme!
"Ah, 'tis too much, (she cried): With all
these charms
"You've conquer'd me!,"—and fell into my arms.

Continues p. 33

MISS ABRAHAMS

I sent for you, Miss Abrahams, today,
Wherefore it is superfluous to say,
A glance upon the table shows the cause,
Your slight infraction of scholastic laws,
You know would not have set us two at odds,
Had you not lied, necessitating rods.
From any other fault, your age would free,
Here whip I must; and soundly whipt you'll be
'Tis pain to tell you so, nor am I one,
To joy in doing that which must be done.
While I admit your general conduct good,
This crime by promptest means mus be withstood.
Mercy were weakness, liars have their part,
Scripture declares, in everlasting smart.
Only the giver absolution grants,
This law I execute.
Let down your pants.

removed from the school, not because of the whipping itself, but on account of some of the accessories. The lady principal's practice is to make the elder boys kneel on a flogging block, she then undresses and prepares them herself; straps their knees firmly to the block to prevent them rising, seats herself facing their heads, and holds the boys in position by pressing her knees firmly on each side of their necks. She then birches them very slowly and securely, with a great deal of lecturing. The boy resumes his jacket and waistcoat, but instead of his own nether garments he has to don for the rest of the day a pair of his governess's prettily worked drawers of red flannel or white longcloth according to the season.

11. A KEEN GOVERNESS

ONE CAN ONLY speak of what one knows, and I must say I do not approve of whipping for children, either girls or boys—that is, I have never known any children who seemed to me bad enough to need it.

I was a chubby, stoutly-built little boy, now some twenty years ago, and for some months I was in charge of a young governess, who never seemed happy unless she had me over her knee. She would sometimes keep me there nearly an hour, birching or spanking me almost all the time. She liked me to kick and struggle and cry a bit, as it seemed to be her great desire to conquer me, as she called it.

Worst of all to me was when she brought in one of the maids, who was a great friend of hers, to witness and sometimes to help in inflicting my punishment.

It may be asked, why did I not tell my parents? I can only say that I had the feeling of boyish honour, that it was mean to tell tales. Under this severity, I grew morose and ill-tempered, until, fortunately for me, an accident revealed the state of affairs to my mother, and the governess was summarily dismissed. Ordinary, kind treatment soon made all the difference to me. Can it be wondered at that I do not approve of whipping children?

But, and here is my point, I do approve of whipping adults. I know, by experience, what an excellent discipline it is, both mental and physical, dissipating often, as if by magic, the vapours and humours which arise from our artificial town life. It is a tonic, both for mind and body, which deserves to be generally known.

12. A PLANTATION SPANKING

I AM VERY fond of all animals, especially cats, and any cruelty to a dumb creature always makes my blood boil. So feeling very angry, I rushed down to the edge of the water, and picking up the half-drowned kitten when it had again managed to reach the shore, I placed it on the bank, hoping that the poor thing would recover. But the creature had been injured by the stones; it was at its last gasp, and in a few seconds was dead.

I was now more angry than ever, and going to the two children, who had not attempted to run away—not that flight would have saved them—I took each of them by the hand, and led them into the summer-house intending to give them both a good spanking.

They were slaves and belonged to the house, therefore they were under my authority. As I have said before, I think that all children need corporal punishment at times, and in my opinion the two children who had stoned the kitten to death richly deserved a whipping for their gross cruelty. The girl especially, as she was old enough to have known better, and it was she who had led her little brother into mischief. I scolded the young wretches heartily, winding up by telling them that I was going to give them both a good spanking. They did not appear to be very much frightened, but stood staring at me with their large brown eyes, without saying a word. I suppose both had been often spanked before, and I knew that three weeks before, the girl had been well beaten by Dinah, by order of Randolph, for pilfering. They were both very light-coloured; the boy was a sturdy little fellow dressed in a white cotton shirt and trousers; and the girl was pretty, with long, curly, dark brown hair flowing loose over her shoulders. She was dressed in a pink print frock, reaching a little below her knees, and showing her legs clad in clean white cotton stockings. Sitting down upon a chair, I took off my slippers, then told the boy to come to me, and he at once obeyed my order. I had never spanked a child, but I remembered the position in which my father used to place me for punishment, so seizing the boy, I laid him across my knees. I then unbuttoned his trousers, pulled them down to his knees, and tucked up his shirt, laying bare his posteriors.

I gazed at the chubby little bottom laying upturned on my lap, and passed my hand two or three times over the smooth, olive-tinted skin... Holding him down with my left arm over his loins, I applied the slipper smartly to his plump little bottom, each smack leaving a red mark on his skin, and extracting a howl from him. He kicked up his heels and wriggled about, squealing lustily and trying to roll off my lap: but holding him tightly, I spanked away steadily till the whole surface of his bottom was red. Then I stopped, and placed him kneeling on the floor with his trousers down and his bottom turned towards me, telling him not to move until I gave him permission to do so. He did not attempt to stir, but remained where I had put him, crying loudly, with his fists in his eyes, while his little red buttocks shook with the sobs that were bursting from him. While I had been spanking the boy, his sister had looked on with a

SQUIRE HARDMAN

from page 31

Yet not from that day does our rapture date:
The truth is, Reader, we could scarcely wait
To hurry on the banns and marriage-rite,
And snatch'd the pleasures of our wedding night
Betwixt discussions of the joys ahead
When whipping sports should ready us for bed.
—Aye, it was nigh two weeks before our dream
Was realiz'd, and that fortnight did seem
Believe me, quite the longest in the life
Of Squire Hardman and his lovely wife.
Howe'er, at last the business was behind,
The workhouse visited, the papers sign'd,
And three fine bastards to our tender care
Committed, with a deferential air.

I pass the pleasures of th' initial night
(There are some joys too sacred to indite):
Suffice to say our mutual sympathy
Was not exhausted till the sun was high,
And sleep at last weigh'd down the languid eye.
Yet still, ev'n as I slept, I seem'd to hear
A sound of thongs and thrashing in my ear,
Mixed in a rich and comfortable chorus,
As if my Love and I had still before us
The self-same blubbering and breechless boys
Who'd launch'd us on the ocean of our joys;
Until at last the noise of strokes and screams
Was mingled with the transports of my dreams,
And I awoke to find the morning sun
Was nigh o'erhead—and Mary Anne was gone!

I started up, but ere I'd time to rise,
She entered: rosy cheeks and sparkling eyes
Told of some early morning exercise;
Her hair still plaited in a modest queue,
She wore the same neat riding-hood of blue;
And as I felt my Soul with love expand,
I saw the supple thong she had in hand.
"My dearest Love, (she cries) while
you've been napping,
"I've just been giving Tom another strapping!
"You may have overheard, for by the Mass,
"The child has lungs that might be made of brass:
"I did not rouse you, but you should have been
"On hand to see how well I broke him in."
So saying, she cast off her capuchin,
And clasp'd me to her with a deep-drawn sigh,
"He's nicely warm'd by now—and so am I!"

From that day forward all was sheer delight,
With whipping morning, afternoon and night.

Continues p. 35

perfectly unmoved countenance, and when I told her to come to me, she did so without hesitation.

Taking hold of her, I placed her in position, saying to myself that I would make her show some signs of feeling before I had done with her. I whisked up her short and scanty garments, at once baring her bottom, as she wore no drawers: everything she had on was perfectly clean. Although the girl was only a little over thirteen years of age, she was remarkably well developed. Before taking her up, I had noticed that her bosom was already showing a slight swell under her thin bodice, and now on looking at her bottom, I was quite astonished at its size. It was well-shaped too, the plump, firm cheeks standing out in rounded curves, and her thighs also were fairly well rounded. She had good legs for so young a girl; her skin was soft and smooth, and of a pretty olive tint…

I began to spank her, laying on the slipper with considerable force, making her wince and writhe, but she bore several smacks in silence, and then bursting into tears, began to squeal and kick, at the same time putting both her hands behind her to shield her bottom from the hot slaps. Catching hold of her wrists, I held them tightly with my left hand and went on spanking her, as she wriggled, twisted, bounced, and bawled: her olive skin growing redder and redder every moment, while the summer-house echoed with her shrill squeals, and the smacking noise made by the slipper as it struck her bottom, the flesh of which was as firm and elastic as possible. But I felt no pity for the cruel little girl; so, quite regardless of her cries and her entreaties for mercy, I gave her the soundest spanking she ever had in her life; and when the punishment was over, her bottom was a dark red colour from the loins to the thighs.

I made her kneel beside her brother, and hold her petticoats above her waist; and then I put on my slippers and leant back in the chair, taking breath after my exertions, which had been considerable, for I had found it no easy task to keep the struggling, kicking girl on my lap while I was whipping her.

While resting, I looked at the red marks of my handiwork on the children's bottoms. The boy had ceased crying, but he still sobbed at intervals, while the girl, who must have been smarting dreadfully, wailed aloud. After a short time, I told them that they might go, and they at once stood up, with the tears trickling down their cheeks; the girl letting her petticoats fall, and the boy buttoning up his trousers. Then they slunk out of the summer-house, and went off home.

13. The Willow Rod

GRAN: "… WILSON had returned unseen by me, and had laid her burden somewhere out of sight. She now stood at the half open door; when she flung it wide two maids entered bearing a sort of wooden couch with stool attached, such as was used in most of the great schools. This they set down when told, and stood one at each side of it, in sleeveless bodices and skirts of serge, for servants were servants then and dressed for work not show. These two were strapping wenches chosen for their strength in case a big girl should refuse the rod. They smiled furtively, whispered to each other, and then looked at me. About Mary's condition there could be no doubt, she being already seized. Miss Grace and Miss Priscilla, whose business it was to strip, walked her between them to the upper end where the block was, and commenced the work with savage zeal. Wilson stood by with pincushion in hand."

JANE: "Was there much stripping?"

GRAN: "I might say yes or no to that. Buckram and Farthingale were out, and in revenge the rising generation looked like dolls and scare wore anything but shift and gown. Stays there were none, the waist served up the breasts as on a dish, and were clasped behind between the shoulder blades, the skirts adhering to the shape below. This led to shocking scenes in girls' schools, where, as I said before, it was customary to whip those of quite a marriageable age. To insure a thorough strip little more was needed than to take down the web drawers, which hooked in front and came up breast high to keep the vitals warm. This was seldom done without more or less resistance, and when done the skirts were furled to the armpits front and rear, and fastened round the throat. The nudity of the bath would have been decent compared to these fights and the sexual exposure they involved."

JANE: "But if the strippers stood in front, they must have hid the view."

GRAN: "Not during the twists; besides I have not done; when you know all, you will understand how impossible it was to hide what ought not to be seen. There were two junior teachers there, poor young women apprenticed to Miss H., who made no scruple to flog them before us all. After their heads were hid, we could tell which was which by only looking at them from behind."

JANE: "La, what a shame! Mama will soon be back; get on with the story, please."

GRAN: "Mary was too sensible to fight; when her things were fixed in the manner I have described, she was handed to the maids, who placed her on her knees upon the stool and gently pushed her body down till her mouth touched the cushioned part. The sisters then returned for me and dragged me up, inclining to one side so as not to intercept the view, the schoolgirls being ranged in rows behind, some mounted on the forms. When we reached the whipping place they took off my scarf and sash, but did no more just then, being intent on what was going on.

"Mary had yielded sullenly, and lay motionless upon the block; deep silence reigned. Miss Horseman left her desk, tramped up the room, and took her station to the left and rear. She drew the glove from her right arm and handed it to Wilson, who advanced with the long rods."

JANE: "Why do you call them long? Were they birch rods?"

GRAN: "No, my dear, Wolver is not like this shire where birch abounds. With us canes of all sorts and sizes were in use. For trifling faults the culprit got it with a slim rattan on the bare hands and arms; for graver ones she was held upon a form and beaten on the broadest part with a thick bamboo over the thin clothes. These punishments, though painful, were not reckoned much of a disgrace, but we were to be treated in a different fashion. For crimes so flagrant as ours was reserved a weapon of exceptional severity. This consisted of a short stout stick, to which were attached three lithe willow wands, that, when flung, extended some feet in length and gave a triple whiplike cut that lapped round the loins."

ALICE: "Ow–wow!"

JANE: "Did not your flesh creep?"

GRAN: "My dear, I was so scared I

SQUIRE HARDMAN

from page 33

Fir'd by the spectacle and exercise
Of wholesome flagellation, by the cries
And leaps and plunges of subjected boys,
Our loves were constantly refresh'd, our joys
Expanded and increas'd—O blessed noise,
Of discipline, O dear domestic clamour,
Who can express thy captivating glamour?
Alas, whene'er I try, I seem to stammer;
But this I will avouch, Thou wert the source
And origin of all the intercourse
That made our honey-moon a constant round
Of pleasure—and Thine too, ev'n now, the sound
That wakes me, as the trumpet does the steed,
To Love's encounter with unfailing speed.
How often, on each bright succeeding day,
Was I rous'd by that jolly reveille!
And no less often were my afternoons
Enliven'd by the same enchanting tunes
Bringing, thro' windows, passages and doors,
The news that Mary Anne was settling scores.

For you must know my Wife has taken care
That there should be occasion and to spare
For constant punishment, and to this end
Declar'd that she herself would condescend
To bear the trouble of their Education,
And see it should be fitted to their station.
In his resolve I heartily concurr'd;
And thus we gain'd the neighbourhood's good word.
"How generous," the local Ladies cried,
"How truly Christian shews her lack of pride,
"How conscientious is the Squire's bride!"

Aye, she is conscientious, I can swear:
If anyone will doubt her zealous care
They should survey the schoolroom, and its fittings
Plann'd for all kinds of academic sittings.
Indeed, dear Reader, if you could but view
The chamber for yourself, you'd say so too:
And whilst I speak of it, why shouldn't you?
There's no one round to spy or oversee:
Come, step upstairs and look at it with me.
See, here's the room itself: a goodly spot,
Light, airy and well furnisht, is it not?
Remark the oaken desks, the sturdy stools,
The globe and blackboard, and the cap for fools.
Aye 'tis a model schoolroom, Sir, and here
Occasion never lacks for whipping-cheer:
Observe the nice and necessary gear,
And you'll agree that each appurtenant
Bespeaks the well-experienc'd flagellant.

Continues p. 37

scarce knew whether I stood upon my head or heels."

14. An Impassioned Lover

"You deserve to be whipped," she would say; and down he would go on his knees, and kiss her white hands, and clasp his arms around her to caress away her anger, while she submitted to his endearments, nothing loth. After a few encounters of this sort affairs grew more serious, and her fancy for whipping her interesting pupil could be restrained no longer.

"I shall whip you this time," she said at last, after a more than usually blundering performance of her scholar.

"Not this time", pleaded he, casting himself at

A Demon Schoolmaster

Oh, hour that comes too late and goes too soon,
My day's delight—my flogging hour at noon;
When I count up the boys that stay behind,
And class their bottoms in my cheerful mind!
I whipped him yesterday, the first to-day,
He's the *bonne bouche* with which to choose the play.
For nothing charms the true school-master more
Than tickling up afresh the half-healed sore.

What! here's a virgin deaf & dumb with dread—
Now he shall lose his schoolboy maidenhead;
I'll switch him softly, which will lead him on
To some great fault before the week is done.
When two fine birches shall address his rump
Till every twig is broken from the stump;
With the whole school about him gaily gathered—
To see the "new boy" gloriously lathered.

My third's an amateur. But I must try,
Who first will cry "Peccavi*"—he or I;
But then his hide's so tough, his a—e so thin,
It's scanty satisfaction if I win.

The next's a roarer—e'er his skin is clipped,
He howls as if he were already whipped, —
"Oh dear! my bot-bot-bottom!—No, I can't—
Can't bear it—oh, my a—e! I'll tell my aunt.
Pray, pray, not there—I'm fainting; I'm so ill;
Oh, it's so sore! I'll die—I will! I will!"
And all this uttered with such strange grimace,
You'd die of laughter could you see his face—
Such wild contortions o'er his features pass,
He should by rights be flogged before a glass.

My fifth's a miracle—the biggest fool
And plumpest breech I've got in all the school;
Sent with a solemn charge that I must fain
Reduce his bottom and improve his brain—
But either effort hitherto in vain.
I use all means—I beat him like a drum;
I tie him up for hours with naked b—m
Where all the lads may lash him for a lark;
Shoot with their steel pens at him for a mark;
Aim their sharp pea-guns at his rosy h—e;
Lick him, and kick him with the thickest sole.
Then I, to finish; furiously rush in,
And work the rod on his obdurate skin;
Which, after some three days' relief from pain,
Heals up, and all is jolly soon again—
He must be now superlatively sleek—
Not having tasted birch above a week;
But I've got fun enough before me here—
So I'll reserve him for my evening cheer—
Then make an onslaught on the fatted fool,
And with a birch-rod slash him round the school.

So much for this day's task. To-morrow's levee
Will be more numerous, and my hand more heavy—

For there's a fair this afternoon, I know,
To which my pupils are forbid to go;
But to which most will hasten all the same—
To my great profit in the flogging game.
Sorne pedagogues are only strict for books;
My bottoms blush for manners, words, and looks—
Nothing a gentleman's demeanour teaches
More than a graceful downfall of the breeches.
Does a boy giggle? birch him till he's grave;
Won't sing? a rod will soon bring out a stave;
Won't eat? excite him with some strong birch tea;
Greedy? make his b—m a fricassee;
Wants purging? bleeding will relieve his guts;
Breaks wind? just break his skin with fifty cuts;
Wants—or has—spirit? keep to the same plan—
Till the child learns the endurance of the man;
For the brave youth who owns the double grace,
A pouting bottom and a cheerful face,
And licks the milksop who, unused to pain,
Dares hardly raise his fist to strike again,
Wins from my favour many a pleasant boon
Refused to the insipid lean poltroon—
Whom I rejoice to see his comrade dogging,
To kick the hinder part I've just been flogging.

* *"I have sinned" (Latin)*

her feet, and clasping her plump, white hands, which he covered with kisses.

"Yes, now. Stand up, and take down your trousers."

"Oh, no! I will try and do better; I will indeed."

"No excuses, sir," she said, with feigned severity, while the maid listened intently, and marked how her eyes flashed with excitement. "At once, sir," and she took off her dainty slipper, affording more than a glimpse of her handsome leg as she did so. The young man fell at her feet, and embraced them, and kissed them; but it was all to no purpose—she was inexorable: she made him undress, and bestowed upon him a smart slapping with the slipper she held. But this only gave her a more decided zest for the rod; and when she informed her scholar that the next time he transgressed he should be whipped with a rod, and severely, too, he kissed her eyelids and her rosy mouth, and intimated that he was ready to submit to anything she chose to do with him. The maid held her tongue about this, but not about the more ceremonious whipping which took place shortly after, and of which she was also a witness. Before Mr B arrived, she was ordered to fetch a box out of her mistress's dressing-room, the contents of which she was very well acquainted with, and place it in the

SQUIRE HARDMAN *from page 35*

See where the canes of rattan stand arrayed,
As nicely "si~'d" as soldiers on parade;
Look, where the supple straps in order hang,
Like curling tongues that silently harangue
The recreant scholar; while beside them, see
What fills his heart with dread, but mine with glee,
The stinging whips to sign his b—m's degree!
And there, God bless it, stands the flogging-horse,
The public school's traditional resource,
A famous piece of furniture, in sooth,
Which generations of our British youth
Have found that schoolmasters won't do without:
Mark well the weighty irons and timbers stout
With which 'tis brac'd and buik, and
the smooth saddle
Whereon your little scholar lies a-straddle,
With straps to bind his ankles and his wrists,
So that no matter how he turns or twists
His lively b—m is always well toward,
And tho' half scarified, will still afford
What a midwife would call, with fond elation,
"An easy and convenient presentaton.
"Now also cast your curious eye towards
That other engin'ry of wheels and cords
Whence hang two leathern cuffs, a fine invention
Whereby your culprit's kept in nice suspension,
What time his a—E receives your full attention.
—Aye, Reader, here's my Mary's room of State,
Here is she sovran and inviolate,
And here she spends her mornings, well content
With tasks of teaching and of punishment,
Adept at each, a true-born Pedagogue,
Well pleas'd t' instruct, and still more
pleas'd to flog.
So I can say, whate'er the seasons bring
Of snow that stifles or of rains that sting,
The climate of our Love is always Spring;
And ne'er more vernal than when Winter hangs
His gloomy curtain o'er the world, when twangs
The bitter north wind and the days are short:
'Tis then, in fact, we take our finest sport.
What is more lovely than a Winter's eve,
When all the dying tints of twilight leave
Their soft impression on the inner sense
That now retires to breathe their influence,
And all is given to dear domestic Peace,
To social converse and instructive ease?
Now stir the fire, and close the shutters to,
(As comfortable Cowper bids us do)
Let fall the curtains, wheel the sofa round,
And while the bubbling and loud-hissing sound

Continues p. 39

boudoir. This she did, and then took up her post of observation. The young gentleman came as usual, and began his studies, blundering egregiously in a very short time. She made him stand before her like a little boy, lectured him severely on his carelessness, and ordered him to bring the rod. In vain he begged and prayed, kneeling before her, and kissing her feet, covered only by a thin silk stocking. She commanded him to stand up and prepare, which he did, still begging and praying to be released. Mrs A—would have no mercy, and his trousers were quickly taken off. Then he was bidden to bring the rod, then to kiss it, and finally, the lady laying him across her knee, administered a thorough whipping, till he fell on the floor, smarting and exhausted. All this the maid saw, not once, but many times, and, after the fashion of her class, did not hold her tongue about it. The result of all this was that Mr B grew so wildly in love with his fair instructress, that he became in danger of ruining himself for her. There was no limit to his extravagance, and Mrs A—was a lady of expensive tastes. Gifts of all sorts began to find their way to her house. Gems which he would swear could not rival the lustre of her eyes—dainty slippers which he would fit on, and kiss the exquisitely shaped foot they were made to adorn—articles of vertu, and sumptuous feminine adornments of all sorts, were almost daily delivered at her door, and the affair became a matter of public scandal. Guardian of the infatuated young man remonstrated with him on his extravagance without effect, until a bill for £2000, for a parure of emeralds, opened their eyes to the true state of the case, and they refused to pay for the jewels. Mrs A—as stoutly refused to give them up, and the result was an exposure of the circumstance, which resulted in Mr B being at once despatched to his estates in Ireland, and the lady having to make a hasty retreat to fresh fields and pastures new where she might perchance pick up another wealthy innocent to minister to her whims and passions."

15. A Smacking in the Park

My dear, I've just had such an unexpected treat. Walking in the park I noticed a nursery-maid in conversation with a soldier by the Serpentine. Her charge—a boy of about nine—had wandered away from her, and was walking along the brink of the water. The conversation with her companion was too absorbing to allow her to look after the boy, who was pleased enough to take advantage of her being otherwise occupied, and was amusing himself with sailing such little bits of stick as he could pick up. Suddenly a cry from him informed her that while stooping forward to sail one of his extemporised vessels he had overbalanced himself, and fallen forward on his hands and knees into the shallow water.

Beyond getting wet he was in no danger, and to catch him up was the work of a moment for the girl. "Oh, you naughty boy," cried she, red as fire with vexation and rage, "won't I make your arse tingle for this!"At these words I approached her and said, "I think you are right; such dangerous tricks should be put a stop to at once by a good whipping." She, pleased to find that I agreed with her in laying the fault on the child, curtsied, and said, "Yes, sir, and that he shall have, I'll warrant, before another minute." And in a twinkling she had his breeches down, and putting her left arm round his head and shoulders, inflicted a shower of heavy slaps with her right hand till she was out of breath with the exertion. The child bellowed and kicked lustily, and I was afraid lest his screams should cause some of the passers-by to interfere, but nobody seemed to think the matter any business of theirs, and I had the pleasure of enjoying the sight of as sound a whipping as I could wish to see. The minx had an arm like a sledge-hammer, and when she had done, the boy's bottom was as red as her face, which was the colour of beetroot.

"There, you little beast," she cried, setting him free at last, "if ever you get into the like mischief again I'll flay you alive."

The effect of this scene upon me you may imagine, and I was unable to move from where I was standing for some time afterwards. Approaching the girl, I gave her half-a-crown, telling her to accept it as a token of my regard for the excellent discipline with which she managed children. "I should think," said I, "your mistress must highly value you as a nurse-maid."

"Lord bless you, sir, missus would send me away at a minute's notice if she knowed as I flogged one of 'em!"

"Then are you not afraid of his telling his mamma?""asked I. "He dare not, or else he would fast enough," answered she with a grim smile; "the first time I whipped him he stamped and said he would tell his mamma when she came home. 'Will you?' said I, having him across my knee in a jiffey, 'will you, will you, will you?—not until I've flayed your arse for you, though,' and I kept on spanking it, sir, for a good quarter of an hour in spite of his promises not to tell."

"But I should have thought," interrupted I, "he would have told all the same when his mother returned." "Not he, sir, for I didn't let the matter rest there, but told him if ever he said a word to his mamma about the whippings I gave him, Mr Jones, my young man as he was then, would come as soon as he went to sleep, and carry him off to a place where they whipped little boys with red hot wire, and as my young man was in the kitchen at the time, I called him up to speak to the truth of what I said, which he did. So you see, sir, I've that child's bottom as much at my disposal as if it was my own, and it's only by spanking of their behinds as you can do anything with children."

Wasn't this a charming morning's amusement, dear?

16. A LOUISIANA SCHOOLMA'AM

I HAVE FOLLOWED with considerable interest the discussion in your columns on whipping. I fail, however, to see why you should describe that time honoured mode of punishment as indecent. Is it indecent for a hospital nurse to wash and otherwise attend to the wants of the patients? Then why should it be thought indecent for a governess to perform certain duties with regard to her pupils? I would ask those who condemn the use of the rod whether children at the present time are more obedient, well-conducted or morally pure than were their fathers and mothers in childhood? Yet it was the rod now quite tabooed, in the fear of which the fathers and mothers were brought up. My advocacy of the judicious use of the rod is based on no mere theoretical grounds. I can speak from experience

SQUIRE HARDMAN *from page 37*

Of fragant punch gives notice to the ear
Of coming cups t'inebriate and cheer
And warm to doughty deeds of discipline
So let us welcome peaceful Ev'ning in.

How often in my uncompanion'd past
This self-same hour had found me quite downcast,
Dull, moping, out of sorts, and in distress
How best to cheat the evening's idleness:
But now, how chang'd the prospect! Blessed hour
Of fellowship and jointly wielded power,
With what anticipation do I hail
Thy coming, and the ev'ning's long regale!

For now, remark the grave, dissembled air
Which lovely Mary well knows how to wear,
As she discourses on the naughty ways
Of Tom (our youngest) for the past few days:
See how we sit awhile in sober chat
On the behaviour of the little brat;
Until when some ten minutes have gone by
In sad discussion of his deviltry,
I shake my head and with a deep-drawn sigh,
"My Love," I murmur, "I am much afraid
"The little fellow needs the timely aid
"Of some correction, wholesome and parental,
"Not too severe, of course, yet not too gentle;
"And tho' I know the task is far from pleasant,
"I really think there's no time like the present."
"Alas (sighs Mary) I must e'en admit
"You are, as always, in the right of it:
"Aye, Sir, you point me where my duty leads;
"We'll have him down, and whip him as he needs."

And so the touzle-headed lad appears,
Clad in a nightgown that befits his years,
A garment brief and simple, and well plann'd
For execution of the work in hand;
And see, by Jove, the cunning little sweep
This very moment has begun to weep,
As if he felt his skin already smart
And hop'd his tears might soften Marrs heart:
Vain hope, my luckless Tom, and vain those tears:
Your b—m's account is too much in arrears!

Now Mary smiles and speaks him tenderly,
Bids him approach and takes him on her knee,
And fondling him with motherly affection,
Informs him that his temper needs correction,
And the bad habits into which he's slipping
Must be arrested by a nice warm whipping;

Continues p. 41

most personal. Those of your correspondents who have stated or implied that sensuous desires of a certain kind are created by whipping, I assure you that, as far as my recollection goes (and my remembrance on the subject is very vivid), the only effect the rod had on me was the strongest possible intention to avoid in the future the offence which had brought its infliction upon me.

At fourteen years of age I was about as good a specimen of a spoilt child as can ever be found among the present generation of children. The only son of a wealthy planter, surrounded by slaves, who from infancy had treated me with all the deference due to their future lord, I had grown up ignorant of any will but my own. My father's death placed me under the guardianship of an aunt, who entered me with the least possible delay in a school of some note in Southern Louisiana.

This establishment, conducted by a Spanish lady of good family, consisted besides the school for young and backward boys, of a seminary for ladies, and to this latter was attached an infant class for both boys and girls too young for either of the other two departments. But very few days passed before by disobedience to the governess of my class I had earned the privilege of a private interview with madam. I had already become quite aware of the fact that disobedient children in that establishment were whipped, but even when summoned to madam's room it never entered my mind that anyone would dare, or daring be able, to take such liberty with me. Judge therefore, my astonishment, indignation and fury when, after a very brief struggle with two maid-servants, I found myself stripped to the shirt, fastened face downwards to the sofa. Madam having issued her orders, remained an apparently unconcerned spectator indifferent to my cries; but the use of certain words, which I had been in the habit of applying to offending servants at home, brought upon me the further inconvenience of having a kerchief tied over my mouth.

Madam waited till I lay quite exhausted with the vain efforts to free myself, and then with great deliberation began to lecture me on my evil deeds, especially that culminating one, resistance to her chastisement. "For this, my child, you will receive twenty strokes with this rod." She placed the long slender bundle of twigs almost under my nose. Again I fought and kicked, but to no purpose. When I had convinced myself of the futility of all resistance, madam proceeded with the same deliberation with the punishment. It need but very few strokes to reduce me to the frame of mind she desired. Not heeding my cries or petitions for mercy she went to the end.

Unfastened from the sofa I now knelt before her, and with the greatest readiness obeyed her slightest command. The repetition of a certain formula used on such occasions, acknowledging the fault and thanking madam for the punishment, kissing the rod and finally madam's hand seemed to come quite natural. But a much severer test of that new born obedience followed, when, instead of being allowed to resume my clothes, I was dressed in the costume of a child three or four years old—drawers, petticoats, short dress, all beautifully embroidered and ornamented, and when this toilette was completed I was placed by madam in the Kindergarten class. Of course, it is extremely humiliating for a big boy to be dressed like a little girl, to be made to play with little children, to have to repeat their infantile lessons, to be put to bed at seven o'clock, and, worst of all, to have to submit to a great deal of teasing from the older girls, who delighted in making me carry a doll, and submitting to other indignities; but all aided in producing the one effect desired—prompt obedience to all in authority. When madam considered that

lesson had been sufficiently impressed upon me, I was restored to my place in the boys' class and allowed to resume the ordinary dress. I remained a considerable time under madam's charge, but never again incurred punishment for direct disobedience, though like the rest, boys and girls big and little, received punishment for minor offences. This, madam, having placed the culprit across her knee, after letting down trousers or drawers, administered with a short rod. Such whipping, though by no means to be incurred lightly, is not to be compared to the birching I have described as my first experience.

Madam's influence over her pupils was unbounded and lasting. I thoroughly believe, were she to confront any of them to-day, grown men or women, those well-remembered words, "My child, again have you been disobedient; bring me the rod, take off, etc. etc." would be received with unhesitating obedience, even to assuming the position needed to receive the punishment.

17. GUSTAVE THE PAGE

FIFINE THREW THE dress across her knees, and set the coquettish little hat on the top of her dishevelled hair, that she might see the effect of the colours against her brunette complexion. Certainly the result was ravishing.

"Take them away," her Highness said; "I'll wear that dress this very morning to the croquet party. I'll put it on as soon as ever I have whipped that boy. Put down that glass, sir, and take off my boots."

Not only her boots but the stockings did she make him take off, and he made no mistakes this time; it was wonderful how quickly he had adapted himself to his new position, and acquired the little arts and graces so necessary to the making of a lady's page. This done, she made him bring the rod and kiss it, delivering it to her upon his knees. To prepare him was the work of a minute: it was only to fasten up the skirt he wore

SQUIRE HARDMAN

from page 39

Whilst, as she speaks, the cowering urchin's eye
Is fixed upon the table standing by,
Where lies, all ready coil'd, the supple strap
Whose sting he knows full well, poor little chap!
And I in turn survey the pleasing scene
In expectation silent and serene,
So when the lecture rounds unto its close
My spirits are at the proper height, God knows.

But now 'tis time the real game began,
The sport that warms the English gentleman
To amorous play, —and in a twinkling, see
How Tom is stretched across my good right knee,
His trembling legs close gripp'd between my thighs,
His hands secur'd in mine as in a vise:
When Mary whisks his shirt up to his waist,
How more expertly could a boy be plac'd?
I smile to see her raise the strap, for who
Has now a better vantage-point and view
O' th' spheres of operation than I do?
And when the thong with an impetuous hiss
Begins to fall, who can describe my bliss?
I mark each rosy welt the leather makes,
I see the chubby flesh that shrinks and shakes,
I hear the screams and sobs, the desp'rate pleas,
And feel each bound and struggle 'twixt my knees;
While as th' unhappy urchin leaps and squirms,
My Mary lectures him in formal terms,
And with a store of comfortable saws
Improves each moment when she makes a pause.

—And here, dear Reader, give me leave t' admit
I much admire this heavy schoolroom wit;
I love those florid nursery platitudes
From whose old-fashioned eloquence exudes
A certain homely, staid hypocrisy
Which suits the temper of my lechery:
How pleasantly they fall upon the ear
When mingled with the sounds of whipping-cheer,
Half drown'd by shrill invigorating screams
Such as my wanton appetite esteems,
And punctuated by the hearty smack—
Slow, regular and solemn as the clack
Of an old water-wheel—which pliant leather
Makes when a strap and b—m are brought together!

Another ev'ning, and 'tis Bobby's turn;
For certain, every eight-year-old must learn
The salutary influence of pain
Thro' contact with the thin scholastic cane:
This is a fix'd opinion I maintain.

Continues p. 43

round his neck, and there he was almost naked. Strangely enough, he made no protestations on entering, but a queer light came into his eyes as the lady's hand passed over his bare shoulder, with a gesture that was almost a caress. Fifine and I held him down over the ottoman, and her highness administered a sound flogging to him, measuring every stroke with a precision that I knew from experience only made the smart the harder to bear. He roared enough now, and writhed and twisted, till at length, after some dozen blows, he fairly struggled himself free of our hands, and slipped on to the floor. Then he clasped the Princesse's feet, twining his arms round her bare ankles, and looking up into her face, implored her pardon. She did not grant it till she had given him a good many rapid stinging blows, and then she allowed him to get up. In spite of his roaring and crying, I could see that the boy liked the discipline he had received at her hands, and I saw his lips on her feet too while he lay there clasping her ankles, but she took no notice of it. When she had done with him she would not let him go; she seemed to like to see him writhe and twist, and ordered him to bring the rod once more. It was my turn now, and I knew she was going to whip me before him, but it was no good to say a word.

She rested a little, for she was out of breath, and then she ordered me to kneel and bring the rod. I could have strangled the little monster of a page, for the sight of me being prepared for whipping seemed to do his smarts a mighty deal of good, and he ceased squealing and rubbing himself when he saw what was going on. The Princesse made him stand behind the sofa, with a rod in his hand, while she whipped me, and told him if he stirred she would turn him over to Saunders for another dose. He had a horror of Saunders, but if she had proposed to whip him again, or delegated the task to Fifine or me, I verily believe he would have disobeyed her on purpose. I'm sure I heard him snigger when I knelt down, but when her highness turned sharp around, there he was looking so preternaturally solemn that she laughed herself, and there he stood as if he was carved out of a block of wood while she whipped me. I need not write of how she did it: she can whip; and it was all I could do not to slip down on floor and roll and scream as the boy had done. I managed not to, however, and contrived to take the rod and leave the room without crying out, but my face was all working; I felt it and when we got into the passage that wretch of a boy pointed at me and burst out laughing. I couldn't stand that, my dear, and I flew at him and shook him, and boxed his ears till he roared more than he had done at the princess's whipping. He has been respectfully afraid of me ever since; and though, since he has been down stairs amongst the men, he has learned a great deal of impudence, he seldom favours me with any of it. They can't teach him much he doesn't know already, for a more precocious boy I never saw; and yet no one can help liking him that comes near him.

I daresay you think, from the tone of my letter, that I have altered my notions about whipping; and so I have. While it was all punishment for me, to please the whims of the ladies, I could not see the enjoyment of it, or feel it rather, but now I can. Nor does the Princesse feel half the pleasure in whipping me or Fifine, or even any of the sisterhood, which she has when she gets Gustave across her knee to birch him. I've seen her pause in her whipping, and pass her hand over his firm flesh, lecturing him the while, as if she would prolong his punishment for her own gratification, and the little wretch keeps quite quiet, and likes it all the while. As for me—well, there, I suppose I may confess it to you, but I'm fallen in love with the boy, or something very like it. I like to have him near me—to be able to touch him when I choose—to caress him when I please—and, above all, to whip him when I can find occasion: that's by no means seldom, for he is always in mischief. I sometimes think the little wretch does all sorts of wicked things for the sake of getting a whipping from me—for there's no mincing the matter, my dear, he is as fond of me as I am of him. He knows a handsome woman when he sees her as well as anyone, and I don't think I'm so very bad looking. My feet are as well shaped as any lady's among them; and the Princesse couldn't feel flattered if she saw how her page kisses them sometimes, when I have been punishing him for some of his vagaries. Ah, my dear, our whipping escapades among ourselves, as girls, were all very well, but there's something like enjoyment in having a fine strapping boy always at your beck and call on whom you can practise when you like. There's real pleasure in getting hold of a plump, firm boy like that, with a skin as soft as satin, and laying him across your knee, especially when you know that he likes it—and you.

18. A LECTURE ON RODS AND POSTURES

"MY DEAR LADIES! The means at our disposal for corporal punishment are manifold. The most commonly used, however, are the hands, the carpet beater, the birch rod and, but only as an exception, the whip. People blessed with an exceptional imagination make use of a whole assortment of the most bizarre implements, including chains, paddles and a whole variety of instruments, simply too many to mention here. The carpet beater is primarily used in France and is only infrequently used in our country, though I must admit that I often make use of it in order to impart a slight Continental flavour to the education of the pupils entrusted in my charge. Only when forced, in extreme cases, do I make use of the whip, and even then, very sparingly. Normally I give a small dose at the end of a punishment, two or three lashes at the most. To use the whip for a prolonged punishment would be very unwise indeed, because even with what one might think are light blows, it is very easy to rip open the skin and cause gashes that leave scars forever. Even the firmest *derrière* is apt to be literally torn

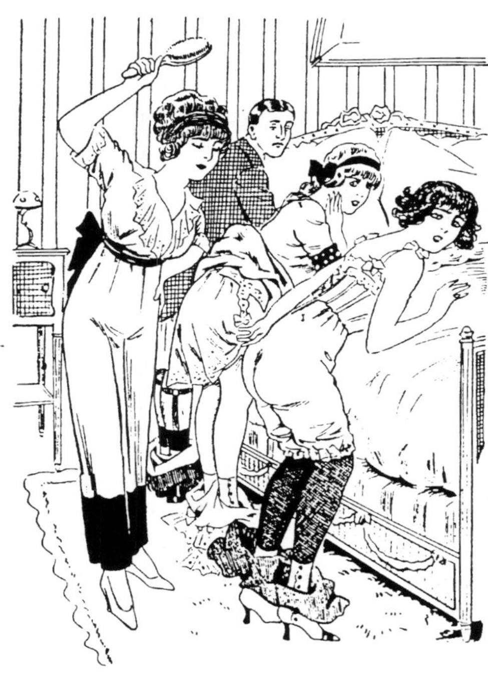

SQUIRE HARDMAN *from page 41*

Indeed it seems to want no demonstration
The best thing for a boy is flagellation:
The doctrine need not exercise our wit;
'Tis shewn, by Reason and by Holy Writ,
That Education all amounts to this:—
A good sound whipping never comes amiss.
And so we need no reason nor excuse
To put the rod to its appointed use:
The world has found, whene'er it means to flog,
That any stick will serve to beat a dog;
And Mary Anne and I have found, with joy,
That any pretext serves to flog a boy.

Therefore when Bob is summon'd I commence
By sounding him upon his rudiments;
I press him closely, and to each reply
Vouchsafe the doubtful tribute of a sigh;
At last, with low'ring brow, I bid him sit
And work some problem well beyond his wit,
Or find the answer to a monstrous sum
Whose figures stretch from here to kingdom come.
—Then comes the sport (of pleasures not the least)
Which serves as appetiser to the feast:
Delightful game! to watch a lad essay
Some hopeless task you've set him, to survey
The fix'd and furrow'd brow, the anxious air
With which he brings his little pow'rs to bear,
And as they flag, to note the trembling limbs,
The cheek that flushes and the eye that brims;
To mark how well the moist and quivering lip
Bespeaks his mounting terror of the whip,
And how the very fear of flogging serves
To dull his wits by harrowing up his nerves!
Aye, gentle Reader, trust me when I say
This homely scene is better than a play.
Meanwhile dear Mary sits demurely by;
Calm is her brow, but sparkling is her eye:
I note the conscious swelling of her breast,
And smile to see the symptoms that attest
A Woman's sympathetic interest—
The speaking looks that fix themselves, in turn,
Now on her pupil's desperate concern
And now upon the limber cane that lies
All ready for her favourite exercise.

"Well, Bob, your time is up," at length I say:
"Come here and let me see your answer, pray.
"—Why, what's the meaning of this silly scrawl?
"Is this what you've to shew me? Is this all?
Mary, the little wretch deserves the rod,
"And he shall have it here and now, by God!

Continues p. 45

to shreds by this horrible instrument.

"Unfortunately, there are many Ladies who use the whip exclusively, but it cannot be denied that they are by nature hard-hearted and jealous creatures, using this inhuman instrument of torture only to revenge themselves. Cruelty for cruelty's sake should never find a place in our mode of punishment. That is why we should only very seldom, and then sparingly make use of the whip.

"In general, it is sufficient to use the hand where little girls are concerned. Since the misdeeds of little girls are never very serious, it follows automatically that the punishment should never be too severe. Of course, whenever the little one suffers a relapse, it is advisable to use the rod. However—I cannot repeat this too often—sparingly, Ladies sparingly. The birch easily tears open the tender skin and one should know when to stop before this happens. Obviously, the blows should be felt, and it is proper to make the little behinds swell up a little bit, but under no circumstances should the tender skin become damaged. Hitting with the hand is, in itself, painful enough and should be more than sufficient for a little one's behind.

"Larger girls who are in need of punishment should in general be punished with a birch rod after they have received, for various reasons which I will explain later on, several solid whacks with the hand. As my esteemed colleague, Mrs. Skin-Tear, has so thoroughly demonstrated to all of us, one can make much longer use of the rod when the skin of the buttocks has been thoroughly prepared. Sometimes use of the hand is more than sufficient, even when one had in mind using the rod. Many sensitive behinds cannot stand punishment of the hard blows to which the rod is capable. It is all a matter of experience and good sense. Suffice it to say that it is sometimes easier to punish a *derrière* with sensitive skin by hand than it is to whip a thicker skinned one with the rod.

"Finally, and this is also a very important matter, the position of the penitent is of the utmost import. To punish a victim one can take her between the legs across the lap or under the arm. Young girls have as you already know, an inborn sense of shame, and they suffer the pains of hell when we make them feel ashamed. Especially after puberty. Their young faces will cover themselves with a purple blush which sometimes goes all the way down to their pretty little behinds. It is a delicious experience for the delight we feel in punishing our victims and it lasts much longer if we execute our punishments very slowly, permitting us to delight in their confusion as long as we possibly can.

"Punishing adults—and most adults we have are our maids, cooks, and so forth—can be extra pleasing if we treat them as if they were little children. The punishment of these delinquents can be very severe, provided they possess physical charms. The area to be punished can be the entire *derrière*, the small of the back and the thighs. In short, with delinquents of this sort it is possible to give free rein to one's fertile imagination. Even though I am of the firm opinion that one has to take the maidenly ears of our little charges into consideration—after all, the education of the little dears has been entrusted to us—I do not think that such considerations have been taken into account toward those persons who are in our employ. I see no reason on earth why we should be ashamed for our female servants. Moreover, the use of certain less-refined expessions can be very, very exciting. We can bring ourselves into ecstasy with them. If we call certain bodily attributes and functions. by their proper English names, one can say almost anything and at the same time achieve considerable nervous relief.

"Whenever I have to beat the behind of an adult offender, it gives me considerable pleasure to attack my victim also with the harshest words I can find in my vocabulary.

"It is imperative, when using the rod, to deliver the first blows as lightly as if they were caresses. It is easy to increase the strength slowly, which saves the executioner from becoming tired too soon. Moreover, greater emphasis is given to the punishment by prolonging it, and finally it is possible to wind up with the delivery of several hard and severe blows which will stick in the memory of the patient for a long time to come.

"As I have already stated, I use the carpet beater very sparingly and only then when I have the victim standing in front of me, completely in the nude. I only use it when I want to beat my victim from top to bottom. It is possible to derive maximum pleasure from this form of punishment if the victim is beaten slowly from the shoulders on down to the ankles and then from the bottom on up back to the breasts. It it easy to let the straps wander all over the body; they cause considerable pain and yet they do no permanent damage. The skin on the inside of the thighs is very sensitive and lends itself marvellously for a treatment with the carpet beater.

"I use the whip only on very sturdy delinquents and only them when they truly deserve severe punishment. Moreover, the punishment has to be almost over before I resort to using the whip. I only use it two, at the most four times, though there have been a few exceptional cases where I was forced to mete out up to six lashes. The delinquent suffers an almost unbearable pain and sometimes cries for hours afterward.

"Depending entirely upon the imagination of the executioner, the positions of the victims during punishment can differ. It is impossible to lay down any firm rules regarding position. In my opinion it is most logical to select positions that serve the purpose at hand best.

"Personally I would prefer to hold little girls under one arm or to take them across my lap, whether they have to be beaten with the hand or with the rod. It is immaterial which mode of punishment is used, but the skirts should always be lifted and the drawers should always be held open. It is important with little ones that the punishment does not last too long. If a small girl is very stubborn it is recommended that her drawers are taken off and that the girl receives a few very painful lashes across the buttocks and in repeat cases across the legs, where the skin is more sensitive. The dear little ones quickly learn that it behoves them to be very obedient during punishing sessions and the next time they frequently volunteer to hold open their own drawers, offering their behinds eagerly to the punishing hand or the rod.

"If the delinquent is pretty and her physique is such as to give considerable pleasurable excitement, I would recommend keeping her between one's thighs. If the dear little one is not already in the nude, I would advise strongly to peel off her drawers.

"Unfortunately it is impossible to use the same method with the large girls,

SQUIRE HARDMAN *from page 43*

"There's but one proper med'cine for a dunce,
"And so—down with your breeches, Sir, at once!"

The little fellow, with a fearful gaze
At Mary, gasps and trembles, and obeys;
And there, all taut and trembling, is his rump,
Divinely rounded, exquisitely plump,
And wearing still in tell-tale indigo
The signs that 't has been whipt not long ago;
But shewn t' advantage by that bending stance,
The welted surface of the wide expanse
But whets our ardour, and in accents plain
Invites the rod to cut and come again.

For sev'ral minutes we drink in the sight
Approve his posture and enjoy his fright;
And then my Mary, rising from her chair,
Makes her cane whistle softly in the air.
O lovely sound, more pleasing to my senses
Than any that an Orchestra dispenses,
Sweeter than vernal jargoning of birds,
Than bells at ev'ning or than lovers' words,
How sweetly that precursive swish alone
Evokes a quiver in my gluteal zone,
As if I were, myself, the sans-culotte
And whipping-boy—which (thank my stars) I'm not!

"Well, Bobby, (cries my Dear) you scatterbrain,
"Speak up now! Are you ready for the cane?"
And with the words she cuts the air again.
I smile to see the o'er-expectant thighs
Contracting as he stammers and replies,
"Y-yes, Ma'am, Mrs. Hardman! B-but pray
"Have mercy! You have whipt me twice today—"
"—And must once more, ev'n tho'
  it draw the blood!
"Remember, you are whipt for your own good.
"And now, no further prating: turn your face,
"Look straight before you—and in any case,
"Keep your hands properly upon your knees,
"And do not change that posture, if you please."

He whimpers and obeys; then trembling-tense,
Awaits in a fine fever of suspense
The moment when his caning shall commence.
But Mary, mistress of the flogging art
In all its branches, knows the proper part
Played by a culprit's sense of blows to come,
And still defers the onslaught on his b—m:
Four times the whistling rattan cuts the air
A nail's breadth from that cow'ring derriere,

Continues p. 47

even though we have to forego a tremendous pleasure. Those girls, however, are capable of putting two and two together, and it would be very unseemly if they were to discover that our disciplinary actions, which are so necessary for their proper education, have a twofold purpose, namely our pleasure first, their education second. The titillating delight such a girl gives us should, alas, be sufficient for us.

"The punishment of the larger girls, and they are capable of suffering a prolonged beating, can be more complicated and therefore more fun. First of all, their drawers can be opened and a beating with the hand can be administered. If the girl is unwilling to hold open her drawers herself to receive the rod, the drawers should be unbuttoned and taken down. Then the girl is to be placed in a position where it is most comfortable for the beater to administer the blows. One may let the girl kneel in front of a stool or a chair and tie her.

"Personally I suggest the use of a chair and make the penitent sit astride it. Her drawers have to be taken down and she has to be tied to the chair, her behind sticking out and her wrists tied behind her back. She should then be forced to bend over and her skirts and chemise should be tied around the waist. Of course, it is far more practical to undress the victim completely. Because of the fact that the girl is bending forward, the greater part of her behind becomes accessible to the carpet beater.

"I prefer this instrument for this position because the skin is so tautly stretched across the flesh that any other would make it burst. The carpet beater, however, causes incredible soreness, redness, pain and discomfort, but the straps do not break the tender skin tautly stretched across the buttocks. But to really enjoy the type of punishment I just described, it is necessary to have the big bottom of a big strapping girl, like for instance the cook or a chambermaid.

"Since adults are usually punished only for true sins, it is obvious that one can make them run the entire gamut of humiliations. One may make them undress completely and lightly slap them all over the body, a procedure which causes great discomfort, especially when an occasional stinging blow is delivered. They never know when to expect the next one. Simultaneously one is able to taste the delight of causing humiliation and the excitement of viewing a body which is fully developed in all its delicious splendour."

19. Hold Out Your Hand

Mr. Davis gave a portentous "hem", and said, in his most impressive manner—

"Young ladies, you remember what I said to you a week ago. I am sorry this has happened; but I never allow my rules to be infringed, and I never break my word. Miss March, hold out your hand."

Amy started, and put both hands behind her, turning on him an imploring look, which pleaded for her better than the words she could not utter. She was rather a favourite with "old Davis," as, of course, he was called, and it's my private belief that he would have broken his word if the indignation of one irrepressible young lady had not found vent in a hiss. That hiss, faint as it was, irritated the irascible gentleman, and sealed the culprit's fate.

"Your hand, Miss March!" was the only answer her mute appeal received; and, too proud to cry or beseech, Amy set her teeth, threw back her head defiantly, and bore without flinching several tingling blows on her little palm. They were neither many nor heavy, but that made no difference to her. For the first time in her life she had been struck…

20. An Evil Disposition Firmly Checked

I own, as you see, one of the most honoured names in England, and call myself "Gratitude", because I am anxious to show my gratitude for the fact that I owe my present position as a useful, happy English lady to the firm discipline I experienced at the very turning-point of my life. I was brought up in a loving home, I had every possible advantage; but amidst it all I became sullen, self-willed, and disobedient and idle. I was the grief of my parents and a byword to my companions. However, soon after I was fifteen I most fortunately was sent to Mrs—'s school for young ladies, in Brighton, where I showed the same evil disposition which I had evinced elsewhere, but where, most fortunately and happily for me, it was checked and cured. In school and out of it, during the first month, Mrs— and the other teachers reproved me, set me tasks, and "kept me in." But I only grew worse and one night, after I had refused to do an "imposition" as boys call a punishment lesson, Mrs— came and sat in my room, after I was in bed, and talked to me most impressively. The next day, however, the impression of what she had said wore off, and I was as bad as ever. But a change was at hand, for in the evening, when we had just gone to our bedrooms, Mrs— again came to me, and said, "Miss W., you will tonight occupy the dressing-room adjoining my room. I will show the way." I was half inclined to disobey. However, I followed my governess through her bedroom and across a small sitting-room which opened out of it into a room comfortably furnished, in which was a small low bed, and telling me to undress and go to bed, Mrs— left me, locking the door after her. I had been in bed about a quarter of an hour when Mrs— came to me, holding in her hand a long birch-rod. Placing the candlestick and the rod on the table, she told me that but one course was now open to her after my behaviour, and that she was going to flog me, and I was to get up. But though the twigs of the birch-rod stood out in ominous shadow in front of the candlestick, and while I noted the thin, closely-wrapped handle of that rod, and its fanlike-spreading top, I never attempted to obey. Three times Mrs— told me to get up, but I stirred not. She then very deliberately turned down the bedclothes, and again told me to get out of bed. I began to feel that I was going to be conquered, but yet I stirred not. Mrs— returned to her own room, and came back with a small, thin riding-whip, and said, "Must I use this?" There was something about her which quite awed me—it was more her manner than her tall, powerful figure—and as she swung the whip about in her hand I at once stepped out of bed and stood before her. "Give me your hands," she said, but I put them behind me, when slash across my shoulders came six or seven smart strokes of her whip, and screaming I put out my hands, which she fastened together with a cord by the

SQUIRE HARDMAN *from page 45*

And each delusive stroke, with threat'ning sound
Makes the affrighted flesh leap and rebound—
A sight at once so pleasant and so droll,
I cannot choose but laugh, upon my soul;
When all at once, and with no farther warning,
The cane makes contact with the seat of learning
In strokes so rapid, brisk and sure of aim,
Th' astonish'd skin is suddenly aflame
Almost before 'tis conscious of the same!
But laggard sense soon catches up with pain,
And hearty yells acknowledge that the train
Of warm impressions, though awhile delay'd,
Has been completed, and the charge convey'd.

But best of all I find our eldest lad;
For Dick has spirit, and I love, by Gad,
To see he's neither milksop nor poltroon:
Indeed, I've seen him flogg'd into a swoon,
His skin from waist to ankles strip'd and swoln,
Ere he'd admit to having lied or stolen—
When he was innocent! I love to see
Such indications of Integrity,
And how a stubborn will can match the power
Of a good horsewhip laid on for an hour.
The boy, God bless him, has a temper too,
Which even the fear of whipcord can't subdue,
A fault we claim most thoroughly to detest,
But which in sober truth (be it confess'd)
We like of all his qualities the best.
For how comely 'tis and how refreshing
To cap a youngster's tantram with a thrashing,
To raise his choler by your ridicule,
And then exasperate the little fool
Until his sullen silence or his rage
Brings down the punishment that fits his age!

And, once you have him hors'd and
strapped in place,
What sport it is to taunt him to his face—
Aye, ev'n as he is writhing 'neath the whip,
To stand and ply him still with gibe and quip,
Till you're unable to distinguish plain
His howls of anger from his shrieks of pain.

So when we have our ev'ning interviews
'Tis never long before I find excuse
To criticize Dick's carriage or demeanour;
I eye his hands, remark they could be cleaner,
Find fault with his attire, or break some jest
Upon his latest whipping, and protest
His silly bawling interrupts my rest.

Continues p. 49

wrists. Then making me lie down across the foot of the bed, face downwards, she very quietly and deliberately, putting her left hand round my waist, gave me a shower of smart slaps with her open right hand—a proceeding which so surprised and humiliated my proud self that I could hardly believe in my own identity, and as I screamed and struggled, she merely said, "This is for not doing now as I told you, and it will not only punish you for that, but will increase the pain of the birching I am now going to give you." Mrs—then, as I lay, spoke to me for a few minutes with great kindness and earnestness. She then rose, took the birch in her right hand, and stooping over me, pressed her left hand tightly on my shoulder so as to hold me as if I were in a vice; then raising the birch, I could hear it whiz in the air, and oh, how terrible it felt as it came down, and as its repeated strokes came swish, swish, swish, on me! yet I felt, spite of the terrible stinging pain, that I deserved it all—and it was painful. I was a stout, fair girl, and very sensitive to pain. I screamed, I protested, I implored, but it was of no avail; Mrs— heeded not my cries, but held me down and birched on till she had finished a whipping which seemed to last an age, but which quite changed my character. At last it was over. I was permitted to rise, my hands were unbound, and, burning and smarting, I raised my tear-stained face to my true friend's, on whose face no sign was visible of the slightest anger or passion. Calm and serene, she wished me "Good night," and left me conquered. Henceforward I was a different girl; and though a few weeks afterwards I relapsed, yet another night spent in Mrs—'s dressing-room, and another similar application by her of that wonder-working birch—I did exactly as she told me this time—sufficed finally to cure me. I became cheerful, obedient, unselfish. My parents and friends the next holidays could hardly believe that I was the same girl. I stayed three years with Mrs— at Brighton, leaving her when I was nineteen with much regret. I am now twenty-four, and hope to be married at Easter to the best man in the world, who never could have loved me had not sensible, wholesome discipline changed my evil nature, as the means under Higher Power of doing so. I am thankful to publish my experience, and so to express not only my gratitude, but confirm what others have so well said and told on this subject.

21. CHOOSING A SWITCH

MY SCHOOL DAYS began when I was four years and a half old. There were no public schools in Missouri in those early days but there were two private schools—terms twenty-five cents per week per pupil and collect it if you can. Mrs. Horr taught the children in a small log house at the southern end of Main Street. Mr. Sam Cross taught the young people of larger growth in a frame school-house on the hill.

I was sent to Mrs. Horr's school and I remember my first day in that little log house with perfect clearness, after these sixty-five years and upwards—at least I remember an episode of that first day. I broke one of the rules and was warned not to do it again and was told that the penalty for a second breach was a whipping. I presently broke the rule again and Mrs. Horr told me to go out and find a switch and fetch it. I was glad she appointed me, for I believed I could select a switch suitable to the occasion with more judiciousness than anybody else.

In the mud I found a cooper's shaving of the old-time pattern, oak, two inches broad, a quarter of an inch thick, and rising in a shallow curve at one end. There were nice new shavings of the same breed close by but I took this one, although it was rotten. I carried it to Mrs. Horr, presented it and stood before her in an attitude of meekness and resignation which seemed to me calculated to win favour and sympathy,

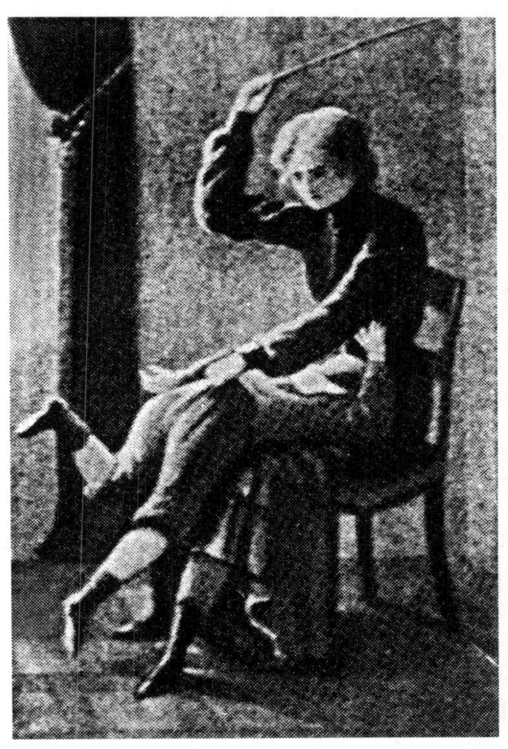

SQUIRE HARDMAN

from page 47

Thus by degrees I activate his bile
With cutting comment and sarcastic smile,
Till, grown at once both angry and dismayed,
He speaks—and there's occasion ready made.
"What's that you say, Sir!" I inquire at once;
I turn his explanations to affronts,
Then lead him on to make some statement rash:
Whate'er he answers, he must have the lash;
While if he holds his tongue, 'tis all the same
(Silent or speaking, he must lose the game):
"What, in the sullens, Dick?' cries Mary then,
"I really think you must be whipt again."
"Aye, aye, my love, there is no other course,"
I interject. "Come, Dick, to horse, to horse!"
And with these words we carry him upstairs,
Where you can guess how pleasantly he fares,
Stripped to his shirt and strapp'd down on his face
To have his b—m whipped for an hour's space.

But sometimes, for variety and spice,
We use that other notable device
The schoolroom so conveniently affords—
I mean the Whipping-scale, whose cuffs and cords
Hang always ready for our little wards.
And then, observe how temptingly Dick stands,
Drawn up on tiptoe by his fetter'd hands,
With all his backside, gloriously nude,
Presented in the natural attitude!
Indeed, I think that, as a Connoisseur,
This posture is the one that I prefer;
And when the flogging starts, you may agree
'Tis more diverting when the legs are free.

But come, see for yourself (along with me),
As Mary bares her arm and takes a grip
Upon her long and slender riding-whip
An instrument well fitted to instill
The categories of a woman's will,
To dress the wayward, to control the wild
And quell the humours of the naughtiest child.
And mark now, how that limp and lifeless thing
Assumes an animation and a spring,
Quiv'ring thro' all its smooth and limber length,
As rapiers do to feel the swordsman's strength:
How, once 'tis grasp'd in Mary's practis'd hand,
It seems to come alive, to understand
Its finest role to flog a boy in style.
And when, with no preamble save a smile,
My fair tormentress brings it into play,
You see th' unequal contest under way.

Continues p. 51

but it did not happen. She divided a long look of strong disapprobation equally between me and the shaving; then she called me by my entire name, Samuel Langhorne Clemens—probably the first time I had ever heard it all strung together in one procession—and said she was ashamed of me. I was to learn later that when a teacher calls a boy by his entire name it means trouble. She said she would try and appoint a boy with a better judgment than mine in the matter of switches, and it saddens me yet to remember how many faces lighted up with the hope of getting that appointment. Jim Dunlap got it and when he returned with the switch of his choice I recognised that he was an expert.

22. A Boys' Prison Birching

NEXT MORNING I walked behind this boy, a white-headed youngster of ten, when we were being exercised in a batch in the yard, and in a whisper I had with him I learnt that we had not had our punishment yet because he had still to be examined by the surgeon. His sentence was fourteen days and a whipping, for heaving stones at a peeler. He had sobered down since the evening, but had regained some of his perkiness, and, like me, had never had a penal whipping before and was in a similar tremble of anticipation. But soon after we were taken back to the cells I heard him being marched off to the surgeon, and I knew then that it would not be long now. In half an hour or so I heard the youngster being brought back, he was howling pitifully, so I at once knew that he had had his turn. I heard him locked in his cell, his howls answered with scoffs from the corridor warder, who threatened to report him if he did not stop his noise, and get him put on bread and water. The warder then opened my door. "Come on," he said, "they're waiting to make a young nightingale out o' you too." Words that made me quail, and the moans that swelled from the youngster's cell as I passed and followed me down the corridor further chilled me. The building sounded empty, nearly all the boys being either in the shed picking oakum or otherwise employed, and we passed out across a yard into another similar building, which also sounded empty, and I was led into a large isolated cell in the fore-part. There I at once saw the hurdle on which I was to suffer in position against a recess in the wall, and I was greeted thus. "Here comes the other young blackguard to be whipped, sir"

The governor, the gentleman in a frock-coat whom the Prime had addressed, and who was smoking a pipe, gave me the curtest of glances, then turning to the surgeon, asked how many strokes I was fit for. The surgeon answered that I was fit for as many as the governor had in mind for me. "The governor now exchanged a word with the Prime, and then ordered him to give me twenty strokes. The Prime touched his cap, and the governor, after signing to the Prime to carry out the punishment, then withdrew, the surgeon following him out. having apparently something to discuss with him. At a nod from the Prime the warder with me now pulled down my trousers, and he and the warder who was to be the whipper, a loutish man of pugnacious cast, started to fasten me to the hurdle. The board on which the middle of my body rested had to be fixed for my height, and my hands tied with a cord on a pulley attached to the two posts of the hurdle and then pulled forward, which had the effect of keeping my body stretched, a strap going round my waist, below which I showed by shapes, my feet being strapped to the bottoms of the two posts. Meantime I was contemplating the fearsome birchrod, the handle being very long and the twigs in the form of a thick bush, that was standing against the wall. A bucket of water stood close by. The only words spoken while I was being fastened up, there was nobody but those three men in the cell, were by the whipper, who asked me in a gruff voice if I had said my prayers, because if I had not, I had best do so at once.

"I could not have described the punishment, the pain was so acute, it deprived me of my critical faculties, I merely felt an ever increasing smarting in my tail and in spite of my manly resolves I could not help crying out pitifully, though the strokes were hurting more than injuring me. After ten had been counted by the Prime there was an interval of a few minutes, during which the surgeon came back, examined me with some care, and then pronounced me fit for the second lot. He remained while these were inflicted, in slow enough time to let me lie quivering on the hurdle in dread of the next stroke, and I sought relief by squirming and straining in the straps, my cries now becoming more of a continuous moan. But when it was over, though my tail was much swollen and bleeding freely, and I was still moaning a little, I was surprised how sound I otherwise felt. When the Prime said, "Well boy, you've been well flayed, how d'you feel?", I was able to answer him, quite truthfully and in a broken voice, "Not too bad, sir," And the surgeon's comment after he had examined me further was, "A wonderfully hardy youngster for his age." He then gave me a touch on the shoulder as a sign that I could pull my trousers on, and said, "Now, boy, let this be a lesson to you." The warder then took me back to my cell, remarking on the way that I was not nearly such a nightingale as the other youngster had been. "Do boys always sing under the birch, sir?" I had the spirit to ask him. "The younger 'uns mostly do, that's sure," he said.

23. A SEVERE TUTOR

THERE WAS A strong feminine element in Bertie Seyton; he ought to have been a pretty and rather boyish girl. The contrast would have been greater then: now he looked at times too like a small replica' of his sister, breeched and cropped.

Faithful history, desirous that the character and training of one actor on her stage should be duly understood, may be allowed to look after the boy a little and record the result of his small adventure. Entering the house before dressing-time he encountered his tutor. The wet hair, the face still salted from the sea and breathing at every pore of sea-water, the stained tie and dishevelled collar, gave damnatory proof against him. Passing over any form of question, Mr. Denham simply let one sentence drop from pale and close lips: "Tomorrow after breakfast, my boy, before we begin work." Herbert passed him without appeal. The evening wore through much as usual; but some inflexion in the boy's voice as he said good-night irritated the restless nerves of his tutor, who fell asleep upon a resolution to pay him off thoroughly. At breakfast Lady Wariston noticed in her brother's manner a certain shyness that was nei-

SQUIRE HARDMAN

from page 49

See how the smooth and waxy whipcord twines
In artful circles round the quiv'ring loins,
As each soft whistle of its airy round
Ends in a sharp, excruciating sound!
See, too, what leaps the nervous buttocks make,
How the skin shudders and the muscles shake—
And hear the howl that follows, to proclaim
How well the lash succeeded in its aim!
Now up, now down, now counter, now crosswise,
Lashing the hips and licking round the thighs,
The active cord industriously flies;
While Mary, sovran mistress of its course,
Pois'd in the grace of majesty and force,
Induces with each flourish of her arm
Still lovelier movements of her lissome form;
And I, well plac'd t' enjoy the double view,
Divide my greedy glances 'twixt the two,
Admire, with rising flesh and rapture dumb,
The dancing bubbies and the writhing b—m.

And when Dick's hinderparts can take no more,
There's still some livelier punishment in store:
Now you shall see how cunning 'twas to leave
His legs unfasten'd—for you'd scarce believe
The sport he'll shew us when the lash begins
To do its business on his calves and shins.
—Aye look now at that whip-begotten prancing,
Those kicks and pirouettes, a kind of dancing
Full of the maddest leaps, the wildest twirls!
The reeling hips recall an Indian girl's
In fine disorder, but the feet below
The "cake walk" of a Nigger Minstrel Shew—
And hear how well those piercing screams enhance
This schoolroom version of St. Vitus' dance!
And still the work goes on, the blows descend,
Until poor Dick, whose shrieks and sobs contend,
Must wonder if the thing will never end.
But, back'd by watchful eye and cunning wrist,
The busy lash leaves ne'er an inch unkiss'd,
No crease exempted and no cranny miss'd,
Until it has picked out, from waist to heels,
A splendid tracery of crimson weals;
And there th' exhausted culprit hangs at last,
Flogg'd to the most exacting Husband's taste.

Thus, Madam, do my wife and I prepare
For th' adequate performance of our share
Of those connubial duties which, you know,
The Wife and Husband to each other owe;
For who so lickerish as my lovely spouse
After a pleasant, punitive carouse,

Continues p. 53

ther insolence nor timidity but very like both.

"Is Bertie in trouble again, Mr. Denham?" she said when they rose. He smiled. "The face speaks for itself, Lady Wariston."

It was pale and visibly hot, with tightened lips and tremulous eyelids.

"This won't do at Eton, you know, Herbert," said Lord Wariston as he passed.

"Poor old Bertie," said his sister. "Come and tell me about it when it's all over. And don't flog him within quite an inch of his life, Mr. Denham, please."

There was a singular light in the man's eyes as they followed her passing out after this speech; a sharp hard look with a cruel edge to it, but full of hidden heat; the light and heat of dumb desire, of desperate admiration, of bitter and painful hatred. Something too of wayward and hopeless pleasure was in their dark grey globes, latent and tacit. Suffering, self-contempt, envy, and the rage of inverted love and passion poisoned in the springs, all were absorbed by the keen delight of a minute while her skirt brushed him and her eyes touched him. A pungent sense of tears pricked his eyelids and a bitter taste was in his tongue when she went out. Her godlike beauty was as blind and unmerciful as a god. Hating her with all his heart as he loved her with all his senses, he could but punish her through her brother, hurt her through his skin; but at least to do this was to make her own flesh and blood suffer for the pain inflicted on himself. His feet were cold, his head was full of hot and sickly fancies his heart beat as hard as Herbert's when they entered the library, though his will controlled and quenched the agitation of his nerves. The likeness infuriated him; but he subdued the fury; eyes of cold anger and judicial displeasure followed the boy's movements. Bertie winced under them, but saw nothing singular in their expression; there was no fierceness in its gravity, no variation in its rebuke

He made a last appeal, looking up in Denham's face.

'Please, sir, I wasn't in the water long. And it wasn't rough—not very. I promise I won't bathe again this year by myself."

'I don't think you will, Herbert. I mean to make sure of that: and I advise you as a friend not to keep me waiting, or I shall have you hoisted; and then you must take the consequences. Go down"—and poor Bertie "went down" after the manner of schoolboys at the block.

"Now mind, I mean to punish you severely; after an offence like this you can hardly expect to come off as easily as usual."

He spoke in a clear harsh note, with brightening eyes and tightening lips, as he watched the boy wince; his words had edges and cut like a harsh look.

"Must I tie your hands? or will you promise not to resist?"

"I won't move; or put my hands back: I won't, on my honour", said the boy: but the first stroke made him leap and writhe, catching his breath with a sharp sob: Denham knew better than to flog too fast; he paused after each cut and gave the boy time to smart.

"Will you tie my hands please—or I'm sure I can't—keep my word?" quoth Bertie in a sharp small shaking voice, turning half round and holding his wrists out. Denham was rather moved for the minute; but the cold fit of cruelty was upon him. He tied the small wrists tight and laid on the lithe tough twigs with all the strength of his arm. There was a rage in him now more bitter than anger. The boy sobbed and flinched at each cut, feeling his eyes fill and blushing at his tears; but the cuts stung like fire, and burning with shame and pain alike, he pressed his hot wet face down on his hands, bit his sleeve, his fingers, anything; his teeth drew blood as well as the birch; he chewed the flesh of his hands rather than cry out, till Denham glittered with passion. A fresh rod was applied and he sang out sharply: then drew himself tight as it were all over, trying to brace his muscles and harden his flesh into rigid resistance; but the pain beat him; as he turned and raised his face, tears streamed over the inflamed cheeks and imploring lips. It was not the mere habit of sharp discipline, sense of official duty or flash of transient anger, that impelled his tormentor; had it been any of these he might have been more easily let off. As it was, Denham laid on every stripe with a cold fury that grew slowly to white heat; and when at length he made an end, he was seized with a fierce dumb sense of inner laughter; it was such an absurd relief this, and so slight. When these fits were on him he could have taken life to ease his bitter and wrathful despair of delight.

"Here," he said, contemptuous of the boy's brief bodily pain, and half relieved by the sight of it; "give me your hands to untie. You've felt the last of this rod, my boy. Come, stop crying. I hope you'll never have anything worse to cry for;

you'll be the luckiest fellow I know."

But Herbert, after a double dose of flogging, was not in a condition to see this: he did readjust himself, with sundry sobs and pauses and then stood tingling and crying, with hidden face and heaving shoulders: only looking up when he felt his tutor's eyes on him. His own as he raised them were as full of light as of tears; the light that comes into the eyes of one still fighting against pain, hot with fever and brilliant with rebellion, shot out under the heavy eyelashes fringed thickly with tears. Denham flinched in his turn; his eyes fell, and he smiled. He had never seen the two faces so like before; the eyes were hers now that pain had brightened and tears softened them...

24. THE GOVERNESS TAKES CHARGE

MISS EVELYN, FOR some reason or other, was out of humour that morning, and more than once spoke crossly to me for my evident inattention. At length she called me to her, and finding that I had scarcely done anything, she said—

"Now, Charles, I give you ten minutes longer to finish that sum, if not done in that time I shall whip you. You are exhibiting the mere spirit of idleness. I do not know what has come over you, but if persisted in, you shall certainly be punished."

The idea of the beautiful Miss Evelyn whipping my bare bottom did not tend to calm my excitement, on the contrary, it turned my lewd thoughts upon the beauties of her person, which I had so often furtively gazed upon.

It was close upon four o'clock, at which hour we always broke up for a run in the garden for an hour, and during this period I had resolved to begin instructing Mary in the secret mysteries I had so lately been a witness to. But fate had ordered it otherwise, and I was to receive my first practical lesson and be

SQUIRE HARDMAN *from page 51*

And who so happy as the ardent Squire
When his dear flagellant and he retire
To slake their mutually arous'd desire?
Aye, who so blest as I in such a wife?

Who, from such vision of impassion'd strife
Betwixt a woman and a naked boy,
Can pass straightway to more substantial joy?
And now for nigh five years my lot has been
Cast in the pleasant places you have seen:
With such prime urchins and with such a wife,
I live, indeed, an enviable life;
For, put aside the gust which amorous play
Receives from flagellation, night and day,
Consider what is gain'd another way—
When all the rubs and crosses and longueurs
Which matrimony's heir to, and what's worse,
The female spleen that breeds domestic jars,
The humours that make wedded life a farce,
Are work'd off promptly on some luckless a—e!

Indeed, so fortunate in every sense,
I've grown th' uxorious man par excellence;
For who from such a Wife would choose to roam,
Or even spend a night away from home?
Not I, in truth—and when I'm call'd to town
On tedious business which will tie me down
For a fortnight or more, I count each day
As lost, as absolutely thrown away:
A hundred times I rail upon the chance
Which parts me from my little miscreants
And my dear paragon of flagellants;
A hundred times I call into my mind
A vision of the joys I've left behind,
Until my tears (I do confess it) flow
For the domestic bliss I must forego,
And the sole comfort of my sad condition
Is to project that Orgy of punition,
That festival of infant suffering
With which I'll celebrate my homecoming.

However, my downcast and anxious air
Is not unnotic'd, as I'm well aware;
And thus throughout the neighbourhood I've won
The excellent regard of everyone As the best
Husband underneath the sun;
As Guardian, also, of three foundling boys,
I find my fame is making such a noise
That I'd not be surpris'd if I were sent
At next elections into Parliament.
—But who so well admir'd, so far renown'd,

Continues p. 55

initiated on the person of a riper and more beautiful woman; but of this hereafter.

At four o'clock I had done nothing with my task—Miss Evelyn looked grave: "Mary and Eliza, you may go out, Charles will remain here." My sisters, simply imagining that I was kept in to finish my lessons, ran into the garden. Miss Evelyn turned the key in the door, opened a cupboard, and withdrew a birch rod neatly tied up with blue ribbons.

Now my blood coursed through my veins, and my fingers trembled so that I could hardly hold my pencil. "Put down your slate, Charles, and come to me." I obeyed, and stood before my beautiful governess, with a strange commixture of fear and desire.

"Unfasten your braces, and put down your trousers."

I commenced doing this, though but very slowly. Angry at my delay her delicate fingers speedily accomplished the work. My trousers fell to my feet. "Place yourself across my knees." Tremblingly, with the same commixture of feeling, I obeyed.

Her silk dress was drawn up to prevent its being creased—my naked flesh pressed against her snowy white petticoats. A delicate perfume of violet and venain assailed my nerves. As I felt her soft and delicate fingers drawing up my shirt, and passing over my bare posteriors, while the warmth of her pulpy form beneath me penetrated my flesh, nature exerted her power… I had but little time, however, to notice this before a rapid succession of the most cruel cuts lacerated my bottom. "Oh, dear! Oh, dear! Oh, dear! Oh, Miss Evelyn. I will do the sum if you will only forgive me. Oh, oh, oh," etc.

Holding me firmly with her left arm, Miss Evelyn used the rod most unmercifully. At first, the pain was excruciating, and I roared out as loud as I could, but gradually the pain ceased to be so acute, and was succeeded by the most delicious tickling sensation. My struggles at first had been so violent as to greatly disorder Miss Evelyn's petticoats, and to raise them up so as to expose to my delighted eyes her beautifully formed silk-clad legs up to the knees, and even an inch or two of naked thigh above. This, together with the intense tickling irritation communicated to my bottom, as well as to the friction of my cock against the person of Miss Evelyn in my struggles, rendered me almost delirious, and I tossed and pushed myself about on her knees in a

state of perfect frenzy as the blows continued to be showered down upon my poor bottom. At last the rod was worn to a stump, and I was pushed off her knees.

25. MADAME DE BERROS

MADAME DE BERROS then clapped her hands, when two of the female attendants, who were always in waiting in the ante-room, came in through the folding doors and courtesied. "Bring me a rod," said madame to one of them. "Prepare Miss B," she motioned to the other. The culprit scarcely even changed colour, and, seeming to know that all resistance would be in vain, resigned herself at once to her fate. The maid having brought in a long birch rod of very slender twigs, handed it to madame from a salver, with a courtesy, and then proceeded to aid her confrere in the unrobing. Having courtesied to madame, and kissed the rod—a ceremony which was never omitted upon the occasion of a flagellation—one of the maids took her gently on her shoulder, turning round at a little distance from madame. It being my first appearance at a flagellation, I felt a mixture of emotions which I cannot describe.

All being ready, madame, flinging back her arm, brought the rod down gently on the culprit, who at once uttered an exclamation as if she had been plunged in a cold bath. About a dozen stripes equally gentle followed, and then madame, as if warmed by the exercise, concluded in a way which brought the lady to tears. Being at length let down on an ottoman, her hands were released, when, after kneeling down and kissing the rod, Miss B—retired with a profound courtesy, the attendant carrying her petticoats and robe into the anteroom.

26. THE VIRTUES OF CEREMONY

A WHILE AGO I undertook to bring up two nieces, of the ages of twelve and fourteen. I soon found them to be most stubborn tempers and impudent. Thus they have often caused me much trouble and annoyance. Though not an advocate of corporal punishment, I was much struck with the description by "A Schoolmistress" of a most ceremonious method of inflicting punishment that I determined to follow exactly the same method and try it the same morning.

I prepared a woollen dress; not being able to procure a birch I sent and had made a pair of very long pliant leather taws. In the afternoon I found the eldest of my nieces in a gross fault and on being found fault with she was very pert. I therefore took her to my bedroom and made her don the garment and follow me to the drawing-room, she never thinking for a moment of what was to follow. I then quietly told her of her bad conduct for some time past, and that I was determined to try what a whipping would do.

On ordering her to lay across an ottoman she distinctly refused. I told her if she did not at once comply I would ring for a servant to compel her. Still refusing, I rang for assistance. Hearing the servant coming upstairs, and seeing me determined, she lay down, rather than be seen by the servant in this predicament, wherefore I went to the door and sent the servant back. I then fastened her across the ottoman and then proceeded to administer a few

SQUIRE HARDMAN

from page 53

As the Squire's Lady in the country round?
What praise for all the pains she takes—and gives—
To educate her little primitives!
Her Spartan regimen, so well approv'd
Hath made her name respected and belov'd
Throughout the county, and I've even heard
Talk of a Testimonial being conferr'd
Upon us for our work of Christian charity—
A piece of news that fills me with hilarity.
And here's the finest irony of all:
Our Dick himself, now grown a stripling tall,
Has ta'en to bragging of how well he stands
His daily martyrdom at Mary's hands;
Exalts her strength, exaggerates his own,
And swears, by God, that he can make it known
His are the best whipt hurdies in the town!
I smile to find his pluck is such a byword,
And that, in the same manner as young Siward,
That likely youth of whom his father blunt,
Merely inquir'd, Were all his wounds in front?
Our Dick his no less honourable scars
Displays in triumph on his swollen a—e.

However, as the hast'ning years go past,
'Tis clear the situation cannot last;
For, as we see, the melancholy truth
Is that our eldest lad is now a Youth,
And soon must pass from our devoted care
To find a home and discipline elsewhere.
Indeed, his mind's made up, and to our joy,
He's set on 'listing as a drummer-boy,
Meaning to serve his Country and his King
By making a good cat-o'-nine-tails sing—
A life, you'll say, or which he seems ordain'd,
For to what business was he better train'd,
And for what work is he so well equipp'd?
The taste for whipping comes from being whipped.
—By Heav'n, I can already see the lad
Engaged in punishing some hulking cad
With all the regiment on dress parade
Drawn up to watch the jolly drama played;
What time the victim, naked to the waist,
His limbs to the triangle firmly lac'd
And writhing 'neath the salutary lash,
Is learning, from each skilful cut and slash,
That the new Drummer-boy, whate'er he lack
Of other lore, already has the knack
Of doing justice on a comrade's back.

Yet as that vision fades, I boldly face
The fact that someone else must take his place;

Continues p. 57

strokes of the taws, which soon elicited cries for forgiveness and promises of future good conduct, but being determined to try the efficacy of this method, I continued until I had given her a severe flogging.

I then allowed her to rise, and on her knees to thank me for the correction, then sent her off to bed for the day. Up to this time the perfect subjection and submission of this girl is such that I most heartily recommend all parents and guardians to try the same method in all cases of disobedience. I think that in all whippings of grown children a large amount of cool ceremony is most effectual."

27. A Master of Spanking

He executed all or nearly all the punishments, whether by spanking on the bare buttocks or by caning on the palm of the hand or by swishing on the posterior. I remember well all three experiences. He was a master of spanking, though he used to say that it hurt him nearly as much as it did us. I remember that it was at about the fifteenth blow that it really began to hurt, and from thence the pain increased in geometrical progression. The largest number of smacks I ever received was, I think, forty-two. But comic to relate, I still remember the delicious feeling of warmth that ensued five to ten minutes later when the circulation had been thoroughly restored and the surface pain had subsided… with the birch he never gave me beyond ten or twelve strokes—and that for some peculiarly grave offence—in his bedroom at night.

28. A Wardress Recollects

"Yes," said Cunigund soon afterwards, "only a few years ago Helen, whom I have just punished, would have got the birch in the morning. Every little domestic fault that I could put a stop to summarily with a few stripes was then punished in that manner. In the early morning I have gone along… to the bedside of a culprit and, while she was held down by her comrades, have given her a proper thrashing. And then there was order, great order, far better discipline than at present; therefore I was always glad to do it, and I gave such satisfaction that I was often called into the men's quarter to give the birch to some big lad, sometimes sixteen or seventeen years old. Ah! I delighted to lay on the stripes on a naughty boy's trousers, and I always thought then of the wise Solomon and Jesus Sirach, who order us not to spare the rod on wicked children, particularly boys.

"You'd hardly believe it, girls, how I did lay into them! Then as now the public was allowed to be present—for what have lads like that to show?…

"But, oh, you should have seen, children, how the great ladies, who never fail to be present at great 'Welcomes' and 'Farewells,' how they rush into the hall when it was announced that the 'Welcome' or 'Farewell' was to be given with birch to a lad… Oh, how often would one or other of them come and shake my hand, leaving in the palm of it a bright piece of money, and how often did I hear them say: "Yes, today good Cunigund has done her work downright well; wherever did she get her strength? Yes, she delivers her strokes as if they were measured with a compass, and the marks on the skin look as if they had been traced with a ruler!'"

29. Reluctant Cruelty

"SEVERIN, I WARN you for the last time," began Wanda.

"If you love me, be cruel towards me," I pleaded with upraised eyes.

"If I love you," repeated Wanda. "Very well!" She stepped back and looked at me with a sombre smile. "Be then my slave, and know what it means to be delivered into the hand of a woman," At the same moment she gave me a kick.

"How do you like that, slave?"

Then she flourished the whip.

"Get up!"

I was about to rise.

"Not that way," she commanded. "On your knees."

"I obeyed, and she began to apply the lash.

The blows fell rapidly and powerfully on my back and arms. Each one cut into my flesh and burned there, but the pains enraptured me. They came from her whom I adored, and for whom I was ready at any hour to lay down my life.

She stopped. "I am beginning to enjoy it," she said, "but enough for today. I am beginning to feel a demonic curiosity to see how far your strength goes. I take a cruel joy in seeing you tremble and writhe beneath my whip, and in hearing your groans and wails; I want to go on whipping without pity until you beg for mercy, until you lose your senses. You have awakened dangerous elements in my being..."

30. A Severe Flogging

THE SUMMER AFTER you left, while sharing with your sisters the instruc-

SQUIRE HARDMAN *from page 55*

For Mary Anne and I well understand
That we must have at least three boys in hand:
Our constant need to flagellate a b—m
Prescribes this figure as a minimum.
But here, I'm happy to relate, we've found
That subjects for the vacancy abound:
The Foundling Home, the workhouse Governor,
A dozen neighb'ring families and a score
Of bustling Widows offer us our choice
Of lads to take, and with persuasive voice
Extol the merits of some graceless brat,
Some unlick'd stripling or spoil'd dandiprat,
Whose urgent need of horsewhipping or caning
Is the best reason (as they keep explaining)
Why we should take the youngster into training.

But to each tempting offer I am blind:
The truth is, I have something else in mind.
I must confess (now, Madam, do not smile!)
I have a yearning towards the Infantile:
The image of a chit of three or four,
Arrayed in tucker, bib and pinafore,
Has haunted me for the past month and more,
And filled my head with genial fantasies
Of plump posteriors and baby thighs,
Divinely rosy, generously form'd,
And only waiting to be nicely warm'd!
For what is Home without a little child,
So gaily bold, so innocently wild,
Whose various peccadilloes may be made
The source of pleasures n'er before essayed?
Oh, how I long to see one ta'en in hand
By Mary Anne, and made to understand
The causes and effects of discipline
Applied in season to his infant skin!
For Parents, as I've notic'd with disgust,
Seldom correct their children till they must;
Most brats are whipp'd too little or too late,
And pay for faults at but the current rate:
Is not the wiser way t' anticipate

The naughtiness they're certain to commit
By thrashing them ere they're aware of it?
And so I lose myself in contemplation
Of all the forms of infant fustigation—
Those nursery spankings, where the female hand,
Softly insistent and severely bland,
Imparts to tender skins a crimson blush;
Those merry smackings with a smooth-back'd brush
Design'd to make the little buttocks burn;
And that old method, humourously stern,

Continues p. 59

tions of Miss Prim, I had witnessed the administration of the birch by that most modest and good-humoured of young ladies. Prize medallist of her college, learned and accomplished, the only objection to her as a governess was her youth, which might detract from her authority over her pupils. To obviate this, she had your mama's commands to punish freely, and for the sake of example, always in our presence. When resort to the rod became inevitable, Prim, blushing to the roots of her blonde hair, would retire with the culprit to a remote corner of the schoolroom, where, after a moment of unseen preliminaries, she would sit down facing the wall, the skirts of her book muslin fantailed round her waist, and her fat shoulders so square to the spectators that little of the other party to the transaction was visible but a flushed face and slippers in convulsions. Among so many there were various degrees of reluctance or otherwise. Philly, in especial, would cry, "harder yet," and drub the ankles and bump upon the lap, till Prim, in self-defence, was obliged to put forth the full force of her well-rounded arm. As a guest I was not subjected to this discipline, which did not seem to me to be very formidable. Who can judge of the unseen only by the seen, and on this model I had formed my notions of school punishment. Brought for the first time face to face with the naked facts of the Screechery, I felt a blending of awe, astonishment, and disgust, the latter feeling so powerful as almost to turn my stomach.

I shall now, as far as I dare, describe what I saw. The object that had scared Patty proved to be a heavy stool, rivetted, I believe, to the floor, with an upright front, in shape somewhat like an executioner's block, whereon the culprit knelt low and erect to receive the discipline. This block was covered with black cloth, and rested on a carpet of the same under the sky-light, so that the flesh-tints exposed on it, contrasting with the sombre ground, came out with photographic distinctness. The floor around was strewed with the fragments of a broken rod; Patty, her petticoats still pinned about her neck, dancing a sort of sob-saraband which left the spectator in no doubt as to the cause of her gyrations. On the block knelt Helen, my own Helen, in the hands of the Philistines.

Stays being inadmissible in the supreme moment, hers had been removed and lay upon a pile of her upper clothing. Wanting this support, the over-wide chemise had dropped to the middle of her back, where being met by the upturned tail and twisted into a rope, it formed a belt of white sufficient to show that she had been covered. At either side of the block and a little to the rear stood Armstrong and Atchinson, Steinkopf having been made by Martinet to yield her place to the latter in the present instance. These two held the rope lightly, rather to support it than to confine the culprit, whose arms they left free, with a dependence on her pluck which was not belied by her looks, for her cheeks blazed, her breasts heaved, and her eyes shone like carbuncles with the expression.

On Martinet I dared not look; being, however, aware of the motion of her arm, I turned aside my head and covered it with my apron.

I said that Patty's screams alarmed me, but I was even more horrified at the stoic silence which allowed every lash of the many-twigged rod to be heard cutting deep into the flesh with monotonous rhythm, interrupted only by occasional rasps against block or the dress of the assistants.

There is a pause at last—my head reels, for my own turn will come next—nay, my own turn is come!

"Once more I order you to come here and stand before me."

I was dropping to the floor, when Renardeau caught me by the neck and thrust under my nose a bottle of some pungent essence which instantly revived me.

"*Va qu'elle te chatouille!*" she hissed into my ear, givlng me a shove to hasten my movements.

Martinet's dreaded voice could indeed make me stand trembling before her, but no power could have induced me to look her in the face then. Even her shining shoes on which my eyes rested, seemed replete with menace.

"Dora Doveton."

Her tones were preternaturally calm, like the senators in my dream, and frightened me far more than angry scolding.

"Scarce ten days arrived here, you find your way already to the whipping room. And on what charge? For participation in a crime so wicked and at the same time so disgustingly obscene, I cannot pollute the cars of those present by even hinting at its nature. Such deeds, though nameless, require public and exemplary chastisement. It is now my painful duty to see if I cannot scourge that demon out of you. —Fetch two of the No. 6 rods, and unlace her, if necessary."

Renardeau darted her hand beneath my clothes and reported that I wore no stays. Nor do I now; my waist is naturally small, and a little stiffening in the body of the dress suffices to keep my breasts in order. Steinkopf, who had resumed her place, and Armstrong, then laid hold of me, and despite my prayers and tears, while one held my hands above my head, the other opened my dress behind, and stripped off skirt, pet-

SQUIRE HARDMAN

from page 57

Which Nurses love to use when unprepared,
That fine impromptu when the brat is bared,
A knee is angled, and a leading role
Played by the slipper's smooth elastic sole;
Nor do I overlook the covert sport
Of brawny nursemaids, who love to extort
The howls and screams which lighten their
"dull care"
By homely switchings in the open air,
As with the play of lithe unbudded twigs
They teach young feet to dance precocious jigs.
Then, mingled with the sounds I seem to hear
Of all this smacking-sport and spanking-cheer,

I half believe I catch the childish treble
Of my imaginary little rebel,
Rais'd in the accents of a sweet distress
Made doubly dear by its own artlessness.
Thus to my fancy I become a thrall
Until, as slumber wraps me in its pall,
My ear creates the loveliest sound of all,
And superimposes on the midnight's calm
The crick-crack of a woman's naked palm
Applied *con brio* to a bare backside:
Darkling I listen, and grow half-deified
To hear that cadence, regular and slow,
And all the time, between each stinging blow,
The ululation of infantine woe.

Nor have I been in any manner chary
Of retailing these fantasies to Mary:
"And see you not, my dearest," I conclude,
"The gain arising from his babyhood?
"At such an age the undevelop'd tot
Can sleep in our own chamber, in his cot;
"And then Farewell the worry and distress
"Born of maternal conscientiousness,
"And all those nightly doubts which on you prey,
"Whether or no you've whipp'd enough that day:
"Those carking fears of having been too lenient
"Will vanish—for consider how convenient
"'Twill be to have the urchin at our side:
You've but to rise and reach him in one stride,
"Then whip him soundly till his screams allay
"Your doubts of duty unfulfill'd that day—
"When, eas'd by such well tim'd severity,
"You may return, in peace of mind, to me."
And then so eloquent do I become
Upon the subject of an infant b—m,
That she herself by now is quite agreed
A little child's exactly what we need.

Continues p. 61

ticoats, and drawers; then with one shameless drag she furled up my shift in front and rear, and pinned it over my shoulders.

The next moment I was forced upon my knees on the block, with four hands grasping my arms and pressing my neck down. The breeze from the sky-light fanned my back, and I felt that the eyes of all present were rivetted on my naked person. Could it be that I was thus subjected to such indignity? Though my arms were squeezed, I felt it not; all my sensation seemed to have retreated to another quarter. My skin is so tender that even when bathing I tremble to expose it, and here was I fixed as in a vice, with nothing intervening between that thin skin and the murderous implements behind me.

A pause, it seemed to me an hour long, ensued, till my spine grew cold as ice twixt fear and waiting. Something had rattled on the floor, but the sound had died away, and still the expected blow came not. I looked round with half a hope. Martinet was leisurely re-adjusting a bracelet on her rod arm, her eyes the while devouring my form with a wild impassioned gaze like a lover's.

Can she be relenting?

Alas! the brows contract—

—the grasps of the holders tighten on my arms—

—Whir—r—r—Whisp!

"Yah! Yeou! Yeoiks!" Oh! the unspeakable agony of that first murderous lash! Legions of scorpions fastened on my flesh and dug their fangs into my vitals. Vainly I hung back and screwed my front against the block, rear would not recede; I could only diminish its width by muscular contraction.

Whir-r–Whisp! Whir-r—Whisp! Whir-r-Whisp!

Nature cannot endure the pain; I struggle to my feet, receiving a fifth rasper in the act, and my shrieks rival the loudest howls of Patty.

This was the "whipping proper," a few strokes more of which would probably have killed or maddened.

The two strong women soon resumed their clutch and dragged me to my bearings on the whipping stool—less reluctantly—for already the charm had worked; the mere act of rising seemed to have brought relief, and a change next to miraculous took place in all my thoughts and feelings. I noted the impressions shortly after they occurred, and shall endeavour to describe them.

Fear and shame were both gone: it was as though I was surrendering my person to the embraces of a man whom I so loved I would anticipate his wildest desires. But no man was in my thoughts; Martinet was the object of my adoration, and I felt through the rod that I shared her passions. The rapport, as the magnetisers have it, was so strong that I could divine her thoughts; had she wished me to turn my person full front to her stripes, I should have fought and struggled to obey her. Then, too, there was a thrill in a certain part, I knew magnetically, of both our persons, which every fresh lash kept on increasing. The added pang unlocked new floods of bliss, till it was impossible to tell in my case whether the ecstasy was most of pain or pleasure. When the rods were changed, I continued to jump and shout, for she liked that, but—believe me or not—I saw my nakedness with her eyes, and exulted in the lascivious joy that whipping me afforded her. This state would have continued as long as my strength, for I had no power to quit the spot till my other self willed it.

The punishment over, I broke from the assistants, and from Atchinson, who, crinoline on arm, would have acted as lady's maid, and rushed towards Martinet, intending, I believe, to throw myself at her feet, when my course was forcibly arrested by Helen. With a whispered Steady! she unpinned my shift, and directed my attention to the last act in this day's drama, which was now commencing.

31. A Cruel Aunt

At the age of seventeen I was sent to a fasionable boarding school, near Exeter, in Devonshire. I was sent there owing to the influence of my aunt, who was always praising this establishment up to my mamma, and strongly recommending it as a finishing academy for young ladies. My aunt was a maiden lady of forty, a fine, tall, handsome, buxom woman.

Neither myself nor my mamma ever thought she was an advocate for the rod, and liked administering, and seeing it administered. It turned out afterwards, as the narrative will show, that she was really in league with the schoolmistress, and would frequently call at the establishment and indulge herself in her favourite pastime, for which she no doubt paid large sums annually, being a strong and fervent advocate for corporal chastisement, at times an unseen observer and with some of the elder young ladies being the operator. In all there was twenty-four young ladies in this fashionable establishment, their ages varying from twelve to nineteen. I was as tall, fine-shaped, and handsome as any young lady in the school, and no doubt when my mamma gave her consent to my leaving home, my aunt thought there was a great treat in store for her.

A few days after arriving, I soon found out what sort of lady principal I had to contend with, and her assistants were not much better. The first sample I saw her administer to one of her pupils was after I had been there four days. A young lady, about fifteen, had committed some trifling error, for which madam told her in plain terms that she should give her a good whipping when class was over, and this she did and in front of the whole school. She was taken by the arms and legs by two of the assistant teachers, and thrown face downwards over a desk sloping each way, and firmly held there. Madam then approached with a flat piece of wood about an inch-and-a-half in thickness, and shaped like a hair-brush, but much bigger. After addressing a few words of advice to us, and admonishing the culprit, she took hold of her garments at the bottom, then without any further to-do, she lifted the "spanker," as this piece of wood was called by my schoolfellows, and inflicted a tremendous "spank" across the girl. A loud yell followed, and a strong effort to free herself from the grasp of her tormentors, but all of no avail, for who, no doubt owing to their previous experience, could hold a young lady in any position. She received about a dozen stripes before she was released.

We had a system of making so many marks, and if any young lady had not made so many by the end of the week they were sure to receive a whipping. I have known as many as seven young ladies whipped on a Saturday. It was at these whippings that my aunt and her

SQUIRE HARDMAN

from page 59

And now, good members of my audience,
I'll take you all into my confidence,
By telling you my choice has long been made
Among the neighb'ring children I've surveyed;
And that I've ta'en already, with discretion,
Such steps as put the brat in my possession.
—But soft! There is a secret, dark and deep,
Which it behoves us from my Wife to keep.
Touching the little fellow's parentage;
For you can readily conceive her rage
Did she suspect he well may be my own—
Although of that there's nothing certain known.
The fact is, that about five years ago,
Ere I was wed, or thought of being so,
I would work off the humours in my blood
Upon a damsel of the neighbourhood,
And oft I thought, "Thank G—d that
  England breeds
"Such girls to fill the squirearchy's needs!
"This Polly in her humble bed of straw
"Gives me the pleasure of a Persian Shah
"And so she did: the only drawback was
There were well-nigh a dozen other Shahs;
And I discover'd soon, to my chagrin,
I had two rivals from the village inn,
Another from the forge, and two or three
From various farms in the vicinity—
All whom, in turn, my Polly entertain'd,
Their lusts invited and their vigour drain'd.

The day when I surpris'd her in the act,
I bore myself with dignity and tact;
I made pretence of being purely griev'd:
"By Heav'n, (I cried) 'tis scarce to be believed
"The parish holds such an abandon'd quean!
"Never was heard the like of it, nor seen:
"O fie, O shame upon you, Polly Green!
"Look ye, to punish your behaviour lewd,
"I'll see your annual lease is not renew'd."
And when, but three months after this decree,
She bore a handsome boy, it was to me
A source of satisfaction doubly sweet
To turn her and her bastard into street.
Since then her progress to the common sewer
Was (as I had expected) swift and sure:
A fine example of the classic pattern
Of wanton metamorphos'd into slattern.
Ere two weeks had gone by, this rustic fair
Was grown as common as a barber's chair;
Inside a year her face and features coarsen'd,
For beauty fled as her condition worsen'd;

Continues p. 63

friends were present as unseen spectators, through the medium of small glass panels being inserted in a door to an adjoining closet.

In fact, during my two years at this establishment I was whipped several times. I shall never forget my last experience. I think the lady principal had made up her mind that I should be flogged on the Saturday, for at the early part of the week, however good I did my lessons, fault was found with me, and I got careless towards the latter end. On the Saturday I found my name on the "Black List," as it was called. I was number three on the list, my two schoolfellows, both young girls about fourteen, had gone in and received their portion, and, as usual, had been dismissed to bed after their punishment. I was then ordered in. I need not tell you that I entered the room trembling from head to foot. Madam called me by my Christian name "Emily," and informed me she was very sorry to have to inflict punishment on such a big girl as me, but the rules of the school must be enforced, winding up by ordering me to prepare for punishment. I dropped on my knees in front of her, and begged of her to take into consideration my age, size, etc.; in fact I hardly remember what I did say. She was inexorable, and, with a smile on her face, ordered me to obey, or she should have to call assistance, and my punishment would be much more severe. I made some remark, when she seized me by my beautiful long hair, and beat me about my ears, head, cheeks, and arms, with the birch, until I was compelled to give in and promise obedience in future.

Soon after I found means to send a letter to my mother, informing her of the circumstances related above. She accordingly took steps for my early removal, and I was soon afterwards married, but my mother and aunt have never been friends or spoken to each other since.

32. Virtues of the Rod

Most lordly gentlemen and noble ladies, voluptuous flagellation is a constant thought in the minds of all refined votaries of Venus, while in high society this rapturous pastime gains ground daily. Let us be pleased at such progress, for 'tis the game of the gods! It is the supreme expression of a lover's adoration for a divine mistress; the ideal of mysterious intoxication. Woman is a mystic rose, and the man who loses his senses when inhaling the fragrance of the feminine flower, must also quiver naturally beneath the sharp prick of its thorns. What greater voluptuousness is there for a fervid lover than to bow down at his adored sweetheart's feet and vibrate beneath the magical caress of her rod?

In such a case, do you know what are a suitor's sensations? He is deliciously tormented by contrary emotions dragging him hither and thither, so to speak, between the fear of the sacrifice and his ardent desire to submit to it. He trembles at the sight of the formidable implements with which his mistress threatens him; he retreats affrighted, and yet dazed with delight is impelled to throw himself into the furnace. All his willpower crumbles away in a fit of bewildering weakness, as he feels himself humbled and crushed. He rolls on the ground at the feet of his inexorable charmer who renders him powerless by binding him with ropes abolishing all resistance. Obediently, like an attentive and submissive slave, he awaits his doom. His mistress's will is his, and she, implacable, soon resorts to extreme measures. Seizing the birch, she encircles him in flames, licking and burning his flesh. He tries to escape, or flee, but he cannot extricate himself from the grip that holds him fast. The imperious loving woman is actively plying her rod. Nothing can stay her hand—neither his prayers, nor his shrieks. Pain, however, inflicted by her—the radiant idol of his maddest dreams—is akin to joy, and suffering becomes voluptuous delirium.

33. A Shaming Punishment

Some of the best characteristics of our greatest men and women have had their beginnings in the discipline of a good mother, and those who wield the greatest influence over their children will be they who show themselves most in sympathy with the methods of our mothers, who before putting us to bed would punish us for our misdeeds in a very practical, if inelegant manner. I am a father of five, and by the request of their mother I leave them entirely to her for punishment, and I feel sure she would resent any interference on my part in what she regards as exclusively her domain. Indeed I have always regarded this birching as more a woman's topic than a man's. If a mother who is mentally and physically well and strong cannot manage her own children, I am sure their father cannot. From the beginning it has been conceded that the mother's influence over her children far outweighs the father's, at least up to 15 or 16.

My own father held this view, and gave the absolute control of those under that age to mother, who even then, in a case of flagrant misconduct, would not hesitate to unbutton our nether garments and cane us severely, afterwards making us beg humbly for forgiveness. Now I do not maintain that the physical pain of such a punishment is in itself alone calculated to do all that is required in reforming a bad boy or girl of 14; but at that age children are self-conscious, and regard themselves as "grown-up", and quite above such minor considerations as politeness. In a case of this sort I know of no more effective and positive remedy than that which was always resorted to by my mother, who regarded it as a "safe cure".

Up to fourteen I was a "model boy", tall for my age, and possessing some good traits, but falling in with a few evil companions older than myself soon began to develop the above symptoms, to which might be added bad language, smoking and late hours. This was soon to have an end!

A neighbour, whose fifteen year-old daughter I had kept out late, complained to my mother and demanded that I be punished. This was promptly acted upon, and the same night in my mother's bedroom, with the door locked, I was laying across her lap, clothed only in my nightgown. After a severe caning I was sobbing out my repentance, and giving very sincere promises "never to do it any more". I seemed as weak in her hands as when I was a baby. Her magnetic influence made it impossible to keep anything back. She made me confess to having appropriated a small sum of money, and with it having taken the aforesaid young lady to a music hall. In my undignified and repentant position across my moth-

Squire Hardman

from page 61

And as her eyes became more dim and sunken,
Her cheeks more bloated and her breasts
more shrunken
She added to her charms by turning drunken;
Till now, behold her at her hovel door,
With hair dishevell'd and eyes bleary'd o'er,
The very picture of the Village W—e.

But strange to say, the issue of her shame,
Her sturdy bantling (Joseph is his name)
Has grown in health and beauty, all the same.
Nay, there's no child in all the country round
So well look'd after, or one better found:
So nicely wash'd and comb'd, so sprucely drest,
The little fellow always looks his best.
But with all this, you never saw a child,
So far indulg'd, so cosseted and spoil'd,
So sharply pert, so impudently wild:
Shameless in speech, inveterately base,
He has become the Village's disgrace,
His attitudes the scandal of the place;
He never speaks but what his baby mouth
Is full of gibes or filthiness, or both,
And every second word a swingeing oath.
But worst of all, this wretched little creature
Has my Phys'ognomy and trick of feature,
Which gives much colour to the village talk
That Joey Green's "a bud from off my stalk;"

And tho' I've done my best to scotch the rumour,
Each time I hear it puts me out of humour:
Whether he's mine or not, I do not know:
What's certain is, I have it in for Joe!
And so today I spoke to Polly Green,
And told her I had come for her squireen.
Ev'n as I spoke I mark'd her looks of dread,
And tho' the pallor that her cheeks o'erspread
Soon chang'd to indignation's lusty red,
I feign'd to notice neither till I'd done:
"And so, you see (I said), the little one
"Will be well look'd to—for, as you're aware
"My Lady makes it her especial care
"To give a boy a proper Education—"
But here all Polly's powers of execration
Break forth, as raucously she intervenes:
"Foh, Education! I know what that means!
"'Tis only whipping him that she'd be at!
"I've heard about her special care for that,
"And how she keeps those three poor lads of hers
"Howling all day, just like so many curs!
And if you think I'll let her take my Joe

Continues p. 65

er's lap it was impossible to conceal the truth, so with a flood of tears I confessed everything.

My caning had been a most severe one, calculated to make anyone sob and appeal for mercy in a louder key than I had done; but I had a fearful dread of betraying to some listeners, giggling at the door, the manner in which I was paying the penalty; but my mother's intention was to make me thoroughly ashamed of myself. She talked very seriously for five minutes; then commenced the most mortifying part of it all.

Previously, the cane had been the silent instrument of torture, but mother decided, for the edification of the listeners at the door, to use her open hand. The unmistakable sound this produced made it known to everyone in the house that I was being chastised in the manner adopted with naughty children in the nursery. This was the most bitter part of it all; but as I knew afterwards, it was the great factor in effecting my cure. I had previously held some high opinions of myself, but mother had, in her own words, "taken the nonsense out of me", by letting me and all the family know that I was still regarded by her as a big naughty child, and as such treated me.

34. An Encounter with the Horse

Up to twelve years of age I was brought up by my aunt, who kept up my father's house (my mother died when I was very young). During this time no attempt was made to correct by physical pain (except of the mildest description) my many evil propensities and bad habits; but after I was twelve, my father married again, and I was sent to a boarding-school in Norwich, where, when I had been about three weeks, I had my first whipping. I had been guilty of gross misconduct, and told a lie to screen myself. And the punishment inflicted on me was the beginning of my entire reformation. I shall never forget that first whipping, how I was told after prayers to go to Mrs. S.'s private sitting-room; how, after a most loving reprimand, I was told that as reproof had failed to do me good I must prepare to be whipped; Mrs. S. then rang the bell, and giving to the maid who answered it a long woollen dress, which she took from a hanging closet, bade her see that I put that on and came back to her. The maid, an old confidential servant, took me into Mrs. S.'s bedroom, made me undress, and don the long woollen garment, which fastened round the waist with a band and was open down each side from the waist to the feet. I then was bidden to put my feet in a pair of list slippers. This being done, the maid, carrying off all my clothes to my own bedroom, requested me to go back to the room where I had left Mrs. S., and give four knocks at the door. Instead of doing this, I lingered in the passage, where the maid found me a few minutes afterwards. She said, "You must follow me." I did so, and she remained till I had knocked four times at the door. On being told to enter, I found Mrs. S. sitting at a table reading, but on the table lay a long, lithe birch-rod. Pushing the table on one side, Mrs. S., taking up the rod, pointed to a long narrow stool, which I afterwards knew as "the horse", and told me to lie across it. The previous preparation, and Mrs. S.'s manner, so awed me that I submitted. I then found myself buckled across by a strap across the horse. I heard Mrs. S. fasten the door and draw a heavy curtain across it. She then very quickly folded the back part of the woollen dress—which was loose on each side from the waist to the feet—above my waist; then very briefly speaking of my faults, she grasped the rod, and gave me very deliberately a most severe birching. Of course I screamed, and shrieked, and implored, but the rod pursued its destined course, and wielded by Mrs. S.'s strong arm, it did its destined work. The stinging pain, the after-feeling and marks, the present shame, the necessary submission, the ceremony observed—all did their work; and as I took my course to bed, I felt the first overthrow of the old rebellious nature. From

that time till I was sixteen I had to pay seven similar visits to Mrs. S. in that same private room, and to go through even more severe whippings. But behold the fruit. At nineteen I became a teacher in the same school; I remained for ten years Mrs. S.'s much-trusted assistant. I have now for very many years had a school of my own, and I myself administered corporal punishment with the birch-rod in precisely the same way as I have described my first whipping, and we have never known it to fail. By "we" I mean Mrs. S., myself, my teachers, the parents of my pupils; and dozens of pupils, in their happy after lives, have, in most grateful terms, thanked me for my discipline.

35. A VENGEFUL GUARDIAN

A HAND PULLED my long curly hair. I tumbled over on my back and saw Mrs. Smythe standing erect before me. She was trembling with rage and as I sprang to my feet gave me two stout slaps in the face nearly knocking my little head off. I saw a shower of sparks. She then turned to Lizzie and dealt her a similar brace of smacks; afterwards driving us both brutally before her into the house.

Without another word I was at once bundled into an empty room. The door was locked and I was left for an hour to reflect upon my dreadful plight… My daydreams were disturbed by the entrance of the housemaid who took me straight to the bathroom. As I entered I saw the worn stump of a rod on the ground amid a quantity of broken twigs from which I concluded that before I had been fetched Lizzie had passed a rough half-hour.

I pitied the poor girl who was innocent after all but Mrs. Smythe's harsh tones cut my musings short.

"Young man", she said, "I can find no words to qualify the act you have committed. Your crime is so monstrous that

SQUIRE HARDMAN

from page 63

"To use so heathenly, I'd have her know
"His breech is not for her to fricassee
"What's more, you tell your Lady straight from me
"That tho' she've been a Governess and sich,
"She'm nothing but a nasty flogging b—!"
And then the boy himself appears, to swell
His mother's clamour with insulting yell;
And words obscene, in one unending yap,
Run from his lips like water from a tap.

Altho' distasted by the rowdy scene,
I bore the deluge with impassive mien;
While to myself I said, "Aye, sirrah Joe,
"Curse while you may! Your babyship will show
"Another face within an hour or so!
"Those working features and abusive tongue,
"That infant energy and strength of lung,
"Will serve for other uses before long,
"When you shall sing another kind of song."
And then, when both are out of breath at last,
I show the papers drawn this fortnight past,
Where all is settled, and the Court commands
That Joseph Green shall pass into the hands
Of Squire and Mrs. Hardman—for his good;
His present home not being all it should.

No sooner had I broke this piece of news
Than Polly still'd her torrent of abuse,
And the poor creature thought to change her tune
By falling in a counterfeited swoon,
From which emerging, she turn'd on the tears:
Now pray'rs, instead of oaths, assail my ears;
She howls and blubbers, calling Heav'n to witness
Of her chaste habits and maternal fitness;
Till, seeing all her arts of no avail,
She wrings her hands and breaks into a wail:
"O my dear Joey, O my pigsney Pet,
"And must thou leave me? Ah, not yet—not yet!
"Dear lovely Squire, give me one day of grace,
"One little day! Ah, no? That threat'ning face,
"Those angry looks, that harsh and gloomy brow!
"You did not always look upon me so—"

Here she breaks off, and falling on her knees,
Assails me with the fury of her pleas;
While Joe himself, now catching the infection,
Makes his own imitative genuflection,
And adds his blubb'ring to his mother's blether.
—I listen'd for a while to both together,
Till, tiring of the dull unequal sport,
I seiz'd the lad, and cut his mother short

Continues p. 67

I ought really to send you packing back home to Paris at once. I do not wish, however, to grieve your kind parents. They have delegated to me all their rights over you while you reside under my roof, comprising permission to punish you as I may think fit when you deserve to be corrected. I have therefore decided that your wrong-doing shall be expiated by corporal punishment as proportionally severe as your great fault deserves. You will thus learn that an Englishman respects all women, and more than any, an innocent young girl. I warn you that I shall flog your naughty bottom mercilessly. I also tell you at once that it will be best for you to submit with due humility to your deserved punishment. Should you resist my authority, I shall take forcible measures to restrain you. Here I have everything necessary for subduing a young scamp such as you are!"

I uttered not a word in reply, feeling quite dazed, not knowing whether I ought to be overjoyed at tasting at last the caress of the magic rod, or be alarmed at the rigour of the chastisement the young mother threatened in such despotic terms.

My impassibility seemed to increase her ill temper. "Undress!" she commanded, clutching my arm and shaking me furiously.

Suiting the action to the word, she helped me to obey by tearing off my garments.

I was soon in my shirt, blushing to have to stand thus, half-nude, in the presence of this beautiful woman, who looked quite young. My shame, however, was not devoid of lascivious pleasure.

She pushed me towards a heavy armchair and made me lean over its seat. Then she fastened me securely to this piece of furniture, in the proper position for enduring my torture. I could not take my eyes off my lovely hostess, whose irritation increased the beauty of her features, giving fresh life to her good looks, causing her to appear bold and fearless. Every time her silk skirt touched my naked flesh or her soft hand skimmed over my skin, a delicious thrill ran through my frame.

From the pail, she chose a long rod, and after having shaken the superfluous moisture from it, she wiped it on a towel, and made it whiz through the air, as if to try its elasticity.

"You'll now see," she said, coming close to me, "what happens to a boy of your age who takes indecent liberties with a young lady!"

The rod began its wild saraband on my buttocks. I throbbed and bounded beneath the ruthless onslaught, unable to prevent myself from groaning with real pain. My lamentations evidently excited the rage of my severe flogging hostess, and she kept on hitting me with still greater force. I trembled in every limb, making desperate efforts to get loose. But I was tightly tied, entirely at the mercy of cruel young materfamilias who continued to birch me with a firm hand, unheeding my cries and prayers for forgiveness.

When her birch had been worn away to a stump, she desisted—but not till then. The violence of her beating had caused every twig of the bundle to be broken. My fright increased, because I saw her return to the fatal bucket, and I greatly feared that she was about to take another rod and continue my martyrdom. But she only dipped her practised hand in the cold water for a few seconds; her fingers being benumbed by the tension of her grip, and her palm slightly scratched by the thorny ends of the branches forming the handle.

36. Unusual Entertainment

"Have either of you any particular fancy? We can give you plenty of variety in this house. You can go to bed with one or more girls if it pleases you to do so. If either of you is fond of the rod, I have a room fitted up with everything necessary, where you can tie up and strip any girl you fancy and give her a little birching; or if you like it better, you can see a girl birched by another. Or would you prefer to see some Tableaux Vivants? I pride myself especially upon them.

"I can show you tableaux with scenery, and with the girls dressed in character; and I can show you some tableaux of statuary, with the girls naked; and I can also show you some very naughty tableaux."

Ford and I consulted together for a moment, then I said: "We should like to see a selection of tableaux: some of all sorts."

"So you shall. Are either of you fond of seeing the rod used?"

We both admitted that we had a liking for such a sight.

"Well then," she said, "I will show you two tableaux of whipping; then a couple of tableaux from mythological subjects; and finish up with two naughty tableaux."

Both of us were perfectly satisfied with the programme she offered, and we said so.

She then told us to take our seats on two easy-chairs which were placed a few feet distant from the curtains, and she added that we should have to wait a short time, as the scenery Had to be set, and the girls dressed for the first two tableaux.

Then she made a sign to the girls, and went behind the curtains, followed by the whole troop of laughing damsels.

As we sat waiting for the entertainment to commence, we could hear the girls bustling about, chattering to each other in low tones, and occasionally laughing as they dressed themselves.

At the end of about ten minutes, Mrs. Leslie called out in a clear voice: "The first tableau will represent, 'The Birching of a Nihilist in a Russian Prison.'"

Immediately the curtains separated in the middle, drawn aside by unseen agency, and the tableau appeared, brilliantly lighted from above, so that we could see the smallest details. The scene showed a large, bare, prison cell, with whitewashed walls, stone floor, and grated window. In it were six figures, five "men" and one woman, all attired in costume, and personating, respectively: the governor of the prison; the surgeon; a prison warder; two soldiers—and the Nihilist lady. In the middle of the cell there was a long, curved wooden structure, upon which the "Nihilist lady" was bound in a bent position, her feet resting on the floor. Her arms were stretched out one on each side of the "horse," her wrists being secured to rings: and her ankles were strapped together, and fastened to a bar at the lower part of the structure. She was dressed in prison costume, consisting of a loose, blue serge frock, the skirt of which, as well as her petticoats and chemise, being rolled up to the middle of her back, and she had been divested of her stays and drawers. The "Nihilist

SQUIRE HARDMAN

from page 65

With threat of summons to the next Assize,
Then carried off my weeping little prize—
While as I hasten'd homeward, Polly's bleat
Pursued me half way down the village street:
"O my poor honey, O my sugar-plum!
"Dear Mr. Hardman, spare him till I come!
"Poor blessed darling, O poor little b—m!"

And here I sit, within my study brown,
As the sweet summer Ev'ning settles down
And paints the landscape in those tender hues
Made to inspire the fancy, and infuse
Ev'n such as I with motions of the Muse.

Hail, gentle Ev'ning, Thou who bring'st to all
Such partial happiness as may befall
The sons of men! Whose Star, as Sappho sings
Leads Lovers back to their beloved things,
Sheep to the fold, the child to Mother's breast;
Thou bring'st to weary limbs the boon of rest,
To weary brains the sleeper's vacancy,
To brides their happy bridegrooms, and to me
The prospect of my Wife's severity.
—And oh, this ev'ning, what a special treat!
By Heav'n, but I can scarcely wait to greet
My Mary with the news that all our pray'rs
Are answered, and an infant lock'd upstairs.
Already I can see her lovely eyes
Candescent with ingenuous surprise,
The colour richly mantling in her cheek,
The sudden joy that will not let her speak
Save in a modest sigh, and with all this,
The chaste dissimulation of her bliss—
For she's still constant to the smooth pretence
That the sole motive of her punishments
Is justice re-inforc'd by common sense.
And hark! What sounds come floating thro' the air,
Borne to me from across the courtyard there?
By God, those whistling strokes, that rowdy-dow,
Tell me that Mary's at her task, ev'n now,
Of teaching Tom and Bobby something new
Thro' application of a good bamboo—
A welcome noise, from which I can condude
My darling's in a proper flogging mood,
And can foretaste the joy when—from my Wife—
My bastard gets the thrashing of his life.

Now for a moment (as I take my tea),
I plunge in Philosophic reverie;
I contemplate my pleasures and I see
They're but a Type of what the gods intend

Continues p. 69

lady"—whom I recognised at Edith—was a plump, shapely damsel, with a fine big bottom, large thighs, and good legs cased in black stockings, which contrasted well with her white skin.

At the left side of the "culprit" stood the "warder" who was inflicting the punishment; a bearded "man," wearing a uniform consisting of a dark green tunic, with trousers of the same colour tucked into long boots reaching to "his" knees; and a round flat cap with a peak. "He" held high in the air a thick, bristly birch rod, which seemed just about to fall on the "culprit's" bare bottom. At the other side stood the "surgeon," a whiskered, moustachioed "man," in a plain, dark blue uniform, and beside him was the "governor," with a fierce moustache, dressed in an imposing uniform, with medals on "his" breast. A little in rear of the horse stood the two "soldiers," with cross-belts and side-arms. The "culprit's" bottom had been most skilfully "made-up," so that the whole surface of the skin, from the loins to the upper part of the thighs, appeared crimson, and striped all over with long livid weals, and spotted with blood, which also appeared to be trickling down the "victim's" white thighs. She had her head turned to one side, and she was glaring with eyes full of intense horror at the uplifted rod; her face was scarlet and distorted with pain; her mouth was wide open, with the lips drawn back from the teeth, as if she were screaming loudly; and the tears appeared to be streaming down her cheeks. The whole scene appeared so intensely real, that I actually waited, with a feeling of suspense, to see the rod fall on the bleeding bottom, and to hear the victim's shriek. Since that time I have seen many "Living Pictures," but I have never seen one better done.

In another moment the curtains were drawn, shutting out the scene. Ford and I applauded vigorously, clapping our hands and crying out: "Brava! Brava! Well done! Very well done!" Then, turning to me, my companion whispered: "It was splendid! The illusion was perfect. I have never seen anything to equal it, in Paris or Vienna."

After a rather long interval, Mrs. Leslie announced: "The next tableau will represent punishment as inflicted in a boarding-school for young ladies." The curtains were parted, and we saw that the recess was now fitted up as a schoolroom, with desks, benches, a blackboard, globes, and maps on the walls. In this tableau there were ten figures; seven of them, dressed as schoolgirls, in short frocks, and with their long hair flowing loose over their shoulders, were sitting on high forms, so that we could see their pretty legs, cased in silk stockings of various colours; and in two or three cases where the petticoats happened to be very short, we caught glimpses of the lace frills on the girls' drawers. In the middle of the "schoolroom" stood a stalwart young woman, who was evidently one of the servants of the establishment, in her ordinary attire, consisting of a black frock, with white apron, cap, collar, and cuffs. She was bending forward, "horsing" in the orthodox position the girl named Ethel… The skirt of her short frock, and her dainty little white petticoats were pinned up to her shoulders, and her pretty lace-trimmed drawers were hanging down about her knees. She had a most lovely little bottom with round, firm-looking, plump cheeks; and her delicate skin was as white as snow, except where it had been artificially marked with pink streaks, and small red dots, representing the ravages made by the rod. Her thighs were fairly well developed; and her small but shapely legs were clad in long, brown silk stockings, gartered with bows of black satin; and she was wearing neat, buttoned boots on her little feet. The "schoolmistress" in a grey wig, and with spectacles, was personated by Mrs. Leslie, who held over the girl's delicious bottom, a long, slender birch rod, prettily ornamented with blue ribbons.

Ethel played her part well. She was looking over her shoulder, her face was red, she appeared to be crying loudly in pain, and her eyes were fixed with an appealing glance on the stern "schoolmistress." The other "schoolgirls" were looking on at the punishment with various expressions on their faces; some appeared to be rather amused at the sight; others seemed to be perfectly indifferent; and others were looking very much frightened. The girls had been well drilled in their parts. This tableau, like the preceding one, looked wonderfully real…

37. ON THE PEG

BOTH MY BROTHER and myself were spoiled, in the fullest sense of the word. My father spoiled me, and my mother spoiled my brother. However, when I was fourteen years of age my parents were compelled to go abroad for

mamma's health, and I was left under the guardianship of a maiden aunt, who quickly decided that a strict school was the best place for me. To a school in Hertfordshire I was accordingly sent, the schoolmistress having been previously informed that I was "a child of wayward disposition." I had not been there a week before "the spirit of opposition which pervaded me," as my aunt used to term it, got me into hot water, and I was ordered to bed. I had not been undressed many minutes when Miss Margaret, one of the principals, came into the bedroom, and after well lecturing me on my conduct, told me she intended to whip me. She then rang the bell, and one of the maids brought a birch-rod, and I was told to prepare, which I flatly refused to do. As I was rebellious, the maid tied my hands together with a towel, the end of which she fastened to a peg high up on the wall, so that I could only just reach the floor with the tips of my toes. Miss Margaret then gave me a severe flogging. Finding I was obstinate, after a minute or two she desisted and left the room, leaving me with the maid. I tried hard to get off the peg, but could not. When Miss Margaret returned she asked me whether I was sorry. "No!" I shouted. "Then I must whip you again," she said, suiting the action to the word. This second whipping was too much for my spirit, and I begged for forgiveness.

SQUIRE HARDMAN

from page 67

For him whose taste perforce must condescend
To watching children flogg'd when they offend:
What are they but the pastime of a soul
Design'd by Fate to fill a Tyrant's role
And bring mankind beneath a like control?
Aye, every Amateur of whipping sport
Was born a man of the despotic sort,
One meant to be the scourge of humankind
Had not his inclinations been confin'd
Within domestic bounds where, Lord of all,
He still can be a Phalaris—in small.
—Well, that's the part that I'm content to play:
I ask no other, more extended sway
Than o'er the infant skins I love to flay:
Give me but urchins, and good whips and canes,
And let Ambition addle other brains!
Wide as the Ocean, varied as the Earth,
Extend the joys that flogging brings to birth;

And as I stand, like other Debauchees
Rapt in the vision of their ecstasies,
I raise my hands, I fall upon my knees,
And humbly here invoke, with streaming eyes,
The only Deity I recognize:
Genius of Flagellation, O incline
Thy countenance, severe and yet benign,
On us thy worshippers! Do Thou infuse
Our spirits with lusty vigour to abuse
All weaker beings plac'd beneath our sway!
Grant us yet more occasion, night and day,
To wreak fresh torments wheresoe'er we may;
Inform our wits with cunning to invent
Still new varieties of punishment:
Bless Thou our arms, hallow each instrument!
Provide more helpless victims, fresh and fresh,
To feel the greedy and insatiate lash;
Till the whole world acknowledges Thy power,
And multitudes agree in a blest hour
To let the host of humankind become
A kind of Universal naked b—m,

Gross, like the measure of all natural crime,
Naked, as Nature form'd it in her prime,
And destin'd only to be lash'd thro' space and time!
Enthrone on high Thy flagellant elite,
Lap them in joy forever keen and sweet,
And all the rest cast down beneath their feet,
Mid fire and smoke and exhalations foul
Confounded all together in a common howl.

FINIS

The rest of the day I did not cease crying, not so much from the pain as from mortification that I had met my match and been conquered. Strange as it may seem, from that day to the present I have loved Miss Margaret, and felt her to be a true friend. As I believe great benefit has resulted from corporal punishment, I think it right to advocate it, for I know from observation that if our faults are not corrected when we are young, we generally suffer in a far harder school when we grow up.

38. The Nun, the Drawers & the Birch-rod

With the onset of biological maturity the pupils of the boarding-school were no longer allowed to wear the closed "children's drawers." According to school regulations they now had to be newly furnished with six pairs of open flap drawers, so-called women's trousers, made of a hardy chiffon. That year my sister and I were also required to be provided with the regulation "women's drawers" for the beginning of the new school year. The step-mother ordered the seamstress to come to the house where she sewed for us the twelve pairs of regulation drawers. At first I was horrified over these "brazen" trousers, as I called them, but I soon calmed down because I did not have to part from my short closed drawers for the time being.

Since our departure from home, my relations with the step-mother and to father remained cold and formal. It became impossible for me to indulge in any intimacy with my parents since to me they seemed to inhabit another world. Consequently, vacations bored me and I was always happy when they drew to a close. The monastic life pleased me incomparably more, because there I found the stimulus which my sensibility sought. The beginning of school, therefore, was a happy expectation! Secretly I had sworn eternal loyalty to my beloved friend, Dionysia, and I was impatient to see her again.

Dionysia already wore the trousers prescribed for the big girls and was punished very often. Now it was no longer a matter of unbuttoning drawers, but merely of pulling apart the flaps to the right and to the left after which the full, round, girl-bottom emerged shiningly in the white frame of the drawers. The ravishing Dionysia gave the teachers continuous cause for dissatisfaction, for which reason not the slightest bad behaviour on her part was overlooked. Her voluptuous beauty provoked the rod. Once, during the needlework lesson, the teacher forced Dionysia, by way of increasing her punishment, to kneel in a corner facing the wall and to bare her bottom, red from flogging, to the whole class. Her dress was raised high and fastened to the shoulders with pins; the two open flaps of the drawers were pulled apart like a curtain and she was ordered to hold the edges of the flaps on both sides wide apart in order to prevent her from closing them again over her bottom.

Dionysia, sobbing, obliged with trembling hands. Thereupon, the short chemise in the fly was yanked upward and likewise pinned on the back of her dress. The needlework teacher prepared this scene, so humiliating to the incorrigible pupil, with obvious pleasure and then stepped aside with a satisfied expression on her face. Oh! what an unforgettable, madly exciting sight! The whole class stared with fascination on the girl-bottom shining fiery-red like a pæony in full bloom from out the dazzling white frame of the wide-open, gaping flaps, and whose well-contoured buttocks, divided by a deep, mysterious furrow, quivered lightly from shame. Sweet Dionysia, weeping and heartrendingly trying to repress her sobs, kept her head deeply bowed and buried her face in her folded arms while a convulsion coursed through the whole of her young body… Gradually, I awoke from the intoxication of my senses and was restored to reality. Dionysia was sent back to her bench where, her mouth set defiantly, she sat working at her knitting-pattern like an offended beauty. Oh, after such punishments she felt an especially intimate need to be "consoled" by me. And how gladly I would have done this with abundant tenderness! But the strict daytime supervision of the pupils prevented any such possibility. In the evening, however, in the dormitory when the lights were put out and everybody was asleep, I soundlessly crept to the bed of my beloved friend and lay down at her side…

On the next day in the classroom we could not pay attention to the lesson. My thoughts dwelt on Nysia and my glances tried to read her lovely face. My absent-mindedness, my absolute rapture in the sight of this school mate was discovered, my negligence reprimanded and the wrong answers which I gave were severely censured. I was unaffected by these reprimands and indifferent to them and after the lesson I was punished.

After being led to the punishment chamber, I received a stern warning from my teacher-nun as well as the birching on my bared bottom which I had merited. I knelt down on the punishment bench and tilted the upper part of my body forward submissively in order to receive my punishment. The nun flipped up my dress in the back, burrowed her hands for a long time searchingly in the padded folds of the drawers in order to pull the flaps apart to right and left so as to bare my bottom. Her hands vainly sought to find the fly. After a while she noticed that the edges of the flaps running from front to back were sewed together. This was an open violation of the regulation to wear open drawers. I had grievously transgressed against it by sewing the gaping flaps together! Delighted as I was to see drawers cut in this fashion on the other girls, much as they charmed me when I spied upon them under their short dresses and saw the long tongue of the chemise peep out of the open fly, I simply could not endure these "brazen and naughty" drawers on myself, and I wore them with extreme reluctance. I always sewed together the open fly of my "trousers" despite the punishment that I inevitably drew upon myself by so doing.

The nun waxed indignant over my self-willedness, ordered me to stand up and to remove my drawers entirely. I stood up, frantic and ashamed that as the result of removing my drawers I would have to lie there before the nun's eyes not only with bared buttocks but also with bared thighs. Slowly and hesitantly, I guided my hand under my dress, loosened the ribbons around the waist and let the flap of the drawers slide down to my ankles. Thereupon the nun, with the birch in her right hand, instantly seated herself on the punishment bench, pulled me toward her and forcibly stretched me across her knees. Then she lifted my dress high and in a twinkling my bare bottom came into view, and my thighs also hung naked, unprotected and without drawers over the lap of the stern nun.

An instant later I already felt the smarting kisses of the birch rod sear my skin. While the nun rained twenty lashes, slowly but forcefully, upon my buttocks and thighs, I howled and wailed in pain and shame. My struggling hands sought a support and in boundless excitement I clasped the nun's leg under her smock and clung to it firmly. My hand conjured up for me the bond with mother, and my wildness was transformed into a yielding love that cleansed my mind and soul. All wickedness vanished from me, and I felt myself freed from all the conflicting demons that dwelt inside me. I was now suffused only with a feeling of infinite surrender and attachment to—mother...

39. HOW WE DO IT HERE

I WAS INVITED to tea by the directress... After we had gone over all the details of the daily instruction programme, we came to the question of discipline... "And now," she continued in a tone of great solemnity, "it is my painful duty to explain what happens when they come before me. Since the founding of our orphanage in 1851, according to regulations, corporal punishments for serious infractions have been administered solely by the directress, and the instrument of punishment has always been the birch rod. A visit to the directress, therefore, is always viewed by the pupil as a sign of the greatest reward and likewise of the severest punishment. This has been the will of the founders. Therefore you must know that if you lead a girl into my office, she will inevitably receive a birching. This is administered to her exposed bottom, after she has been ordered to unbutton her bloomers. Little girls under ten are punished with willow soap-rods; for the older ones a birch rod soaked in salt water is used. I always administer the punishment alone, without an assistant.

"After the teacher has registered her complaint with me, she leaves the office and the culprit remains. And now I shall show you how and where the punishments take place. My office is on the second floor, and adjoining it is a small room which in the beginning was set up as a punishment area. Please come with me."

We climbed the stairs and entered the office. From [here] a small door leads to the punishment chamber. It is very small and cramped, partially slanting under the roof. A skylight with six panes occupies this slanting part of the roof. The floor is covered with a thick rug, and a felt curtain hangs over the door!!! Below the window there is a sofa-like piece of upholstered furniture which in our language we call a "puff". Approximately in the middle of this item of furniture two leather straps are attached, whose function is obvious. A chair and a low closet in the corner complete the

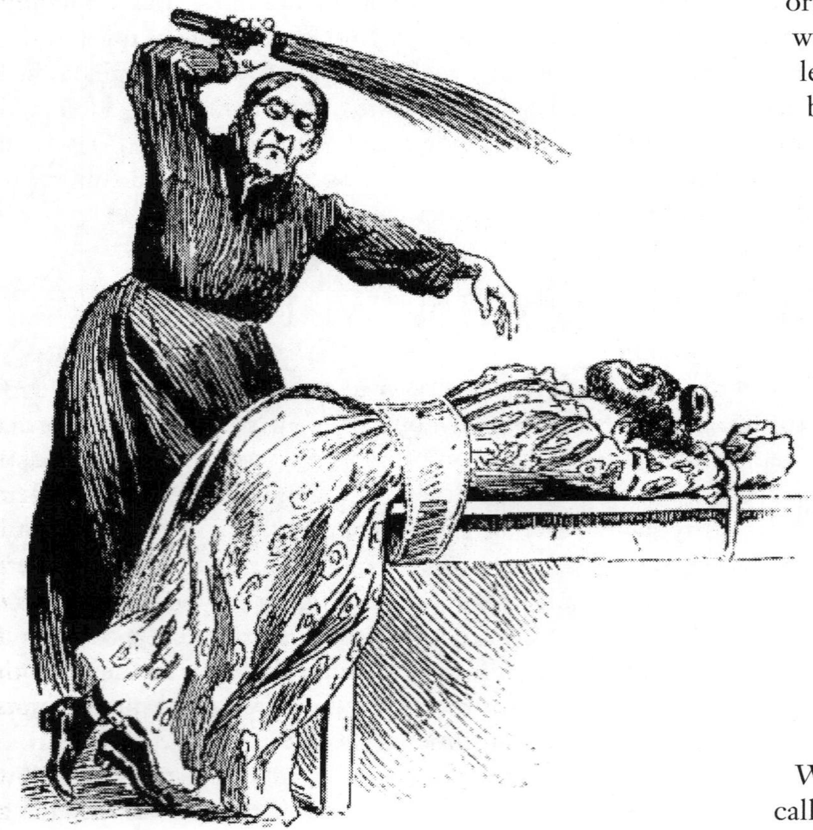

room's appointments.

The directress opened the closet and showed me her rods: a few small willow soap-rods and many birch rods in different sizes, which were being softened in a tall jug of salt water, so as to be in constant readiness…

40. Mixed Motives

I WAS A weak and delicate boy and was sent by my parents to a school in the suburbs kept by a lady. The school contained only small boys of ages varying from six to fourteen. I was twelve years old. The Principal was a tall, thin woman, exceedingly plain but very smart in her dress. The two governesses were in awe of her and obeyed her implicitly in everything. They were not to punish us in any way, but they had orders to present a report of our behaviour everyday. At twelve o'clock the principal used to enter the school room in a black or brown satin dress and take her seat for the Bible class, the only class she herself held. The governesses then read out the names of the boys on the punishment list, who were ordered to stand up. The principal then read a chapter in the Bible, after which she ordered one of the boys to fetch a whip. For slight offences during lessons she would whip the smaller boys across her knee, after removing their clothes, and the bigger boys on the palm of the hand. For graver matters, however, the delinquent was sent to the punishment room for a private whipping. Many a time have I gone through this ordeal, which took place in the following way. The principal first would order me to take off my jacket and trousers, and then I was made to kneel over a low block, with red satin. She would then lift up her petticoat and place her left leg over; and whip me slowly with a birch rod. Between every two or three strokes she admonished me, and made me promise to obey her. When this operation, which she called the correction, was over, she sat down, and I was made to kneel before her, and to kiss her feet, the skirt of her dress, and the rod and then to thank her for correcting me, and to beg her to be so good as to whip me for having been so naughty. Sometimes she was not satisfied with this, and would administer a few more strokes with the birch in the same manner; but when she considered I was sufficiently subdued she turned me across her left knee and slapped me with her hand or slipper. After which she always said: "Now join your school-fellows; the next time you are reported to me I shall whip you more severely". I think two or three of us were whipped every day in the school room, but as only the five elder boys received private whippings, the punishment room was only used about once a fortnight.

41. Spanked by the Maid

WHAT AN unconscionable time Phyllis had kept me. I had never for one moment intended being so late. I kennelled my dogs and entered by the back. I walked into the hall. The dining-room was silent. What a relief! Mademoiselle had forgotten all about me. Come? I would have some supper.

There were no men servants in the house so

that in the hall I encountered a maid. She looked slyly at me with an intolerably quizzical expression that I saw at once meant—mischief and that made me most indignant. She informed me quite impudently that Miss Lisette wished to speak to me.

I felt still more uncomfortable but disguised the fact as best I could. Lisette was Mademoiselle's own particular maid.

A strong buxom country girl. I felt instinctively that I should be no match for her.

"Where are Mademoiselle and my Cousin?" I asked Ellen.

She answered they had gone out to dinner adding that Mademoiselle had been expecting me all the afternoon (whereat I smiled) and that she had left directions about me with Lisette who had desired to be informed the instant I came in. I felt my face grow long at this.

"All right Ellen, tell Lisette I am going to get some supper and she will find me in the dining-room if she wants to."

There was nothing to eat in the dining-room. The table and the sideboard were both clear.

What rubbish, I must have some food. These idiot girls. I angrily and violently rang the bell and in the meantime took out a bottle of Burgundy and filled a large glass as I felt a long drink was decidedly desirable at that juncture: Just as the bumper touched my lips Lisette walked in. She was smiling with a very complacent air. She had not had anything to do with me before and I believe was pleased that her turn had come to last. I offered her a glass of wine. It would be well to be on good terms with her. A little gallantry might win her over to my side. I held the bottle and was in the act of pouring out a second glass, having set down my own untasted for the purpose, when she calmly took the bottle out of my hands put in the cork and quietly saying: "Merci M'sieur" drank off what I had poured out for myself. She laughed in my face when she saw my auger and began hustling me about. I quickly lost my temper whereupon she followed suit and catching me by the collar bundled me off before her giving me violent thumps in the rear with her knees as she did so. She did not vouchsafe me any information whatever. When I proved refractory she gave me one or two sounding cuffs on the head much severer punishment than Mademoiselle's slaps. I soon found all attempts at resisting this virago useless.

I had not the necessary strength. She conducted me into Mademoiselle's bed-room and through it into a good sized closet opening off the bed-room. There was I noticed a firm wooden bedstead but no clothes on the bed which consisted only of a piece of stout rough canvas laced to the sides and ends of the wooden frame with cord.

At the head there was a bolster. There was no crockery in the room. The window was small and quite ten feet from the floor. The sash was shut or opened by means of a pulley and rope. Lisette showed me into this den so roughly that I felt the tears rise in my eyes. She gave me no chance whatever of making friends with her. The impetus of her push made me fall across the seat, she went round it and drew up the window muttering something about my being a dirty little *coquin*, a miserable *garçon*, and inquiring how I dared set my governess at defiance, she caught hold of my arm and seating herself pulled me towards her, divesting me of my jacket, waistcoat and trousers before I knew where I was. Turning me round with a vigorous movement of her arm I speedily found myself face downwards across her lap, with my shirt over my head in front as well as behind receiving such a spanking from her massive hand as I had never imagined possible. The pain was fearful, her hand was so hard and heavy. She had got me well up between her legs and was plainly intended to obtain as much pleasure for herself as possible. She ceased, rested and began again, keeping me tightly down in the interval. I thought she would never stop. I knew I should be black and blue. I expected she would pound my flesh into a jelly. I was still very sore from the birching. I prayed for mercy. I cried and besought and protested and promised. All to no purpose, I could not escape. She told me if I did not take my punishment quietly she could only give me more and would not cease until I ceased yelping. Finally I cried quietly. At last she threw me exhausted on to the floor and gave me one or two kicks. Then she tore off my shirt and vest. She held up the first and examined it of course discovering the stains on the front from what Phyllis had done, and she said she would direct Mademoiselle's attention to it. She then strapped my hands behind my back, bundled up all my clothing under her arm told me I did not require any supper and left the room locking the door behind her and leaving me stark naked.

42. First Use of the Rod

Beloved! In your last letter you write of how excited you were moments before you were to give your first punishment, and that you were barely able to wait for the end of the instruction period. I understand this completely because the very same thing happened to me. I had to force myself to eat my lunch at twelve. I could hardly swallow a bite and literally sprang up the stairs to the office. I was breathing heavily and my heart beat as though I were possessed. I went into the punishment chamber and checked everything: whether the leather straps on the puff were solidly in place and the rods fresh. I took one from the jug, caressed it, brandished it in the air in order to make the water spurt from the branches, struck the puff with it experimentally and at the same time dreamed many sweet dreams.

The doorbell rang! My heart beat madly, the veins in my neck throbbed in unison with it. I felt dizzy and I had to lean against the closet for support and make a great effort to keep my self-control. After putting the rod back in the jug and closing the closet door, I rushed breathlessly down the stairs and opened the door…

There stood Fraulein Lauritzen, the teacher of the second section, and next to her stood Mathilde… Fraulein Lauritzen reported to me that Mathilde had a very sloppy way of sitting at

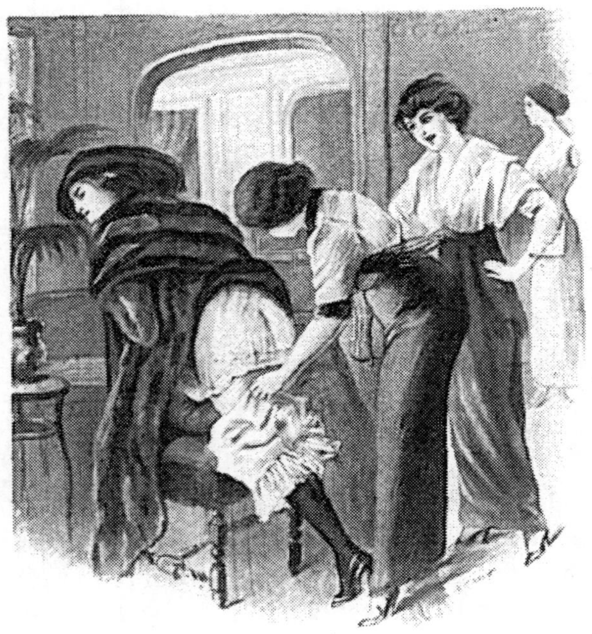

her desk, for which she had been repeatedly reprimanded. This morning, upon being called to order, the girl had impertinently answered: "Now what?" In my excitement, I completely forgot to invite the teacher to come inside. After she registered her complaint, I said with forced calm: "Thank you very much, Fraulein. And you, Mathilde, come with me." Fraulein Lauritzen withdrew and I closed the door.

At first Mathilde began to cry, since she had obviously hoped that the new directress would be more lenient than her predecessor. Slowly it began to dawn on her that dark clouds loomed on the horizon… I said: "Up the stairs with you, naughty child, I'll teach you better manners. Now, quickly!"—and I shoved the reluctant girl in front of me forward and then upward.

Following behind her, I peeped under her clothes. I saw her well-formed legs, which disappeared beneath her skirts; her lace-edged white bloomers, which at that time were longer than they are now, reached almost to the knee and could be followed up to the middle of her thigh. I noticed how her well-rounded bottom arched under the petticoat, and I already bared it savagely in my mind's eye. Mathilde was almost fully grown and her body was voluptuously contoured; she was pretty without being a beauty. I flung open the door into the office, grabbed Mathilde by the arm, and propelled her inside.

Once we were in I locked the door. Mathilde completely broke down at this moment. Tears poured down her cheeks and she gave a heart-rending and lowing plea for clemency. The upshot of her protestations was that I recovered my self-possession; the more urgent her pleas, the calmer and more calculating I became in my thoughts. I sat on a chair, drew Mathilde to me, and held her firmly by both arms. Outwardly calm and in an icy voice I scolded her and spoke in detail about her infraction of the rules which I, of course, solemnly viewed as very serious. I cold-bloodedly changed my voice and expressions: now I spoke in a friendly, almost caressing tone, now with extreme severity and inflexible hardness. I enjoyed the changing moods that were mirrored in Mathilde's face. When I spoke in friendly tones, a ray of hope suddenly beamed in her eyes; the tears no longer flowed, indeed a secret smile stole across her features: "I'll go scot free." But then when I spoke again in authoritarian tones, the tears began to flow again, and Mathilde understood that she should abandon all hope.

But only I knew that the latter consideration was correct and I became so excited that little by little I felt that I could no longer withstand the rising tension. My cheeks glowed red-hot, my senses were in a tumult... While I was severely scolding her, I spontaneously slipped my hand under her clothing. I was completely calm and did this with a sure instinct.

When Mathilde noticed this she broke into sobs, so that her whole body was shaken by her desperate weeping. She begged, and swore never to break the rules again; she became more hysterical when she felt my finger on the buttons of her bloomers... I said nothing, all my thoughts and my whole sensory apparatus at this moment were in my fingers. In her fear and despair Mathilde did not notice that my hands were lightly stroking her buttocks, as I pulled down the flaps on her bloomers. Now I released her in order to escort her to the punishment chamber. The unbuttoned black flap of her bloomers showed under her dress when she staggered through the door into the Holy of Holies... Mathilde's spirit was completely broken and she let herself be led to the puff, unprotesting. I grabbed her by the shoulders and forced her down upon her bed of pain.

When I threw her dress back over her head, she resumed her desperate pleading, but by now I was so excited that I could scarcely stand. As though intoxicated I clasped the straps around her waist and crammed her petticoat and chemise underneath and around the straps. At last her beautiful, well-rounded, stark-naked bottom offered itself to view.

My eyes ecstatically drank in the wondrous sight. Now I could belabour her at my pleasure with pitiless blows from the rod. My gaze fastened itself on the smooth bottom with its deep, mysterious furrow between the quivering hillocks. How these provocative dull-white buttocks needed the rod anyway! I forcibly tore myself away from the fascinating view in order to fetch the rod. I dragged the chair toward me and sat next to Mathilde and saw literally only her wonderful bottom. It was my whole world!

43. WHOLESOME PUNISHMENT

THE SINS OF childhood are seldom grave, but if left unchecked, they may soon become so, and parents who, from whatever motives, neglect their correction have only themselves to thank if they have something more to answer for when they have passed beyond their control.

The mother who, in the safe seclusion of the boudoir, takes her naughty child across her knee, may be forgiven if she does so with a with a single eye to the good of the moment; but in a pet, the results are much wider and more permanent. Incessant scoldings, repeated admonition, and the irritating withdrawal of small indulgencies are worse than futile. They leave no lasting impression, and often sow the seeds of secret enmity between parent and child. But a whipping lingers in the memory long after the smart of it has passed away, and seldom fails to justify its infliction on the minds of those who are benefited by it.

The opinion on this subject of a friend of mine to whom I showed the last number of society may perhaps be of interest to your readers. As I expected, the title of the correspondence, "Should Children Be Birched?", raised a smile. "I do not think," she said, "that I am of coarser fibre than most people, but I have never been able to understand why, if children are naughty, they should not be punished; or, if they are to be punished, why they should not be whipped.

"This punishment has been a tradition in our family for years, and tens and twenties of years. My mother countenanced no other, and it certainly never occurred to me that I should be punished in any other way. It was always inflicted after the old-fashioned method—over the knee, *cotillons retroussés, caleçons retirés.*"

I myself was never birched when a child, but, as our American friends have it, "spanked". Once only was a slipper used—a dainty instrument of correction enough—but it was meant to hurt, and it did. Later, when I was about twelve, if I had to be punished, I was allowed to choose whether I would be whipped or not; but as the alternative was deprivation of some pleasure I did not care to forego, I think I chose wisely. I was punished then in much the same way as before, only with a light birch, and extended full length on a sofa, over a cushion, with my skirts and petticoats firmly secured with a ribbon above my waist, and the rest of my "dersons" conveniently disposed.

I don't think that shame or disgrace enter into the question, privacy being maintained. The punishment is a wholesome and natural one, and the time-honoured method of inflicting it the only wholesome and natural mode. If whipping were abolished, I don't think the world would be either better or happier. I am certain it would be a much less pleasant place than it is.

Whipping has not made me faultless, but I know myself too well to doubt that I should not be as happy as I am if it had not been for those sharp, short, tingling lessons of my youth, which braced and prepared me for the rougher experiences of the world.

If it were more generally practised, and its virtues better understood, I think we might perhaps hear less of those enquiries for schools where the birch is a *sine qua non*, and where correction, because it is administered by the hands of strangers, and not by those whom true affection and tenderness move to its use, is often harsh, brutal and ill-judged.

44. A Cruel and Voluptuous Birching

A SORT OF MESMERIC influence seemed to have crept into me from that intensely feminine garment which had been in such close contact with Mademoiselle's own person and then so long over my head and face as I stood disgraced in the corner. It seemed to have sapped my strength and all my powers of resistance, to have undermined my self-respect, to have rendered me contemptible in my own eyes; in short, to have completely emasculated me. I had felt my virility ebbing away during the hours I had stood with the red thing enveloping my shoulders, touching my eyes and nose and mouth, conscious all the while that it was a woman's petticoat which had been worn, and that a thing so essentially feminine had, willy-nilly, been forced upon me. I had gradually, step by step, to give in to the flood of feminine associations which rushed upon me, and yield by degrees to the power of woman. I was keenly aware that nothing could save me, that all opposition was useless and hopeless, and I was slowly drifting towards the knowledge that I must sooner or later abandon myself absolutely to it. I stood before Mademoiselle, cowed and humiliated, not so much at the prospect of the beating as at the sense of my own helplessness in her hands, because she was feminine and could therefore do with me what she liked.

Whatever it was, I knew I had no power left to resist, and trembled at the inevitable acknowledgment of this fact to myself. She seemed the embodiment of triumphant womanhood as I was hustled into her presence, shaken and pulled about by another woman, to be whipped by her. As I stood before Mademoiselle, my hands still tied, my ears red and tingling from Elise's rough usage, panting and out of breath, my back sore from the rude thumps of Elise's knees, my courage gave way and my eyes filled with tears, which the poignant sense of my abasement caused to overflow. I could only hold my head and yield in silent resignation and despair. Let not the reader, however, imagine that I was subdued at once. No, there was many a reaction. A constant revolt of all my manhood which required many severe lessons to quell and conquer finally. But I must confess that as time went on, my disgust lessened, these revolts were divided by longer intervals, and at last I became a wretched petticoat-slave. Mademoiselle looked on haughtily. Her form dilated and expanded with the sense, so agreeable to a woman, of power over something male. She looked like a magnificent bird of prey, a regal and feminine eagle, about to swoop upon her victim. She stood erect, her head thrown back, consciously displaying her well-developed bust and elegant figure; her air of determination and pretty wilfulness much enhancing her charms. There was something arch about her manner as she quizzed me upon my first introduction into a lady's bedroom. She asked me, as she significantly handled a light, long, and elastic birch, how I liked the prospect of my first assignation. She remarked that I had been introduced in all due form by her maid to whom she proceeded to give a guinea out of my pocket money (which Mademoiselle had charge of) in recognition of her services. Mademoiselle produced a sovereign and a shilling and gave them to Elise before my eyes, to my intense and ill-concealed annoyance, which increased her merriment, and Elise thanked me with mock politeness and gratitude.

Mademoiselle promised me by way of consolation, that the maid should be sent out and that consequently I should have the advantage of an entirely private *tête-a-tête* with her, and enquired whether I was not rejoiced at my good fortune? I do not know what it was, but something or other in these words, or what they suggested, quite changed my mood, and I let my eyes rest on her affectionately and admiringly, and said that I indeed appreciated the favour; a remark which brought me a sound slap in the face. Again disconcerted, I determined that nothing should allow me to be made a further fool of, and resolved not to utter another word.

The room was a large one and very handsomely furnished. The extremely pretty bed stood under a heavy silk canopy across the angle of the room farthest from the fireplace, the canopy suspended from the ceiling and the carved oak bedstead standing clear of the walls. There were several quaint, cosy-looking chairs about, and bowls of spring flowers. Mademoiselle stood between me and the light, tall and graceful in her severely simple black mousseline de laine dress, displaying her womanly figure to the fullest advantage. As I contemplated her in my wretched condition I felt yet more abjectly humiliated. A novel sensation of awkwardness again replaced my habitual self-possession, an inveterate stupidity my ordinary sprightliness and vivacity. There I stood, a great boy, trussed like a fowl, with nothing to conceal my bare legs but a shirt, which did not reach to my knees.

Mademoiselle ordered Elise to place a long carved bench of black oak, about a foot wide, in the middle of the room, and to put upon it a feather bolster which Elise, by means of tapes, tied to the bench. I was then compelled to stand across one end while Elise strapped my ankles close together underneath and then left the room. Mademoiselle went to the door, shut and locked it, and then turned full upon me. I could not but note as I trembled how her whole form glowed with smiling and triumphant satisfaction. She walked deliberately up to me, lifted my shirt up behind, and, to my intense shame, intently contemplated my back for some seconds; then, still holding up this undergarment and standing a little way off, she took up the birch and gave me some stinging lashes with it. I had never felt anything like it before. I had no idea that it would hurt one-tenth as much as it did, and was compelled to cry out.

Mademoiselle then, to my horror, unbuttoned my waistcoat and lifted my shirt with both hands high up in front. I could not move. I was speechless, as she stood facing me and examining my most secret possessions over which and along the front of my things she several times passed her dimpled hand. Then she let the shirt fall, untied my elbows, and taking up a lady's jewelled riding whip, she remarked that I should be flogged naked. Standing at my left side she ordered me to take off my jacket and waistcoat. I hesitated and fumbled. Looking round she gave me a touch of the whip on my bare legs. If the birch smarted, that vicious little thing bit like fury. I yelled and clapped my hands to my legs, but only to get them lashed also. She went on until, in desperation, I tore off my jacket and waistcoat.

"Now your shirt! Quick!" Up went the whip, her eyes sparkling savagely. This time, without an instant's hesitation, and without thinking about it, I whipped off my shirt more quickly than ever I had done before. And there I was, perfectly naked before her, red and overwhelmed with shame and smarting with pain. She leisurely regarded me, evidently intending not to spare me a single pang. She moved her hand along my back and shoulders, remarking that she thought the whip would mark my skin easily, and, by way of experiment, she gave me several more smart cuts with it on various parts of my body, each stroke causing me intense anguish. I cried out, and implored her to desist; but she merely gloated the more over my torture.

"Now," she at length said, "your bottom must be put in a proper position for me to punish."

"Oh, Mademoiselle, forgive me! Oh, I am sorry for my disobedience and folly! Do forgive me… "

"I never forgive! Lie down on your face."

I saw there was nothing for it but compliance; so, with a sigh like a gasp of despair, I obeyed her. She placed her hand on the back of my head and pressed it into the bolster. The wide bench separated my thighs, pressing my most sensitive parts cruelly. She fixed a strap round my neck and passed it under the bench, placed another round the seat and my waist, and lastly fastened my hands together underneath the bench. My posture and the soft bolster (which soon became pleasantly warm) gave me a certain voluptuous feeling soon, however, to be dispelled by my sufferings.

"Now we shall see whether a girl can properly punish a boy's bottom!!" How she dwelt on the shameful word! "Whether a youth is or is not to be subject to feminine discipline and rule and to his governess… " Her skirts caused me an electric shock each time they touched me. The feminine characteristics of her form, as she stood over me, became indelibly stamped upon my being, and acquired for her and for the rest of her sex an absolute dominion from that moment over me. A look or the rustle of petticoat is enough for me now. At either I tremble.

This sway was established and emphasised by the cruel punishment of the most secret portions of my body which I then underwent at her hands. Regularly and deliberately was the birching given; the methodical administration of which I could not interrupt. I protested and swore; but I had to learn how cruelly women can punish—how relentlessly they slake their vengeance—what a lust they have to satisfy, when they have a male at their mercy, to deal unmitigated torture out to him. How they exercise that dominion over him which is so real, although often unacknowledged. Men are not subject to these motives and never punish so cruelly as women.

Only once was my torture stayed. Mademoiselle had flogged me from my right side and from my left. My sobs had given place to screams and yells; but Mademoiselle said she should insist on my taking punishment quietly, at which threat I gave a delirious laugh. She calmly opened a drawer, and took out a plum-shaped piece of wood with a leather loop at its thickest end, through which loop she slipped one of her scented handkerchiefs. Then she forced the plug into my mouth, and tied the ends of the handkerchief tightly behind my neck. I was nearly choked, and effectually gagged. Perfectly indifferent to my sufferings, she resumed the punishment, merely remarking that I should have ten minutes more of it for making the gagging necessary.

When the ten minutes had expired there came an interval when the strokes, which had fallen with the even regularity and swing of a pendulum, the swing of which I had ascertained to the fraction of a second, ceased. I hoped it was over. I could not express the hope in words, so I groaned. Mademoiselle had been whipping me across both ways. She now came to the top of the bench at my right, daintily lifted her skirts, and put her right leg across me. Then, almost sitting upon my neck and smothering me with her petticoats, the back of which fell to the floor over my head, she proceeded to flog me lengthwise. She was looking down my back, and I knew that behind me the wardrobe mirror reflected my open thighs. Although the strap had been loosened I could scarcely move my head; when I tried to do so, however, she pressed me more closely. I can give no idea of what I felt at my novel posture underneath a young woman. She now struck lengthwise, more slowly but more viciously; the strokes cut like hot iron, and, as the pliant ends of the birch hit what lay between my thighs, I felt I was being murdered. The anguish was maddening, and if I recollected what she could see by lifting her eyes to the glass, it was with utter recklessness to the exposure.

"There, Master Julian, that's enough for the first time. I think I have whipped you pretty severely. You will not care to set me at defiance again," she complacently remarked, throwing herself into a great saddle-back easy chair, apparently somewhat exhausted.

I lay utterly prostrate, powerless to speak even had I not been gagged; all my strength was gone, and I smarted as though I had been scared with red hot wires. Presently she unstrapped and ungagged me, I could scarcely move. I was in a cataleptic or comatose state and only semi-conscious.

She resumed her seat, and bade me kneel at her feet. I obeyed mechanically. Had she bade me walk into a fire, I think I should have done so. I was thoroughly exhausted, my head sank upon her lap, and my tears flowed softly, but I soon began to feel better. She then bade me kiss her hands and the remains of the rod, and thank her humbly, but sincerely, for whipping me. Whatever she ordered I at once obeyed, deprived altogether of my own volition. She made me stoop down and kiss her feet and legs; for one delicious moment she held my head in soft imprisonment between her thighs. Beside myself from the effect of the pain, I am astonished still at the recollection of how my feelings towards Mademoiselle then underwent a most unreasonable but complete alteration. I loved her as violently as I had detested her before. I fell hopelessly in love with my cruel governess. I loved her because of her cruelty and became suddenly enthralled by a strong and anxious desire to press and fondle her. I worshipped the very ground on which she walked. Why was this?

45. MRS LESLIE & MISS DUNDAS

IN ABOUT AN hour's time, Mrs. Leslie and her sister came into the room: I jumped off the bed, and stood before them, feeling very frightened, but firm in my resolve. Mrs. Leslie asked me if I would do as she had told me? I replied, with the tears streaming down my cheeks, that I could not; then I implored her not to whip me, saying that I had never been whipped in my life.

She made no reply, but seized me and laid me across the bed: Miss Dundas immediately taking hold of my wrists and holding them tightly. Then Mrs. Leslie turned up my short frock and petticoats to my shoulders, and unfastening my drawers, pulled them down to my knees. I did not struggle to escape, nor did I again beg her not to whip me, as I knew it would be no use; but I felt very much ashamed at being turned up in such a degrading manner; I also dreaded the pain before me, and a sort of creeping sensation passed over the flesh of my bottom as I lay on the bed, in dire suspense, waiting for the punishment to commence. Mrs. Leslie leisurely took off one of her slippers, then she held my legs with her left hand, and began to spank me very severely; and as I had never before received a blow, I felt the pain acutely, but I tried to bear it quietly. The stinging slaps fell in quick succession all over my bottom; the pain grew sharper and sharper; I could no longer contain myself, and I began to struggle and cry. She went on spanking me relentlessly; my bottom seemed to be burning, and I screamed loudly at each slap.

At last she stopped, and put on her slipper; then she and her sister left the room, locking the door on the outside, leaving me lying on the bed, with my petticoats up and my drawers down, crying with shame and pain. When the smarting of my bottom had somewhat subsided, I wiped the tears from my eyes, got off the bed, and fastened up my drawers, then I lay down again, and buried my face in the pillow, feeling very wretched.

About an hour after, Miss Dundas brought me a cup of tea and some bread and butter, telling me that I should get no dinner that night; and she added that I was a young fool. She then went away, leaving me locked up.

Next morning, after I had dressed, I was waiting to be let out; but I was not. Some breakfast was brought to me, and later on, some lunch. At five o'clock, Mrs. Leslie and her sister made their appearance, and I was again asked if I would consent; and again I refused. Then for the second time I was laid across the bed and severely spanked; and as my bottom was still sore, I felt the stinging pain of the slaps more acutely than before, and I struggled more violently, and screamed louder than on the previous day.

When the punishment was over, I was again locked up.

At five o'clock next day, for the third time, they came into the room, and for the third time the question was put to me. Trembling, crying, and wringing my hands in utter despair, I exclaimed that I would never consent. Then, for the third time, my sore bottom was laid bare, and the spanking was begun That time the pain was most intense; I winced, writhed, and shrieked at each stroke of the thick slipper. I struggled hard to get of the bed, and I tried to kick; but Miss Dundas held my wrists tightly, and Mrs. Leslie held my legs down, at the same time spanking away, without paying the least attention to my shrieks and entreaties, until she was quite out of breath. Then she put on her slipper, and went away with her sister; locking me in the room as on the previous days.

My flesh tingled and throbbed painfully: I was hoarse from screaming; my cheeks were furrowed with tears, and I lay on the bed, crying and sobbing in abject misery for quite ten minutes. Then I got up, and bathed my burning, still smarting bottom with cold water, which greatly allayed the pain. I then gathered my short petticoats up above my waist, and standing in front of the glass, I looked over my shoulder at my bottom, and saw that it was very much swollen, the skin being shiny in appearance, and a dark purple colour; it was also so tender that I could not sit down comfortably. It afterwards turned black and blue.

I was kept locked up, and scantily fed, for three more days, but I was not again spanked. On the fourth day of my imprisonment, Mrs. Leslie came into the room, and said that if I would not do as all the other girls did, she would turn me out of the house. The threat startled me a good deal, but I again said that I would not sleep with a man.

She glared angrily at me; then, after telling me that I was to leave her house within twenty-four hours, she swept out of the room, leaving the door open.

46. Governess Triumphant

"As to the children, I have reached a climax with them, and do not think I shall have any more trouble. Yesterday occurred my battle royal with Master Hugh Dysart, and it is my opinion—yes, I really think—that, upon the whole, I came off victor. He is a young savage, this master Hugh Dysart, and from the first he has continually done all he dared to defy and annoy me. But yesterday the crisis arrived. He brought into the school-room a dog I hate (and secretly stand in fear of), a big-fierce-looking creature, belonging to Sir Roderick. and he also brought a whip with which he teased it. I ordered the dog out, and told him to bring the whip to

me. He told the dog to remain, and refused to bring me the whip. I am afraid of the dog, as I tell you, but my temper was stronger than my fear; so I went to the animal and took it boldly by its collar and led it out myself. Then I returned to my seat and commanded my young Sir Roderick to come to me, as I had done before. The two girls dropped their books, and sat and stared at me. I really believe there was something in my face which frightened them. For fully two minutes the boy sat in his seat, laughing at me a horridly wicked laugh,. and then a sudden passion of fury seemed to seize upon him. He sprang up and ran towards me, all at once, and before I could touch him his whip had struck me across my face.

"You cannot imagine, unless you have once received such a blow, what its effect was upon me. It is already agreed between us that my temper is not a cold one, and between the sting and the humiliation, and my perfect conviction that my time had come, I will confess that it got the better of me. In two seconds I had wrenched the whip from the little animal's hand, and held him with all my strength, and then I beat him—and beat him—and beat him! I beat him until I felt that even the amiable Sir Roderick might have considered I had distinguished myself; after which exploit I flung him upon the floor, broke the whip into half a dozen pieces, and threw it at him where he lay..."

47. In Front of the Maid

"Come here at once, James," she summoned the boy.

The unlucky youth caught his breath.

"Miss!", he began to whimper, "Forgive me!... not... in front of... Bridget."

"Don't argue! Come here!" commanded the governess.

James tried to go, but his legs refused to move. Meanwhile Barbara fixed him with her eye—he had to obey. Trembling, he stumbled over to her and she seized him by his hands.

"I shall not give you your full punishment immediately," began the teacher, "I want merely first of all to show Bridget how one handles naughty boys, no matter what age they are."

She spread her legs apart and clamped James between her knees, turned him round, bent him over her left thigh, and held him firmly around the waist with her left arm. James found himself in the classic position of boys about to receive the rod.

James made no resistance, for he knew, that it was perfectly hopeless and would only make his position worse.

But the humiliation was dreadful to him, and not only the humiliation. To receive the rod at all, let alone undergo it in the presence of the housemaid! He thought he would die when he felt Barbara's fingers unbuttoning his trousers and underpants and taking them down to his knees, and could not suppress a despairing squeal as the governess pulled up his shirt.

"You see, Bridget, that it isn't difficult to take a big boy's trousers down," instructed Barbara. "Do you not think that he would rather sink into the earth for very shame? Oh, James, shame on you! Think—to be prepared for the rod, to have to display your bare bottom in front of two women and then to be beaten on it by my hand! Will you steal chocolate again? Answer me! Will you?"

"Oh no, no, Miss! I'll never do it again!" whimpered the boy in his excruciating position.

"And you shall receive the rod, and really be punished for your fault. You will get a respectable number of strokes, but only a sample of what awaits you tonight. Then at bedtime you will receive your full punishment. With birch and strap!"

While Barbara has been speaking to the boy in this fashion, she still had not begun to beat him.

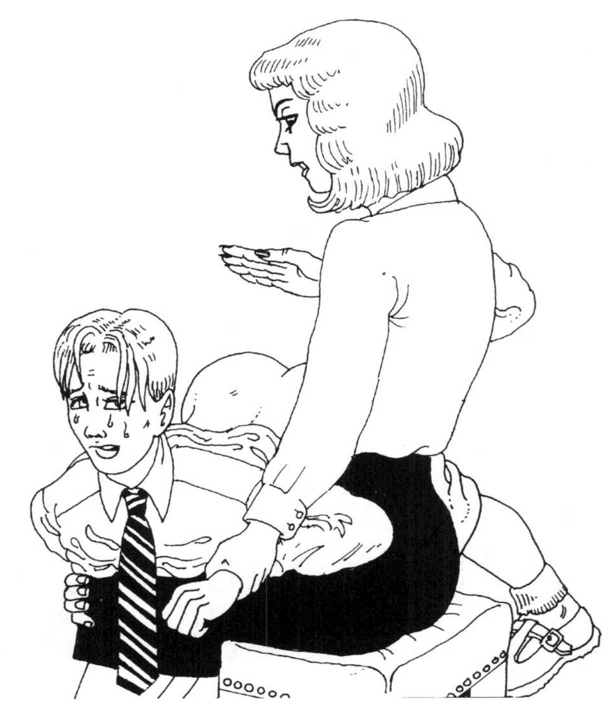

She now commenced to draw his underpants a little further down, and his shirt a little further up; she pressed his legs a little tighter between her own, and her hand, lying on his bottom, moved softly up and down; for him the contrast between the coolness of the air and the warmth of her hand brought home to him the shame of his nudity.

48. The Whipping Dress

I have been much interested in the correspondence on corporal punishment in your paper. I think myself that all children are whipped, whether with or without the parents' consent. I have known many cases in which the mother disclaims any such punishment and yet knows perfectly well that her nurse whips the children daily. I do not object to the whipping, but think it ought to be inflicted by the mother and not by the nurse. The best mother I ever knew used to whip her children, young and old, in the good old-fashioned way—that is to say, across her lap—and spanked them more or less severely, according to circumstances. She always made a serious business of it, and put on what she called a whipping dress, which was a soft black satin. This was always ready, hanging in her cupboard, and the culprit had to bring it to her, which was part of the business.

I may tell you that this same mother in her earlier married life strongly objected to whipping her children. She was converted in this way: one of the children was impervious to all other persuasion, and at last nearly put his brother's eye out by playfully striking him with a nursery knife. This settled matters, and his mother for the first time took him across her knee, and in her impetuosity more than soundly spanked him. The boy was a reformed boy from that time, and the mother slapped all the family from that time with the very best results.

49. A Drunkard Thrashed

I consider that a good whipping is the one—and the only one—remedy for faults committed; and in the case of those inebriates who so frequently reappear at our Police Courts on a charge of drunkenness, if they were sentenced to a good birching, instead of imprisonment, it would not only save the country much expense but do them far more good, as they would not be so likely to come up for another dose if it were well and properly administered.

I know of one case which occurred in my own family, where this remedy proved effectual. One of my relatives—a very good fellow in all other respects—had a distinct failing for getting too much to drink which led to quarrels between him and his wife, and was likely to end in separation.

The wife at last resolved to stand it no longer, and made up her mind to leave the husband, and when he found out she meant it, he begged of her not to go. She replied she would consider about it, and consulted her friends, one of whom said he deserved a jolly good hiding, and if it were her husband, that's what would happen. Struck with the idea, the wife resolved upon acting on the advice given her, and informed the husband that on condition of his undergoing a thorough good birching, and promises of amendment in the future, she would continue to live with him to see how he would go on.

The wife having previously procured a well-made and pliable birch-rod, which, upon the suggestion of her friend, she steeped in a pail of water, in which was dissolved a large quantity of salt, the next evening he received his punishment. The wife laid it on with such effect that it was some hours before he could sit down but he has not got drunk since.

50. Girls Enjoy Smacking

I have not been to school myself, but from conversation with girls who have, I have deduced this fact—that in an establishment where the rod is used, the conversation and manners of its inmates are apt to savour of birch, and the example of authority spreads down the ranks. What I mean is, that girls hail any occasion of acting as governesses, and one of their number who has committed a priggish or underhand act is not sent to Coventry, but stretched on a bed by half a dozen of her schoolfellows, and subjected to a "smacking". Naturally, might is right.

There is another example of this tendency. Girls left for an afternoon to "take care" of some young cousins, or indeed any children, frequently amuse themselves with a little amateur whipping. A girl of nineteen told me seriously that there was nothing she enjoyed more than to slap a chubby boy of about eight years old across her lap. I have no doubt many of your correspondents will confirm what I say.

51. A Busy Woman

I LUCKILY MET once again the disciplinarian matron of the neighbouring school, who had so rigorously birched the young chambermaid at my boarding-house. The flogging lady was alone this time, and I had to summon up all my courage before I dared address her. I stammered out my request quite timidly, but I had hardly uttered a few words before she flatly refused.

"No, sir, I don't whip men for their pleasure! There are heaps of women who make a business of this sort of thing. Go to them!"

I persisted, telling her that I prized a beating at her hands, because she was no common whipping woman, and that to be punished by her was almost an honour; a privilege possessing peculiar piquancy.

"No, no, I cannot consent," she said, "except on one condition. Had you committed some fault that really deserved chastisement, I might see things in a different light."

Her declaration caused a glimmer of hope. I fancied I had found a way to realise my secret longing idea by mentioning some trivial motive, but I had hardly opened my lips than she stopped me.

"You are about to invent some foolish story. It won't go down with me. If you should do something deserving punishment, write to me at the school. I shall then reflect. If I judge that the nature of your backsliding permits me to intervene, I will drop you a line to that effect."

She turned on her heel and left me rather puzzled.

I imagined a thousand things, rejecting them soon afterwards one by one, until, at last, I recollected perfectly well that a few days before I had indeed been guilty of an error that was worthy of expiation.

I bought some gloves and neckties in a large drapery store, paying with a hundred-dollar bill. The young woman who served me had handed me fifteen dollars too much when she gave me my change. I saw the mistake soon after I left the shop, but out of sheer carelessness, I did not go back to reimburse the lady assistant.

I therefore wrote to my stern governess accusing myself of this slight sin of heedlessness. I awaited a reply with a feeling of great anxiety, but a note soon reached me. It ran thus:

> Sir, What you call negligence is real larceny. You had discovered the mistake and knew who would have to suffer for it. Your education and your social position ought to have rendered you incapable of such lightheaded conduct, causing you to neglect to set that striking example a man of your rank in the world should always be able to show his inferiors. There is not the slightest doubt but that your duty is to return without a moment's delay the sum of money you dishonestly appropriated to the person to whom it belongs. I will chastise you. You deserve severe corporal punishment. In order to endure it, you will present yourself at the school tomorrow, Saturday, at three o'clock, after the pupils have left. The janitor will show you my office. My fee is one dollar.

I had attained my ends. I was to be deservedly birched by an official whipping matron, almost a legal flogging governess, if I may venture to say so. The modest figure of her emoluments proved that she deemed herself invested with honourable functions and did not seek to make money. When I reached the school, a boy between twelve and thirteen, holding a letter in his hand, was talking to the janitor, who, as he led me to the office of the disciplinarian schoolmistress, told the lad to follow him as well.

The flogging teacher, without troubling about me, except by replying to my respectful bow by a slight nod, glanced at the note brought by the youth. "Quite well, Harry?" she said. "Your father and mother ask me to give you a good dressing down. Come along here, I shan't be long over it!"

On hearing these threatening words, the little chap started as if he had received a shock from an electric battery, and began to sob.

"Oh no, please ma'am! Don't whip me! Oh don't, I pray you!"

"I shan't be more than ten minutes birching this young fellow," she said coolly, addressing me. "I will attend to you immediately afterwards."

She opened the door of an adjacent room and dragged the boy, still lamenting and struggling, in with her. "Down with your pants!" was the order given to the weeping lad.

"Oh no, please forgive me, ma'am! I'll never do it again!" howled the child.

The door had been left ajar. I could see distinctly what was going on in the other room, where there was a heavy form and a heap of birch-rods piled up in a corner.

"Didn't I tell you to let down your pants?" repeated the matron in an authoritative tone.

"Yes, ma'am. But oh!—do pardon me. Never again will I be naughty!"

The wretched boy trembled like a leaf, and the impatient woman slapped his face with such force that his head waggled about on his shoulders for a few seconds afterwards.

"So you won't take down your breeches?" she said. "I'm letting them down—I am really!" stuttered the youth.

Without allowing him to complete this necessary act of partial disrobing, the termagant, in a rage, threw herself upon him. Gripping both his hands, she tied them together at the wrists. She then threw him brutally on to the bench, passing a thick rope over his loins so as to bind him securely face downwards. She then tore off his trousers completely, and wound a second stout cord round his legs, while he never ceased struggling and howling. Catching up a strong rod, she set about flogging him with might and main, hitting him with real vigour. The lad yelled as if mad, bounding and writhing, despite his bonds. The terrible birching lady paid no attention to anything but her task. It looked to me as if she had lost her wits, for putting for her entire strength, she literally covered the brat's little bottom with formidable slashing strokes.

It was a thrilling sight—this tall female, as frenzied as an enraged lioness, mercilessly cutting these palpitating boyish buttocks with practised, mighty blows of her stout birch. Her victim roared with acute pain. I trembled in every limb, thinking how in a few minutes, I also should be bound down on the same bench, to be birched still more brutally, as I was older, and able to support still greater agony.

Nevertheless, the sensation that benumbed my entire being was not devoid of infinite voluptuousness. I struggled against a natural impulse prompting me to fly from such severe correction, and yet I remained as if my feet were nailed to the floor, incapable of movement. I was actuated by a furious desire to endure the torturing ordeal.

The spectacle became very thrilling; the teacher going on with her fierce birching, and her captive twisting about under the burning twigs, as he uttered heartrending cries. Bits of birch flew about all over the room, and when at last the female executioner threw away the worn stump of her rod, I breathed again. She unfastened the ropes and bundled the boy outside, without even giving him time to adjust his disordered garments.

Passing in front of me, she gave me a look that made me shudder.

"Go in the corner and undress!" she said roughly.

Just as the little boy left, a girl of about fifteen years of age came in. She brought a letter that the governess glanced over after tearing it open impatiently.

"What! More punishment?" she exclaimed. "Can I never have a moment's peace?"*

The Twentieth Century

1. Recollections of Domestic Discipline

In those days over ninety percent of all Frenchmen and -women were "peasants". Louise was no exception. In the year '00 she had been born, third child of a family of nine, to the wife of a Normandy *fermier*. The farms of Normandy are rich, but this was a small one, and there was no question that when she became of an age she would have to go out into the world and earn her own living (in this way she was situated almost exactly like her English colleague, Dorothy Baxter, also the child of agricultural parents, and similarly with no chance whatever of inheriting even the smallest piece of land).

Louise had supposed she would go eventually to Paris, into service naturally, but in fact her first real live-in position was as the *bonne* in a household kept by a widow in Chartres. She was then just fifteen. The widow was not the deceased husband's first wife but his second; she was still quite young, in her forties, and had been left pleasantly-off. This allowed her to keep a small but well-furnished house in the best district of the great cathedral city, to move in Chartres society, to entertain on a modest but pleasant scale, and to pay for the education, upkeep and clothing of her stepson Maurice.

"He was I suppose about thirteen," said Louise. "A black-haired boy, a little plump perhaps, with soft brown eyes and long lashes; his hair fell over his eyebrows like a girl's. When first I saw him I curtseyed as one must but he seemed more embarrassed than I and almost ran past me. At the time I did not understand."

One morning, not long afterwards, Louise was on her knees, cleaning the grate in the salle de réception, while the lady of the house sat in an armchair and smoked black cigarettes. She was waiting for a particular friend to call—a Madame de Trébizon. There was a mild thump and crash from the hallway. Louise got to her feet and went to the doorway to investigate. She came back and knelt down to her task again.

"What was that?" asked her employer, idly turning the pages of a ladies' journal. Louise thought she did not sound very interested, and saw no reason why she should not say—in any case, it was a light enough matter.

"Monsieur Maurice, madame," she replied. "I think he slipped when he came down the stairs. He's all right now. Not hurt at all. Nothing broken."

"Be so kind," said the widow, without looking up, "as to ask my stepson to join me." Not a note of her voice conveyed anything but mild boredom.

Louise got to her feet, went into the hall, caught the boy on his way back upstairs, and delivered her message. She saw his face change—it went oddly wooden—but she thought little of it and followed him back into the salon.

The conversation between the boy and his stepmother was conducted with Maurice standing in front of his *belle-mère*'s armchair, hands behind his back, head drooping, while she, without once looking up from the magazine so far as Louise (who had meanwhile returned to her task by the grate) could see, interrogated him about the recent mishap in a lazy, uninterested manner.

What had he been doing to cause the noise?

He had been descending the stair, *maman*, and slipped near the bottom.

At what speed had he been descending the stair?

Perhaps a little quickly, *maman*, but he had wanted—

Never mind what he wanted. He had many times been forbidden to rush about like a barbarian in the house, which was full of valuable objects. Was that not so?

Oui, maman.

"At this moment and not before," said Louise, "she put down her reading and fixed him with her gaze. She was a handsome woman with rich black hair, coiffed *à la mode*. She had cold blue eyes. She looked calmly at him, through him, almost dreamily, I thought.

"By this time I hardly had attention for the fireplace. The air was electric. I was convinced something was going to happen. And I wasn't wrong!

"The widow said: 'Tell me again what you were doing. Start from the moment you arrived at the top of the stairs and describe every single step you took from that moment. Begin. ' And as she said these words—they were not said harshly—she reached languidly forward with both her long pale hands and, tugging him gently closer, turned him to his right and began to unfasten his trousers, which were high-waisted, close-fitting and knee-length, buttoned down each hip in the Spanish style; dark blue velvet, with ornamental buttons at the hem. Very expensive trousers, not the sort a boy of thirteen can readily play in. They were the only sort he was ever allowed to wear.

"He stood still and let her do it. I wanted to see his face but it was turned away from me. I could not believe this big boy would let her undress him in front of the maid without so much as a protest. But I give you my word that is what he did. And as she had bidden, he spoke throughout this procedure, his voice quivering as he tried to obey her, while all the time she was making preparations to punish him!"

For it was now plain to Louise that something of this nature was in the offing. She wondered when the mistress would notice her, tell her to go, but she did nothing of the kind. And when she had undone enough buttons on one side she rotated Maurice back to front, so that he was facing the other way, said "Continue", and began, methodically, and with the same lazy deliberation, to undo the other buttons, one by one.

Louise felt sorry for Maurice—not because she didn't think boys of his age should be spanked when they need it, but because it didn't seem to her to be such a severe offence. She could now see the boy's face quite plainly—eyes lowered, lips parted, mumbling his futile and near-inaudible relation of unimportant events.

"Continue!" said the stepmother, again, and so of course he had to ("not that she really wanted to know, you understand?" said Louise). She now turned him to face her and even while he was miserably admitting he had taken the last three stairs at a single leap, she was carefully, contemplatively, caressingly, easing the trousers, now freed from all support and restraint, down his legs, over his knees, to his calves, where they subsided into an expensive, pathetic, softly crumpled heap. The boy stood quietly in his shirt, totally passive, head drooping, and awaited events.

Louise fell silent. "Well?" asked Dorothy impatiently. "Well?" asked Mary, leaning forward tensely over her teacup.

The widow laid her stepson across her knees in the classic position. He offered no resistance. His forearms rested on the ground and his shins brushed the carpet. He was a tall boy for his age, and the chair was quite low.

It seemed to Louise as if the arms of the deep chair might impede the forthcoming execution but the widow had clearly done this exercise many times before, for she simply eased herself forwards a foot or two so that she obtained good clearance for her palm and forearm. Then she unbuttoned her cuff and rolled back her sleeve to the elbow, staring into the middle distance with that same abstracted look on her face, as if performing some wholly automatic task like kneading bread. Her stepson lay still as a stone.

Then the doorbell rang. Louise, anxious not to miss anything, answered it as quickly as she might, and followed the visitor back into the salon, having first relieved her of her furs and cloak. It was Madame de Trébizon, as expected.

"Forgive me, my dear, if I do not rise to greet you," said the widow, smiling upon her well-to-do friend, "but as you can see I have a small matter to attend to first."

No further preparations had taken place during the brief hiatus. Maurice still lay silently across his stepmother's knees. The tail of his shirt concealed the upper part of his posterior; the lower part and the upper thigh were still clad in close-fitting linen. It dawned upon Louise that the boy was perfectly resigned to the humiliatingly public circumstances of his imminent punishment—had certainly experienced such chastisements before.

"At first I thought it was self-control, and admired him for it," said Louise. "Later I thought it was terror. Today, I am not sure what it was. But to continue: having bidden Madame de Trébizon to a chair, my mistress lifted up his shirt, right up his back. Then she… took down his knickers! What else? *Voilà!* All the way to his knees. I could hardly believe my eyes.

"She began to spank him with the palm of her right hand. I have said that her fingers were long

and graceful—Madame played the pianoforte very well, did I mention that?—and although she did not smack him very hard, as it seemed, his flesh turned very pink very quickly. Her hand simply rose and fell, with no particular to-do. And yet it made a good sharp noise, and there was the reddening, and after a while the wriggling, and soon after that the usual sounds one hears… so I suppose they must, after all, have been very hard smacks! It is an art, to make it look so easy, to give the impression that you are doing nothing more strenuous than fanning yourself. I have always tried to copy her.

"And then, just when I thought she must stop, she began to talk. I mean: converse! On the subject of discipline, *bien sûr*, but in an easy, polished way as if around a dinner table. She talked to her friend, saying how often Maurice needed chastisement—that was her special word, chastisement, *la châtiment*—and the other woman was agreeing with her. Emphatically! It seemed plain they had played this game before…

"And then, to my amazement, she spoke to me! All without stopping for as much as a moment!

"'Louise,' she said—smack!—'when you were younger'—smack!—'did your *maman* punish you'—smack!—'in this manner?'

"I said: 'Yes, madame, many times.'

"'Just like this'—smack!—'with the bottom bare?'

"'Yes, madame," I replied. I have no doubt I blushed.

"'I have heard it said', interposed the other lady, 'that in the country the mothers use nettles to whip their children. Is it true?'

"'Yes, madame'.

"'Do you hear that, you naughty boy?' she asked, addressing the hapless culprit. 'How lucky you are to have a kind *belle-mêre*, who would never dream of doing anything so cruel!'

"My mistress drily remarked (without ceasing to chastise) that nettles were not necessary in a house whose grounds contained willow and (smack!) birch trees as well as (smack!) hazel thickets, and within whose chambers many useful items like hairbrushes (smack!), bedroom slippers (smack!), washing paddles (smack!) and soap-rods (smack!) were to be found without difficulty.

"'And'—smack!—'there is also the table-crumber, is there not, Maurice?' she added.

"Finally she let him get up. I suppose he may have received about fifty good spanks. He was weeping, but not loudly.

"She then made him stand before her in his shirt and repeat a phrase he obviously knew by heart. I remember it began: 'I thank you, madam my stepmother, for my chastisement… ' A formula. I can't remember it all.

"Then she told him he might button up. When he had done this, she kissed him, and off he went. He did not look at me. But I noticed he had already stopped crying."

At this point in her story Louise stopped, and thought for a moment. Then she said a curious thing: "Maurice was the most exquisitely punished boy I ever knew."

"How do you mean," said Dorothy, "'Exquisitely'?"

"She was an artist, that woman," explained Louise. "She really enjoyed punishing him, and she brought into his punishments all the charm and beauty that she understood so well through her music. There was nothing of the barbarian about her! Though she certainly did not whip him over-gently. A good collection of stripes from the birch, if she had used one. A red bottom, always, especially after she had used the table-crumber, which made broad marks and was probably the most severe weapon she used. How she could 'colour up' that youth where he sat down! He was a boy who blushed a lot. Those who go red in the cheeks when they are ashamed or shy are also those who blush most easily and notably in another part! Have you not found this to be the case?"

Dorothy considered. "Never really noticed, or thought about it," she said apologetically.

"And you, Mary?" asked Louise, perhaps with a touch of malice.

Mary said, stammering: "Me? I've never smacked anybody in me life! How would I notice such a thing!"

"You're blushing, Mary!" cackled Dorothy.

"I am not!" But she had been, all the same, and she knew it.

2. A Severe Young Schoolmistress

"Go in front, Wright," she said.

She was trembling in every fibre. A big, sullen boy, not bad but very difficult, slouched out to the front. She went on with the lesson, aware that Williams was making faces at Wright, and that Wright was grinning behind her. She was afraid. She turned to the map again. And she was afraid. "Please Miss, Williams—" came a sharp cry, and a boy on the back row was standing up, with drawn, pained brows, half mocking grin on his face, half real resentment against Williams—"Please Miss, he's nipped me,"—and he rubbed his leg ruefully.

"Come in front, Williams," she said.

The rat-like boy sat with his pale smile and did not move.

"Come in front," she repeated, definite now.

"I shan't," he cried, snarling, rat-like, grinning. Something went click in Ursula's soul. Her face and eyes set, she went through the class straight. The boy cowered before her glowing, fixed eves. But she advanced on him, seized him by the arm, dragged him from his seat. He clung to the form. It was a battle between him and her. Her instinct had suddenly become calm and quick. She jerked him from his grip and dragged him, struggling and kicking, to the front. He kicked her several times, and clung to the forms as he passed, but she went on. The class was on its feet in excitement. She saw it, but made no move.

She knew if she let go the boy he would dash to the door. Already he had run home once out of her class. So she snatched her cane from the desk, and brought it down on him. He was writhing and kicking. She saw his face beneath her, white, with eyes like the eyes of a fish, stony, yet full of hate and horrible fear. And she loathed him, the hideous writhing thing that was nearly too much for her. In horror lest he should overcome her and yet at the heart quite calm, she brought down the cane again and again, whilst he struggled making inarticulate noises, and lunging vicious kicks at her. With one hand she managed to hold him, and now and then the cane came down on him. He writhed, like a mad thing. But the pain of the strokes cut through his writhing, vicious, coward's courage, bit deeper, till at last. with a long whimper that became a yell, he went limp. She let him go, and he rushed at her, his teeth and eyes glinting. There was a second of agonised terror in her heart: he was a beast thing. Then she caught him, and the cane came down on him. A few times, madly, in a frenzy, he lunged and writhed, to kick her. But again the cane broke him, he sank with a howling yell on the floor, and like a beaten beast lay there yelling.

3. A Cruel Governess

In the second year of the reign of Mademoiselle, the scene changed from London to a lodging-house at Eastbourne... Before leaving us our mother expressed a pious hope that we might be speaking fluent French on her return. This hope produced a grievance; Mademoiselle considered that it reflected upon her prowess as a teacher. She said that I never knew my lessons nor seemed to take an interest;

if we could not yet speak French it was no fault of hers. I was lazy, stupid and obstinate, a discredit to any teacher. She was tired of my sullen unreceptivity and resolved to beat it out of me. Peter also should be beaten, but not as hard or often. Boys she considered less hateful than girls. Peter did not look so sullen, he was more bearable. Accordingly at the first provocation I was ordered to my room and told to undress. I did so, wonderingly. Mademoiselle called in the housemaid who stood inertly and said:

"Fancy now! And you being such a naughty little girl, who'd ha' thought it?"

I am not sure which I minded most, the beating with a wooden spade or the indignity of being seen with no clothes on by the housemaid. A latent class consciousness was bitterly aroused.

Another day Peter was beaten with the wooden spade, but his punishment was for some offence of mine. This represented another effort on the part of Mademoiselle to drive the wedge between us. Peter, who knew my agony of mind, tried not to cry, so that I would not think he was being hurt…

Every morning we did our lessons in the wood, and this was preceded by a systematic ritual: as soon as we had arrived at the habitual spot, Mademoiselle picked up a stick and hit it against the nearest tree trunk to prove whether it was brittle or not. If it withstood the test she then threw me to the ground holding me up by my heels, and proceeded according to habit. This, she explained, was in order that I should know my lessons.

4. THE APPRENTICE GOVERNESS

UNTIL THE AGE of fifteen, I was ignorant of what is called flagellation: the many severe corrections that my mother had inflicted on me until my tenth year had left me with only disagreeable recollections of this sharp form of maternal love.

At fifteen, a boy of middle height, well built, intelligent, with a docile character, but sensitive, I went to stay for a while with my aunt, who lived in a nearby town. There I attended a special school and, for the duration of one year, prepared for an examination. My aunt, an unmarried lady, was not much occupied with me, leaving me alone often in the afternoons, to go for a walk or to visit friends.

One beautiful day, my aunt was advised of the return of her Goddaughter, having finished her studies in Switzerland, Germany and England, was coming to London to seek a situation as a lady's companion or family governess. My aunt had invited her to stay until she found suitable employment.

The young lady of 19 arrived. Not having seen her since her fifteenth year, I was agreeably surprised by her svelte beauty distinguished by regular features, a beautiful blonde head of hair, wide eyes, a well-formed and energetic mouth, and fine build with provocative curves.

The sympathetic sentiments with which I greeted the young lady were reciprocated and she asked me, the first day, to call her by her first name Denise. I performed many small tasks and services for her; and for her part, she assisted me with my French lessons—she knew that language very well.

I remember well the occasion when she exclaimed: "Oh, what a great number of faults! If I were your aunt, I should whip you, you lazy creature!" I took this remark—and others like it—for teasing and took my revenge by means of practical jokes; one time, for example, I dropped a wet sponge on the back of her neck.

She called after me: "If I catch you, I'll spank you! Rogue!" But afterwards she seemed to have forgotten her threat.

Two or three days had passed since the first incident, when at a certain moment I was leaning out of the window, looking at the business and activity of the street below. All of a sudden, I felt a sharp smack on my backside. This burning contact penetrated like a small thunderbolt. I was startled to see Denise still stooping over me. She laughed.

"What was that for?" I stammered, though without straightening up. "Well," replied Denise, "that was for your provocative pose and also for the wet sponge."

Excited perhaps by my apparent submission, Denise took hold of the thin material of my trousers, while saying in a dry tone: "Wait! I'm going to give you a spanking. Truly you deserve one!"

"No, no," I replied. "People can see us!"

"Not at all," answered Denise "There's only a garden opposite." And immediately, I felt a series of powerful smacks falling on my surprised bottom.

"Is that warming you up?" she said. "I hope

you're going to be more respectful towards me—in fact I'm sure of it. But next time, I'll take down your trousers and give it to you on your bare bottom!"

Faint with shame, I murmured: "But what if I tell my aunt?" Immediately Denise released me. "That's horrible! I don't love you any more—go away!" She turned away, visibly offended; but I took her in my arms. "Don't be angry, Denise, forgive me, I won't say anything about it to my aunt." Denise looked at me with suspicious eyes. "Promise?" "I promise you, dear Denise."

"Even if I take down your trousers?" she answered, after two seconds of silence. Blushing, I murmured: "No." And then, under the influence of a sensation altogether new to me, I added: "You can do everything!"

"No," answered Denise. "That will be for next time. But your threat has earned you a severe extra spanking over your trousers. Quickly! Bend over the table… "

Once I was in the required position, Denise took firm hold of my trousers, then administered sixteen good smacks, well placed, after which she

ordered me to leave the room.

Arriving in my little room, I lowered my trousers and examined my whipped backside… I experienced singularly delicious emotions… And, from that day, my ideas turned, ardently, to the waiting renewal of a similar correction!

But one, two, three days went by, without the dreamed-for event taking place. It seemed that Denise didn't notice my practical jokes, vainly intended to provoke her. But, the third day, on returning from school, and crossing the corridor in order to enter my room, I saw Denise's door opening just as I passed. The young lady, standing on the threshold, motioned for me to enter.

"You have continually been teasing me lately! The moment has arrived for your correction. Yesterday you slipped a horsehair brush under my bedclothes! It's the right moment. Your aunt is out until seven. Take off your jacket and let down your trousers!"

Even while I protested at this, Denise hunted in a drawer where she found, hidden under some lingerie, a short and supple birch-rod of yellow colour which was of a different texture to birchwood, as I could tell by sight.

I removed my jacket; but embarrassment prevented me from carrying out the remainder of her command. "Must I help you?" Denise demanded and, without further ceremony, she began to unbutton my breeches. This done, she started work on the buttons at the back. I protested: "Oh, I can do it myself"—"Then hurry up!"

Then, the trousers arranged, Denise pulled me towards her. Seating herself on a chaise longue, she took me across her knees and, holding me under her left arm, tucked up my shirt. "Oh, what a pretty bottom! What a beautiful white backside laid out for me to look at—like a well-built girl. I'm going to do it justice, this bottom, you'll see!"

During these comments, she kneaded and fondled my excited flesh, and stroked it softly with her light hand. I felt, for a moment, her fingers slipping between my buttocks.

Then she began to apply firm and regular strokes, growing more rapid. "I'm going to warm it it properly, this bottom, villain! That will do you nicely. One must always whip them, boys of your age—and of all ages! Smack! Smack! But he isn't afraid of mere smacks. Nobody sees him, nobody hears him!"

Her sermon continued, along with the smacking,. interrupted only from time to time by a short pause. I find it impossible to describe the emotions I was experiencing. I was like a fiery furnace, and I felt sure I was giving proof of my feelings against the left thigh of my punisher.

Then she took the birch and whipped me with rapid strokes, across, along, to the left, to the right. Holding me still more tightly against her body, her left arm entangled with mine; her left hand, underneath, supported me, and I felt, beyond all doubt, the contact of her fingers...

5. FORBIDDEN READING

"A BOOK OF Voltaire!" exclaimed Mr. Bordumien, recoiling, "And where did she get that?"

"I have not yet had time to ask her," replied his wife, "But we will do so at once. In any case, Marie deserves punishment. Claire has received hers. I want you to whip her severely; I am not strong enough to manage such a big girl, and besides, coming from you it will have a much greater effect."

"My dear, you may be sure that she will get a whipping and a good one... A book of Voltaire... did you ever... Yes, she certainly deserves something... Good heavens, good heavens! What shall we come to when our children start reading Voltaire!"

Mr Bordumien choked with indignation.

"Come up with me to Marie's room," concluded his wife, "You will punish her up there... "she added as she handed to Mr Bordumien a bundle of twigs she had just pulled out of a new birch broom.

The two parents went towards Marie's room, and the latter felt her heart sink with apprehension when she saw her mother come into her room, and her father, his face an apoplectic red, carrying in his hand the famous birch, whose disciplinary functions she was well acquainted with, having often had experience of them, and not so very long ago. Madame Bordumien spoke first: taking the little book from her pocket she held it out to Marie, who felt the walls of the room swimming round her. "Can you tell me, Miss, where you found this horrible thing?" Marie, instead of replying, commenced to cry. "Will you tell me, where did you get this?" insisted her mother. Marie hid her face in her hands: her mother, advancing towards her pulled her arms apart. The young girl, her face bathed in tears, stubbornly looked on the ground.

"Very well! Very well! You will not tell the name of the person who lent you this book... once... twice... all right... three... Good, your father is going to whip you and in such a fashion that you will remember it all your life."

Mr Bordumien, birch in hand, took a step towards his daughter.

"No! No!" cried the latter, quite frantic at the prospect. "No... papa... papa... do not... whip... me... I will... tell you... the truth... it was... Al... Alice... Mur... ray who gave it to me... she told me not to... speak about it... I have not read it... I swear it... I gave it... at once to... Claire..."

"Why did you give it to Claire instead of returning it to your friend Alice?" demanded Mr Bordumien.

"I don't know... hi, hi, hi!"

"You don't know... I think your mother was quite right in asking me to punish you, and I am going to do it... get ready... now then!"

"No, papa, no... Oh!"

This oh! was occasioned by the fact that Mr Bordumien, without more ceremony, had seized the maiden by the waist, bent her in two and tucked her under his powerful arm as in a vice, in a position which held her body in a right angle, so that even her feet did not touch the ground. Mad with shame, literally overwhelmed by this awful catastrophe, the fair Marie permitted herself to be placed by her father in the classic pose

THE MANXWOMAN

There was a young woman of Manx
Whose nephew was full of rude pranks
So she took the young chap
Across her broad lap
And gave him six good stinging spanks.

It grieved her, she said, to get wild
And whip such a fine chubby child;
Then she made him feel sore
With three or four more
And when he begged pardon she smiled.

Her smacks made so quick an impression
She gave them for every transgression
So often he got 'em
He's never forgot 'em
And this is that boy's own confession.

of a child who is going to be spanked. Ah! She was a very light weight under the strong arm of her father. The knowledge of her helplessness paralysed her. With her mother it would have been another matter, she would have struggled, would have screamed, thrown herself on the floor, but now…

"Ah! No… papa! Not… there!" These exclamations were caused by the fact that Mr Bordumien had just turned up her skirt and petticoat. Madame Bordumien assisted her husband by fixing the turned up clothes with a safety pin, then the father raised his hand over a plump, curved bottom, carefully wrapped like an exquisite bonbon, in the dainty covering of a school girl's little drawers, quite plain, with a little lace round the knees. "Won't you take off her drawers?" asked Madame Bordumien. "No, she is too big: besides that won't prevent her from feeling what I am going to give her."

And Smack! Smack! Smack! The heavy hand, big as a shoulder of mutton, fell regularly, ding, dong, sometimes on one, sometimes on the other cheek of the filial behind, painfully exposed to the blows.

The thin material of the drawers, if it did to some extent protect the extreme modesty of the little one, was certainly no defence against the blows.

Each smack as it fell on her bottom hurt her horribly, a frightful smarting sensation making her yell.

Twisting her supple body, kicking her legs to right and left, in spite of her most desperate efforts she did not succeed in protecting her fleshy parts from that rain of blows which with horrible regularity always fell on the same place.

A heavier smack than usual drove her frantic, she gave a piercing scream and, with a mad, unconscious movement, she turned half round and bit her father's wrist.

At the pain, Mr Bordumien almost let her fall.

"She has bitten me!… She has bitten her father," he cried. "Suzanne, pass me the birch…"

she has bitten her father!... Ah!"

Without a word Madame Bordumien obeyed her husband and handed him the article he asked for.

Mr Bordumien grasped the bundle of twigs in his hand and prepared to whip his daughter's bottom soundly, having replaced her in position with a twist, grasping her waist till she could scarcely breathe.

"Wait a moment," said Madame Bordumien to her husband. She approached Marie, whose pretty white-stockinged legs were waving in the air, and whilst keeping clear so as not to be caught by one of the unhappy girl's lunges, she slipped her hands under her belly, and untied her drawers, which she drew down to her ankles, despite the appeals and cries of shame from the lass.

The chemise covered her bottom with its light batiste curtain. The mother raised this last veil and tucked it over the hips of the victim, then she withdrew and Mr Bordumien had before him, insolently naked, exposing its already scarlet cheeks with an indecent arrogance, the prettiest female bottom that anyone could wish to see.

Before this charming spectacle Mr Bordumien hesitated a moment, he could not but be affected by the graceful proportions of his daughter. A glance from his wife called forth the necessary energy; he seized the birch in his hand and laid it on with a will, cutting into the appetising apple, the beautiful, delicate moon, the ravishing buttocks whose central furrow, shaded with warm tones, curved inwards towards the thighs in a darkness full of perfumed mystery. At the first cut of the birch, striking squarely across her bottom already swollen by the previous spanking, Marie screamed with all her might, so loudly that the servant came upstairs and opened the door. But when she saw it was only the young lady getting a whipping she went down again to the kitchen.

6. In Front of the Girls

"YOU WOULD have liked that place, Paulette. Its name was Picquigny, and it was in the country, not far from Amiens. We had relatives there. My father, mother and I were staying at my aunt's house. We used to arrive on Sunday morning and leave the same evening. Sometimes, however, we left the following morning.

"The kid I mentioned was the son of neighbours on the road which led to Airennes. One

day, after lunch, I went to their house with their daughter. She had called to ask me to come and see a hat she had decorated. She was sixteen, and we spent the time talking about fashion because I wanted to be a milliner. I can still remember how ugly that hat was, with its forget-me-nots as trimming!

"The boy had answered his mother back. She was in the yard, and became very angry. It was obvious he was going to get a terrible punishment!

"His mother dragged him into the house, into the dining room, where we were talking. She held him under her arm and took his trousers down in no time at all. She really did it quickly!

"And then she spanked him! How she spanked him! But she didn't hurry in the least. She didn't say a word, although she was in a real rage, a cold rage, and the more she spanked the more she wished to spank. You should have heard the slaps! She was a big woman, and as strong as a horse.

"The spanking lasted a long time. It was more than an ordinary punishment: much worse than what you call a good one, Paulette. I can remember it clearly, and now I wonder if the woman's feelings weren't a little suspect. Especially as his sister told me that he received lots of spankings—and spankings like that one: never less severe!...

"A fortnight later we returned to Picquigny. My aunt's neighbour was just punishing her boy when we called. Unfortunately I didn't see any of the detail, but Fernande told me all about it.

"When we got into the house Fernande's mother was no longer in the dining room. She had seen us cross the road and had hurried off to change her dress. My mother said to the boy:

"Why are you crying, Emile? Have you got toothache? Are you in pain?"

His sister burst into a roar of laughter, and when she had finished, she said: 'It isn't his teeth that ache! Ask him yourself where the pain is! It isn't his face that's smarting! He looks so red because he's ashamed. Mother has just been giving him a spanking. If our window hadn't been closed, you would've heard the slaps. She was just pulling his trousers up when you came in… '"

7. A Governess Reminisces

"When I was thirteen, we were living with a family in Knightsbridge, in a grand row of buildings opposite Hyde Park. The family, named Peterson, had two boys: Martin, who was two years my senior, and Simon, one year junior to me. Every week day, I took my lessons with them, learning all the academic subjects, just as you and Michael do now. My mother, believing she should prepare me to make my own way through life as a governess, felt is was necessary for me also to master the feminine arts; so in the hours I wasn't studying with the boys, I was learning my stitches or perfecting a piece on the piano forte. Sometimes my mother would have me act as apprentice to one of the staff, so I might understand the domestic skills required of my future female charges. And she was very insistent we should all be in possession of good business acumen. I remember the time we pretended to buy stocks and shares, and calculated our earnings over a period of time.

"She really was a very progressive thinker, especially when it came to girls. It was her conviction that girls are superior to boys, not in the sense they are better, but that the traits they possess, which belong solely to our gender, are the essential traits that allow our species to attain the highest degree of civilisation. This is not to say that the traits boys possess are unnecessary, but more that they are the consequence of this primary mission. She was quite a believer in theories of social Darwinism, you might be surprised to learn, and very often characterised the development of a child to an adult within this framework.

"Girls, she would tell me, matured much more quickly than boys; a boy's behaviour and attitudes might be half those of a girl his chronologic equal and, just as frequently, one might find a girl's maturity to be in excess of her chronologic age. She saw this as perfectly natural, an outcome of the evolutionary pressures on females to bear and mould the next generation. Using the same sort of theorising, she explained the critical need for the finely tuned balance of nurture and stringency in the female, which is often completely lacking or only marginally developed in the male.

"I suppose, if I think about it closely, the notion that the female possesses and is capable of articulating this delicate and necessary balance was the cornerstone of her whole ideology. Everything she set out to teach me, or inculcate in her charges, regardless of their gender, stemmed from a belief that nothing happened successfully without the proper mixture of love and firmness. A situation might demand more of one than the other, but neither should be completely neglected. Such an oversight could only lead to ruin."

"And do you believe this to be true?" Kitty sounded in awe of these radical thoughts.

"I'm not sure, my dear, that I would make as much use of the Darwinian motif, but then, we have tended to move beyond much of the deterministic thought that was a part of that generation. I don't suppose the whys really matter; what does matter are the observations of behaviour, for in that my mother was clearly well-grounded. Whatever you might say, in the final analysis, girls grow up very differently and certainly more quickly than boys. If you are charged with raising and educating a child, you absolutely must accept this."

"So, being a woman is much more important?"

"Oh darling, it would be folly to assume that. So many of the fine and noble traits that define us as human beings come from the male. I am thinking of things such as courage, loyalty, a sense of justice. Wonderful, beautiful aspects of the human spirit—we'd be lost without them. But the traits that females possess, applied appropriately, make the expression of these fine ideals possible. You can't have one without the other, as my mother would say."

Michael watched his sister's head nod in thoughtful agreement as Miss Victoria continued.

"As you might imagine, the boys were often quite a handful. Simon was a human butterfly, unable to stick with any one thing for very long. And Martin, he was a moody, sullen boy, totally unable to live up to his parents' high expectations. Sometimes I felt badly for him, thinking it must be very difficult to go through life being unappreciated for who you really are. Actually he was a very good musician, much better than I at the piano, with a beautiful singing voice.

"My mother had a talent for bringing out the best in people, and she certainly gave these boys the full benefit of her skills. But, of course, there were many times when one or the other had to be reined in—Simon would get so out of hand and Martin could be positively obnoxious. She found herself spending increasingly more of her day delivering punishments that proved rather ineffective in the long term. She would spank them, or use a strap or cane on their bottoms; she would assign them lines to copy or have them stand against the wall, and while the boys would refine their behaviour briefly, it had little lasting impact.

"One day, she decided her pattern of thinking stood in need of revision. She felt she had been reacting to situations as they presented themselves rather than addressing the cause and what she really needed was a programme of prevention. So she devised what she called her 'Motivation Appointment.'

"The routine was this: each morning the boys, individually, would report to my mother's sitting room, still wearing their night shirts. She would be waiting for them, seated in an over-stuffed chair, and they would have to stand before her and ask, politely, for their lesson, which is to say they were to ask for a spanking. Depending on the nature of their conduct the previous day, my mother would select either a thin, leather-soled slipper or a hairbrush with which she would administer their motivational lesson.

"You might notice that these are two quite feminine implements—and indeed the whole ritual was very maternal in nature—and there was a reason for this, although for my scientifically-minded mother, I thought it rather mystical. She told me she believed it would impart a feminine balance to their lives.

"It really was a simple strategy, and it was completely private. The boys had simply to keep their appointments and no further mention of the event was made. Mother felt to add further shame or embarrassment to the undertaking would redirect its energy when she wanted their minds focused on this one experience."

"Do you mean the boys got a spanking every single morning?" The notion seemed to overwhelm Kitty.

"Yes. Every morning."

"And did they hurt much?"

"You've never been slippered or spanked with a hairbrush?" Miss Victoria seemed a bit surprised at Kitty's naivety.

"No, Miss." She blushed, as if she were embarrassed to admit it. "Actually, Miss, the only spanking I can ever remember is the one you gave me."

"I see."

"But I have been given lines. And once I had to scrub the entire schoolroom floor," she said hopefully, as though these might compensate for her dearth of experience.

"Well, I do believe if one is to be a successful disciplinarian, one needs experience of both sides of the coin. Just as I suspect the best Doctors are those who have also been patients. But there I am back at theory again, and you've asked me a specific question. Let me see… a slipper with a thin leather sole is a very stinging implement, but it hasn't much weight, so the sensation is mostly applied to the surface of the bottom and tends not to linger long. Whereas the hairbrush is a more formidable weapon. It is heavier and thicker, so not only does it sting, but it is capable of leaving one bruised and sore. If my mother felt an extra measure of motivation was needed, she'd choose the hairbrush and then spank longer or harder, depending on the circumstances. So, yes, Catherine, either way they did hurt quite a bit.

"Once she had made her selection, my mother expected the boy to pull up his nightshirt, beneath which he should be wearing a clean pair of pants. These she would lower to his knees, carefully inspecting them to see that all was in order, then nodded. This meant the boy was to position himself carefully across my mother's lap. She would then inform him how many smacks she intended to administer and direct him to keep the count aloud. She required of the boys a strict code of conduct: they were not to plead or even address her directly, neither should they scream or wriggle wildly, although if they felt the need to cry she did not object. Better behaviour, even within the session, won the boys fewer smacks. You should understand, however, that it is very difficult to keep still and quiet under the punitive force of a hairbrush.

"The spanking concluded, the boy was expected to raise himself off her lap, return his clothing to a state of repair, and finally offer his sincere thanks. My mother was a stickler for this—I once saw her tip one of the boys back over her knee for giving an insincere response. After this, she would draw the boy into her arms and give him a most loving hug. And that was the ritual."

8. Spanked by Nuns

"Many details I'd forgotten come back to me now. Among the pupils I particularly remember the daughter of a little shoemaker who lived lower down the street. She was fifteen and her parents came from Auvergne. Her name was Maria and she was a tall brunette with a well-developed bust. She still lives in the district and I often see her when I go to visit my mother.

"She and another girl had been going out with boys. The girl's mother discovered what had been going on and asked the Mother Superior to keep an eye on her daughter for the last three months of the school year. The Mother Superior did so, and during those three months Sister Jeanne carried out the orders given to her: every two or three days the culprit received twenty of her terrible smacks.

"Because Maria sat at the front of the class, there was no need to treat her in the same way as those who sat at the back. All she had to do was step forward onto the platform where the desk was. She was then in full view of all the pupils there, and they didn't have to turn around to see her punishment. The Sister who was in charge used to leave her chair and stand by the first row, where the Mother Superior joined her.

"Sister Jeanne took hold of the big girl in the same way as she did everyone else, and the punishment that followed was no different. Maria's knickers were taken down, and Sister Jeanne raised her chemise to her waist. As was her custom, she did this without hurrying, and when she had finished there were two large buttocks in full view..."

9. The Maid Takes Charge

When the two girls were left alone, Maria advanced towards Isabelle: "Now then, Miss, you heard what your father said... submit yourself... you will have to do so."

"Idiot!" replied the big girl, looking the servant up and down.

"Idiot, that is perhaps your idea, Miss, but nevertheless you are going to receive the whipping."

"You dare touch me!"

"Oh! We will soon see about that." The struggle commenced. Maria threw herself on the young girl and grasped her in her arms, lifting her off the ground and bending her backwards. They both lost their balance.

Isabelle fell on her back, dragging with her Maria, who immediately tried to turn her over in order to lay her on her stomach.

Without uttering a word they continued to struggle: as soon as Maria made her turn half over, Isabelle, quick as lightning, re-established herself in the defensive position destined to protect her buttocks from the degrading fate which menaced them.

The young girl was pale with rage. The servant, on the contrary, was red from the result of the efforts she made.

The contrast between these two girls was as extreme as could be, but at the moment, neither the one nor the other gave a thought to the aesthetics of her attitude. The brunette struggled to defend herself and the other to overcome her.

After several unsuccessful attempts to get Isabelle into position, Maria adopted a brutal stratagem. It had to be accomplished somehow.

Seizing Isabelle's arm vigorously, she began to turn it round. The young girl gave a shriek of pain. She tried to resist. Maria continued the movement and, little by little, Isabelle was obliged to give way to the pressure applied by her torturer.

She lay down on her stomach. Without releasing the arm, Maria took up a leather cushion which had fallen to the ground during the fight, and slipped it under her young mistress's belly, which had the result of bringing into prominence the behind which shaped clearly under the light, thin material of the clinging skirt.

All was ready. With a bound, Maria straddled her victim backwards, her face turned towards the goal she wished to reach; settling her big sit-upon on the young girl's back, she pinned her with all her weight to the carpet.

Isabelle felt that she was beaten. She resigned herself and did not attempt to struggle when she felt the hands pull roughly at her skirt to turn it up.

The drawers were immediately underneath. In order to be thinner, more in the fashion, the young girl was not wearing a petticoat. Maria attacked the frail envelope which covered the condemned parts. She did not take the trouble to open the slit, but proceeded to remove the drawers entirely.

First of all she unhurriedly piled the skirt over the loins, then she searched round the waist for the string of the drawers. When she found it she untied it carefully, then slipped the dainty drawers along the thighs. She next lifted up the chemise and looked at the little plump bottom, with its deep crease, almost a boy's bottom, rather more rounded though, with a bold line that gave it an impudent air.

The white silk stockings and same coloured garters set off admirably the dull golden skin of the lovely brunette. The cushion placed under the belly threw up the bottom which opened out, emphasising its furrow of warm shade, proffering itself in its most favourable amplitude to the thorough spanking which it was fated to receive:

"Look out, my beauty, I'm beginning..."

The warning, to say the least, was unnecessary. The first smack sounded clear and joyful, the hand bouncing from the young and elastic bottom. Then there came an uninterrupted shower. Slap! Bang! Slap! Bang! Here, there, right, left, in the middle and across.

Maria's robust hand spanked with a desolating power. Isabelle braced herself, alternately opening and closing her buttocks, but still without uttering a sound.

Her moon reddened under the blows. With her slender thighs still white and the bottom of her loins also untouched, visible under the edge of the turned-up marine-blue dress, this crimson behind resembled a brass kettle-drum. The heat made it shine, completing the likeness of this somewhat unbecoming comparison.

Isabelle had already received about thirty slaps. She did not cry out... Her breath came pantingly, her body bounced on the cushion, her knees were gripped tightly the one against the other, her feet contracted in their little white kid high-heeled boots, scraped the floor.

Sometimes, under a more spiteful blow, the victim weakened, her muscles relaxed their tension, the bottom opened like a big rose in the sun, the knees grew limp, and the young girl seemed to surrender herself, forgetful of all decency, until, quivering again, she stiffened herself once more in a short-lived effort of all her nerves.

Maria, with dilated nostrils, conscientiously applied the spanking she was charged to give.

She soundly slapped Isabelle's behind about fifty times, without wringing a cry or a moan from the obstinate victim.

At last, the big red-headed girl's plump hand began to hurt her, she stopped, rose nimbly to her feet, and put up her hair, which had come down in the course of the struggle.

"Now then, Miss, that's over; you can do up your drawers … aren't you ashamed to stay like that with your moon in the air?"

But Isabelle was not ashamed. Now that her hindmost mystery had been so thoroughly exposed to view, she saw no particular object in hiding it so quickly; with her face in her hands she gave a glance between her fingers and replied. "Since you took them off, put them on again yourself."

"Very well, come here," said Maria, smiling strangely.

Isabelle got up, turned her back on the servant who, kneeling behind her, put up her drawers. Suddenly, Isabelle leaned quickly forward, and her bottom came into violent contact with the servant's nose, so that she almost fell over.

Thereupon Isabelle burst into a merry laugh, did up her drawers herself, and looking Maria in the eyes, made a face at her.

What mysterious fluid, what invitation, what secret thought, was expressed in that smile? At all events Maria in turn smiled and blushed to the very roots of her hair. Without a word, Isabelle ran up to her room, turning two or three times to see if Maria was following her.

"Miss," said the latter, lowering her eyes with an hypocritical air, "if you would like me to tend you…I will apply a soothing lotion if you wish…"

"Come up then, stupid," replied Isabelle, "but another time, when you spank me, I beg you not to hit so hard, because you have hurt me."

And they both burst out laughing like the two little madcaps they were.

10. A German Boys' Home in the 1900s

The cane was not the ultimate sanction, more the daily bread, and I was astonished at the indecent way in which both the headmaster and the teaching staff used it. For me it was barely credible, how a schoolmistress could apply the rod to a girl without blushing. That boys could be dealt with in this way by women in front of others was past understanding.

The first time I was about to leave the schoolroom, when my senior colleague was going to punish a schoolboy. She ordered me to remain, so that I could learn how these matters were dealt with. I submitted therefore and stayed, but I did not believe what I saw. The Mistress ordered the culprits to come forward to us at the desk; then one after the other they had to lean over the bench; and my colleague said to me:

"Watch me exactly, in order to observe the right way to do this. The boy has no right to resist—if he does, ring for a servant to hold him fast. We achieve this by severe discipline. This boy here may keep his trousers on. For this purpose we pull his jacket up—so—and take the trousers tightly in a bunch—see how I do it?—and stretch them tightly—can you see?—so that no creases remain. The boy must place his hands under his chin and may not remove them. And now that he cannot move, take the cane and thrash with full strength like this… ssst… ssst…"

To me this was utterly unbelievable. I saw the boy obediently lying across the bench and his bottom with the tightly stretched trousers thrust out, accepting his humiliating punishment without a movement.

But there was still something else to come. When the next boy came up the Mistress declared: "This boy is due for a sharper punishment and therefore must take his trousers down." The amazing scene that followed was nothing short of unbelievable, for he hastily loosened his short trousers and let them down to his ankles. He stood there in his tunic and shirt and I thought that by his instant acquiescence he retained some honour. But there was still more to see. The Mistress commanded the waiting, sobbing boy to lie across the table, while one of his comrades held his hands, and another his feet.

"You must not be embarrassed," said my colleague to me. "The sight of a naughty boy's bare

bottom won't kill you."

With these words she pulled up the lad's shirt and uncovered that part of his body on which he was due to receive punishment.

I hardly dared to intercede and I myself was not in a position to prevent the punishment. The bare skin quivered gently, like the haunch of a young horse, and the provocative pose with the taut divided flanks strengthened still more the painful effect of the nudity.

Here I must stop, for at that time I was unusually prudish and had never had any experience with male bodies, not even as a schoolgirl with boys, and found everything strange, even forbidden…

Gradually I became recognised as an independent teacher and it became my duty to apply the punishment for every trifling fault entered in the book as "Hosenspanner" [caning over tightened trousers]. The boys made no resistance worth mentioning, laying themselves across the bench, allowing me to thrash them across their tightly bent bottoms over the trousers with the Spanish cane. Also I learned how to apply strokes across the bare bottom, and I must confess that it became for me more and more of a tingling excitement, when the boys took their trousers down, I lifted their shirts, and the taut bottoms became visible…

11. Richard's First Spanking

THE OLD GRANDFATHER clock struck eleven as Harriet finished setting the tasks for the afternoon. She closed her book and rose. Richard followed suit; trembling in every limb, he was devouring his governess with an anxious and supplicating gaze.

She went to the door, drew the bolt, gave a turn of the key in the lock, and then calmly turned the sleeve of her right arm and folded it above the elbow. Richard followed these preparations like one spellbound, as if barely able to conceive the reality they betokened. The young woman looked at him with a faint smile.

"Now, Richard, you will take down your trousers and kneel on that armchair again."

"Oh Miss," he panted, clasping his hands in entreaty, "please—please, I—I couldn't! Please, Miss, —don't beat me!"

She looked at him for an instant with absolute impassivity, her eyes glowing. "I must, Richard," she said. "It is for your own good." For the first time she seemed moved, her voice shaking slightly. "You must be punished. I have decided upon it. And do not expect ever to soften or divert me, Richard," she said, her tone suddenly becoming harsh. "You do not know me yet, I'm afraid! I am very strict, and I do not change my mind. And you, you need a firm hand over you, as your father said—do you remember, Richard? Well, my hand will be firm, you need have no doubt of that. Come, now." She carried rather than led him to the black leather chair. In her hands, he felt his strength desert him entirely, he let her do as she wished with him, weeping with great infantine sobs, repeating through his tears almost mechanically, "Please, Miss! Oh please, please no!" Once he was on his knees she did not wait for him to prepare himself; she herself drew his trousers down to his ankles. Richard felt as if he were about to faint. "You will be better without your jacket, too," she said calmly. "We are quite

alone, there is no one to disturb us." She unbuttoned his jacket and waistcoat, and pulled them off; then with a swift and expert movement she drew down his short drawers.

But Richard, feeling the chastisement drawing ever nearer, began to writhe; he tried to retain his drawers as Harriet drew them towards his ankles.

She paused. "Richard," she said coldly, "you are being a very foolish boy. Do you really believe such stupid resistance will do you any good? I have told you, once before, that your punishments will be carried out in a seemly manner. —Now, sir, will you cease that struggling, or must I fasten you down?"

"Oh no, Miss! Don't do that! I'll be quiet..."

"Very well. I advise you to do so." She lifted his shirt and; drew it up around his shoulders; then, stepping back, she contemplated him for an instant. "Do not think for a moment that I enjoy having to do this, Richard. I am simply acting in your best interests, and I have seen there is only one course to be taken."

She passed her hand slightly over his bare flesh; Richard gave a sigh, a sigh that was more like a gasp, at the contact of this hand which seemed to be taking the measure of sensitivity in the region to be punished. "I am sorry to have neither cane nor martinet as yet, Richard. But how was I to know you would put me to the necessity of whipping you? So, I shall have to correct you this time with my hand—as if you were a baby!—Now, are you sorry for refusing to obey me? Answer me." "Yes, oh yes, Miss..." Richard sobbed, forcing himself to turn towards her a face tormented with shame and anguish. "Then you must beg my pardon." "Oh Miss, I—I do! I beg your pardon!" "Very good. And I trust you are ashamed of yourself, Richard. At fourteen and a half, almost fifteen years of age, to have to be punished like this! I would not have believed it. Now sir, lower your head!"

He obeyed, shaken with great sobs. Bending over, the governess encircled his waist firmly with her left arm, and her open right hand, rising high, fell smartly on his skin with a characteristic sharp report. The flesh leapt under the blow; the hand rose and fell again—and again... Harriet had become rather pale; short, languorous sighs escaped from her with every stroke she gave; the bridge of her nose was furrowed with a small wrinkle, her nostrils quivered, flaring widely as if she were breathing some intoxicating odour, and her tight-lipped mouth was twitching with emotion. She struck hard, the flat of her hand descending evenly, methodically, first on one side and then on the other. Under the vigorous, stinging blows the delicate skin took on a scarlet hue, warm and vivid, deepening more and more towards purple; the flesh quivered and shook under the strong hand, the loins twisted, the legs kicked involuntarily, while the boy himself, his head turned back over his shoulder, his eyes wild, moaned and sobbed desperately. Harriet, thrilling to the medley of sounds, experienced a still keener emotion from the contact of her hand with the firm flesh, so that instead of applying only a dozen strokes, as she had intended, she kept prolonging the correction. Indeed, she could not make up her mind to stop, so exhilarating did she find this exercise... But her palm had become burning hot, her shapely arm, strong as it was, was growing tired.

She exhaled a final sigh and straightened up. If at that moment she had thought to look in the mirror, she would have seen that her own cheeks were almost as red as the quivering flesh of her pupil. She drew a deep breath, obliging herself by a powerful effort to resume her calm.

"Now you must cease that crying and sobbing,

Richard," she said. "It is all over now. I hope this correction will bear fruit—but I must warn you that I am resolved to punish you frequently from now on. You require, I can see, the firmest handling—and from now on I shall see that you have it."

She stepped in front of him, bent over and wiped his eyes with a delicately-scented handkerchief, and then pressed her hand, the hand which had beaten him, to his lips. "Kiss my hand, Richard," she said calmly. "That is an excellent humiliation for you. When I whip you with a cane, it is the cane you shall kiss. Now get up and put your clothes in order."

He obeyed, finding himself almost unable to stand. He was as if stupefied; an intense heat was devouring his beaten flesh, seeming to penetrate to his marrow and his inmost being; he felt an overwhelming disturbance of his nerves, and the impression of shame dominated every sensation.

"Well," said Harriet, smiling at him. "You are not so badly hurt, are you?"

His tears redoubled; he felt as if he were suffocating. "N-no, Miss..."

Harriet continued looking at him with a faintly mocking glance. "I have forgiven you," she said. "And you will try to behave better in future, will you not?"

"Yes, Miss."

"Then come here and kiss me, Richard. We shall forget this first spanking I have had to give you. That is the way all your punishments will end—with a kiss."

It was she, however, who kissed him. Taking his head between her hands, the one cool and soft, the other still burning from its vigorous efforts, she pressed her lips to Richard's and closed her eyes, so sweet was the sensation she received from the contact.

"And now we will go to luncheon," she said.

12. A LADYLIKE BIRCHING

I LOOKED AROUND for possible instruments of torture and my eye fell on a pair of alarming-looking coiled springs cased in metal, lying on the desk. What could she possible do to me with these?

I was still wondering when Cousin Daisy produced a bunch of twigs that I recognised as coming from the weeping birch outside the front door. I thought of her going out in her tweed suit and toque, perhaps this morning to pick these particular twigs, choosing them carefully for having already lost their leaves, and perhaps testing them against her own thigh. I wondered whether she had perhaps picked too many, and dispensed with a few, throwing them lightly aside on the grass, or whether she had thought her bunch too meagre, and so gone back for more.

"Pull down your drawers," she interrupted my thoughts by saying, "and kneel down."

13. RETRIBUTION FROM THE CHATELAINE

MADAME DE CORRIERO made a sign to Dorothy and remained motionless for a moment. She then quickly approached the youngsters and restored Claire to a decent posture, as Pedro who seemed very embarrassed, tried to escape.

"Stay there, sir," she said sternly. "And you, young woman—tell me what you were doing, you brazen creature? You will get a lesson straight away which you won't forget in a hurry."

"It was Pedro who wanted it," the girl moaned.

"That's as it may be, but it's no reason to do his bidding. Dorothy will immediately administer punishment which will teach you to be less compliant when boys make demands of you."

Julia broke off a few twigs from the bushes round the mass of neighbouring trees, gave them to her lady's maid and told her to raise the skirts of the culprit and cane her hard.

Dorothy without a moment's hesitation took Claire by the waist, raised up her petticoats and her shift, and with one hand laid her on the grass bank which had witnessed the crime, while with the other she conscientiously inflicted the punishment.

"Now," Julia said, when the girl scrambled tearfully to her feet again, "see that it doesn't happen again."

Claire immediately ran off to the house.

Meanwhile Pedro had been silent, while sheepishly standing on the spot where Julia's gesture had stopped him.

"As for you, I don't suppose you think that matters will be left as they are, and that you will get away without paying for what you have done. Claire was wrong to have yielded to your desires, but you are even guiltier than she in having asked her, so you will be punished, too. Dorothy, go and find the gardener."

Dorothy picked up the flowers she had plucked in the greenhouse and went off.

"Why are you sending for Pierre?" Pedro asked gloomily.

"To punish you."

"I shall strangle him if he touches me."

"Oh, we'll see about that."

"If I need to be punished," the boy said, strangling a sob, "it won't be by him; he isn't my father, he is only a servant."

"Perhaps so, but as you have no father he will take his place."

"That man will never touch me. As you took me on, I am like your child and you have the right to punish me. I'll take anything from your hand but not from him."

"Well, all right—but, mind, you won't gain from the exchange. Let's get on with it and stop making such a fuss."

Julia went up to the delinquent. Then, thinking that the sounds of the severe punishment she was determined to inflict would be heard from the garden, she decided it would be better to go indoors.

"Walk in front of me," she said curtly. Pedro did so slowly, and they went towards Madame de Corriero's dressing-room. In spite of his reluctance, he had to step into this charming retreat, the door of which Julia bolted. The room was at the end of a corridor which at that time was deserted. There nobody would be able to hear the protestations she expected.

In fact, while they were on the way to the place of torture, Pedro had put on a reasonably good face and all he did was to weep silently. But when he saw his protectress taking off her hat, rolling up her sleeves and pushing a large pouffe into the middle of the room, he understood that the critical moment was upon him and he threw himself on his knees asking for pardon with pitiful cries.

Julia was adamant: it would have been grossly unfair for Claire to be the only one to pay her debt to morality. "If you don't submit, I shall send for Pierre," she said in a merciless tone of voice. And, as Pedro did not hurry to obey, Madame de Corriero quickly undid the hooks of the lad's trousers, which slid to his heels in spite of his efforts to keep them up. She then quickly seized Master Pedro and reversed him with her left hand and lifted the shirt-tails which covered his fleshy parts. Then, with a white and soft but dry hand, she administered twenty hard slaps which brought a livid red colour to the culprit's buttocks and made him sob heart-rendingingly.

Madame de Corriero was made breathless by the exercise she had just taken and sat down on a couch. She glanced at Pedro and was very surprised to see that, though he was upset and sobbing, he made no effort to dress. He held his painful buttocks in his two hands but did not move.

14. School Discipline in 1900s France.

At the age of five years, the working-class child enters infant school. Everything there is done in the maternal style, particularly corrections. Girls and boys are together—at this age, there is still no real gender difference—and the mistress or supervisor lavish bare-bottom spankings to one and all. However on this occasion the young gentlemen have their trousers well and truly taken down, and if the young ladies are wearing, as is the style in Paris, closed knickers, these too are taken down, their chemises are lifted, and they are smacked.

The executioner sits on a chair; on her knees, the victims, lying face down and tightly held, kick and howl, while some of the watching children—precocious philosophers—laugh; others, terrified, tremble; but all who watch miss nothing—and forget nothing—of the spectacle.

The child remains at the infant school until he is seven. In such suburban schools with eighty pupils, there are twenty-five or thirty similar executions each day.

15. A Luscious Punishment

One day, in the course of a reception Claudia was giving, Edward dressed himself very sumptuously and his stupidity made him redouble the affectation in his way of walking. To punish him, Claudia took the young man by the ear and made him ask pardon of each of her guests. To mark the depths of his abasement, she made him kiss the tip of each guest's shoe…

Without taking her gloves off, Claudia completed the lesson by giving Edward a volley of blows on his fingers and palms and which drew tears and cries from him. Then, judging it necessary to go further in the way of severity, she sent a chambermaid to find the "coffer".

The coffer! This was a rectangular wooden box, painted white, which contained a complete assortment of the instruments used to teach impertinent young gentlemen the respect due to ladies.

Ranged in the order of their effect were birches made of broom, willow, rushes and birch. There were three martinets made of pigskin, a leather tapette, shaped like the sole of a shoe, a Scottish tawse, and an American paddle, inspired by the Japanese.

While the ladies passed the instruments from hand to hand to examine them more closely, Edward, his face full of apprehension and shame, pleaded with his terrible cousin, rubbing his tortured hands together, still on his knees in the middle of the implacable group.

Claudia dragged him to a sofa and stretched him over her. While Margaret joyfully came and held his wrists, Louisa held his ankles. Behind the back of the sofa, Diana leaned forward. She was well placed. In front and a little to the side, sitting on the white velvet carpet, Bess, the devotee, was ready to hand the different instruments in the box one after the other to Claudia.

This scene was one of the best composed in the film, and Monsieur Horace thought highly of it.

The subject was worth the trouble taken to get it right. The final shots were perfect. The removal of Edward's trousers was a double pleasure; for underneath the velvet shorts he wore, there was a pair of knickers made of lace which must have cost a fabulous sum…

16. Prep School Smackings

Three fairly senior boys came up the stairs, grinning with bravado, halted outside Bungey's domain (he hadn't arrived yet) and announced to us, through the open dormitory door, "We're going to get spanked." Naturally we all felt, while waiting, a certain amount of vicarious tension. Eventually, Bungey came loping up the stairs, two at a time, strode down the passage and invited the culprits to step inside. For what seemed a long time we could hear only his low voice talking, though one couldn't distinguish any words. Then, suddenly, we heard him cry out, in a tone of impatience and excitement, "No, kneel, kneel, kneel, kneel!" Then followed the sound of the blows. They told us afterwards that they had each been required to crouch upon the carpet, with their bare buttocks elevated, while Bungey beat them sitting in his armchair.

"Spanking", as we called it, had a kind of tabu aura around it. It was the subject of bated-breath jokes, little doggerel rhymes and so on, rather taking the place of sex jokes among boys too young to know about the latter. ("My son, my son, it must be done. Down with the trousers, up with the bum.") The instruments used were personal and various. Mr Stow used to spank on the bare buttocks with a thing called a fives bat, which is rather like a table-tennis racket but bigger, and longer in the handle. Bungey used to use the "jack" of an old-fashioned wooden shoetree—the removable, handled bit that is thrust into the middle. He, too, beat on the bare buttocks. Mr Liddell, as I have said, used a cane.

For very serious offences there would be what were known to us as "public spankations". Of these, there were only two during the four years I was at the school. The first took place after a weak assistant master had entirely failed to control a prep. which gradually dissolved into a general, anarchic rag. Everyone was wondering why the master was apparently doing nothing. In fact, he was taking names to report to Mr Stow. After evening prayers that night three of the principal offenders, picked at random, were told to come up to the front and take down their trousers. They were then beaten hard with the fives bat, before the eyes of the whole school. The second occasion was when three quite senior boys, members of one of the classes who were supposed to do their prep. uninvigilated in their classroom, climbed out of the window and went for a night walk on the near-by common. As ill luck would have it, they ran into the Headmaster's brother, Sir Alexander Stow, who happened to be taking a walk. Naturally, he reported them. They, too, were publicly spanked—five each with the fives bat. One thing about this I have never forgotten. Mr Morris's place at prayers was at the back of the big schoolroom where we assembled. During the pause while the culprits were taking down their trousers and Mr Stow had gone out of the room to get the fives bat, the silence was broken by the sound of Mr Morris shambling up the length of the room. He drew out a bench and placed it exactly at a right angle to the desk over which the three boys would have to bend. On this he sat down, leaning forward with his elbows on his knees and his hands together, with the air of a connoisseur who was not going to miss anything…

Everybody nowadays talks about the "humiliation" of corporal punishment, cuffing and so on: but we never felt humiliated. A cuff was neither here nor there, if you knew it was merited. As for a spanking, you felt rather proud of having endured it well, and would hasten away to describe it in detail to your friends. I remember walking over to Horris Wood with "Paddy" Ewart, on the evening when he had been one of those publicly spanked.

"Did it hurt, Paddy?" I asked.

"Yes, it did," he replied in a casual tone. "Quite a lot, actually."

17. A Lover Loses Patience

Infuriated by her barbarous response to his advances, Michel grabbed her by the nape of the neck and jerked her forward with such force that she lost her balance and fell face down across his knees.

"You must be taught how civilised people behave toward each other," he said.

While he held her head down by the back of the neck she was helpless, for all her kicking. He pulled up her skirt and under-slip to reveal a rump clad in almost transparent rose-pink silk. Her struggles became more frantic and her hands were pulling at his fingers to release herself. When that failed, she scratched at the back of his hand with her nails.

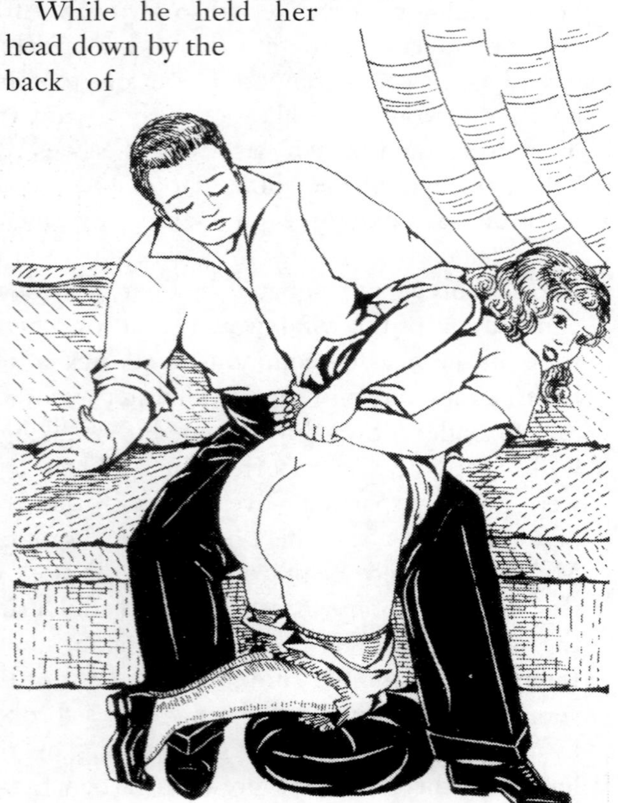

"Ah, would you!" he said, gripping all the tighter and wrenching her flimsy underclothes down to expose the pale skinned cheeks of her bottom.

"You behave like a badly brought-up child and you will be disciplined like one," he said loudly.

He raised his hand and smacked her hard. Ninette squealed and lashed out futilely with her feet, Michel was thoroughly caught up in the comedy. He laid into her soft bottom with his open palm, changing its pallor into red blotches. How many times he spanked her he did not know. He stopped only when her struggles ceased and she lay across his knees sobbing quietly.

18. Board School Discipline in the 1920s

"Wot's the gime?" Fred exclaimed, and promptly punched Pat Kelly on the nose. The boy grunted and felled Fred with a swift blow in the stomach. Pat Kelly's schoolmates ran up, three Luxton Road boys ran up too, and in a moment there was a savage free-for-all. Pat Kelly, big, raw-boned and furious, laid about him, and, after knocking three boys silly, was himself knocked cold by the combined onslaught of Fred, Ted and a beefy boy called George Street. They in their turn were laid out flat, at which point Mr Bolton appeared, followed by Jeremiah, cane at the ready.

"Stop!" Mr Bolton bawled in his loudest voice. The boys fell apart, abashed. Mr Bolton seized Pat Kelly by the collar and dragged him to his feet. "It's you again, I'll be bound!" he thundered. "I've a good mind to thrash the hide off you. What's the explanation this time?" "Please, sir, I didn't do nothin'." "No, you never do." Mr Bolton turned to Richard. He was physically intact, but his nerves were jangling like out-of-tune bells. "Did he strike you, Nash?" "Oh, no sir," Richard said, rather too quickly. "It—er—was just a misunderstanding." Mr Bolton looked at Richard searchingly, then glared round at the others. "I don't want to have to cane the lot of you on my first day here," he said, "but if this deplorable behaviour is repeated, I shall have no alternative. Now, all of you, shake hands and make it up." He turned on his heel and went in.

Fred said, "The new 'ead's rather a sport. That sod Caneall would have let us 'ave it!"

Later that day Baldy was taking a lesson in "essay" writing. Grubby hands were laboriously scratching in exercise books; young brows were knit in mental pain wondering why, whe n it came to it, Britain ruled the waves. Twenty minutes had already passed and Richard, glancing over at Pat Kelly, saw that the boy had so far ground out half a sentence ornamented with a blot. Richard had himself filled two pages with specious reasoning, and thus had time to meditate on the futility of brains versus brawn in the cruel world of boyhood. At that moment the door opened and a tiny boy of five came in. He was trembling from head to foot. Everyone looked up as with slow and hesitant steps he went up to the headmaster's desk.

"'E's a kid from the preparatory," Fred whispered to Richard out of the corner of his mouth, while he kept a sharp eye on Baldy. "'Spect Miss Sourpuss 'as sent 'im for the kids' cane."

"What's that?" Richard whispered out of the side of his mouth, keeping his eye fixed on Baldy. "It's a bit thinner than the one they use on us," Fred said.

"Stop talking, Nash," the chill voice of Baldy interrupted. "I shan't tell you again." Richard's throat went dry: but out of the corner of his eye he watched the small boy ask Mr Bolton for the cane. Mr Bolton gravely selected one from his comprehensive stock, and handed it to him, together with the punishment book. The kid, painfully aware that every eye was watching him, began to cry. With nervous, jerky strides he ran from the room. "Get on with your work," Baldy said. They resumed the agony of composition. About ten minutes later the door reopened and the boy re-appeared with tear-stained face and frightened eyes. Slowly he went up to Mr Bolton's desk and handed to the master the cane and punishment book in which his crime and punishment were recorded by his female flagellant.

After the little victim had gone, Richard sat staring at his unfinished essay. Quite suddenly he had lost all interest in it.

19. A BRACING VACATION

ONE DAY, SOON after this conversation, Harriet saw fit to further improve her position with her employer.

"It is now midsummer, sir," she said. "Living in town, in this heat, is not good for a boy of Richard's age and delicacy of temperament. We ought really to go to the country for a month or two. Did you not tell me, sir, that you had a small property somewhere in the country?"

"In Hampshire? Of course!" exclaimed Mr Lovel. "In fact, why don't you go down to Christchurch with Richard? That will do him a world of good, upon my word! Exactly, Christchurch. An excellent idea, don't you think?"

Harriet cloaked a smile of triumph. When she broke the news to Richard, he too seemed deeply moved.

"We will go to Christchurch together," she said. "Down there, I shall have you under my authority even more firmly than here. I will make you a well trained boy indeed, Richard!" She looked at him affectionately. "Well, are you glad to be going down to the country with me? To live there with me, just the two of us alone?" "Yes! Oh yes, Miss!" he breathed. She took him in her arms and kissed him with such warmth that his head reeled.

Mr Lovel wrote to the old couple whom he employed as caretakers of his house at Christchurch; and in a few days Harriet and her pupil were ready to set out. She packed the boy's trunk with him; and she also made him carry a parcel containing the ruler and a new rattan: the first cane had long since been worn out, and already at least a half-dozen had succeeded it in turn.

"I think," said Harriet with a kind of bantering gaiety, "that we shall be able to find in Christchurch everything necessary to whip you with, but it is better to be on the safe side. I have packed my strap, and I may need the cane as soon as we arrive. On the way down, my voice and hand should be enough to keep you in order..."

The trip passed without incident, except that Richard leaned out of the train window and caught a cinder in his eye, and the governess declared, in the presence of two very elegant women in the same compartment, that he was a foolish boy and would be soundly thrashed for

fly. As soon as they arrived she summoned Molly, the caretaker's wife, and gave her instructions in her duties. The governess had already planned their life in the country, and she now organised matters accordingly. Molly was to do the housework in the early morning and prepare the breakfast, and neither she nor her husband were to set foot in the house at any other time of the day. The old couple occupied the small lodge at the entrance to the grounds, and thus had no further business in the house itself. A caterer in the town was engaged to bring the meals twice a day; Harriet would simply plan the menu and leave her instructions. In this way she and Richard would be always alone and undisturbed.

While waiting for their luggage to arrive, the governess and pupil went on a tour of inspection of their new home, as pleased with it as if they were a newly wedded couple. The house, standing in the midst of heavily wooded grounds encircled by a high brick wall, enjoyed the greatest seclusion and privacy. At the end of the garden the

his imprudence as soon as they arrived at their destination. This announcement had the immediate effect of gaining the favourable notice of the two ladies who, extremely distant heretofore, at once entered into conversation with Miss Marwood without deigning to acknowledge any further the existence of her companion.

They arrived at Christchurch in the evening. Mr Lovel's house was situated a little beyond the outskirts of the town, in the middle of the country and not far from the Stour, the pretty river which flows into the Avon a short distance further on. The old caretaker was waiting for them at the station; Harriet left him to see to their luggage, and set out at once with her pupil in a hired

wall was pierced by a small door which led to the park itself, a pretty stretch of woods made up mainly of oak, ash and birch. From the lawn behind the house, where she was standing with Richard looking at the trees, Harriet observed the white satiny trunks of the birch-trees, and pointed them out to her pupil.

"See," she said, with a little laugh in her throat, putting her arm around him, "at least we shall not lack for rods!"

He sighed: it might have been a sigh of trepidation or of pleasure. He was still suffering from the cinder which had lodged in his eye, and he had not forgotten the promise which Harriet had given him in the train.

After the trunks had arrived, and under Harriet's superintendence, the clothes had been unfolded, shaken out and hung up; and the linen unpacked and laid out in the drawers, there was still a good half-hour before dinner.

"Now let us look at that eye of yours," said Harriet, drawing Richard to the window of her own room.

She explored the underside of the eyelid, and after patient effort succeeded in removing the unlucky cinder; when this was accomplished, she bathed the eye carefully, and then, having dried his cheek with her own handkerchief, she murmured with a smile: "But after all, I might have saved myself the trouble of bathing your eye, since you will be shedding tears in a few minutes..." He raised to her a glance full of anguish and appeal. "Have you forgotten what I promised you in the train?" she said pleasantly. "Your imprudence deserves a sound whipping, and naturally you are going to get one."

She looked around her thoughtfully. The cane and ruler were already unpacked and Lying on the massive mahogany table placed in the middle of the comfortable old-fashioned room. "Unless you are fastened to my bed," she resumed, "I can hardly see how to place you so I can whip you properly... No, wait: you will lean over this table and hold on to the far edge with your hands. That is the best way." He obeyed, whimpering; but when he was standing in front of the table, stripped to his shirt, he looked at Harriet pleadingly. "Miss, please! I've never travelled on a train before... I didn't know—" "That is doubtless an extenuating circumstance," she replied. "But simple common sense should have told you one does not lean out of railway coaches... Bend over at once, sir—very good. Now reach out and hold on to this edge. Excellent!" She stepped back and surveyed him with satisfaction. "Suppose, Richard, that at the moment you put your head out, the train was entering a tunnel! You would have been decapitated, my boy—just like that. The correction I am going to give you may serve to put a little sense in your head for the future. It seems indeed, Richard, that the whip is the only language you understand..." During this brief lecture she had raised his shirt above his shoulders, and emphasised her remarks with a few ringing slaps which made his flesh shake and quiver. Then, picking up the cane, she proceeded to flog him vigorously for almost five minutes. He wept and writhed, but took good care not to release his hold on the table.

"Very well, Richard," she said at last, laying down the cane. "You may get up now. And now come here and kiss me, and promise to be more sensible in future." His face still bathed in tears, he kissed her smiling mouth as she had ordered, feeling the same disturbance he always felt in bestowing this salute—this kiss which was, in fact, designed at once as a stimulus to his adolescent sensuality and as a last refinement of humiliation.

20. PARIS DECADENCE IN THE 1920S

WHEN MY TWO charming nieces and Rose returned, Madame conducted us to the Whipping Room. It was a large room hung with dark yellow velvet. Ladders of varnished wood, the bars of which were here and there provided with straps, a wooden horse covered with soft leather, a cupboard containing every kind of instrument of flagellation, a long wide sofa, a narrow oak bench, both of them furnished with straps, and finally the whipping chair formed the furniture of this comfortable apartment from which no cries or appeals could escape.

Not that it is a room of torture, far from that, but, as I explained to the girls later, there are certain refined voluptuaries who never feel the supreme pleasure so keenly as when they have been severely scourged by a female hand.

We must of course admit that there are tastes of all kinds.

As soon as we had entered the room Madame left us to the tender care of Rose who alone had accompanied us.

My little friend invited us to be seated and then said:

"I must tell you, young ladies and Monsieur, that it is a rule of the house that no visitor may enter the Whipping Room without receiving a whipping. It is a tribute which must be paid! With which of you shall I begin?"

Evelyn and Nora, crimson with confusion, declared that they would be much too much ashamed to be whipped before me.

At this Rose laughed heartily.

"Really?" said she. "Perhaps you are afraid that your uncle would be shocked at the sight of your charms?... If that is so, you may banish all fear.

Monsieur is no novice I can assure you. He has seen many a whipped bottom. And I don't mind admitting that he has seen mine dancing under the rod not so very long ago.

"But", objected Evelyn, "it must hurt terribly!"

Rose's laughter increased.

"Not at all, not at all!" said she. "Please remember that we are here for our pleasure and not for our pain! Don't be alarmed, young ladies, and make up your minds to go through it. One thing is certain, and that is that you will not leave this room without having had a whipping, nor will your uncle either."

"Oh, for my part", I said, "I will gladly submit to the rules of the house."

"Then", said Evelyn, "you have it first!"

"No" said Rose, "that would be breaking the rules. We must always begin with a visitor who is making a first visit to the establishment."

"Evelyn", said I, "I will give you my word of honour that I will go through it after you and Nora. And besides, didn't you tell me that 'you were prepared for any thing'? If you want to understand things you must learn by personal experience… And I assure you that you won't suffer any pain, but quite the contrary!"

"But you will see me!"—"And have I not some little claim to such a delicious reward?" "—And Nora will have it after me?"—"Yes, after you, and I after Nora!"—"Oh, good heavens, very well then; do with me as you like!"

Assisted by Rose I led her to the armchair. The seat consists, so to speak, of two arms placed close together, hollowed out like a gutter, and thickly padded. We directed Evelyn to kneel down on it and this she did without much hesitation. Promptly Rose fastened her legs to the arms by means of two broad webbing straps, and then directed her to place her arms round the back of the chair: these she fastened securely at the wrists by means of another strap. Evelyn then noticed that her stomach was resting on a sort of velvet cushion fixed at the bottom of the back of the chair.

"What is it placed there for?" she asked, a little frightened without knowing exactly why.

"To support you, darling," I said. "Now, don't be afraid!"

Touching a lever Rose set the back of the chair in motion. It fell slowly, but steadily, backwards, drawing with it the upper part of the astonished Evelyn's body.

A cry of distress issued from her pretty lips, and Nora, frightened too, rose from her seat and seemed inclined to cry out.

"Don't be frightened", I said quickly. "Be a good girl, Nora. I've told you that no harm shall happen to Evelyn: You can have complete confidence in me."

Evelyn, meanwhile, continued to utter little cries of terror which became more plaintive when, the back of the chair continuing to fall backwards, the dear girl found herself falling forwards, quite gently it is true, and without her fastened limbs or her body suffering any pain whatsoever. The downward movement only ceased when the back was almost parallel with the floor, and as the arms had risen as the back fell, Evelyn found herself exactly in the position as if she had been on all fours, that is to say her bottom was raised in a way most admirably adapted for a whipping. This position in itself was already extremely exciting for Nora and me, the spectators, especially for me, but what it compared with what I was about to see!…

The mere idea of this made me tremble with desire. Evelyn, on finding herself thus exposed, felt a very natural agony of shame. She cried out more loudly and her lovely face expressed a regular terror when she found herself thus placed with her head lower than her heels. Rose gently reassured her.

"Oh! Miss Evelyn", she said, "you are not going to cry out like a little baby, surely!… You know that it's only fun! If you really deserved to be punished and if we wished to do so, we should not take so much care to make you comfortable, should we? You will see how curious it is and what strange and powerful emotions this new experience provokes…. Now, be a good girl, and we will begin the operation. Ah, yes! Monsieur Quatrefois will see your pretty little bottom! He will see it birched! And what if he does! I don't suppose that you imagine that it is the first time that he has seen such a thing! I can assure you that your bottom will not be the first that he has seen under such conditions; will it, Monsieur?"

"I'm obliged to confess that it will not!" said I, laughing. But the shame which is inseparable from the "preparation" for a whipping had now taken complete possession of Evelyn. Her face was crimson and sweet little tears appeared on her long eyelashes and this attitude of humiliation, I must confess, gave me infinitely more pleasure than if she had taken the situation as a matter of course, to be merely laughed at.

Rose delicately seized between the thumb and finger of each hand the edge of her light skirt and turned it up slowly over the patient's shoulders. Evelyn uttered such a cry of distress that, if I had not restrained myself, I should have flung myself on my knees before her and kissed her little lips, so pretty in their timid fear, in order to comfort her.

"Oh, what are you going to do?" she sighed.

"I am about to uncover this part of you, miss," said Rose smiling. "You don't suppose that we are going to whip you over your petticoats, do you?"

"Evelyn, darling", I said in my turn, "if you really wish to know everything, you must submit to everything. And it's all the more easy to do this because, I assure you, it isn't a punishment that Rose is about to inflict on you but a most delightful caress!

"Oh, I believe you… But it seems so dreadful! So shocking! Oh, do get it over quickly!" Rose, highly amused, proceeded to raise the soft petticoat and then her light and skilful hands sought out, under the waist and the upturned clothes, the buttons of the drawers.

And, as is always the case, this search was the beginning of the excitement, and what a novel excitement it was, for Evelyn. I could see it by nervous trembling which shook her charming posteriors, still protected by their thin covering.

I could not take my eyes from these splendid rotundities, the bold roundness and fullness of which were thus suddenly revealed to me. The drawers, made of the finest lawn, were open, "as the drawers of every self-respecting flapper should be", and at the bottom of the slit, near the thighs, a little end of the chemise peeped out, and trembled like a little tail…

The drawers, very full in the legs, although at this moment tightly stretched by the jutting out position of their sumptuous contents, were slit up the side to a certain point and this opening was fastened at the top by a large bow of rose coloured satin. Rich Valenciennes lace, forming an edging, fell down over the well-formed calves encased in their charming open-work black silk stockings. They were as pretty a pair of drawers as you could want to see, and I could not help wondering if Evelyn, anticipating what was in store for her, had put them on for my benefit, and if I should find that Nora was equally dainty in her undies when her turn came to display them.

Meanwhile Rose, having found the buttons, slipped the drawers down to the knees, and then slowly, and with gestures which seemed almost religious, raised the fine crêpe chemise and turned it up over the shoulders with the petticoats.

21. BERLIN GAMES

THE LOOK of interest on Madame Filipov's face vanished abruptly as she glared down at Krill.

"Enough!" she said angrily. "You go too far! I gave you permission to kiss my foot. I did not reprove you when I felt your lips touching my knee. It seems that I am too softhearted with you."

"Forgive me!" Krill gasped, his face flushed dark red.

"Your manners are deplorable," she answered coldly,

"God knows what you would have tried next! Your crude attempt on my modesty is shameful and unforgivable. Gretchen—bring me the stick!"

"I try to overcome my failings," Krill moaned, "you know how hard I try… but to be allowed to approach you so closely is more than I can bear without becoming desperate for a small sign of your esteem…"

"You shall have a sign of my esteem," she said, her tone languidly cruel.

She got up and turned her back towards him while she opened her negligée fully and removed the only other garment she wore—a pair of silk knickers cut in the French style, with an edging of lace round the wide legs. Manfred was treated to a view of her body, breasts, belly and the patch of dark hair between her pale-skinned thighs. Meanwhile the maid had pulled out from behind the dressing-table a long and flexible cane. Madame Filipov dropped the silk underwear she had taken off on to the seat of her chair and turned to take the cane from her maid. "Now, Herr Krill, since you are so anxious to obtain a token of my regard and because I am a good-natured and obliging person, there before you lies something of mine, something more intimate than you dared to hope for."

Krill shuffled on his knees to the chair and put his face down on to the silk garment. "Oh!" he moaned loudly, "I can feel the warmth of your body, Madame!"

Presented with so easy a target, Madame

Filipov swung her stick and laid it with a crack across the seat of his trousers. To Manfred it sounded most painful, but he had not the least doubt that Krill was enjoying it. The energetic way in which Madame Filipov applied herself to thrashing her adrnirer's broad backside made her open negligée swirl about her and showed off her naked body to Manfred and the Baron to very fine advantage. "Oh..." the Baron whispered, hugging the silk slipper to his heart, "the delight of this stern Amazon destroying her victim... I shall faint with the joy of it..."

Herr Krill bore his punishment in silence, only his heavy body jerking slightly at each crack of the stick on his rump. Eventually Madame Filipov tired of beating him. "There! That will improve your manners, Herr Krill. Whenever you are here I take a great deal of trouble with you and one day you will be truly grateful to me."

"I am, I am," he babbled, raising his purple-flushed face from the chair. "I am pleased to hear it. You may take your leave of me and go to the room where Fraulein Ellie is waiting for you. She will soothe your pain with her cool hand and relieve your distress in ways that suit you." He kissed both of her bare feet, rose and bowed stiffly, her silk knickers in his hand, and hurried out of the room. Madame handed the cane to her maid and resumed her seat, to examine her hair in the mirror in case it had been disarranged by her vigorous exercise. "He's a dear man," she said, "so devoted to me!"

22. More Berlin Games

The first person I saw was Anni. She was standing in the middle of the room. Arthur cringed on the floor at her feet. He had removed several more of his garments, and was now dressed, lightly but with perfect decency, in a suit of mauve silk underwear, a rubber abdominal belt and a pair of socks. In one hand he held a brush and in the other a yellow shoe-rag. Olga towered behind him, brandishing a heavy leather whip.

"You call that clean, you swine!" she cried in a terrible voice. "Do them again this minute! And if I find a speck of dirt on them I'll thrash you till you can't sit down for a week."

As she spoke she gave Arthur a smart cut across the buttocks. He uttered a squeal of pain and pleasure, and began to brush and polish Anni's boots with feverish haste.

"Mercy! Mercy!" Arthur's voice was shrill and gleeful, like a child's when it is shamming. "Stop! You're killing me."

"Killing's too good for you," retorted Olga, administering another cut. "I'll skin you alive!"

23. THE LITTLE PRINCESS

I KEPT JEROME confined in his room for several days, the only interlude being the uncomplicated spankings. Spankings such as one applies to brats, clothes rapidly re-arranged and placed in the right position for manual correction.

I spoke to him insidiously of the strap and the birch, which would soon be his to taste.

A prisoner, without any connection to the outside world, he was growing accustomed not only to the slippers and dressing-gown, but also to wearing them graciously.

That light attire, which facilitated my flagellations, complicated the morning through my own will.

"In my company, Jerome, would it not please you to take a trip around the garden?"

He pointed to his gown:

"In this outfit?"

"Well, no! It is a little too mild. It is not that you would get cold. If you get cold, I know exactly how to warm you up again! It is not fitting attire for going outside. I have ferreted in the shops for you. You are going to be dressed like a little princess."

It was precisely the right expression.

The finery that I placed at his disposal was feminine apparel. In order to gather together everything of my choice, I must have walked far, because I held firm in my choice of underwear for non-closed knickers. Yet it was that piece of lingerie that caused difficulties, for the totally enclosed knickers had superseded everywhere.

I must have suffered the mocking smiles of a great many of the merchants, but I finally succeeded even though I was pushed almost to the end of my tether in my troubles.

Those for Jerome to begin with!

He made a painful grimace when I laced the corset onto the short and fine feminine shirt. And his emotion became more marked when I buttoned the lace knickers to his waist. I covered that very quickly with a slip and a small black sleeved dress. Black, likewise, were the new stockings that I had matched with patent shoes. Tucked up for whipping, it would be an incomparable symphony of black and white, so delectable to the eyes.

Once dressed, I dragged him to the garden. I had ribbons in my hand and he asked what use I intended for them.

Gathering slender branches here and there, by the time Jerome joined me in the shaded depths of the garden, I had in my possession a pliant handful of switches tied with splendid ribbons.

A stone seat invited his welcome, it was going to be witness to a scene between schoolgirls.

Seated, I lay my young lover across my knees and, without haste, tucked him up like a big little girl. His white knickers entirely opened, my fingers spread the crack, pushing the shirt up onto his loin. When Jerome's behind was quite prominent outside the lily-white batiste, I began by making him writhe with full-blooded smacks beneath my hard and passionate spanking.

His red buttocks contracted, his thighs crossed by suspenders, trembling again, from the lace of his knickers to the edge of his silk stockings, with the correction received higher up, I made the birch hiss. That produced, through reflex, such a contraction of the rump that it seemed, not having the ample round proportions of the female

Continues p. 6

PADDLE POKER

At Sally's cottage, on the bay,
We played "Strip Poker" every day
And as you know it couldn't fail
To get monotonous and stale.
The game is full of spice and fun,
But can, of course, be overdone.
So we were eager for some trick
To give our sport some extra kick.
Ethel got a brilliant scheme
To give these games some extra steam.
For losing, she thought there should be
Some really drastic penalty,

So everyone would play with care
And try not to be the first one bare.
She thought the first player to lose
Every stitch, from hat to shoes,
Should have a hairbrush spank applied
For every garment laid aside.
She promised this would offer sport,
Of a most new and novel sort
And would offer a lot of fun
(Except for her upon whom done).
A few of us had, sometimes, felt
The stern parental paddle dealt
And knew the smart it could provoke
Was not by any means a joke.
Yet our drab boredom was so great
We were inclined to risk that fate.

So, laughingly, we all agreed
And got the cards out, to proceed.
A tense excitement filled the air
And everybody played with care.
But, one by one, the clothes we wore
Were peeled and piled upon the floor.
Our caution, and our luck,
Was such that nobody wore very much,
When Julia lost her final thing
And had to feel the hairbrush sting.
The rest of us, it can be believed,
Were very happy and relieved.
We dealt one more hand to decide
By whom the brush would be applied
And Edna's cards had highest rank
So she had won the right to spank.

The losing player looked real cute
As she stood, in her birthday suit,
Awaiting with a rueful grin
Her hot and hectic discipline.
By counting every single thing,
Each garter, sock, and every ring,
The spanks poor Julia had in store
Mounted up to twenty-four.
Then Edna said, in tones severe,
"Young lady, you come over here."
And Julia went, reluctantly,
And dropped her form on Edna's knee.
She was so pretty and appealing
It gave us all a thumpy feeling
As we stood 'round all prickly thrilled
To see the penalties fulfilled.
For Julia was so smooth and white
She was an artistic delight.
Her fleshy parts were of a mould
It was a pleasure to behold.
And those parts nature had designed
With spanking 'specially in mind
Looked so cute and firm and pert,
It seemed a shame to make 'em hurt.
But Edna told her solemnly
"This will hurt you more than me,
For though we are the best of friends,
On this occasion friendship ends."

Then there was a most awful hush,
As Edna firmly raised the brush.
All eyes were glued, as by a spell,
On Julia where the first spank fell.
It was so very crisp, and clear,
It was a wicked sound to hear.
It was a "lead pipe", and to tell,
It bothered Julia like all h—l!
A hot pink spot began to show,
Very gradually and slow.
I've felt that sort of spot galore
But I'd never seen one before.
Spank number two was then applied
With full force, on the other side.
And Julia had to bite her lip
To keep from letting out a yip.
Then six were laid on good and quick,
They made Julia squirm and kick.
These were followed by a pause,
From a most amusing cause.
Julia thrust her hand to shield
The paddle from its landing field
And Edna didn't have a mind
To have her efforts thus confined
So she said, "Take that hand away,"
Which Julia was slow to obey.
Even then she put it back
As soon as she got one more smack.

Edna snatched the hand aside
And a Jim Dandy was applied.
But Edna had to loose her grip
On Julia's active bobbing hip,
And so to our amused dismay
Julia nearly got away.
We then decided six spanks more
Would be added to the score,
For every time she caused delay
In this, or any other, way.
Julia then resumed her pose
And clenched her fists and squirmed her toes.
Spank! spank! that crisp emphatic sound
Reverberated all around.
Spank! spank! poor Julia's lovely pair
Of legs, in frenzy, beat the air.
Spank! spank! those cute pink spots all spread
Into a solid mass of red.
Spank! spank! and Julia once more darted
Her shielding hand to where she smarted.
This raised to thirty-six the count
And she'd had just half that amount.
At Edna's terse and firm commands
Two of us held Julia's hands
And then Edna got down to action
With vigour and with satisfaction.
Spank! spank!—spank! spank! a steady flow
Of hot and devastating woe.

Spank! spank!—spank! spank!
—boy! she could squirm,
But Edna held her tight and firm.
Spank! spank! she rolled from side to side
But spank on spank were well applied.
We were most awfully amazed
To see the colour Edna raised.
Julia could have posed, in truth,
For a cartoon called "Flaming Youth."
Spank! spank!—Julia like one possessed
Fights to gain a second's rest,
But Edna with a clever wrist
Follows every flounce and twist.
Spank! spank! she's two more still to get.
Spank! spank!—two beauties, you can bet.
We all voted, as you may guess,
The new game was a great success.
Julia did not share this notion
Till she'd been well patted with lotion
And now she's eager as can be
To get a chance to paddle *me.*

(See next page)

rump, to disappear entirely into his truly feminine and unutterable whiteness.

Then I pulled down Jerome's pants completely, from behind, letting the unbuttoned knickers fall to the bend of his knees. The tail of his shirt raised with one hand, the other grasping the beribboned haft of my birch, I lashed his posterior rotundities until they contracted and began bouncing.

Manual to begin with, the birch to finish, this was an excellent double spanking that left him with memories—speckles and stripes on his buttocks.

This was our game repeated daily, morning or afternoon. Sometimes the slit of his knickers was simply parted, other times it was unbuttoned and folded back from behind on his thighs. When I let Jerome have free choice, making him prepare himself, he would unbutton his knickers at the waist before tucking them up himself in a more

The Revenge of the Mothers

The second time we met to play
There was the very deuce to pay,
We played the same rules as before
And Ruth lost everything she wore,
And had with game reluctance spread
Herself face down, across the bed,
And we were waiting, all spell bound,
To hear that thrilling paddle sound;
When our mamas crashed in the door
And Holy Moses were they sore.
We were so startled with dismay
The parents quickly won the day
And each Mama secured a grip
On her bare girl that would not slip.
Then Sally's Mother said that she
Would like a good sound spanking bee
And all the rest promptly agreed
That this would fill a long-felt need.
Ruth's Mother said her girl could wait
And be the last one on the slate,
And my dear Ma was promptly heard
To say that I would get mine third.
Then all the parents were agreed
That Mrs. Wyman should proceed.
Poor Sally was then firmly led,
And placed across the spanking bed.
Her Ma gave terse and crisp commands,
And parents seized her feet and hands.
She still retained one flimsy thing
Too thin and tight to stop much sting
But her Ma's state of mind was such
That even this was far too much
So this was promptly torn aside
So punishment could be applied
On firmly moulded, pink, perfection
With no iota of protection.
The paddle then went into play
In the most emphatic way
On where she was so firm and round.
You bet your life I'd have been glad
If I had been more fully clad.
It was a lead pipe cinch to tell
She didn't like it very well,
Oh Boy! How frantically she tried
To wiggle over on her side
But Mother with a supple wrist
Followed every hectic twist.
And laid 'em on with force and speed
That was disheartening, indeed.
Those sharp, resounding spanks were meant
To carry real true punishment
And hearing that kid raise the roof
Afforded us unwelcome proof
That spanking place was quickly blazing
In a manner most amazing.
And when she scrambled from the bed
I'm telling you that it was red.
Barbara was very vexed
Because she had to take hers next
There was a pretty lively fight
Before they got her laid out right.
The tussle made her Mother feel
A dandy red hot spanking zeal
And Barbara would have to pay
For causing trouble and delay.
That flapper just had on a shirt
Too thin and short to save her hurt
But even this pathetic lace
Was pushed back from the spanking place.
That shapely part—oh futile act—
Tried like fury to contract
Its owner feeling it was posed
Much too awfully exposed.
It was so cute and so appealing
Smooth and soft and full of feeling
It seemed a pity to impart
So hot and desperate a smart,
But sentiments of this mild kind
Never entered her Ma's mind,
Once more we heard the paddle win
Its argument with a naughty skin
Once more the frenzy of a spanking

feminine way each time. For the upright thrashings, especially, with hollowed loins and protruding rump, he found it distressful enough holding the dresses and the edges of the skirts to his shoulders, without adding further to his concern to avoid the closing up of the slit that his contortions and tremblings kept changing.

I made him bathe in an extravagant swimming costume. Opera-glasses were often brought to bear on that young indefinite girl. If they had been able to discover that, with regard to the rump, the costume was cut and the two ends of the jersey held by fasteners, with what curiosity they would have directed their glasses in the expectation of a sudden jolt that would cause the fasteners to fly apart!

Swimming in company, I risked my desire by opening the closed slit in the water. I obliged Jerome to continue to swim thus, me alone seeing his rosy rump emerge from time to time.

Set the bed springs wildly clanking.
Again the swift relentless brush
Spread its Hot and Horrid flush.
Once more wild legs fought to be free
And chum about in ecstasy
A joyless sight I will declare
For one who's awaiting her share,
All out of breath she would implore
"Oh please don't do it any more."
But her Ma paid this no regard
And laid the paddle on her hard.
Oh boy! Oh boy! it made me shiver
To see the quick elastic quiver
Where naughty girl stopped the cruel rush
Of that swiftly descending brush
She choked out "Oh I will be good, '
But her Ma coldly said: "You should. '
And spanked away 'till you can bet
It's one Barbs never will forget.
And now oh dear! Oh dear! Oh dear!
My time has come, my time is here.
My time is sort of in a whirl
I am a panic stricken girl.
The spanking I have seen and heard
Left me terribly perturbed
I lay my tummy on the spot
The others squirming has left hot.
The bed spread is all pulled askew
From paddling the other two.
I make myself, back there, all tense
In my terrible suspense.
Oh boy! I wish that I was through
Like those other smarting two.
My mother stands there with the brush
There is an awful heavy hush.
Her eyes are cold, her lips are tight
And I am in for it, all right.
The paddle cleaves the air and wow!
Words completely fail me now.
Were I endowed with Shakespeare's art
I couldn't half describe that smart.
With number one still going strong
Two and three came right along.
I very quickly flung aside
Any trace of stubborn pride
And I remember like a dream
Hearing myself squall and scream.
Oh boy! I wanted to protect
Where that paddle took effect
And baby! Did I want to cause
Some tiny, tiny little pause.
I flung my hips this way and that
But couldn't miss a single spot
I have been told my paddled portions
Made ridiculous contortions
And I can believe they did all right
At least I tried with all my might.
Boy! it was hot, and it did smart
And Boy! it covered every part.
How long it lasted I dunno
It seemed, to me, a week or so.
But what a soul satisfying peace
When those wild fiery spanks did cease!
Now I am pretty wild and tough,
But, believe me! I had had enough
I was so tamed down that; in Truth,
The spanking they awarded Ruth
Afforded me a lot less fun
Than such a rare treat should have done.
Oh well, they're awful, no mistake
And bitter medicine to take,
But getting spanked will turn the trick
When one is yearning for a kick.
So after all I hope my Mother
Will some day hand me out another.
I couldn't take my eyes away
From that relentless paddle play
And chills ran up and down my spine
Because I'd soon be getting mine
And, anyway, that spanking sound
Was most distressing, so I found.

A Spanking's heaps of spicy fun
Unless you, too, are due for one.

When it rose up, swimming at his side, I would whack and make the round cheeks plunge again. And as our aquatic exercises were often prolonged, before leaving the bath, I closed the fasteners of the costume on a rump spanked almost bright red.

I only whipped him a little in his bathing costume, perhaps once or twice, despite the convenience of the carefully contrived opening. I preferred to delay it until he had taken off his feminine finery. To tug simply on the fasteners was too expeditious.

24. Rules of Engagement

THE IDEA OF a modern spanking is to administer punishment when it is needed—then make up and forget the whole incident. In this way, every disagreement is effectively closed before it has time to ferment into serious discord—to grow into hatred or an indifference which even a great crisis may not be able to heal.

The couple that has every difference out when it arises is not likely to build up an antagonism that can be settled only in the divorce courts.

Also, modern spankings and whippings, correctly administered, tend to improve dispositions, increase domestic happiness, create a much more desirable spirit of unselfishness, and eliminate much other unpleasantness.

The operation of the Plan calls for unselfish devotion to high ideals. It calls for willing submission, and the loyal obedience to a co-operative system of beneficial discipline…

When a spanking is to be given, the wife is directed to go to her room and get ready. This means she is to undress and wait up in her room until her husband comes up to discipline her.

She must not argue about the matter—beg to be let off—or show any sign of resentment. She must obey without a word. When her husband enters the room there should be no delay in carrying out the discipline.

It is best not to say a single word during this period.

The wife should quietly place herself across her husband's lap—after he seats himself on the edge of the bed. Holding her in place, in the age-old spanking position, he begins spanking her. His duty is to do a thorough job—taking the utmost pains to do it right.

The spanking over—and still without speaking—the husband should let his wife up, then quietly leave the room.

It is the wife's duty—after dressing and drying her tears (if the spanking has provoked any)—to go to her husband, then thank him for administering the discipline, and kiss him.

25. Two Husbands, Two Wives

OLGA TREMBLED WITH surprise. She recoiled, her face paling. For at this very moment Pierre had turned on Leonie: "It seems that I am a monster and that you experienced the need to tell as much to your friends!"

"Oh, that awful gossip! Never again will I say anything about us!"

"Well now, so you've already talked to her, have you?"

It was not possible to deny, but, too moved to speak, the young woman continued to nod in affirmation.

"It's unfortunate all the same," Pierre said, "that one can't have confidence in one's own wife!"

"When a wife has abused her husband's confidence, she deserves to be punished," was Jean's opinion, and Pierre echoed: "That's my opinion."

"Well then, why delay?" Jean said. "The place and the moment are equally propitious. The place is deserted. We could flay them alive without anyone hearing them cry out!" Already the wives, maddened with terror, held out supplicating hands. Kneeling on the dry leaves, they begged for mercy.

"What shall we do with them?" Jean asked. "I believe the best idea would be to strip them naked and whip them bloody with a good oak switch."

The terrified women began to sob.

"What a pity that I didn't think of bringing ropes," Pierre said. "We could have tied them to a tree." Now both lovely wives were sobbing loudly enough to break one's heart, and uttering cries of terror and appeals for mercy.

Jean remarked: "I think that for today we must content ourselves with giving them a good spanking."

Hearing this reasonable proposal, Olga uttered a sigh of relief, but Leonie emitted a strident cry. Indeed, while Olga could boast of a certain insensitivity in her bottom, which meant that she had to really be seriously whipped to rouse her, Leonie, on the contrary, had a tender skin which suffered from the very slightest smack. However, Olga was astonished over Leonie's persistent fright; and thus terror, out of sympathy, invaded her too. She imagined, although she had ample experience, that a spanking was really something terrible. The shame also of being spanked in front of another woman dominated her. She did not suspect that the humiliation would go even beyond that!

It began by having each husband stand before his wife and order her to remove her panties. The unfortunate women had to obey. Standing up against the tree, and before the impatient eyes of their husbands who gave them imperious orders, they had to undo the laces of their corsets. It was really a ravishing spectacle. Olga had legs worthy of antique statuary. Robust and beautifully muscled, they were moulded divinely by stockings of mauve-tinted silk and yellow boots which she had worn for the walk in the woods. This gave her a most bewitching appearance, that of a haughty and Amazonian cavalier. As for Leonie's divine legs, they were the legs of a Parisian, slim and nervous, with ankles of unbelievable slenderness and high-set calves, aristocratic legs which inspired desire. Leonie wore grey stockings.

Both women, their cheeks flaming with shame, had to slip their panties down their thighs, then bend over in the same graceful attitudes in order to drag the frail garments below their knees till the panties spilled around their ankles in delicate festoons. But at this point, their decision weakened. Overcome with humiliation and shame, they didn't dare to budge. Now, their cheeks and foreheads fiery red, both women tried to remove the others' panties with one foot.

Pierre interposed: "Don't disturb yourselves! Don't you think that you cost us enough money for your lingerie without spoiling your things that way?"

"Will you use your hands, or shall I use mine?" Jean asked Olga.

The two beauties, still bending over, finally stepped out of the fragile sheaths. Now their white gleaming thighs were revealed in the most suggestive manner. Their plump bottoms tightened and flinched in the suspense of what was about to occur.

Each husband now clamped his wife's neck under one arm, and placed himself in such a way that each woman could look at each other. Their skirts were trussed up and, out of a cruel refinement, they were ordered to hold them up. Then each husband lifted his right hand and brought it down with a violent smack on his wife's splendid naked bottom. In a single prolonged cry, the victims exhaled their suffering. Each husband, stimulated by the other's presence, wished to prove his vigour, an emulation which was highly praiseworthy. But Pierre was obliged to admit to himself that Jean with his strong muscles accomplished much more than he did, while at the same time Jean admired how Pierre compensated by more rapid and more numerous smacks for the vigour which he did not possess. At the outset these gleaming white bottoms became red as cooked lobsters. The birds flew away, hearing the wild wails of the culprits. Finally the ordeal was over. And the two women, hiding their faces in their hands, leaned against the tree and wept.

26. MAKING A BIRCH

NEXT DAY, WHEN we were walking in the coppice, she said "Let's get the twigs now for that birch. You choose them. It's for you, remember." And we chose the twigs together. "No, that's no good," she'd say. "They have to be flexible and springy. They mustn't be too heavy. They've got to sting, remember, not to hurt, to cut, not bruise." We collected about a dozen twigs. "That'll make a very good birch," she said. When we got back to the house, she took the twigs up into my room and hid them in a drawer under my shirts. That evening she brought up some ribbons. "We'll make a pretty birch of it," she said. And she tied up the twigs. She swished it through the air. "This'll do," she said.

27. A COMPOSER WRITES...

WOULD YOU ALSO like to whip me? I have always longed to be beaten as well as to beat. Would you really not mind to whip me—not be bored with it?

We could do it in so many different ways.

26. The one to be whipped shall be tied up firmly and receive a certain number of blows, and afterwards the one who struck shall be tied up and receive the same number of blows; and then

we will see who can hurt most (and make the worst stripes on the body—the best leopard-markings) and who can bear it better. If it was done in that way, who would you rather have bound and whipped 1st, you or I? Or should we "toss up" for who should have 1st innings.

27. Both you and I should take a whip, and both should be armoured over the head, face, neck and hands and wrists, and then we should whip away at each other, and do what we could.

28. Only one should be beaten at one time, and the one to be beaten shouldn't be tied except the hands (but armoured on the head, face, and neck) and be allowed to run away and defend himself as much as possible. "Operations" could be limited to a definite short period of time.

You shouldn't have a single stitch of clothing on your body, but I "as man", must be allowed to wear a shield for the tediously easily destroyed parts of a man's body. I think it must be furiously painful for you to be whipped on your breasts, don't you think? (Couldn't you try on yourself sometime?) If it hurts terribly, you can count more strokes on me. But I can't give up to whip you there; it is one of the greatest longings of my little life.

Would you rather have the performance with or without screams? But tell me the truth, little Karen; do you seriously believe that it will ever actually happen—is it possible?

28. The Indiscreet Film

I COULD NOT believe that this nice couple… She, a vapourous doll, childishly mischievous, with a tormented face, while he worried with childlike pouts. Hands of a small schoolgirl so fragilely white, that nothing, really nothing, could suppose it was those hands that held the rod of conjugal authority.

Nice, fashionable couple, very modern, and infatuated with curiosities. They had invited me into their elegant home to show me their collection of erotic films, of which they were fond and proud, because they were rare, with the women undressed in playful ways.

The projection apparatus could be switched on and left to run, permitting them to sit side by side. She got up only to change the reels.

Suddenly, on the screen, a clearing appeared. Gerard, the young husband, winced in protest.

"No, no, dear! Not that one."

I held him back in his armchair:

"And why not that one? On the contrary I insist on seeing it, as you are causing so much fuss. It must be a little marvellous and suggestive, and I will not tolerate it being kept private."

A few whispered words were exchanged between the two spouses, then the blonde doll laughed.

"Bah! Never mind, Gerard. In the dark who will notice if you go red?"

And the clearing reappeared on the screen.

An elegant figure, the one of my vapourous blonde, came into the field. In summer clothes, she advanced, ran her hands through her hair as she faced the sun, displaying the gracefulness of her arms and the harmony of her curvaceous body. Then she sat on the edge of the bank. The fragile dress fell open to reveal her knees and stockings in the sensuous half-light, allowing us

to see the plump arc of her thighs interrupted by the tops of the silk stockings and the edges of the lace knickers. Stretching her arms, to right and left, and smiling, she pulled towards her some small branches. One by one she plucked away their leaves, until she had collected a bundle of sticks which she tested for suppleness and strength from time to time, smiling as she struck the palm of her hand. When she appeared satisfied with the instrument she had made, with the index she beckoned: "Come! Come!"

Who came?

The man who protested against the projection of this private film, of course.

Gerard!

The erotic films of this era were all silent films, unfortunately. The blonde, becoming excited, specified her whims. The young man seemed to implore restraint, but his partner imposed her will by wielding the bundle. Up to that point, it was charming, because one waited for more. The man entreated, embarrassed, the women became impatient. We saw her anger grow from the agitations of their lips. Then the man yielded. Subserviently he advanced towards her never ceasing to beg her mercy.

"It is very amusing!" I said to the young wife. "And very instructive too!" I added, addressing myself to her husband.

"I beg you, once again…" he tried in vain one last time.

"Hush!" I interrupted.

On the screen, the woman had, at the same time as the complaints had ceased, stretched out the victim across her. On his loins she turned back the black jacket, unbuttoned the clips of his braces, the buttons of his belt and others, and as if she was attending to a small boy, slid down his trousers and removed them completely. As the trousers came down, there appeared, not pants, but a tight-fitting small pair of lingerie knickers, lily-white, with suspenders hanging from the lace, leading across the naked thighs to silk stockings with an impeccable look. And then we saw his shoes with high lacings, that stretched halfway up his calves.

The trousers were rolled up and thrown like a ball. And in its turn the jacket was removed. Beneath Gerard wore a white pullover with big geometric drawings. His partner removed the braces with the jacket and threw them to join the trousers, disposing of all that was male clothing. Gerard had thus the look of a big girl clad in shoes with flat heels, lying across her thighs with a friend playing the severe game of the rigid housekeeper.

And the game became more and more passionate!

The young woman pulled a small end of shirt between the legs of his knickers and lifted his loins, forcing apart the lingerie, slightly, so that only a small section of flesh is proffered for punishment. When, the shirt was completely withdrawn from his knickers and slid beneath the pullover, with both hands she spread wide the slit, equally on both hips, generously baring the chubby cheeks in all their beautiful rotundities, and without a word she applied the birch on the round globes that rose up beneath the stinging caresses, bursting from the open knickers as if out of a shell. The vision of that silent spanking was entrancing. I did not think that the dainty flogger prolonged it a minute too long. She flogged divinely. Sometimes he was twisting so much that the black sheathed calves obstructed the spanking, other times the action was so frenetic that the slit of the lingerie almost closed. She has tamed Gerard so well that whenever that occurred his hands quickly pulled apart the edges of the knickers. And he was the wicked one who wanted to deprive me of this film! No, I did not find the spanking lasted too long.

He begged forgiveness of a laughing whipper. She closed the knickers on the reddened buttocks and continued tapping his buttocks before pulling down the tucked up shirt.

With Gerard standing before her, she draped a scarf around his hips to form the voile skirt to fall as far as his knees, and taking him by the hand led him away as a woman after having made him arrive as a man. Crack! The reel was finished.

"But it is all simply delicious!" I cried out enthusiastically, embracing the flagellant star. "And what is the title of this film that you did not want to show me?"

Gerard, switching on the light, kept quiet. But my vivacity made the little wife talkative.

"I have entitled it after the action which succeeded the stripping of Gerard: *The costume of nettles.* I think it is sufficiently explicit."

"Sufficiently, dear. One could not find better. Now I want to see…"

"Another like it? Alas! It is the only one. Gerard was ignorant of the small camera concealed beneath the trees as it turned on our small

Continues p. 124

THE WOODSHED

As into the woodshed Elizabeth went
To atone for a moment's domestic dissent,
She spied out an object that could cause her some pain,
She spied out an object that looked like a cane.

Why it looked like a cane to her gaze was because
A cane was the actual object it was—
And swung at the end of her father's stout arm
It looked like a cane that could do her dire harm.

It could do her dire harm, our Elizabeth knew,
Having suffered before its weals black and blue,
Having bent her broad b—m for its beastly embrace,
And been altogether in similar case.

Altogether her case seemed lacking in cheer
As her father, observing these symptoms of fear,
States a sentence to set any sinner's ears buzzin'—
"For Answering Back, Miss, the best of a dozen! "

"A dozen, Papa! Oh please, not so strict!
For Answering Back I've ne'er been so licked.
Oh Mercy! Oh Lord! "Twill cut me in two.
Oh please let me off—if only a few."

But let off she's not despite wringing white hands
And a body that's jellyin" e'en there where she stands,
With bosom so tense it might well be in milk
And lilyish thighs whose surface is silk.

Their surface is silky as Father's slick stick
Which now larrups the air so's to make her feel sick,
All her pleas are in vain, elicit a frown,
The click of the latch and a gruff "Take 'em down."

Oh my God she must strip, she must
"take 'em down" quite,
With fumbling fingers bare buttocks so white,
Though not long to remain so is our guess, we fear,
To judge from the way that Dad eyes that rear.

He eyes its appearance appraisingly now
As Betty disrobes with Modesty's bow,
And while Father rolls up the sleeve of his shirt
Her task is to doff (rather slowly) her skirt.

Now bare from the waist, heavy-bottomed and broad,
Betty blushes and stares (rather glumly) toward
That trestle o'er which she must bend her poor base
Soon to be redder than even her face.

Her sense of distress and impending dire pain
Increase at the sight of that gloating gold cane—
"Now get over tight and put it right up;
I'll teach you to lip, ye insolent pup."

"It warn't all that bad," our "puppy" complains,
As that quivering stick now utterly drains
All strength from her limbs, as sickly she turns
To that sawhorse of sorts where her lessons she learns.

Now that sawhorse of sorts has its legs widely spread
And the end where she bends slopes down to its head,
So our Betty is really extremely distended—
An impartial viewer would call it well bended.

Upended, distended, and thoroughly bended,
Our heroine cannot, we fear, be defended
From that terrible trembly hickory stick
Placed in measuring aim to give its first lick.

That wood writes its weal with a grunted-out "One!"
For, Heavens Above, the chastisement's begun
And a flame of white fire courses up that young rump
As the second cut follows with sick'ning thump.

With the thump of her jump our Elizabeth grips
Holding hard to the trestle with in-bitten lips,
Three and four follow sure tho' with plenty of time
For her father—admit it!—knows just how to "lime."

'Tis a father who knows every symptom of pain
Induced by that merciless judge, Dr. Cane
The squirming of skin and the sweating of brow
And that panting relaxing that calls to him—Now!

And now he wraps round her the full of the tip
Whose burrowing ache and blistering nip
Extract his first "music"—a quick stifled cry,
Chastisement's due toll, howe'er hard Bet try.

Brave Elizabeth tries with her might and her main
To suffer in silence the flame of that cane,
But if seven is hell, she gets eight at a run,
Her bottom is blazing, her pluck is near done.

Yes, the pluck of that seat is seen in her face,
When she turns it to daddy as red as her base,
"Oh Father, oh please, ye have set me a-fire;
Oh please can't you possibly come at me higher?"

"Ah please come up higher," she piteously begs,
"Those last two ye gave me were down on my legs.
I'm trying to bear it as best as I know,
But it isn't quite fair to cut me so low."

"It's cutting so low it's quite in the fold
Where it's tender as deuce and, if I might be so bold,
I'll e'en take some extra if higher ye'll come—
In short, Papa, please oh please beat my b—m!"

"I'll beat it," he said, "I'll beat it all right.
Just ye spread it out wide and get it up tight."
And the last strokes he gave her were so terribly true
Betty yelped like a puppy and, come, wouldn't you?

Those last that he dealt her were so terribly strict
She leapt up as if by some mule she'd been kicked,
For a second she seemed with that sawhorse to wrestle,
In the next she had leapt from that terrible trestle.

She leapt up erect as the last caught her well,
Clipping in underneath like some brand hurled from hell,
Biting in underneath where the skin was sore lined,
The most feminine part of our Betty's behind.

Poor prancing Elizabeth holds hard her rear,
Quite lost to all shame is she now, we must fear,
As stamping with pain and mewling her woe
She kneads her young bottom like so much striped dough.

Kneading her chubbies and panting again,
She writhes in the grip of true Punishment's pain;
Her father regards her so, a light in his eyes,
With a grin he confounds her—"Did I say ye could rise?"

For rising before permission is given
Is extra, alas—however you've striven.
In vain poor Elizabeth falls to her knees,
In vain do salt tears now back up her pleas.

Once more she goes over in tearful despair,
Once more her stern parent hews
  that cane through the air,
The dozen's a butcher's—all ways of the word—
"Now off to y'r mother" is all that is heard.

Leaden-limbed, dewy-eyed, and holding her b-m
Betty dresses and hies herself off to her Mum;
Her bottoms are blazing, they seem twice their weight,
The weals thick as fingers whose smart won't abate.

"Mama, I am sorry, I apologise quite,"
And curtseying Betty makes more than a sight
As turning she shows to her mater her seat
Whose lilywhite hue has been barred blue as beet.

She must turn and display the result of the crime,
Transgression's reward and Humility's prime,
The work of her father's ferocious long cane—
"Dear Mama, I shall ne'er Answer Back once again! "

With raised skirt in a corner our sinner must pass
An hour with the Bible, yes, quite bare of... ass,
Reading the prophets, somewhat rueful of face,
One hand rotating just under her base.

Bare of behind and a Bible before her,
Elizabeth's mind is in growing disorder;
Her body's below but her mind's overhead
Where the squeak of a mattress, a protesting bed,

Cause a blush to creep over her velvety cheeks
(Such lusty large lungings and unprotesting squeaks)
As her father, as always after Education's art,
Exerts the due ransom of... another part.

scene."

"Love whipped!" I stated. "No, it is not a second film that I want to see, but the punishment of the protagonist who wanted to deprive me of this treat. To have tried to wrong me in this manner he needs a chastisement and to be made an example of."

I dwelled on the word: Example.

"Of course," the little wife agreed readily. "And in front of you, that will be a truly exemplary chastisement. Do you understand, Gerard? Go and prepare yourself."

"I beg you. It is not…"

The young woman tapped her foot.

"I insist, *compris?* You will have the riding-whip, and it will be my friend who will hold you as a supplement to your punishment."

"And with hands which will be as strong as chains," I stated.

Subdued, while the vapourous blonde withdrew a thin and short riding-whip from a drawer, in a moment it was just as it had been on the screen, with him in a black jacket, silk stockings and white knickers. Kneeling at my feet, he encircled my waist with his arm. I raised his jacket, and the riding-whip of his young woman flogged his rump with stinging blows. The lingerie knickers were neither open nor lowered, it was a batiste so frail that it had the least effect as a protector. The rump was swelling in the tightened fabric, the flounce sweeping across the trembling thighs so that they made the lace shake. Slowly, taking hold of Gerard by the hips, I withdrew the batiste, thinking to make it part gradually. All that was achieved was a greater adhesion of the material. To cover for my resentment, I let out a violent scream which halted the game of the riding-whip and taking control I began to vigorously spank the rump irritatingly covered.

Afterwards, the blonde who knew that my unexpected interruption was due to the audacity of her husband, and braced by that whim of furious spanking that I had administered, pursued the pleasure with blows of her riding-whip in a neighbouring bedroom, where I heard the noisy correction on his naked buttocks intermingled with Gerard's protestations:

"I swear to you! I swear to you, my dear!"

"I swear that you will bleed!" was the only response that she deigned to give him.

And blows of the whip on his nakedness fell afresh, perhaps to the extent of her ferocious promise.

Once Gerard was shut away in the room where his correction had been severely continued, the conversation between us, alone, was as voluptuously agreeable as the vision of The costume of nettles.

"I made that film then as we were engaged to be married."

Such was the exciting beginning of what she wanted to say to me.

"And now?"

"Now? You have seen!"

"Not enough!" I tried to reproach her. But she continued:

"Imagine me making him wear my last school uniform. And not always beneath his suit, you know. He wears the dress, the petticoat too, and the lisle stockings—neither silk, nor lace, that is the strict rule of this house—and little shirts made from fine calico with modest scalloped shoulders, and assorted knickers."

"Closed ones?"

She laughed.

"Of course. It is so much more amusing to unbutton them on the sides, everything done up like a decorous little girl. These days he is my little waiting-maid, helping me with my bath, helping me to take hygienic enemas, helping me to dress, helping me in all that a woman needs to do. I reward him for it. And punish him too."

"In equal proportions?"

"Oh no, the punishments are more numerous than the rewards! It is rare for him to avoid a moist spanking to begin with."

"What is a moist spanking?"

"An excellent method of occupying myself in the bath. My bath is traversed by a board which makes a kind of wooden bridge. Gerard stretches, at my command, on that board, tucked up, his knickers lowered from behind, and his buttocks well within my reach. I correct him with my bare hand, smack by smack, remoistening my hand in the bath after each delivery. That method of spanking is excessively better than a dry spanking, and also the hand does not get hot, by contrast the behind sooner or later begins to sting. For the second correction, because I have told you that the punishments were more numerous than the rewards, it is a birch that I soak in the bath after each lash. That lengthens the chastisement so much that I need a good quarter of an hour to whip Gerard's behind to a treat. Though it would give me more pleasure to unbutton his schoolgirl knickers, if he twists too much I make him remove them and deprive him of a spanking for the remainder of the day." (At that confession, Carlo, my dear, I thought of you!) "If he has brought upon himself that correction, the strap follows with a liveliness. At every turn I raise his dress, petticoat, shirt and whack! whack! whack! I make his big chubby cheeks rear and bound, until red as a peony, before I allow the clothes to fall back. If you want to see how perfect is his feminine education, come for tea on thursday. It will be him who will serve us as the young woman of the house.

"With the greatest pleasure, dear."

And I took my leave thinking ahead of the pleasure that afternoon tea was going to give me.

Next day, Marceline came to ask me, in the library where I was sorting out some notes, if I would like to entertain.

"Who?"

"A man who comes for the first time."

I made her describe him. During the description, I gradually became amazed: it was not possible!

And yet it was possible. It was really Gerard. What did he want of me? Did he come for himself, or else was it my friend who sent him to me?

Introduced, he was very brief on the object of his visit. He desired that I explain frankly about the suspicion that his wife had about my scream.

I looked at him and laughed.

"I am not, my dear, the kind of woman to whom one demands something. I am going to telephone your wife to come here and see the curious visitor I have. No doubt you understand that she will make you taste the whip."

"No, I beg you!"

"Indeed! I want her to come. And then you will explain to her the pureness of your intentions in coming to my house."

"She will not believe me. She will imagine things."

"She will want to whip you, I hope. Hallo, please can..."

He seized my arm to pull the telephone from my mouth.

"I entreat you a last time, do not do it!"

I have taken him far enough into the mouth of the wolf to control him now as I pleased. I abandoned the idea of asking for his number.

"All right. But it will not mean that I will betray the confidence of your pretty little wife by sparing you the correction that you deserve. You are going to submit yourself, or else, it is her who will come."

He went very red.

"Go on! Schoolboy childishness from one who does not want to receive his thrashing, is it? You know what the whip is about, because you receive it often enough. This spanking is not for you, but for me to keep my conscience clear with regard to my friend. Place yourself in the position that your pretty blonde makes you take to receive the birch while I go and seek it."

I left him alone for a long time. When I returned, with a vinegared birch that Marceline had particularly recommended to me, he had dutifully taken off all his clothes that related to his male appearance. His torso lay across a table, offering me his white knickered rump and his naked thighs with the lace of flounce that ended at the silk stockings.

The birch under my arm, I approached.

"Do you prefer that I tie you, or that I have it done by my servant?"

"I promise not to move."

"Everyone always says that! And I am kind enough to give you the choice, when it is straightforward to call Marceline to tie you."

He was quick to decide and pleaded:

"Not the servant."

I took his arms to tie his wrists to the feet of the table, then shackled his ankles, my bundle of rods hindering me in that operation I slid beneath one of his garters, the points of the bundle menacing in the air. Then I excused myself as if I had heard Marceline come.

"A slight second, my dear, I believe there is a new visitor."

From behind a hanging, I took part in the mental torture of his waiting for correction. The cords prevented him from moving. He was too stricken with terror to be surprised in such a humiliating binding. His thighs had nervous contractions. Marceline, who observed him with me, seemed much the more impatient of us that I indicated the birch slid between his thigh and the garter.

"Go on, satisfy your gourmand taste for flagellation, and do not spare him!" It was advice that was superfluous to give her! The vigour always animated her arm. Scorning the birch she took her red riding-whip and bounced into the room, and flagellated the knickered rump until out of breath. Gerard's torso was twisting back and forth on the table when she returned to me, her eyes brimming with happiness, her lips moist and half-open, and her chest heaving.

"Unspeakable," gasped the whipped one when I freed him from his table of torture.

"No, my dear, a lesson by a woman, as simple as that. When a man has the effrontery to come and see me without being invited, I have him whipped by my servant. Marceline has flogged you hard, agreed, but with her you had the advantage of being whipped on your knickers, while with me, it would be on the naked buttocks that I would have given you the birch. Now, if that is your complaint, she can easily begin again but without your knickers this time?"

He had no desire for that, and begged me to leave him to dress, defeated.

29. A Reluctant Mother

Most people, I believe, have some very early memory and it is reckoned that the majority of these haunt the area of a first spanking. That is not my earliest memory, it is my second, when I was three. My earliest is of when I was two and is corroborated by my memory of a view through a window, which establishes the place as Dorking. I was being dried after my bath in front of this window—it must have been summer time as it was open and it was sunny outside. I was gazing down at my four-year-old brother in his smock making a determined attempt to climb the trellis-work. My strong impression is that he did not make any Very remarkable success in this gallant venture. We did not move from Dorking to London until 1910 when I was three. From the age of five until I was nine my Mummy had, more often than it pleases me to remember, to quell the natural anguish which she suffered at what was to her the dreaded prospect of spanking me for one inveterate and seemingly irresistible sin, that of lying. It was apparently impossible for me to resist this temptation. It was a compulsion in me to invent a story and tell it so convincingly that it was believed at first without doubt or suspicion.

After three or four years of the monotonous exchange of sin and punishment, it eventually pierced my sluggish little brain that this operation really did hurt her more than it hurt me. I noticed at last while I was removing the necessary garments that she was in a state of high distress. She caught me staring at her and said, "How I wish you wouldn't persist in making this hateful business necessary. I do detest it so." I resolved that on this occasion I would grit my teeth and not cry out until I could stifle my cries no longer. She stopped after the fourth stroke; I was surprised as I was expecting six. She said, "Yes, it should have been six really but you were so brave I couldn't go on." This amazed me; I had always assumed that if a person did not cry out the punisher would continue, unsatisfied until the expected reaction was brought forth. I thereupon resolved that she should never again be made to suffer in this way and that I would forever remove the cause of it all. And so my habit of lying ceased… for a time, anyway.

I used to wonder why it was that my father did not take on the responsibility, as happened with most sons, but left it to my mother to whom it caused such suffering. I felt sure in my heart, and still do, that she would not risk giving his displeasure full rein in case he did not know when to stop. He had been a schoolmaster with a lasting reputation for severity before taking Holy Orders. How much the nobler, then, my mother's voluntary self-punishment.

30. Still More Berlin Games

Manfred stood up to undress. He had guessed that Magda would want to reverse roles and bind him this time. The prospect was amusing and strange enough to be exciting.

"Kneel on the floor and let me tie your hands," she said when he was naked.

She bound his wrists behind his back with the skill of long practice. She did not truss his body, as he expected, but linked his wrists to one ankle. And that, he realised, was all that was needed to make him helpless, for he was unable to get to his feet or free himself. Magda stood back to stare at him, her head tilted to one side and her hand still caressing between her legs.

"Good," she said, "now for the surprise."

He watched with keen interest as she went to the open wardrobe and bent over to reach into the bottom of it. Her rump was thrust towards him and, between her spread thighs, he could see the dark-curled mound he had ravaged. Its long pink slit was agape and the impression the sight made on him was so lubricious that his limp stem stirred again. His interest turned to surprise, as Magda had promised, when he saw her pull on black knee-length riding boots. Surprise became astonishment when she buckled round her narrow waist a black leather belt, complete with pistol-holster on one hip. And finally, astonishment was overwhelmed by incredulity when he saw her put on a military helmet with a badge on the front and a spike on the top.

Attired in this incongruous manner, she posed before him, a long and thin riding-crop in one hand. She stood arrogantly, legs apart, head back and her fists on her hips, glaring down at him.

"Now, you swine—it's time you found out what happens to scum like you! Straighten your back! Stop drooping like a bag of rubbish!"

Her voice was harsh, her expression cold. Manfred knelt up straight, intrigued by her change of personality and wondering how this version of the game was played.

"Look at you!" she said, "good for nothing! What use are you to a woman with a shrivelled little thing like that?"

"You found it useful enough a little while ago."

"Silence!"

She reached down to prod him between the legs with the end of her riding-crop, none too gently.

"As much use as a punctured balloon."

"It's resting," Manfred told her, "like a boxer between rounds."

"Boxer! That miserable thing couldn't punch its way through a paper bag. One quick sneeze and it's done for! I've seen better on six-year-old boys."

She poked the end of her crop under his limp equipment and started to flick it upwards as she harangued him.

"Up with it! I'll have no laziness here. Do you think I brought you here to doze off?"

The rough jerking had its effect. Manfred's disabled limb began to grow strong again.

"About time too," Magda commented brutally, "I thought it had died of shock after its little performance."

Manfred gazed down fondly at his growing stiffness. His pleasure was cut short by Magda flicking at it hard with her crop.

"That hurts!" he complained.

"Hurts! My God, what a weakling!"

She flicked repeatedly at his uprisen projection, cutting at it from each side in turn. Manfred twisted his body to escape the stinging little blows, but in the end the only way to protect himself was to bend forward, his head down on his knees. At once Magda changed tactics and flicked him across his upraised bottom.

"Kiss my boots," she ordered, "quick—or I'll really lay into you."

31. Public School Punishments

I HAD HAD more than the normal amount of chastisement at All Saints. I had been there about a year when a new master arrived. He was a shell-shocked, wounded hero home from the war—a type most dreaded by all schoolboys at the time. Their heroic gallantry was soon discovered to be wretchedly underemployed and found expression in the indulgence of sadistic tendencies. He had soon fastened his prime interest on me (I reportedly sang like an angel and was as pretty as was needed to attract the worst in certain males). He arrived at the school armed with a specially fashioned strap. We boys thought: "Oh, he's been thinking a lot about punishments then."

The object of his strapping exploits was of course me. With my trousers down I was made to bend over. "Bend more tight, more tight," he always said; angled to his satisfaction, he laid it on to my bare flesh until my screams reached the vicarage across the courtyard. To the vicarage across the courtyard, my adored brother as head boy made his way. He saw the vicar and protested that his brother was being picked out for quite unjust and infinitely more frequent punishment than anybody else. "It's not fair," he shouted at the vicar's raised eyebrows. The highest authority was now apprised that the kind of man spoken of as a "sadist" was on his staff. The wretched culprit disappeared with surprising suddenness; he had only quite recently joined the priesthood and just a few days before this occurrence had celebrated his first Mass.

With my experience of this type of punishment in my old school I saw no reason to feel alarmed by the probability of more of the same at my new one. I was surprised by the size of this miscalculation. The senior prefects of public schools had had enough time and painful personal experience to look forward to exercising this most significant expression of their authority. The strength behind their cane-strokes was so powerful that I suffered pain such as I had not known possible. I never had much of a gift for the stiff upper lip, and in these circumstances I was quite unable to bear it like a man; my reactions were therefore unusually, stridently, vociferous.

Other boys, when they knew that I was for it, would gather in the quad outside the sixth-form room for the entertainment provided by my plaintive performances. It took me almost two years to learn to bear such intense pain in the way that was expected of me.

32. An Admonitory Spanking

Mrs. Wharton slapped the throbbing flesh about a dozen times, always without haste, in a fashion to vex the patient as much as possible, then she stood her on her feet and placed the warm palm which had done the slapping against the girl's mouth. This hand the latter kissed humbly. Once more she took Florence's crimson face between her two hands.

"Now," she said, "I reiterate my question; have you been well whipped?"

This time the girl's shivering was almost imperceptible, and Mrs. Wharton had scarcely any cause to whip her anew. She murmured:

"Yes, Madame... I have been well whipped!..."

"Do you think it will be a warning to you not

to fall back into your habitual faults?"

"Yes, Madame!"

"Very well. Ask my pardon!"

"Madame!" responded the girl, falling to her knees... "I humbly beg your pardon... and I thank you very much... for having given me... a good... sound... whipping... It is for my good!"

33. More Public School Punishments

"Did it give you any pleasure?" "Good heavens, no." "Not even afterwards? Wasn't there a kind of glow?" "I don't remember it. Before we were going to be caned, we used to sit on the hot-water pipes; it hurts less then. Did you know, by the way, that Nelson when he had his arm amputated complained of the coldness of the knife? After that he insisted on having hot water in the sick bay." "It was a good feeling, wasn't it, when the actual pain subsided?" "It was a good thing when the whole thing was over. One felt something of a hero too, you know, like troops coming out of action." "I suppose now and again you had to cane a boy yourself? "I was a prefect for three years." "Did you get any kick out of it?" "I can't say I did. As far as I recall, it rather jarred my wrist; perhaps at first it gave me a sense of superiority, of having the right to beat somebody, but after that wore off, and it wore off very soon, no, I don't believe I got any kick out of it." "But then..." She paused. After that first time she had longed to talk to him, to find out what he had felt, how he had felt it. She had felt shy then; the illusion of punishment had to be maintained. It was different now; but even though he had invited the visit of the secret weapon, there were some things she could not ask. There were, though, quite a few things she could. "Of course you couldn't choose whom you caned. It had to be somebody who had broken a rule of some kind." "Naturally." "You couldn't look down the hall, see a good-looking boy who attracted you and think, I'll give him a good thrashing." "Naturally I couldn't." "And of course they were wearing trousers." "Of course." "Mightn't it have made a difference if they hadn't? If, for instance, it had been a good-looking young boy whom you found attractive."

"That's a very hypothetical situation. I can only say that as far as I was concerned, it didn't happen." "Then would you say that in spite of what the psychiatrists are saying there is no sex element to all these canings?" "Ah, no, I wouldn't quite say that; there are some celibate masters, who are homosexuals without knowing it, who get a kick that way. But for the boys themselves, well"—he paused—"it's something I've sometimes asked myself. My first school was a new one; it started in the very year I went there, when I was nine. At the start there were only six of us. There were forty when I left; now there are a hundred and fifty. We were very ignorant, very innocent; there were no older boys to teach us anything. We knew nothing of the facts of life. We knew how babies were born, but not how they were conceived. Not at least in any detail. But we were oddly enough very interested in whipping. We used to whip each other."

"You did what?"

"Yes, whip ourselves, in the dormitories at night."

"What with?" "Knitted bootlaces or with hairbrushes."

"Which side of the hairbrush?"

"The prickly side. At home when I had a hot bath at night, I used to beat myself and I'd arrange my father's shaving mirror so that I could see the reflection.

"There was a sort of prurient curiosity about it all. We were so innocent at that particular school. I'm wondering if it wasn't a natural development, a normal prelude. I've noticed that old-fashioned school stories used to pander to that prurience. A friend of mine was doing an article on Edwardian school stories. He showed me some of Desmond Coke's. They came out in *The Captain* in 1909 or so. They had very luscious descriptions of boys being beaten. And the publishers reissued after the second war a school story called *Teddy Lester's Chums* that came out in 1960—chock full of it. I'm sure it had a sexual undertone—a premature interest in what doctors call erogenous zones. We used to talk about canings in the furtive way that at public schools we discussed normal cases. Look at this now as an example. As I told you we knew nothing about the machinery of fatherhood. One day when we were in the changing room, about three or four of us, and we were talking about beatings, one of us lifted his shirt and called our attention to himself. He was in a most rampant state. He said, "Isn't it funny that I get like this whenever I talk about beatings?"

Myra chuckled. "It seems to be having that effect on you right now."

34. PUNISHED IN THE TRAIN

At Vime-neuve-Saint-Georges Sir Stephen suggested to O that they return to their compartments. His neighbour, scrambling to his feet, clicked his heels and almost split himself in two bidding O good-bye. A sudden jolt of the train made him lose his balance and sent him sprawling back into his seat. O could not keep from laughing. Was she surprised when Sir Stephen—who had completely ignored her since the start of the journey—had her bend down over the suitcases piled pell-mell on the compartment seat, virtually the minute they were back inside, and raised her pleated skirt? She was delighted, and grateful. To anyone who might have seen her in this position, kneeling on the compartment seat, her breasts crushed against the baggage, completely dressed, but offering, between the hem of her suitcoat and her stockings, and the black garter belt to which they were fastened, her bare buttocks crisscrossed with leatherlike stripes, to anyone who might have seen her thus she could only have seemed ridiculous, and she was well aware of it. She could never help remembering, whenever she was thus made to lie prone, the disturbing, but also the humiliating

and ridiculous aspect of the expression "lift your skirt," even more humiliating than that other expression which Sir Stephen, as René before him, employed at least each time he offered her to someone. This feeling of humiliation that Sir Stephen, or rather Sir Stephen's words, caused her each time he uttered them, was soothing to her. But this sweetness was as nothing compared to the happiness, mixed with pride, one might almost say with glory, that overwhelmed her whenever he deigned to seize and possess her, whenever he found her body to his liking sufficiently to enter it and, for a fleeting moment, dwell therein…

35. THE GUN

BEATING WAS the punishment for a wide range of offences. Merely being a nuisance was enough to earn a trip to the gun. For boys who were caught stealing there was no escape, but they were so hungry that they still took the risk, looting the vegetable garden in which their more fortunate predecessors had worked their own plots. Running away was considered the worst offence, so that the boy who most feared the regime was the prime victim of its severity.

Beatie [Mrs Fry, no pun intended] decided who was to be flogged, "awarding"—her word—up to twenty-four strokes… In 1921, for example, No. 1766, J. Isaacs, was awarded twelve strokes across the gun "for being a General Nuisance". After breakfast the ship's company marched to the gymnasium and were formed into lines to witness punishment. Meanwhile, Boy No. 1766 was conducted to a changing room where he was made to strip naked and then dress in a pair of thin white cotton trousers. When he entered the gymnasium he walked past his assembled shipmates and mounted the gun platform. He stood facing the gun, the barrel pointing away from his midriff like a huge steel phallus. Behind him and to his right was [First Officer] McGavin, a clipboard in his hand bearing a piece of paper. "Sharkey" stood to his left, holding a thick, almost inflexible cane with decorative twine wrappings at its extremities.

McGavin read out the charge and the number of cuts. The greater the punishment, the more likely it was Beatie would be present, standing by the main entrance, looking across the heads of the boys to see that it was done. "Sharkey" ordered the boy to bend over the gun, and on the order "Carry on!" from McGavin he struck with all his might.

The instant the blow fell "Sharkey" would decide if his victim could stand the rest without flinching. Often he could not, and the man laid aside his cane and with short cords tied the boy's ankles to rings on the platform, and his wrists to the gun-carriage. "Sharkey" then took up the cane and continued his work… McGavin dutifully ticked them off on his fly sheet, and Beatie watched impassively.

36. THE WOMAN ON THE STAIRS

SO YOU'D LIKE to know how I acquired the craze for being whipped and abused by those of my choice? Well. I'll tell you.

Every Friday afternoon I used to visit my friend, Juliette, who lived quite a distance from my home, way over in the nineteenth ward. Don't open your mouth to start telling me you understand! You don't understand a thing! My friend has never been… connected with this business. She lived on the third floor of an old, big, six-storey building which had not a single modern improvement. Well, one Friday afternoon. like every other Friday afternoon, I started wearily climbing the stairs to her rooms. Passing the first floor there was nothing unusual. That's not surprising. The din of trolleys and automobiles could still be heard shaking the window-pane in the vestibule door. But as I started up the second flight of stairs I distinctly heard someone crying and the noise of repeated slaps.

I hurried—that is, I took the steps two and three at a time (four is impossible—people do that only in books). But if I weren't curious I wouldn't be a woman. Well, as a recompense for my trouble in hopping so fast that my heart palpitated, I saw, I saw… shaming all decency, a posterior, yes, a bottom, quite bare, on which the hand of a big wide-chested, wide-hipped woman was coming down with terrific force. She was somewhere between thirty-five and forty years old. She was exclaiming loudly in time to the swinging of her arm: "I'll—teach—you—to—whistle—on—the stairs!" How her hand swung! It was a boy's posterior, as I saw from his black woollen knickers on his shorts, both pulled down to his knees, but which did not prevent him from kicking furiously in the empty air.

Sure enough, if his mother chose this means to stop his whistling, it must have been an infallible method, for the urchin didn't whistle any more. Instead, he bleated like a kid, still kicking away, and with good reason, too. He was about eight or nine years old: and the whipping had probably been going on for some time, because his buttocks were as red as two full-blown poppies.

I had seen, especially during vacation time, in the years when I was going to school, little girls of my own age whipped at friends' homes, and so I could make a comparison. The slaps they received were never as stinging as those which fell on the lad's pretty buttocks. I must say he was prodigiously well padded. His rump was like a girl's but harder and firmer, or at least it seemed so while the furious whacking went on, and it rolled from side to side like the sensitive bottom of a girl or woman which is being whipped. I had to wait until this accidental (there I was mistaken) public whipping was over, before I could pass them and ring my friend's bell. The woman pushed her offspring, although he could hardly walk with his trousers and shorts impeding his legs, into the apartment next door.

The whipping put me into a strange state of mind. Do you know how some people feel who have looked at naughty pictures too long? That's the way I felt at the moment, and that sensation didn't leave me.

I rang my friend's bell. She wasn't in. Then, with a sort of impulsive courage, undoubtedly aroused by the excitement I was labouring under, I ran into that woman's apartment to ask her to tell Juliette of my visit but really for another reason. She asked me in cordially. A martinet was lying on the table in the dining room. It had obviously fulfilled its purpose, and the boy's knickers and shorts still lay on the highly polished floor.

We talked a long time, waiting for my friend who didn't return. That's how I learned that the lad's name was Jackie, that he was nine years old (my guess was right), and that he was whipped almost every time he came home. At the moment he was doing penance by being shut up in the kitchen, which was dark, like those in old tenements where you have to turn on the light even at noon time if you want to cook a meal. When I was ready to leave, his mother called him in to say goodbye. With an obedience that should not have surprised me, he came in dressed only in his blouse and a short undershirt that left partly uncovered his terribly red posterior. I picked him up to kiss him, and before I put him down again I lifted his shirt as high as I could. I touched his still hot buttocks, and tapped them lightly—playfully… My emotions were still sizzling in my brain. And what emotions! Proud as I was, I recognised just the same an imperious and sudden need to be humiliated by this creature, so much lower in my estimation than myself. I had been whipped in my childhood, of course. But only a little, and then not after I was sixteen. Besides, were they real whippings I used to get? Real, sound whippings that leave marks, which enervate your soul and blister your skin? That's what I call whipping today. The revelation came to me by the specimen I had just witnessed. That woman was the only one capable of giving me the real good whipping I craved.

I neglected Juliette, multiplying my visits to this woman. And the lickings she gave Jackie in my presence only threw oil on the flames of my passion. I had to make plenty of visits before she reached the point of making mock threats at me. And then the time came when I was almost ready to yield. But just as she took hold of my waist, I couldn't help recoiling brusquely. That day I was wearing very tight bloomers which were attached to my hips by a system of hooks, and I was afraid that she wouldn't bother to unhook them. It was on my naked flesh that I wanted to feel the burning contact of her long, wide, red hand, of her big paws hardened by housework, of her robust arm with its sleeve always rolled up to her shoulder. I had waited too long for this first whipping to let it resemble a doll's being spanked over its panties. So I drew back and said quickly: "No, not today. But tomorrow I'll come early, and you can give it to me while Jackie's at school."

Had she read my face? She took me to the door and said: "All right, let it be tomorrow. But don't fail, or you'll get two the next time you come!"

Fail? I'd take darn good care not to do that!

The next day I put on a pair of drawers—the kind they don't wear any more—very short, and with a long split in the back held together by a single button. I had left off my slip, wearing only my dress and coat on top of it. I was sure she would pick up my dress, but just the same I was still uncertain about the rest. So while climbing the stairs, I took the last precaution of spreading open the flap of the drawers and tucking the hem of my chemise into the girdle which held up my garters.

No sooner did I come in than I was unceremoniously jerked across her knees like a child, and I saw how wrong I had been to put off for a

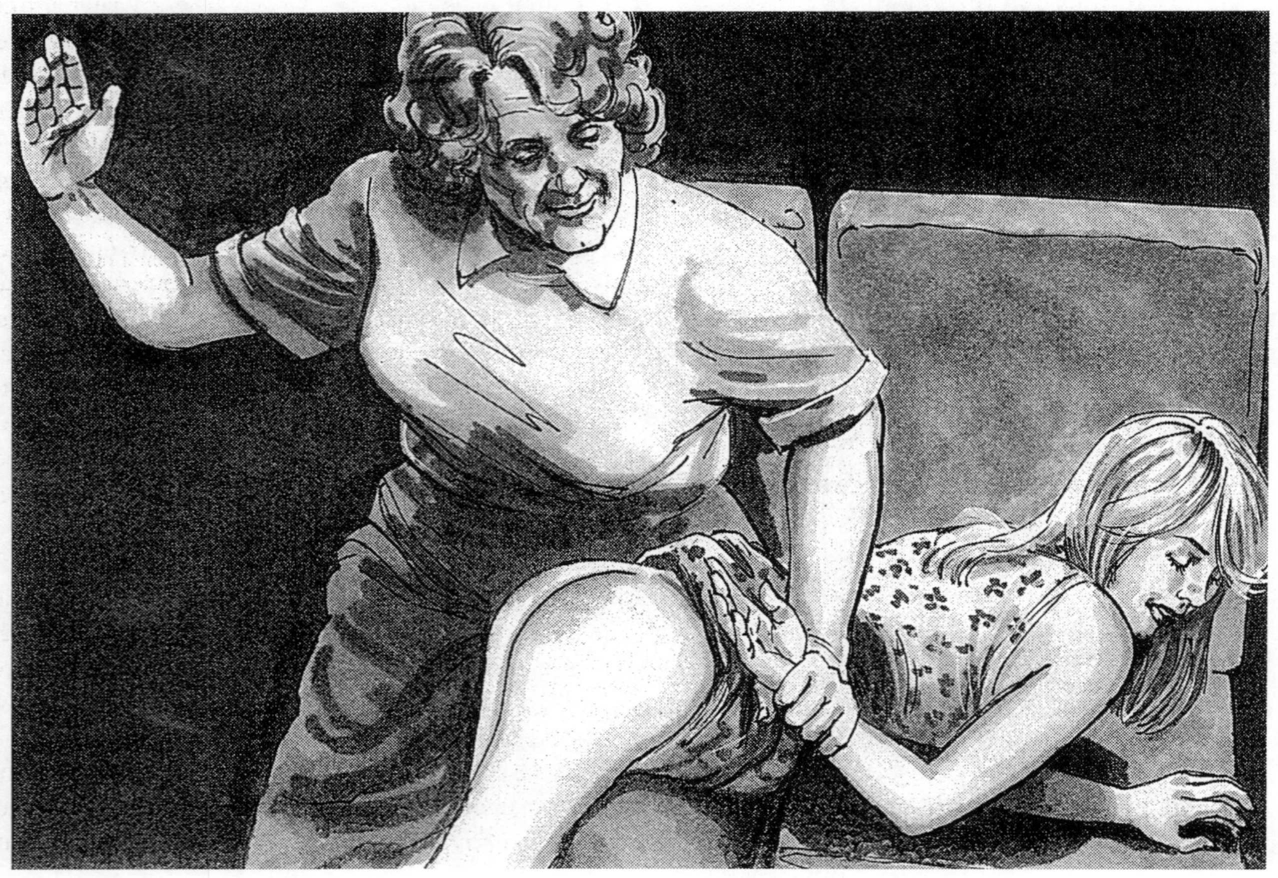

single day the delights of my first real whipping.

Without even commenting on all the precautions I had taken so much trouble over, she pulled my dress above my head, held my arms to my waist with her left hand, opened the buttons of my drawers and pulled them down to my feet with no more ado than if they had been her son's. Her hand which was harder than even I had thought, swung down on my nude posterior as I lay across her knees. The little cries I uttered were drowned out by the noise of the slaps which—I'm not lying—actually flattened my flesh. While spanking me, she chided me as though I were a baby tot, using baby language which made me blush with shame and nearly die with pleasure. But her spanking touched me more than any words she could use. It wasn't long before I began to wriggle about and kick my legs just as Jackie had done on the landing of the staircase. She tightened her arm about my waist to hold me still, and went on smacking me beautifully. My poor buttocks were consumed by hellfire. I don't know what colour they turned, because there was no mirror in the room to reflect the image of a great big girl being whipped. But I don't think I exaggerate when I say that they must certainly have exceeded the most violent shade of red a woman's buttocks could attain under such an energetic whipping.

She didn't stop until I was so breathless that I couldn't even cry any more. My legs were inert and my throat was dry. It was evident that she had enjoyed the game—I felt that especially—and that she would have liked nothing better than to keep on playing, just as long as anyone would naturally want real pleasure to last.

She excited herself to further efforts by voice and deed. When it was over I had to rub myself for at least five minutes before I could revive my body, which seemed as though it was dead. As for my bottom, I hadn't the nerve to ask for a mirror that I might look at it! But it felt like a ball of flame, with red-hot needles piercing my flesh. "That did me good, 'I said, a bit yellowish, but smiling just the same.

A little one, eh? But I don't need to tell you that I went back—over and over again. All preparations on the stairs were now useless, nor was there need to choose between open or closed drawers, because I was always quickly disrobed. And when I wore a simple combination that buttoned between the legs, the business was only further simplified.

I told you of this first whipping. I won't tell you about the others, because they were just like the first. She always spanked me just as hard and just as long, with her big paw and fingers as tough as drum-sticks—Jackie's seat and mine being the drums she played on—his the toy drum, mine the real thing. She would spank me as I lay across her lap, or sometimes she would just bend me under her arm without lifting me off the floor, which she could have easily done, but she preferred to save her strength for the drubbing. Sometimes I would kneel down and put my head under her skirt; she would squeeze it between her legs, which never knew the luxury of a pair of panties. Very often I had to take all three positions in turn.

When she tired of using her hand, she introduced me, for our mutual pleasure, to Jackie's martinet. The idea had already occurred to me several times; and when I was with her I did nothing but obey without a murmur—least of all command. Jackie's martinet, quite pliant from long usage on his bottom, was no laughing matter. It had about twelve blackened thongs at the end of a handle which once had been a beautiful red. But now the handle was brown and only our buttocks were red.

She made me kneel in front of a chair with my chest across the seat. This made my rear jut out quite prominently. While I was in this position she applied the thongs to my flesh. The plump cheeks of my posterior didn't lose a single particle of those stinging caresses. Both buttocks were struck each time by the scattering of the thongs, and it did me no good to hold myself either rigid or relaxed. Every blow told effectively and bit deeply. If I held myself rigid, the thongs nipped like sharp knives and made a big clacking noise. If I relaxed, the blows made my muscles leap, quiver, bound—in a word, dance. For a spectator there is nothing more amusing than to see a woman, or a big well-shaped girl, hold herself relaxed during a whipping. I did that very often, however, for the purpose of encouraging her in her technique. As though she had need of that!

The woman never lacked enthusiasm. Jackie's correction always preceded my own. In his case it was not an act of passion or injustice; the sturdy kid always deserved it. I have heard—and now I know—that there are some people who like to whip boys who are dressed as girls. I can assure you that this good woman didn't need that device to redden completely her son's hard pair of buttocks. She unbreeched him with a twist of her wrist, pulling both his knickers and drawers down to his heels; then with either the martinet or her bare hand, he received a thrashing whose salutary stinging lasted several hours, that is to say, until he was ready for another. After he had been granted pardon, he was allowed to go and play on the street with his little friends. He was never in a hurry to return…

37. A Pretty Penalty

The minutes passed slowly. A little clock upon the mantel-shelf struck the quarter, and afterwards the hour.

"Mayn't I be released now? My feet ache so, arched over high-heels."

"If you knew how pretty and smart you looked, Denise, standing in your corner, you would never want to come out of it," she said calmly.

"But my corset hurts me, it's so tight, and my fetters gall my ankles. Oh Miss Priscilla, I am so unhappy," I said piteously.

"The hands will do as they are," she said. "But still, your feet are hot, and the fetters tight. We can't have your pretty ankles swollen."

She took the little key from the mantel-shelf and unlocked the fetters. What a relief it was! She unfastened the train of my dress from about my knees, and let it drop on the ground.

"Sit down there."

She pointed to the sofa. I stumbled across the room. I sat down; my legs were numbed.

"Give me your feet."

Miss Priscilla knelt down in front of me and with her clever, skilful hands, trained in hospital work, she massaged my ankles, taking the stiffness out of them for a moment or two.

"There! Now the pretty things won't swell," she said.

"Oh thank you Miss Priscilla," I said gratefully.

"Stand up, Denise!"

I obeyed. She unhooked my dress at the back, first taking off my sash. Then, feeling under my cache-corset, she loosened my corset laces. Oh what a joy it was to draw in a deep breath, to be relieved of the constriction about my waist, and of the painful binding about my hips.

Then to my dismay I felt my drawers slipping down. In loosening my corset laces, Miss Priscilla had by mistake, as I thought, untied the strings of my pantalon. I felt a delicacy in mentioning the fact to her. I pressed my thighs together and held the pantalon up at my knees. It was very uncomfortable. But I should soon have my hands untied, I hoped, and I could then slip upstairs and rearrange myself. Suddenly however I felt a violent tug.

"Draw in your breath, Denise, and expel it! That is right," and Miss Priscilla drew in my corsets tighter than ever, and tied the laces.

"Oh, it's worse than before," I moaned.

"Hold your tongue," she answered in her calm peaceful voice, "or I'll lace you up in stay laces from your neck to the tips of your satin-slippers." What a terrible threat! She hooked up my dress, readjusted my sash about my waist and then thrust her hand inside my skirt.

"Where are the frills of your drawers?" She seized them.

"Open your legs, Denise." She pulled the drawers down to my ankles. It was not by mistake then that she had untied the strings. She had meant to do it. Why?

I was soon to know. Miss Priscilla sat down upon the sofa and sedately smoothed her silk skirt over her knees. Then she drew on and buttoned her long glacé-kid shining gloves.

"Come to me, Denise."

I shuffled forward shamefacedly, my pantalon clogging my ankles and lace frills frothing about my satin slippers in the most untidy fashion until I reached Miss Priscilla's side. Then she seized me and with a sudden effort flung me across her knees face downwards.

"Oh Miss Priscilla," I cried startled out of my wits. "What are you going to do with me?" She took up my skirt with its long train and turning it back, heaped the rich satin folds about my back. My thighs, my buttocks were exposed naked.

"Oh, oh!" I protested, my cheeks fiery with shame.

"I am going to slap this white soft fat girl's bottom," said Miss Priscilla, as calmly as if she were in the habit of doing it every day. "I am going to teach you, Denise, not to complain when you are placed in the corner."

"But Miss Priscilla, you yourself admitted that the steel fetters were too cruel."

"I didn't admit that your corset was too tight, or that your pretty heels were too high."

She began to pinch between her kid gloved fingers the white flesh.

"Oh Miss Priscilla, remember that I am eighteen," I protested.

"You must first remember it yourself, dear, and not behave as if you were six." She raised her gloved hand and brought it down with a resounding slap upon my quivering bottom. I could not endure it. The kid-glove stung my tender flesh, but the childlike character of the chastisement stung my soul.

I lashed out with my legs trying to kick my feet free from the delicate fetters of my drawers. But the frills clung about my toes, and caught on the high-heels and diamond buckles of my shoes

"It's abominable," I cried, "to treat me like a little girl." But the kid-gloved hand rose pitilessly again and came down heavily upon naked and helpless flesh. I moaned, I plunged, I writhed upon Miss Priscilla's knees. I kicked, I strained impotently at the ribbons which bound my hands.

38. CANING HIS LOVER

CASILDA SMILED. "YOU know what I'm like, Tony darling," she murmured, and then, after gazing at me fondly in silence: "Shall I fetch the stick? ... I realise I deserve it."

At my nod she went to the chest of drawers, remarking lightly: "The bottom drawer, I assume?" and a hint of anxiety crept into her voice as she added, "this one?" handing me the long, fine, flexible malacca cane.

I pointed to the armchair by the fire. "Bend over," I ordered sharply. An anticipatory thrill of harsh excitement mingled with the dull ache of my jealous indignation and disgust. Casilda knelt in the chair, resting her elbows on the back, and waited. "Not too hard—please, darling", she entreated quietly, as I rolled her dress up above the waist and gently, deliberately, undid her full, frilly panties, which stayed in place and had to be pulled down, inch by inch, over her hips.

I took my time about these preparations—for me far more enjoyable and satisfying than the subsequent infliction of corporal punishment, whereas for the victim herself perhaps enduring the ordeal may prove pleasanter by far than the preliminary suspense attached to it.

Thus I toyed with the intention of removing her girdle, but left it to form a saucy frame, like a flowered border, around the rich, broad, beautiful view of her buttocks.

39. A SCHOOL SMACKING

ME AND A girl called Edna Whitfield were both called out by Miss Swinton. We both got up from our desk and stood in front of her. It was four or five minutes from home time. Miss Swinton said to us both that our handwriting was very bad, [and] that she was going to smack our bare bottoms. She told us both to stand facing the wall until the class was dismissed... I could see Edna Whitfield shaking and her face was pale. She was already sobbing. After the class was dismissed Miss Swinton called Edna to her. She sat on a chair, and she put Edna over her knees. Then she lifted Edna's frock up, and she took her knickers down. Then she began to smack Edna's bare bottom. Afterwards she was told to stand facing the wall.

Then it was my turn. When I got there she started undoing my trousers. She took them down and put me over her knees. Then she began to smack my bare bottom, and tears came in my eyes. I felt my bottom stinging. When it was all over she put me off her knees... It was now half past four and the teacher made me stand facing the wall with Edna, still crying.

40. A PUBLIC BEATING AT PREP SCHOOL

MY ONLY LASTING success at Sandroyd was achieved in my final term when I got a public beating. In all my five years there nothing like this had ever happened. Matron, who rejoiced in the name of Sister Cowe—we were told she came from Berwick-on-Tweed—frequently spanked us with slippers, or Mason & Pearson hairbrushes, in the privacy of the dormitory; but a public caning was unheard of. So to be the first to receive one in my generation was a unique distinction.

The reason for it was "Ma Brown". Ma Brown kept a sweetshop on the edge of Oxshott woods, which we used to pass every Sunday on our strictly supervised walks. She kept the most delicious sweets, including, delight of delights, the newly invented Mars Bar. At school we were only allowed 2d worth of mixed sweets sent down from Harrods, which were issued by the Rev. J.

E. Langdon (known as Bunch) on Saturdays. By the end of the cricket match they had all gone, and come Monday one was yearning for sweets as a drug addict for heroin. One of my contemporaries bet me I would not dare to go to Ma Brown's and buy four Mars Bars. So on Wednesday afternoon (half-holiday and another cricket match) I crept away to Ma Brown's. Unhappily, on my return I ran slap bang into Priscilla, one of the two mistresses at the school, who taught Latin to the eight-year-olds (it was from her that I learnt to address tables and walls in the second person singular, 'O table, O wall' and have found it most useful ever since) and was engaged in order to give us a feeling of "home" when we first arrived. I trusted Priscilla and got on with her quite well, but this stood me in no good stead; she reported me to the HM. That evening in chapel, after the grace of the Lord Jesus and the Love of God had been evoked upon our young heads, there was an ominous hush. I was summoned to appear forthwith in the assembly room; I am rather surprised now that it wasn't in front of the altar. And there, before the whole school and all the staff, my shorts were lowered, I bent over and received ten of the best. From that moment, until I left six weeks later, I was the hero of the school.

41. Caned by his Form-master

It is the primary duty of a commander never to accuse on suspicion, but only upon established evidence. Byno dropped a pencil, stooped to recover it, and, in the fraction of time occupied in doing so, the villainy of Toby was unmasked.

As noon struck Byno dismissed his class, but added the rider:—

"With the exception of Norman, who will remain."

The rest filed out impressively and in silence. The door closed. Addressing Toby, Byno said:—

"You know why, of course?"

"Yes, sir."

"And you know what it's worth?"

"Six, sir."

"On the other hand, Norman, I could cancel your leave during 'Half.' "

"Half" was the half term break, and Sylvia would be coming down—and—oh, lor!

"Couldn't you make it eight, sir? My sister is coming down, and it would be frightfully difficult to explain."

Byno mused over it.

"I'll fog the negative, sir, I swear I will."

"That would be a pity," said Byno. "You exercised quite a lot of trouble and ingenuity to get it, and I might be glad of a copy. Still, rules are rules."

"What about ten, sir?" Toby suggested.

Byno released one of his rare smiles.

"This isn't an auction room, Norman, and no doubt six will suffice."

"Thank you, sir."

"This is your first whacking?"

"Yessir."

"Well, what do you think? Shall we get on with it?"

"Yessir."

So Byno whacked Toby, dispassionately, but with zeal. Toby had had plenty after three. He pinched his nose very tightly to stifle emotion. The rest came and went. Presently it was over. Toby rose and did up his braces. Neither the man nor the boy made any further comment upon the business.

42. A TRIAL RUN

THERE IN THE corner stood the cane. After a moment's hesitation he took hold of it and proceeded to examine it. It was both thicker and more springy than he had imagined. Altogether, in fact, it looked a brutally effective sort of instrument.

Then, idly at first, he began swishing with it. But that taught him nothing—except perhaps to avoid the dangerous backlash, the recoil. If he really wanted to experiment, he would have to hit something. A cushion possibly.

And why not a cushion? There was one, a red velvet one, on the settee in the corner. And, crossing the room with the cane tucked smartly under his arm, he picked it up and arranged the cushion carefully across the seat of one of the chairs. Then he removed his coat and rolled his sleeves up. He was engrossed, utterly engrossed, in this piece of practice by now. And he spat on his hand before attempting to get his grip right.

"Six of the best, I think we said," he observed to the empty air above the chair. "And if the treatment is not effective it can be repeated.

"Six of the best!"

There was a classic ring about it, and he repeated the words, louder and more menacingly.

Then he began.

"One!"

Pause.

"Two!"

Pause.

"Three!"

He was breathing more heavily by now. And the veins in his forehead were beginning to pulsate. But he persisted.

"Four!"

It was just as he was about to deliver the fifth blow—the cane was raised and his teeth were clenched fast in readiness—when he heard somebody address him.

43. AN UNUSUAL SECRETARY

ANNE SAT DOWN and came straight to the point. "How many hundreds of pounds have you embezzled this year, Mr Blake?"

Blake's eyes narrowed. "I beg your pardon?" he said coldly.

"You will save yourself time and embarrassment by admitting it," said Anne. "I have all the proof for four hundred pounds at least."

"Are you mad? Have you gone out of your senses?"

Anne took a paper from her pocket. "Let's just take the last occasion—to show you I know what I'm talking about. Last Monday you submitted to the managing director a claim for £13-8-0. This was signed and returned, and passed to the cashiers for payment. Only it wasn't now for £13-8-0, it was for £113-8-0. You had, as usual, added the figure 1. And I have the dates and figures of three other occasions."

Richard Blake looked at her, the icy fingers of fear clutching at his heart. This would of course ruin him. Even if the company didn't prosecute—and there was no certainty that they wouldn't—he would be immediately dismissed. And his £4,000 a year job... It would be impossible to find another with any other company.

"What are you going to do about it?" he asked huskily.

Anne smiled. "That's better. Don't worry. Under certain circumstances, I'm not going to do anything."

Blake's heart leaped for a moment, and then sank.

"Blackmail?"

"Of a sort, yes," said Anne coolly.

"What sort?"

"Not for money. You can set your mind at rest there."

"But?"

"But for physical submission to me."

Blake stared at her. "Whatever do you mean?"

"I mean," said Anne, "that I now have you in my power, under my thumb, or whatever you like to call it. And I'm going to make you do whatever I want, whenever I want." She took from her pocket the length of heavy, rubber-covered cable.

Blake looked at it without comprehension.

"I'm going to do a number of things to you, from now on, whenever I'm in the mood to do them," Anne went on. "Principally, I'm going to thrash you. I'm going to thrash you very often. Every morning, for instance, when you arrive, you'll receive ten lashes across your naked bottom—with this, or with something else. And every evening, before you leave, you'll have ten more."

Blake's eyes opened wide. "But why, for heaven's sake?"

"Are you being dense?" asked Anne. "Or are

you so innocent?"

"No. Really, why all this?"

"Because I'm a sadist, of course."

"Oh."

Anne stood up. "And now for the first taste. Come round here and take down your trousers. Come on."

Blake opened his mouth to protest, perhaps to refuse. Then he thought of the consequences. Dismissal, perhaps prison. He could neither protest nor refuse. His secretary truly had him in her power. He slowly rose from his chair and walked to the centre of his office.

Anne went to the door and locked it. "Quickly. Down with your trousers."

Blake loosened the buttons and braces, and let his trousers fall around his ankles.

"And your pants."

The pants were removed from their position.

"Now bend down."

Once more Blake opened his mouth to protest. "Really, Miss—"

"Bend down!" There was a sharp note of authority in her voice.

Blake hesitated for only a second more. Then he bent.

"Lower."

Blake bent lower.

Anne pulled up the jacket and shirt, and revealed the naked bottom. She moved into position and raised her piece of cable. She brought it down, hard but not by any means with all her force, across the centre of the buttocks.

Blake exclaimed loudly and jumped into an erect position, rubbing his bottom with his hands. "Good God!" he said. "You can't—"

"Listen," said Anne. "You must get something into your head. You are going to be thrashed from now on, very often. You can't do anything about it, unless you want me to report you. So you've got to take it. And taking it means that you must remain bent down until I've finished. If you don't, I shall increase the number of lashes. I swear that. If you remain bent down now, and don't jump about, you'll get nine more. If you jump about, the nine will increase. And if you make a noise, and anybody hears you, it'll be the same as if I report you because they'll want to know what's going on—and I shall have to tell them. So bend down now, and take your punishment like a man." Blake looked at her with tightened lips for a moment. Then he bent once more. Anne raised her cable again. Emphasising some of her words or syllables with lashes, she said: "Don't worry about my work—I shall remain—a very good secretary—I shall do—all that a good secretary—should do—You'll have no—complaints at all—in that direction." She put the cable back in her pocket. "Now you can stand up and put your trousers on again. And as soon as you want me for the day's letters, I am at your total service." And she unlocked the door and returned to her own office, tingling with excitement.

44. A Burlesque Beating

"WELL?" HOOTED Mr. Quelch.

"I—I think I've got it right, sir!" gasped Bunter.

"You utterly obtuse boy."

"Oh, really, sir."

"If you had prepared this lesson, Bunter, you could not possibly have made such absurd mistakes. You have done no preparation. You are making wild guesses at the meaning of that passage. Your translation, Bunter, would disgrace a small boy in the Second Form. I will not permit such idleness, such slackness—in my form! I have warned you, Bunter, of the consequences of idleness and slackness. I shall now cane you."

"Oh, lor'!"

"Stand out before the class, Bunter."

Billy Bunter rolled out reluctantly. Mr. Quelch picked up the cane from his desk. Billy Bunter eyed it with apprehension.

"Bend over that chair, Bunter."

Whack!

"Ow!"

Whack!

"Wow!"

45. Angela's Caning

AT A QUARTER to three all the pupils and staff had gathered in Great Hall. All were silent. An ominous atmosphere filled the hall. On the stage stood a table on which lay a crook-handled rattan cane, which was three feet four inches in length, and three-eighths of an inch in diameter. To the right of the table, in the centre of the stage was a gymnasium horse. At ten to three the headmistress and her deputy Miss Amelia Rush entered the hall. The headmistress stood in between the table and the horse, Miss Rush stood on the other side of the horse. Both looked resplendent in subfusc with their flowing black gowns and academic caps.

Miss Heaney stood at the open doorway of the little room at the back of Great Hall awaiting the signal from Miss Rush to bring forth Angela. The girl sat miserable and listless, resigned to her destiny. The spirit of defiance which had welled up in her after her first caning had now completely disappeared. How she wished she had accepted that punishment with good grace. She now bore no ill-will towards the headmistress, she simply wanted the Head to be pleased with her.

Miss Eagleton gave a short address to those assembled on the topic of discipline. At five minutes to three she went and stood to the left of the horse, after picking up the cane from the table. She nodded to Miss Rush, who raised an arm to Miss Heaney at the back of the Hall.

"Come, Angela," said Miss Heaney softly. In a daze Angela rose from her seat and began the long walk to the stage. She was pale. Her wide eyes resembled those of a startled fawn, and she was biting her lower lip. In her fear she looked extremely pretty. One would not have thought that such a pretty girl could ever have done something to merit such a punishment. Miss Heaney and Miss Dubois stood on either side of the girl and escorted her slowly down the seemingly endless aisle towards the stage. The walk seemed to last for ever, but they finally mounted the steps to the stage. Angela's knees buckled slightly when she saw the horse and the cane lying on the table, but she was steadied by Miss Heaney and Miss Dubois. All three stood facing the horse. Angela looked straight ahead at the horse, breathing quickly.

"Remove your blazer," said Miss Heaney softly. She took Angela's blazer and laid it on the table next to the cane.

Angela stood, she was pale and she shook slightly. Miss Rush then said: "Bend over the horse. Let your arms hang over the other side." Angela obediently climbed on to the step in front of the horse and lifted her body over the soft leather top. Miss Heaney then raised Angela's skirt and petticoat over her back, so exposing her knickers. Miss Heaney and Miss Dubois went and stood in front of Angela on the other side of the horse. Miss Heaney took hold of Angela's left arm and Miss Dubois of Angela's right to hold her in place. Miss Rush fastened Angela's ankles down with ankle-straps which were attached to the horse. It was now one minute to three.

Miss Rush then looked at her watch and nodded to the headmistress, who laid the cane gently on the girl's bottom several times as she took aim. Every pupil watched intently, each one glad that she was not up on the stage. After laying the cane down gently five times, the headmistress nodded to Miss Rush and drew the cane as far back as possible. The Academy clock struck three. At the third chime Miss Eagleton let fly with as much force as she could muster. The cane flew through the air with a loud swish and thwack as it hit home. Angela gritted her teeth, and managed to remain silent. Miss Rush counted the stroke out aloud. Miss Eagleton impassively drew back the cane to administer the second stroke. Miss Rush looked at her watch, and when twenty seconds had elapsed, she nodded to Miss Eagleton, who administered the second stroke with maximum force. "Two," called out Miss Rush. Angela remained silent, although her face was now red. The punishment continued in the same way, with a stroke being administered every twenty seconds.

After the fourth stroke Angela began to cry out, but her evident distress did not persuade Miss Eagleton to moderate her punishment. She continued remorselessly, calmly administering the strokes with maximum force, deliberately aiming to ensure that the cane hit the lower half of the posterior. Miss Heaney, Miss Rush and Miss Dubois also remained dispassionate, feeling that the punishment was just and in Angela's best interests. The pupils continued to look on in silence, although there were some gasps at the severity of the caning. The atmosphere in Great Hall was subdued, as each pupil realised that she too could also be liable to receive such a punishment. All the mistresses looked on with approval, rejoicing in the new standards of discipline Miss Eagleton had brought to the Academy.

The final stroke was administered. "Eighteen," intoned Miss Rush. Angela had ceased to cry, she merely gasped as the final stroke landed. Although the thrashing had lasted only a little more than five minutes, it seemed like an eternity. She was conscious of an unbearable pain in her bottom, and the intensity of the caning meant that she forgot about the humiliation of being watched by a large audience. When the punishment ended she once again remembered that the seat of her knickers was on display to more than six hundred people, and she flushed with embarrassment, as her bottom throbbed agonisingly.

Miss Eagleton laid down the cane on the table. All those assembled were dismissed and the pupils filed out to return to their classes, as Angela remained bent over the horse, sobbing. When all the pupils had left, Angela was told to stand up. She stood there red-faced and heaving great sobs as Miss Eagleton, Miss Heaney, Miss Dubois and Miss Rush looked on. Miss Eagleton spoke softly to her. "Your punishment is over, Angela, and you have taken it well. Let it be a lesson to you. You have the potential to be a credit to yourself and the Academy. You are an intelligent, personable girl with many fine qualities. I have caned you today in this way in order to uplift you morally so that you may realise your potential. You are excused lessons for the rest of today and tomorrow. You are now to go to the sanatorium to see Matron. Miss Heaney and Miss Rush will accompany you in case you have difficulty walking."

After seeing Matron, Angela was then guided to one of the individual bedrooms in the sick bay where she was to spend the remainder of the day and the whole of the following day in order to allow her to regain her composure and reflect on her misdeeds and her punishment. She lay face down (she could hardly do anything else) and thought about the events of that day. She began to cry again as she thought about the shame of being caned in public. Her behind still throbbed with pain. She thought of Miss Eagleton's calm strictness, the gentleness of all four of the mistresses involved in the administration of the punishment, and a feeling of loyalty to them and a desire to please them began to grow in her heart as she clutched her tear-stained pillow.

In her study Miss Eagleton also pondered on the day that had passed. She considered the caning she administered as one of her duties. It had been onerous, but nonetheless enjoyable. Her mind looked back to the fearsome but just canings she herself received not so many years ago. She was fond of her pupils and particularly of the girl she had caned that day. She even admired Angela's daring in devising such a prank. She had longed to hug Angela after the caning, although of course she had refrained from doing so. The caning had crushed Angela, but this was not like the crushing of a piece of rubbish to be discarded. It was rather something positive, more akin to the crushing of grapes to create a fine wine, or of rose petals to create a fragrant perfume. She would punish the girl again, of that she was sure, and in doing so, she would create a powerful bond of respect and affection that would far transcend the shallow egalitarianism of the modern world.

46. Caning the "Maid"

With my panties at my ankles, it was hard to walk. Mistress sat in a soft chair directly in front of a book filled wall. On a highly polished low table was a fluted champagne glass, a rubber glove and a slender wooden cane. The cane looked rather like an elongated swagger stick with an elaborate leather and suede grip.

Still holding the leash, She looked directly at me. "I am pleased, very pleased with you, Christine. Normally, you would be spanked for whatever corrections I deemed necessary for your deportment lessons to mould into the sort of sissy slave I want. This weekend, as you well know, your submission to Me has become a deeper thing, a new plateau if you will. Gaze well on these objects. In time, the very sight of them will trigger responses in you that I have intended, but you may not have yet comprehended.

"The cane is used for severe punishment Although you do not warrant such chastisement, I want you to drink deeply of it to mark this day in your memory..."

Bewildered, I stood straight, as Mistress also rose picking up the cane and moved behind me. Just after a loud SWISH there was ripping pain. Again and again, SWISH SWISH. Helplessly, I pulled against the cuffs; if not gagged, I would have screamed. Tears began to stream down my cheeks. She lifted my uniform hem and petticoats making me hold them up myself. SWISH-CRACK. SWISH-CRACK.

Muffled sobs accompanied my river of tears. It stung, stung more with each stroke on my bare flaming bottom. M. Ellisia walked in front of me, lifting up the apron and skirts of my uniform. "Do you like the discipline of the cane?" She asked. Emphatically, I shook my head "NO—NO—please." "Very good Christine, then perhaps you will learn to avoid such things if your behaviour meets my parameters." Again the sound and pain, SWISH-CRACK, on my thighs. SWISH-CRACK.

Mistress held the cane in up to my face, rubbing it under my nose. "Note it well, young man", She intoned. Gratefully, I thought it was over; my hopes were false. Four swift strokes fell on my thighs, just over the stocking tops: SWACK-SWACK-SWACK-SWACK. Head swooning, I felt faint, eyes blurred with tears. I didn't see Her move behind me. SWISH-CRACK, SWISH-CRACK on my thighs. Searing spasms shot thru me like electric sparks.

Mistress finally laid the cane on the table, breasts heaving from Her exertions, then relaxed into the chair. Silently, with a wan smile, Lady fixed Her gaze on me. My legs trembled. My eyes met Hers, irrationally, despite what had happened, I adored Her more. After a brief moment my eyes fell to the floor automatically, ashamed of my reaction to the extreme discipline.

47. A JUDICIAL SPANKING

ONE JUVENILE COURT magistrate, very occasionally, used to consider frightening a girl was deterrent enough. To this end, the girl would be ordered to the Chamber, to witness the punishment of a properly sentenced delinquent.

This was reminiscent of the "whipping boy" of medieval times, only here, the boy was a girl, and one who deserved her thrashing for her own crime. Unlike the innocent "whipping boy" who had to take the flogging from an irate tutor of a lazy, inattentive, or misbehaving youngster of noble parentage. This spoilt brat often provoking the tutor, for the amusement of seeing the young serf's bare bottom harshly treated. But this girl knew she deserved a whipping, and was thankful to be spared it. Whilst the other, also deserved her punishment, and was going to get it anyway; before a witness or not; thereby teaching a lesson to both girls for the price of one.

The girl would watch in horror as the offender was stripped naked and draped across the whipping bench. She would share the victim's terror, if not her pain, once the caning got under way. Then, whilst the screaming prisoner was mercilessly thrashed, she would be only too aware that it could have been she herself who was being so severely whipped. Although unpunished for her misdemeanour, the girl would leave the Chamber, often in tears, determined never again to break the law.

The policewomen were always totally against such leniency, and used to go to great efforts to let the girl know that they heartily disapproved of a miscreant escaping her due punishment.

This went a considerable step further, the day the aggressive little policewoman, whose short hair style crowned her head, giving her the appearance of a silky bantam chicken, and whom I have earlier described in Chapter Eight, entered the Chamber, with a sixteen year old girl in school uniform. The girl was reasonably attractive in a quiet sort of way. She had a nice slim girlish figure. Both points I appreciated in a victim, when involved in a thrashing.

Also, she was blonde haired. I always preferred blondes for the whipping bench. Like redheads, they marked so much more easily, and were more smooth and hairless around the area on view, than their brunette sisters. She was very nervous, and I looked forward, knowing that I would not get a turn at thrashing her, at prizing her legs apart, and gazing down at her bottom, whilst the policewoman would be whipping her. However, that was not to be.

The policewoman informed me in most resentful tone, that the girl had been ordered to the Chamber to witness the flogging of another girl, in an effort to make her realise just what was at stake with her breaking the law. Then she turned to the girl and said:

"The whole idea of this exercise is to make you well aware of what goes on in the punishment chamber, without actually flogging you. This, in an effort to make you repent. So you can start off by taking your clothes off, just as any other delinquent would."

I had to smile at the policewoman's ingenuity, and also at the girl's embarrassment. She had thought that she would just be standing fully dressed, watching another girl getting her bare bottom caned, whilst fastened across the whipping bench. But now she was going to be naked for it. She began to shed her clothes as commanded by the aggressive little woman. When she was standing naked, the policewoman instructed her to hold out her arms, and quickly snapped a pair of handcuffs upon the girl's wrists.

"This is to give you some idea of what it is like to be rendered helpless. "

Then we settled down to wait for the next delinquent to be punished. The sixteen year old was very embarrassed as she stood there with her wrists handcuffed in front of her. She was quite aware that both of us had eyed her unprotected bottom, and was truly feeling her helplessness and vulnerability.

At last the knock came to the door, and it opened to admit a young policewoman, who was escorting a very attractive girl of about eighteen. The girl was wearing a blue suit, white blouse, sheer stockings, and high heeled shoes. She was obviously very surprised to see another girl, already naked, in the Chamber. Perhaps she was of the opinion of many young delinquents, that she would just have to take down her knickers for the cane. But the sight of the handcuffed young nudist soon sorted that out for her.

She too was ordered to strip, and immediately burst into tears. The young policewoman repeated the order, and threatened to tear the clothes off the terrified girl. Emphasising the fact that it would be a shame to spoil such lovely clothes, especially when such an action would result in the girl being given extra strokes for her disobedience.

The sobbing girl began to undress. She pleaded for mercy in between the removal of each garment. When she was down to her bra and knickers, the policewoman again had to tell her to take off her bra. It came off slowly, gradually revealing very large breasts. I thought the nipples were never going to appear. At last they popped out, also large and very pink. Then the girl slid her knickers down, to be just the way we wanted her.

The young policewoman and I took an arm each, and led her across to the whipping bench. She put up token resistance, but we soon had her secured in position to receive her dues. She had been sentenced to ten strokes for defacing a government poster. Armed with a cane each, the young policewoman and I took up our positions, one either side of the girl. She was still in tears, sobbing and crying. She begged and pleaded, and became quite frantic when the first cane touched her very full and beautiful bottom, measuring the stroke. She screamed at the first stroke.

This was the ideal model for the young schoolgirl. It was perfect that she should see a young woman so distressed under punishment.

As soon as the sound of the scream faded, there was a loud smack from behind us, and an "Oh." I

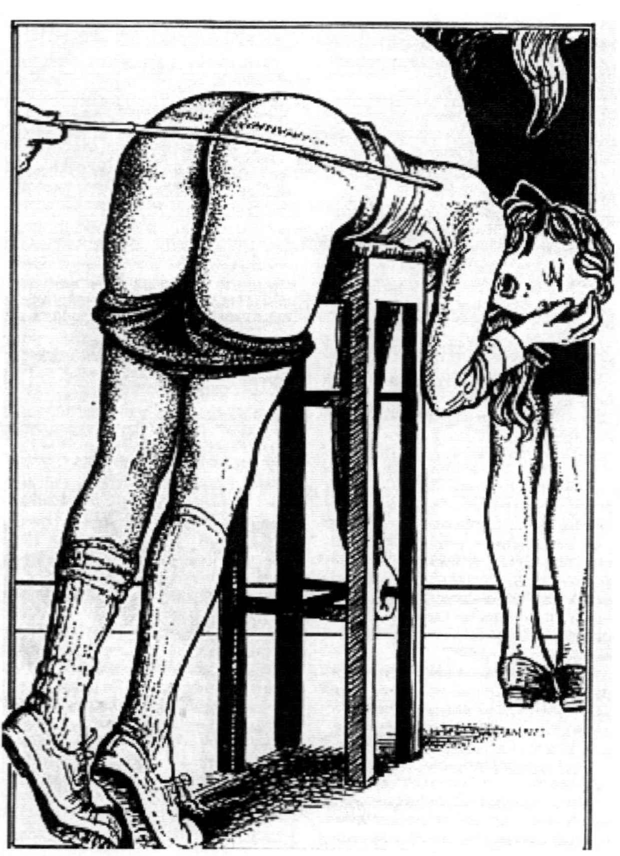

looked back to see the standing girl almost knocked off her feet by a slap across her bottom from the policewoman's open hand. Even though she had a tight grip, holding the girl's upper arm with her other hand.

She spoke determinedly: "Although we cannot use a cane or strap upon you, that is no reason why you should not get your bottom reddened too, Milady." The panic stricken girl spread across the punishment bench, was howling when the second stroke arrived across her protesting and shuddering bottom. Again a scream from her. Then again a loud smack, followed by an "Ouch" as the standing girl got the palm of the policewoman's hand across her bottom. After four cuts, we laid it on slash after slash, watching that scrumptious bottom wobble and gyrate. The victim was screaming her lungs out, and behind us we could hear the smack, smack, smack, smack, and "Ouch", "No", "Aaah", "Oooof" from the schoolgirl. The last two strokes were laid on with slow deliberation, and gained the maximum of screams from the girl, and contortions from her bottom, as her legs flayed the air.

The schoolgirl was also getting her smacking.

When the caning was over, the handcuffed girl was rushed forward to stand directly in front of the thrashed offender. The policewoman believed that the schoolgirl should have been caned, and that her stripping and the smacking of her bottom was allowable and good therapy for the lesson. But ten spanks were hardly enough:

"Right, young woman, you have seen a prisoner being flogged, now it is only right that the prisoner see you being spanked." She immediately positioned the chair in front of the whipping bench, and sitting upon it, told the girl to get across her knees. "Not that way. The offender doesn't want to look at your face. It is your bottom being spanked which she wants to see. Now get over from this side." She pulled the girl across her knees. The schoolgirl's bottom was already bright pink, and only a couple of feet from the shackled eighteen-year-old's face.

The energetic little policewoman then gave the girl about forty good hard smacks, making about fifty in all. Smack, smack, smack, smack, the spanking went on and on, with the girl yelling and howling. She struggled and bucked, but that only made her bottom wobble and shake, encouraging the policewoman all the more. The girl was quite defenceless to protect herself with her manacled wrists stretching down towards the floor in front of her. Smack, smack, smack, smack, as she writhed and squirmed, her creamy white thighs pumping strenuously. The spanked girl's bottom was quite red by the finish, and her face very tear stained. Once the girl was allowed up, she was led by the shoulders around to the rear of the whipping bench. By this time the welts had all risen across the offender's bottom. "That's what a properly whipped bottom looks like. That one will sting for hours, and be tender for days. The marks will stay there for weeks. Take a good look, because that is what will happen to your bottom if you ever have to come here again."

We then allowed the schoolgirl to dress and leave, before even unfastening the eighteen year old. She rose from the bench, bright eyed with enchantment at the sight she had been so unexpectedly treated to. No longer the snivelling young woman who had been conquered and thrashed. She had found great solace in watching the screaming schoolgirl getting her pretty bottom smacked. Her knickers were pulled up over her welted bottom without even a wince. After a little adjustment in front of the mirror, she was ready to leave, and looked every bit the attractive and confident looking young woman she was. It was as though all her welts had been transferred to the bottom of the schoolgirl, she had been privileged to watch being spanked. Although we knew that she had learnt her lesson well, and would never again render herself into the position to make a return trip to our Chamber.

Impressed as I was with the policewoman's interpretation of the magistrate's decision to frighten the schoolgirl rather than flog her, I never mentioned it to any of the other policewomen who brought girls into the chamber as observers. These girls knew that they too could have been in the position of having their bottoms soundly thrashed as they lay pinioned across the whipping bench. Perhaps I was afraid of a complaint being registered. Or maybe I even agreed with the magistrate. Court is a traumatic experience enough, to make any girl want to correct her ways. But to have to visit the punishment chamber and see another girl screaming under strokes which could have been her own, must have been far more illuminating for the watching girl. But that is correction, and not punishment. So the policewoman had a point. And after all, a spanking never did a teenage girl anything but good.

48. Domestic Discipline

It felt a little queer to be a child again and to feel this dread of Aunt Alice. She was in trouble again, that was certain, and as she waited a chill fell over her spirits. Of all things she had least wanted this. She felt, as one often does when taken in a quite different mood, delicate, and as if even a small dose of corporal punishment would be wholly unbearable. Of course Aunt Alice might give her lines; she did sometimes, but that felt no better. The thought of spending hours tomorrow writing out some tedious imposition seemed equally dreadful.

At last the door opened. Aunt Alice was there in her knee-length, straight wool skirt and her blouse and cardigan. She looked very everyday after the glitter of the Brace of Pheasants, as she always did. Annalinde rose immediately to her feet. Aunt Alice made the Brace of Pheasants and art and music and wit seem somehow phantastical, bringing one back to the grey weight of the Real World of duty and discipline and the hard fact that one was a child. Her heart had lain heavily in her stomach as she awaited her aunt. Now it seemed to rise into her throat.

Aunt Alice crossed the room and seated herself on the sofa.

"Come here, Annalinde," she said. "Closer please. Stand exactly there." She indicated a spot on the carpet. "Now, Annalinde, what have you to say for yourself?"

"I don't know, Aunt Alice."

"You don't know. You know to what I am referring, do you not?"

"Yes, Aunt Alice."

"Six Order Marks. Six! And when did I last punish you for Order Marks?"

"Saturday, I think, Aunt."

"Saturday is correct. And your mother has had occasion to give you six since then. Claire is a delicate blonde, Annalinde. She should not have to be troubled with constant misbehaviour from her daughter. And you are a blonde too. You should behave yourself obediently and with gentle grace. A good deal of the time, Annalinde, you behave yourself like a rather unruly brunette. If you were a brunette I should have to discipline you, but as you are a blonde the matter is rather more serious. You do understand the difference between blondes and brunettes, do you not?"

"Yes, Aunt Alice."

"I hope you do. You are getting too old, Annalinde, to behave in a harum-scarum manner. In a child it is allowable, but in an adolescent blonde it is very unbecoming. There is a name for blondes who do not act in a blonde manner, Annalinde. It is not a pleasant name and I should not like to feel that such a name could ever be used of a member of our family."

Annalinde flushed deeply. She did not like to feel that she was risking her good name. Much of her naughtiness took place at home, but it was true that she was sometimes noisy and silly at the cinema. It was true that she sometimes behaved in an un-blonde manner. Perhaps at times she lost a certain connexion with the essence of her femininity—it was a common enough disease in any one who had been exposed to the Pit. Even a brunette should beware of that, but a blonde—

"I see, Annalinde, that something of what I am saying is beginning to strike home. I am glad. It is not just a question of telling you off. You must take stock of yourself. Your un-blonde behaviour has passed as childish fun up to now. But you are getting older. You are reaching an age when the rather—well, rather rough and sometimes indelicate manner you sometimes affect begins to look ungainly and ridiculous."

It was true. She was growing up. It was a fact she had not entirely taken seriously before. After all, her chronological age was so different from her age in Aristasia, that age seemed to be a thing infinitely malleable, and one felt that one could seize at once the privileges of every age from infancy to venerable maturity. But, of course, it was not really true. Different personæ might have different ages, but they must be disciplined and each kept whole and integral: they could not splurge over one another—and Annalinde, her main persona, was definitely growing up. She had gone out with brunettes—well, one brunette. She was starting to be admired as a young blonde. She must not lose the respect of her position. Her remark this evening about petting, for example—and it had been her, not Miss Nightwind—would have been a bit near the knuckle even for a brunette. She excused it to herself on the grounds that it was making a real point, but it must have sounded rather brash and forward and unblondelike.

"This is a small town, Annalinde. A girl's reputation goes with her everywhere. You are admired in some quarters as a charming example of a blonde, and you are such an example at times. Now you must learn to discipline yourself and be charming and dainty all the time, not only when it takes your fancy. I do not mind your being excitable—and even naughty—provided you make certain you are doing it in a blonde way. When I say I do not mind I do not mean that I shall not punish you. Of course I shall. But it is not so vital a matter as maintaining your blondeness. You are not among the newest girls in the district any more. Your job is to set an example. I hope I may rely upon you to set one from now on."

"Yes, Aunt Alice."

"It is not entirely your fault, Annalinde. I blame myself in part. We both know well enough that the traditional method of keeping blondes blonde is to punish them—in particular to whip them. I have not been on hand to beat you nearly as much as your nature requires. We must try to remedy that, must we not?"

"Yes, Aunt Alice."

"Very well, then. Come over my knee." Annalinde obeyed, lying herself across Aunt Alice's lap, her upper body resting on the vacant seat of the sofa. "Put your hands under me," said Aunt Alice. It was her practice when administering a severe spanking to sit on one's hands, thus rendering one immobile and incapable of struggle. Annalinde manœuvred her hands under her Aunt's heavy, grown-up thighs. The straight woollen skirt had ridden up a little and she could feel her upper thigh filmed in gossamer Quinnelle nylon. She even fancied she could feel it grow denser and less ætherial as it darkened at the top. The soft weight of her aunt's legs pinned her firmly, and she was aware of that lady turning back the skirts of her—or rather Miss Nightwind's—elegant black evening dress, exposing the deep-pink satiny petticoat with black edging. She tucked the surplus folds of petticoat between her thighs, her hand warm against her most intimate places, and yet with an impersonal, aunt-like warmth. She knew with what she was to be disciplined. She had seen the hairbrush lying on the seat, and watched her aunt pick it up before she positioned herself over her. In truth, it was not actually a hairbrush, although that is what it was always conventionally called. It was a large, oval-headed Trentish clothes-brush, long, heavy and with a slightly convex back flat enough for its purpose. There were numerous of these brushes in the Empire, glistening in their dark-brown burnished Trentish timber. There was a home-like, quotidian severity about these implements, so ideal for their purpose and versatile enough to brush clothes as well.

Annalinde tensed herself involuntarily as she felt the motion of the first stroke coming. The flat, heavy, stinging shock exploded across her skin, penetrating the satiny petticoat and the matching pink, black-edged knickers as if they had not been there at all. Such delicate protec-

tion was powerless against the heavy thwack of sheening, Trentish wood. Her legs stiffened, her body reared a little, though her hands were pressed immobile by warm, feminine thighs.

"I hope there is not a spirit of resistance in you, child," said Aunt Alice sternly. "We have all night to beat it out if there is. Relax, please. Submit yourself."

Annalinde made her body go limp, letting herself go to the will of her superior. The brush smacked home again, tingling-sore upon the surface, yet deep too. These were heavy strokes. Not the crushing blows that were termed "Victorian strokes", but hard, heavy, full-intentioned smacks. A third, a fourth, a fifth and a sixth fell. Annalinde gasped, tensed, tried to untense and tensed again. She had accepted such punishments better than this in the past, but punishment is a curious thing. In the right mood one can absorb so much, warmly, submittingly, almost voluptuously. Today was almost the opposite. She could hardly bear to be touched. These ringing, tingling flood-waves of pain seemed almost intolerable. She half expected her aunt to tell her again to submit. Sometimes she scolded her all through a spanking. Today she seemed to have said all she had to say. Annalinde knew what was expected. If she tensed and arched herself, the punishment would lengthen. Submission would come in the end.

Unable to help herself, Annalinde, pinioned firmly by the hands, twisted her legs as if to avoid the pain, opening her suspender-crossed thighs in the most ungainly manner. Aunt Alice deftly brought down the hard brush in agonising reproof to the niece's exposed inner thighs. Annalinde squealed like a wounded animal and closed her legs demurely as her only means of protecting this most delicate place of feminine modesty. For the rest of the spanking her legs remained neatly side by side, despite the mounting pain in her bottom and thighs. Even so, that burning soreness would make walking a delicate task next day, as her inner thighs rubbed together, up-gathered above her stocking-tops beneath the modest folds of her skirt.

Aunt Alice was falling into a rhythm now. Hard, swinging slaps falling with easy force upon the pink-sheened bottom and thighs. The flesh was becoming hot beneath its chastisement. Even her own thighs were hot and moist against the adolescent girl's clenching, powerless hands. The girl was sobbing now, but there was less resistance in her sobs. She was resigned to the long, hard spanking.

Angeline, in her little room above was taking off her uniform, unclipping her shiny metal suspenders. She felt glad, at first, that some one else should suffer. She was sore still from her beating at the hands of Betty. Inexperienced as she was, she could tell that it was some hard, wooden implement not unlike the spatula that had been used on her this evening, though heavier. She was still sore from that, used so cruelly over her already-lashed skin, and she slid off the stockings from her thin, girlish legs, enjoying the sharp percussion from below.

She crossed the hall in her petticoat and slippers, washed out her intimate garments, brushed her teeth, cleaned off her make-up all in a leisurely fashion, knowing that the other occupants of the house were otherwise occupied and contemplating the events of her first day in bondage. She was tired, sore, a little shaken emotionally, nervous and even a touch resentful, yet she looked upon all these feelings in a haze of tired detachment and with a feeling strangely pleasurable rather than otherwise.

It was no game; that was, perhaps, the salient sensation of all those in which her mind swum. The idea of being a bonded maid, the District Governess, the sentence, all these had seemed half game-like and half chillingly real. The visualisation of the Kadorian bus-station had made it seem more game-like than ever, though it also added another layer of wistful reality. But today, as it were, the reality had clanged to and the lock had clicked. She was a serving-girl, at the beck and call of her superiors, which meant, as far as she could see, every one. A girl to be ordered about, called hither and yon, to answer bells, to scrub floors, to be slapped and strapped, to be always neat and demure and obedient, to say "Very good, madam" and "Very good, miss" and nothing more. Yet the contemplation of these things was strangely rosy. Even her resentment seemed somehow a shade enjoyable, and the enjoyable part of that resentment was her powerlessness to act upon it in any way, as if she felt a certain—yes, a certain cruelty toward herself. She felt herself clench her teeth and vindictively wish suffering upon herself, as one might wish it on another. Not physical suffering either, but precisely the suffering of resentment. "Yes," a part of her was saying. "Fret in silence when you are treated as a menial slave, denied all privilege, whipped and bullied: fret and resent and cry yourself to sleep, and know that you can do nothing about it." She smiled a curious smile, and, in truth, in the days to come found a certain secret disappointment—secret almost from herself—in the thoughtful, kindly mistress and the reasonable household into which she had been bonded.

Her ablutions completed, she put her things into her sponge-bag and made her way back to her little bedroom. She was surprised to hear the spanking still in progress, slow and rhythmic and hard. Had it been as hard as that all the time she was in the bathroom? Had it been going on at that pace? She felt sure it had. How many strokes must it be? A hundred—no more, probably; much more.

As she settled into bed, she heard the rhythmic strokes, each one accompanied by a high, soulful moan. Annalinde's fingertips were digging deep into her aunt's thighs. The ordeal was far greater than she had expected. The spanking stopped for a moment, and the hairbrush was exchanged for a short, three-tailed strap, hard and heavy, perhaps nine inches long, and made, it seemed, specifically for spanking. It was fashioned from real old leather, dark and shiny with use; clearly an old school or home implement. Its harsh tails cut through the surface numbness created by the long spanking with a new, high-pitched pain. Annalinde squealed.

Angeline remembered Annalinde's commanding her to re-tie her shoelaces, and that gave an added piquancy to this audition of her strapping. She could not see it, of course, but being in the room above, it was almost as clear as a wireless broadcast. She felt sorry for the girl, frightened that such severities were possible in this house, but also she enjoyed it. She enjoyed it especially because of the shoelaces. It would have been easy to think that it was a kind of revenge for her humiliation, but really it was nothing like that. She had not minded serving the young mistress in that way. She had been embarrassed, but she could hardly say she had wholly disliked it. Somehow, though, the sound of this girl who held so much power over her, who could toy with her at will, receiving so sound a spanking gave her an exquisite frisson. Her involuntary squeals of acute distress as hard leather bit already-chastened flesh had an effect quite unexpected; pleasing almost to blissfulness and she found that the pleasure warmed and deepened as she pictured herself kneeling at Annalinde's feet tying her shoelaces. She settled herself to listen to the entirety of the punishment, but in the event she was sound asleep before the leather ceased its harsh refrain and the young lady of the house, sore and subdued, made her own way to bed.

49. A Philosophy of Punishment

For reasons too complicated to go into here, the modern propaganda media have made the whole subject of corporal punishment very controversial and shocking. In particular, they have adopted the strategy of associating it on every possible occasion with sexual perversion, until it is hardly possible to mention the subject in certain circles without producing embarrassed sniggers. We trust that our readers will have the good sense to treat this propaganda with the contempt it deserves; but nevertheless, since it has been successful in its aim of sowing widespread confusion and misunderstanding on the subject, it seems advisable for us to go a little more deeply into the theoretical side of corporal punishment than might otherwise have been necessary...

There are two kinds of corporal punishment: cold and warm. Cold punishment is given without love, simply to enforce a certain kind of behaviour. Olympian society has nothing to do with this kind of punishment. Warm corporal punishment is given with love. It is a form of nourishment; an expression of love, though it is certainly a genuine discipline as well.

Matriarchal cultures say that when a mistress beats her child or her servant, the strokes are like drops of milk flowing from her breasts to feed and nourish the soul. This close association of punishment and love may seem strange to the modern mind, but it is to be found throughout the literature and history of the world. In the Bible it says... that the parent who loves the child will chasten her when necessary, but the parent who refuses to punish the child actually hates her. This does not mean simply that the child who is deprived of discipline suffers in the long term (though this is certainly true), but indicates that chastisement is a real act of love, and that refusal to punish indicates not only a mistaken sentimentality, but a certain coldness of heart.

Punishment, in the context of a disciplined

relationship between two people who love one another, is a warm and passionate experience. It is hardly surprising, then, that in an age which on the one hand is obsessed with sex, and on the other hand is determined to discredit every form of discipline, this experience should be interpreted in terms of sexual perversion. But passion can take many forms, and the passion to submit is deeper and more profound than the passion of sex, just as the passion of love is deeper and more profound than the passion of sex. That is because sex belongs to our animal nature, but both love and submission belong to our spiritual nature.

50. A Punished Servant

HAS HE DEVOTED himself to a higher end, he wonders, standing there in the afternoon sunlight in his slippers and pajama bottoms, flexing a cane, testing it, snapping it against his palm, or has he been taken captive by it? Is choice itself an illusion? Or an act of magic? And is the worst over, or has it not yet begun? He shudders, yawns, stretches. And the manuals...? He is afraid even to ask, takes a few practice strokes with the cane against a horsehair cushion instead. When the riddles and paradoxes of his calling overtake him, wrapping him in momentary darkness, he takes refuge in the purity of technique. The proper stretching of a bull's pizzle, for example, this can occupy him for hours. Or the fabrication of whipping chairs, the index of duties and offenses, the synonymy associated with corporal discipline and with that broad part destined by Mother Nature for such services. And a cane is not simply any cane, but preferably one made like this one of brown Malacca—the stem of an East Indian rattan palm—about two and a half feet long (give or take an inch and a half) and a quarter of an inch thick. Whing-SNAP! listen to it! Or take the birch rod, not a mere random handful of birchen twigs, as often supposed, but an instrument of precise and elaborate construction. First, the twigs must be meticulously selected for strength and elasticity, each about two feet long, full of snap and taken from a young tree, the tips sharp as needles. Then carefully combining the thick with the thin and slender, they must be bound together for half their length, tightly enough that they might enjoy long service, yet not too tightly or else the rod will be like a stick and the twigs have no play. The rod must fit conveniently to the hand, have reach and swing so as to sing in the air, the larger part of all punishment being the anticipation of course, not the pain, and must immediately raise welts and blisters, surprising the chastised flesh afresh with each stroke. To be sure, it is easier to construct a birch rod than to employ it correctly—that's always the hard part, he doesn't enjoy it, nor does she surely, but the art of the rod is incomplete without its perfect application. And though elusive, what else is there worth striving for? Indeed, he knows he has been too indulgent toward her up till now, treating her with the civility and kindness due to an inferior, but forgetting the forging of her soul by way of those "vivid lessons," as a teacher he once had used to put it, "in holy scripture, hotly writ." So when she arrives, staggering in late with all her paraphernalia, her bucket empty and her bib hanging down, he orders her straight to the foot of the bed. "But, sir, I haven't even—" "Come, come, no dallying! The least show of resistance will double the punishment! Up with your skirt, up, up! for I intend to WHAT?! IS THERE TO BE NO END TO THIS?!" "I—I'm sorry! I was wearing them when I came—I must have left them somewhere...!" Maybe it's some kind of communication problem, he thinks, staring gloomily at her soul's ingress which confronts him like blank paper, laundered tiffany, a perversely empty ledger. The warm afternoon sun blows in through the garden doors, sapping his brave resolve. He feels himself drifting, yawning, must literally shake himself to bring the manuals back to mind, his duties, his devotion... "Sir," she reminds him. "Sir" he sighs.

51. "Overs"

EARLIER THAT morning William had been woken from a strange and fitful sleep by the sound of chairs scraping and girls' voices whispering and giggling. At first he thought he was still dreaming. Something felt rather strange—it was as if he had been put over his aunt's knee for a spanking, only it wasn't her knee—it was bigger, wider and flatter; like a kind of soft and padded desk. And the voices—he remembered Lucy and her friends in the drawing-room on that day that the incident had happened. But this time he wasn't being beaten: this time he was just relaxing, dozing. But where was he? Perhaps he was in a field—he could feel cool air on his bottom and the backs of his legs. It actually felt rather pleasant and comfortable, in an odd sort of way.

Suddenly he remembered, and woke with a start. He was bent, face-down, across the end of his bed and his pyjama trousers were down around his ankles. The other eleven boys were similarly arranged. He looked towards the door and saw some third-form girls arranging two chairs at the top end of the dorm. They saw his head turn, giggled, and ran from the room, slamming the door behind them.

"Overs", he remembered. Matron had made them all bend over their beds last night, and had pulled down each boy's trousers in turn. She had instructed them, on the direst pains, to stay like that until they were told to get up, some time the following morning. But what was the meaning of the chairs? And when would they be allowed to stand up and get dressed? Breakfast time came and went. He heard the other children laughing and chattering in the corridors. What a strange punishment this was!

"Overs" was a punishment unique to Linton Abbey and had been instigated by Matron some thirty years before. She had found that while a quick, summary whacking of one or two boys for minor offences could easily be accommodated into a sensible, regular daily routine, some misbehaviour—because of the severity of the offence, the number of boys involved or the lateness of the hour—could disrupt the whole pattern of the day if it were dealt with as it deserved. "Overs" allowed her both to deal with trouble on the spot and to postpone any time-consuming punishments until a more convenient moment.

The girls made their way back along the corridors towards the boys' dorm. Sarah walked in front feeling very important, flexing the cane between her fingers and giving it an enthusiastic swish from time to time. They found Miss Clark standing with Matron at the door to the boys' dorm.

"We thought you'd both got lost!" she said. "Matron was getting quite concerned, weren't you Matron?" Matron maintained a dignified silence. "Never mind: let's go to it!" And with that she opened the door.

To say that Lucy was surprised to find herself suddenly faced with twelve boys' bare bottoms is perhaps an understatement. She gave out an audible gasp. William, having turned his head, like the other boys, towards the door to see who had come in, saw the cane in Miss Clark's hand, then saw Lucy and Sarah and groaned loudly. Lucy, feeling a little guilty, looked down at the floor. Sarah, on the other hand, caught William's eye, held it and gave him what a casual observer might have called an innocent, girlish smile. William, knowing better, buried his face in his bedclothes to hide the tears of rage and humiliation that were welling in his eyes.

There was a slight scraping

sound as the girls sat down in the chairs at the top of the dorm. This was followed by the slow but purposeful footsteps of Miss Clark as she paced the length of the dorm, flexing the cane so far between her hands that Lucy thought it might break. When she reached the far end, she swished it through the air so that it whistled loudly. Twelve boys, bending nervously over their beds, flinched involuntarily and wished fervently that they were somewhere else.

Miss Clark paused for a moment, straightened her jacket and then spoke: "Gentlemen. I hope that I have your undivided attention? Good. One always feels expected to deliver a speech or sermon at times like this, to add to the dignity and the gravitas of the situation. I am not one to disappoint you on this occasion."

She cleared her throat.

"There are many ways," she continued, "to look upon what is about to befall you. Many of you will, no doubt, be tempted to see it in a particularly negative light. I would urge you, though, to consider this as an education and as an opportunity to improve yourselves. For one thing, you will learn an important lesson on the inadvisability of conducting raucous bacchanaliæ at strange hours of the night. You will learn that Matron's sleep is sacrosanct; and that our younger ladies also need what I believe is now called their beauty sleep."

She paused. "You will also have the opportunity to become better acquainted with our friend here." She swished the cane again "The cane. A fascinating item, designed by the providence of nature for the sole purpose of beating small boys. The word comes to us from the French, who took it from the Romans, who, in turn, took it from the Greeks. Kanna was their word, meaning a reed. I hope that you will take full advantage of these remarkable treasures of knowledge."

She gestured to Matron, who came and stood beside her. They turned towards the first bed in the left-hand row: Matron stood to one side of the bed, level with the boy's shoulders while Miss Clark stood diagonally to the rear of his bottom. She touched the tip of the cane lightly to the centre of her target to measure her distance, then moved half a pace back and repeated the process. Satisfied this time, she weighed the cane lightly in her hand, drew it back and then whipped it suddenly and smartly across the boy's seat. He let out an anguished yelp and jerked forwards. Almost instantaneously a line appeared on his skin, white for a brief instant and then a deep, angry red. A second stroke followed swiftly after the first, causing him to squirm and to howl still louder. His hands flew backwards towards his bottom only to be intercepted by Matron, who pinned them firmly to the bed in front of him. The third stroke, which brought the first tears to the lad's face, landed with a loud thwack almost exactly between the marks of the previous two, and the fourth, which whistled and cracked noisily across his behind a few moments later, proved to be too much for him: he squealed and kicked, breaking free of Matron's grip, and collapsed into a sobbing heap on the floor.

"I'd get up if I were you" said Miss Clark, quietly. "Or we'll have to start all over again, and you won't like that at all."

This was not what he wanted to hear: he would have preferred something along the lines of, "That will be all—you've obviously had enough so you can get dressed now"; but seeing no alternative, the tearful boy struggled to his feet and bent, very hesitantly, back over the end of his bed. Matron held his shoulders this time. The stripes on his bottom had grown darker now, and were raised and swollen. Two more strokes followed, each as hard as the last, and the boy sobbed and yelped and squealed and squirmed for all he was worth, and pleaded that he had had enough, and that he was sorry for whatever he had done, and would never do it again, and that it hurt awfully and please would she stop because he couldn't take any more, but Matron had him firmly pinned down and he was unable to get away. When he had taken the full six strokes Matron released his shoulders and he lay, blubbering, across the end of his bed.

The canings continued down the first row and then, reaching the end, started again at the end of the other row. Sarah, who had seen a fair number of beatings in her fourteen years (and given not a few herself with her crop and her hairbrush when her parents weren't around) was fascinated with Miss Clark's style. Where her own mother, who was probably half Miss Clark's age and twice as strong, would whop away noisily for all she was worth until she was red in the face and out of breath, Miss Clark was able, it seemed, to produce far more dramatic results with almost no effort: a short, sharp, considered swing magnified to deadly proportions by a devastating flick of the wrist at the last moment. She was most impressed.

William was awful. Lucy felt thoroughly ashamed that any relative of hers could behave so childishly and so embarrassingly. It had started as soon as Miss Clark touched the cane to his behind to measure her distance. Lucy couldn't decide which was worse: the dreadful noise he made or the way he just wouldn't keep still. No amount of threatening could make him keep quiet or hold the position. Eventually, Matron had to make a small pile of pillows in the middle of his bed and lay him face-down over it. Sarah and Lucy were called on to hold a leg each while Matron held his arms. To teach him a lesson, Miss Clark gave him six hard ones and then, just as he thought it was over, two more stingers in rapid succession "just for luck', as she said, which had him screaming blue murder.

Winters was last of all. His first stroke was as hard as any so far; and although he jerked forwards and gripped the bed tightly, he uttered not a sound. Miss Clark laid the second stroke on harder, and this time he lifted his right foot slightly ("Why do boys always do that?' thought Sarah) and twisted sideways into the bed, his knuckles showing white as his fists tightened on the blanket; but no sound passed his lips. Miss Clark paused for a moment. The third made him squirm still further and hide his face in the mattress, but still he did not cry out.

"Been caned before, have we, boy?"

"Yes, Miss," said Winters through gritted teeth.

"Well, we ought to make it worth your while, then, oughtn't we?"

Lucy was aware of Sarah leaning forward in her seat, a look of the most intense concentration on her face.

Miss Clark took half a pace further back, shook out her right arm, raised and lowered her shoulder a few times, swished the cane through the air and then measured her distance again. This time she brought the cane a little further back and then whipped it across his bottom at terrific speed and with a more pronounced flick of the wrist. Winters gasped loudly through his teeth, his whole body tensing involuntarily. He began to twist as if he were trying to get around to the far side of the bed, then checked himself and resumed the position. Lucy noticed that where Winters had moved his face the bed was wet with tears.

Sarah, meanwhile, sat spellbound, gripping the edge of her seat. It seemed to Lucy as if she were willing him to cry out.

The fifth stroke did it. Winters squealed with pain and then the tears he had been holding back burst forth in a series of terrific sobs. Sarah relaxed her grip on the chair and sat back, an inscrutable half-smile on her face.

"Did we feel that one, boy?" said Miss Clark, pleasantly.

"Yes, Miss, pleeease, Miss, it hurts!" he wailed.

"Does it, indeed? Ready for another?"

"Oh pleeeease, Miss, I can't take another, I really can't"

"I think you can. Don't you, girls?"

"Yes, Miss, I think he can," said Sarah sweetly, a triumphant glitter in her eye.

Lucy looked at Sarah, and then back at Miss Clark. They both seemed to be expecting a reply. She glanced at the sobbing boy and saw the angry weals that crossed his bottom. She could not help but feel at least a little ashamed at her part in getting so many innocent boys into so much trouble. She tried hard to remember what Sarah had told her: every boy has done something he needs to be punished for; and an hour or so later he's forgotten all about his punishment. And what would the alternative be? To admit that she had lied, and that these fearful thrashings were merely a device to get her out of a scrape? To tell on Sarah, too? What would happen then? It really was too horrible to think of.

"I do, too, Miss," she said, hesitantly.

Miss Clark measured her distance one more time. "You see, boy, we think you can."

"Noooo, Miss, pleeease nooo!"

THWACK!

52. AN OLD ACQUAINTANCE

THE PHONE RANG at nine o'clock on a Tuesday night. Agnes decided it had to be one of Sandy's teenage friends, and decided to wait her daughter out on this one. The bell jangled her nerves five times before Sandy gave in and picked up the receiver. With the silence, Agnes relaxed in her chair, and returned to marking student papers.

In a moment, though, she heard Sandy, clumping down the stairs, and then the bored announcement from the hall, "Mom, it's for you."

"Who is it?" she asked, striding into the living room.

"Don't know," Sandy answered, shrugging.

Picking up the phone, she affirmed briskly, "Hello, this is Agnes Warner."

"Agnes?" came a glad voice, "This is Becky Fuller. Remember me?"

Agnes, surprised, lifted her fingers to her forehead.

"Becky! Of course. I haven't heard from you in ages."

"I know, I've been kinda out of touch," Becky rejoined remorsefully.

"Well, where are you? The last time we talked, you were in Alaska."

"Yeah. I left there after about another year, and for the past three years I've been in Kentucky."

Becky's voice continued to sound vaguely apologetic, causing Agnes to wonder if she had not been as welcoming as she ought. She decided, consciously, to turn up the warmth. "Kentucky! My gracious, you really get around. Are you with a church there?"

"Yep. Same thing. Music director. I liked Alaska, but my mom's getting older, and I thought I ought to get someplace that was closer. She's still in Winston Salem, you know."

"That's right, I remember. Well, where are you right now? At home?"

"No. I'm here."

"Here?" Agnes exclaimed. "You mean in Atlanta?"

"Yes, at the Renaissance Hotel, you know, on Peachtree near Ponce de Leon." The prospect of immediate contact, as usual, left Agnes uncertain. She liked Becky, but, at the moment, she wasn't much in the mood for visitors. Still, she realized she had little option. "Sure.... Well, how long are you going to be here? Can you get out to Decatur?"

"That's what I was hoping, if it would be all right with you."

"Well, of course it would. It would be terrible for you to come to Atlanta and us not get together."

"I'm at a conference, but I'm also taking a little vacation, so I don't have to leave anytime particular."

"Great, that's just great." Agnes crinkled her brow, thinking. "Well, let's see. Tomorrow's not good. But you know what? Thursday we're having a morning meeting, and I'm off in the afternoon. Could you come for tea?" "I'd love it." "About three-thirty, or four?"

Agnes was relieved when Thursday afternoon finally came round. She got home at two, and took the trouble of baking fresh scones, Then, in a fit of neatness, she scrubbed the kitchen counter, before going upstairs to freshen herself and change from her teacherly skirt and blouse into a housedress. She was still primping at her mirror when she heard the doorbell ring.

Becky hesitated just a moment when the door opened, then came eagerly to Agnes's open arms. They embraced naturally, but with a longer, closer hug than Agnes was used to, though she found nothing unpleasant in it.

"Goodness, gracious, come in here and let me look at you," Agnes exclaimed cheerily, drawing the young woman into the foyer. "Why, you haven't changed a bit. It's like you were back in school."

Becky colored slightly, and looked down, not knowing what to say. Finally, she managed to meet Agnes's gaze. "It's really good to see you again. For years I've been meaning to call."

"Well, why didn't you then, foolish girl. You know I'm always happy to hear from you."

"I know. It's just that... uh, you know. The days go."

As they stepped into the living room, Agnes noticed that Becky's figure was sturdier than it had been, but not in the way of added weight so much as in seeming to be firmer, stronger.

"I wonder," she thought, "if she's become one of these 'health club people'?"

First relationships are amazingly tenacious. When a former pupil gets together with an old teacher, no matter how many years have passed, it is the teacher who asks, the student who reports. Becky's report went on for nearly an hour, until Agnes remembered her duties as hostess and invited her into the kitchen for tea.

Placing her guest at the breakfast table, she moved easily to put the kettle on, and to drop two tea bags into her special Minton pot she had taken from the china cabinet for the occasion. Neither said anything for a few minutes, and the silence was becoming noticeable when Agnes heard Becky remark, shyly, "You really look good; you know that?"

Agnes looked up, slightly flustered and smiled.

"I mean," Becky continued awkwardly, "I thought you might be an old lady by now, and you're not." The rosy tinge on her face deepened. "I mean, not at all."

"Well," Agnes responded lightly, "I'm certainly getting in that direction."

"No, you're not," Becky said, almost fiercely. "Not even a little bit."

"Thanks. That's nice to hear."

The younger woman seemed to be under some kind of self-directive. "When I was in school, I thought you were the most beautiful woman I had ever seen."

"Becky!" Agnes laughed. "I didn't know you suffered from such severe delusions."

"Oh, don't be modest. You know you're a beautiful woman. Old Mr. Simpson used to slobber just to see you walking down the hall."

Agnes laughed again. "Poor Mr. Simpson. His options were so limited, he would have been aroused by anyone out of the grave."

"I had a terrible crush on you. Did you know that?" Agnes looked at her levelly. "How do you mean 'crush'?"

"A schoolgirl crush. You were elegant, and beautiful, and sophisticated, everything I wanted to be myself, and knew I could never be."

"My gracious, child, you really were in a limited world then, weren't you?"

"I was. But I wasn't wrong about you. Nothing I've seen since has caused me to change my mind."

Agnes began to feel uncomfortable, at the same time admitting to herself that she liked the flattery. She placed the teapot on the table, and carefully poured two cups.

"We're very impressionable in school," she said, "and pretty much see what we want to see. That's the wonderful and the terrible thing about being a teenager."

Becky laughed. "Yeah. It's a kind of insanity. That's why I was anxious about coming this time. I was afraid all the magic might be gone from you."

Normally, Agnes would have brushed such a remark away. She was a beautiful woman. A part of her knew that, though it was something she didn't think about much. She had had enough experience with suggestive remarks from men to know how to fend them off. But this afternoon a tiny nugget of adventure began to form in her heart, so, instead of dismissing Becky with light diversion she asked simply, "And?"

"It hasn't," Becky answered. "It's just as strong as it ever was."

Agnes paused, gazed steadily at Becky for several moments, then reached to take her hand.

"Becky. I... uh... I sense you'd like to talk about something more than gossip. And that's all right. But, I have to say that I'm... uh... I'm pretty much what you see. I don't have... I'm not..."

She trailed off, unable to complete the thought.

Becky looked at her, and smiled. "It's not like that. I'm not like that. I still like men," she added. "If that helps."

"I see," Agnes responded, relieved.

"But you're right. There is something. Maybe even worse."

"All right. Want to tell me about it?"

"Yeah, I do. That's what I had on my mind in coming here. But, before I do, can I get you to promise something."

"I don't know."

"Will you promise to just hear me? And not answer right away? Just let it roll round in your mind for a while? I'll call up tomorrow and see what you think."

Agnes deliberated for quite a long time. "I guess I can promise that. Sure. Why not?"

Becky breathed a great sigh, and for a long time the two women sat quietly, sipping their tea.

"Do you remember," Becky asked finally, "the afternoon you kept me after school because Linda Baker and I kept giggling and disrupting the lesson?"

Agnes smiled, and shook her head. "I really don't. There have been so many giggling girls I've had to keep after school."

"You kept Linda too. But you let her go first 'cause you thought I was the instigator."

"Was I wrong?"

"No, you were dead right about that."

"Well. That's a relief. I'd hate to think you had been resenting an unfairness all these years."

Becky linked her fingers and squeezed hard. "After Linda left, you said something. If you don't remember the afternoon, I don't guess you remember that either?"

"Fraid not."

"You said... these were the exact words. You said, 'It's a good thing for you, young lady, that it's not fifty years ago, because if it were, you'd find yourself across my knee. "

"Goodness! I said that? I must have been awfully provoked."

Becky grinned. "You were. You were so stern I was really terrified."

Agnes leaned back in her chair and smiled, still puzzled.

"How do you come to remember just what I

said?"

"Because I've thought about it every day, from then to now."

"Every day?"

"Yeah. That night in bed I lay awake thinking what if it had been fifty years ago, and you had spanked me? How would it feel across your lap? How much would it hurt? How embarrassing would it be? And the more I thought, the more it came to me that it should have been. It would have been right to be spanked by you. And not being spanked by you meant I was missing something, something almost essential."

Agnes leaned forward. "Becky, I..."

"Remember your promise," Becky prompted.

"All right," Agnes relented.

"The crazy thing is I still feel that way. I still feel it should happen, or else I will miss something that was meant to be. So, I got to thinking that we're both grown up women now, and, so, why not? Why shouldn't I come here and ask you to turn me bare bottom across your lap and wear me out? What would be wrong with it? You can refuse, of course, but I don't think it's wrong to ask. At least that's the conclusion I came to."

Agnes felt completely unable to speak, both because of her promise, and because she was unsure what to say even if she hadn't promised to say nothing.

Becky sat looking down before going on, now more quietly. "I don't know why I want it. I don't know what it means. I just know that I do, and that I can't see anything wrong with it. And, if I didn't ask you now, I never would, and then I would hate myself. And I hope you don't hate me for it."

This last she said in a rush, and ended, gazing imploringly at her former teacher.

"I don't think it's breaking the promise to say I don't hate you at all," Agnes answered quietly. "And, I'm glad you told me."

Then Becky began to cry.

Agnes watched helplessly for several moments before stepping round behind her, to place her hands on the shaking shoulders, and croon soothingly. "There, there. It's all right."

She stayed, massaging gently, looking out into space, while Becky's sobs quieted. After a quarter hour of silence, the younger woman reached for a napkin, stared down into it, and blew her nose vigorously. Shaking herself erect she said, "I've got to go now. Can I call you tomorrow?

"Of course. Why don't you make it about eight in the evening. Lawrence is away for the weekend, and Sandy's spending the night with a friend. She'll be off by then, and we'll have time to talk."

"Okay." Becky looked away, shyly. "Just one other thing. I brought you a present."

"Oh?"

Becky reached in her purse and brought out a box from which she took a flat wooden hairbrush. "It'll be useful even if..."

Her voice dwindled away as she passed it to Agnes.

Agnes took it naturally, saying simply, "Thank you."

Then, Becky was gone.

Agnes glanced at the clock. The visit had lasted not even an hour and a half. Yet the short appointment seemed to have brought her to the verge of another world. She poured herself a cup of tea and sipped it thankfully, trying to empty her mind of everything except Becky's anxious face as it had revealed its secret. Agnes had a well-ordered mind, so she didn't have to think long before she found the question resolving itself into three parts. Was it wrong for Becky to ask? For a person of Agnes's deeply moral nature that was naturally the first part to arise. It was unusual, of course, some would even say shocking. But was it wrong? Agnes was not so naive as never to have heard of the desire Becky was expressing. She had not encountered it in real life, had never expected to. But, in reading of it she had never felt the need to condemn. So, why should she now? Gradually this part became a certainty. There was nothing wrong in Becky's request. Could she comply? This was more perplexing. Not having considered the act, at first she was unsure. Yet, she quickly saw there was nothing complicated about it. Furthermore, it wasn't an entirely foreign act. She had herself been spanked when she was a girl. Everyone was spanked in those days. To say she was incapable of performing the act would be absurd. In this case, pure common sense provided the answer.

Finally, how would she feel about it? Here she had to face a surprise. As soon as she discerned what Becky was leading to, she had felt a thrill run through her. And, when she was sure, the thrill had flowered into a warm feeling of anticipation. Inexplicable as it seemed, she was charmed by the vision of Becky across her lap, waiting fearfully to be smacked. She couldn't any longer doubt herself. Yes, she would enjoy spanking the girl, enjoy spanking her soundly.

There was one small thing: Becky must understand that if this were to be, it had to be real. Agnes felt a shudder of revulsion at the thought of a play spanking. She had no better grasp of why that seemed odious than she did of her attraction to real punishment. Yet she was as sure of her feeling on that score as she had ever been of anything. Becky must be told that if she wanted the experience she had to be prepared for a sore bottom.

Agnes picked up the hairbrush, studied it carefully, then smacked it briskly against her thigh. Through the material of her dress she could feel the sharp sting spreading intensely. She waited a moment, then lifted her skirt to watch the rosy mark define itself. Placing her hand on her leg, she felt the heat pulsing into her palm. "Yes," she mused, "this will do nicely."

Becky, in her rental car on the way back into town had begun to sob again. "Have I made an utter fool of myself? What if she won't even talk to me when I call? What if she tells me I should seek help?" Or, what if she says we shouldn't speak of this anymore? Or—my God!—what if she says yes?" She was in such a state by the time she got to the parking garage she had to sit half an hour in the darkness before she dared to enter the brightly lit lobby.

All through the next day both women had little on their minds other than the coming conversation. Agnes had to take herself firmly in hand to listen to what her students were saying. As for Becky, she scarcely left her room, merely lay on the bed, staring at the ceiling, with little tremors running up and down her spine.

The call came promptly at eight. Agnes was waiting in her bedroom, where she had been relaxing for an hour, since Sandy had got off to her friend's house, running over in her mind how the conversation might go. She wasn't at all sure how Becky would be, but she felt she could handle her end of the talk fairly well. She had even committed some phrases to memory. "Agnes? This is Becky." "How are you this evening?" "I'm all right, I guess. To tell the truth, I've been miserable."

"Becky! You shouldn't have been. That was foolish."

"I've been so worried, wondering what you might be thinking of me."

"I told you, didn't I, that it was all right to say what you did, and that I wasn't offended."

"Yes, but ..."

"But nothing. When I tell you something, I expect you to listen. Understand?" There was just enough teacherly sternness in Agnes's voice to send Becky back to the sixteen-year-old she had been, leaving her able only to mutter, "Okay."

"Now, do you still want an answer?" Agnes asked. Becky felt a great hope rising. "Yes," she said anxiously. "Yes, I do." "Well, if you're sure about what you said, I think I could take you in hand as you asked. But I want you to be very clear about one thing?"

"Uh... What?"

"If I do this, I'm going to do it just like I were an old-fashioned mother or schoolmistress, and you were a girl who had misbehaved pretty seriously. And that means, young lady, that you'll end up with a well-spanked bottom. It won't be just a token punishment."

The voice at the other end of the line was silent.

"You hear?" Agnes asked firmly.

"Yes ma'am," came the answer, dropping unconsciously into the patterns of twenty years before.

"Well, are you still of the same mind?"

"Oh, yes," Becky responded breathlessly.

"All right. Now, do you have plans for this evening?"

"No. No, not at all."

"Fine. Then I would like you to come out here and spend the night with me. I'm alone, so we can have plenty of time together. How soon can you come?"

"Oh, I ... uh," stammered Becky. "Uh, right away."

"Okay. Then I'll expect you here by nine o'clock. Don't be late."

"I won't. I'll be there. Uh... are you sure it's all right for me to spend the night?"

"I said that I wanted you to spend the night, didn't I?" came the answer in a measured tone.

"Uh... yeah... well, okay, I'll he there."

"I'll be waiting for you," Agnes said, then placed the phone on the receiver.

She got up, went into the bathroom, undressed, and stood in her underwear, brushing her hair full about her face with the brush Becky had given her. Finishing, she stood sideways to the full-length mirror on the door and studied her figure. "Not bad," she thought to herself, "for an old lady." She took off her bra and turned to face her image, glad, as usual, to note that her breasts were still full and firm. Padding back to the bedroom, she laid the brush prominently on her dressing table, and pulled on a thick flannel gown. Slippers and robe finished her costume. She turned off the light, closed the door, and went downstairs. She sat in the window-seat looking out on the driveway, waiting for Becky. She had no desire other than to watch and to wait. Becky had said she would be there in less than an hour. But the time didn't matter. Agnes was content to wait quietly.

She almost wished Becky would be late, giving her the chance fully to drink in the dark and the anticipation. In the event, Becky was punctual. The little rental Chevrolet rolled into the drive at five till nine. The headlights went out, and then there was a long pause before the door opened. Agnes waited patiently, still content.

Finally, Becky got out, holding a small overnight bag, and started hesitantly up the walk. Agnes didn't move, waiting for the bell. She realized that Becky was standing on the porch, summoning her courage, and smiled at the thought. "Let her stay as long as she wants," she whispered to herself. "She'll have to come in sooner or later." Another five minutes, and then the bell did sound. Agnes got up and walked easily to the door.

"So, you're here," she said coolly, as Becky stepped into the hall.

"I'm here," Becky answered quietly.

Agnes took the small suitcase and set it by the staircase. She placed her hand on Becky's waist and guided her toward the living room.

"Step in here, in the light. I want to have a look at you." Placing Becky in the center of the room, she moved to the side of the sofa and leaned against the arm. Becky stood, looking down, her hands limp at her sides.

"Turn around," Agnes ordered.

Becky obeyed.

"You look very healthy. Is that right?"

"Yes," Becky said over her shoulder. "I've been fine." Agnes studied the figure for a minute or so before stepping around to lift Becky's chin with her hand. "A girl like you is in need of correction every now and then, isn't she?" she said quietly.

Becky lowered her eyes. "Yes ma'am, I guess so."

"I don't think there's any doubt about it. So tonight I'm going to punish you, both for the little snip you were when you were in my class, and for not getting in touch all this time. It really provokes me that you didn't call to tell me you had moved."

"I'm sorry," Becky said contritely.

"Well, in a bit you're going to be even more sorry, you hear?"

"Yes ma'am."

Leaving the young woman standing shyly, Agnes moved to the chair facing her and sat, legs crossed, tapping the toe of her slipper lightly on the carpet.

"I don't know why you think you can get away with being so thoughtless. You have a responsibility to the people who care for you to let them know how you are."

"I... uh... I wasn't sure you wanted to know," Becky said hesitantly.

"Well, I did, and I do," Agnes responded firmly.

She sat for a couple moments more before adding, "Gracious! I really am out of sorts with you. And I see no reason for putting this off. You come with me," she said, rising to take Becky by the wrist. "I'm going to paddle you now."

Becky followed her out of the room, up the stairs and down the hall. The first thing she saw when the light went on in Agnes's room was the hairbrush lying starkly on the dressing table. It sent a shiver coursing down her spine.

Agnes stepped to pick it up before seating herself on the side of the bed. "I'd like you to get undressed now," she directed quietly.

"Completely?"

"Yes, completely."

"Okay."

Slowly Becky began to remove her clothes. Now that the moment she had dreamed of was here she found that she was horribly afraid. She took off each garment carefully, deliberately, wanting to postpone as long as possible the event that was moving to reality. Still, regardless of the pace, she had to proceed, and the moment inevitably came when she found herself standing in her underwear, absurdly undecided whether her panties or bra ought to go next. For some reason she took the unorthodox choice, and slipped her panties down before reaching behind to unsnap the hooks of her bra. She let it slide off her arms and down onto the floor.

Agnes had been watching her steadily through the whole process. Becky turned, resolutely toward the bed, as if to say, "I'm ready," and was met with the directive, "Come here."

She stepped up to her teacher, boldly now, drinking in the sight of her. Agnes displayed the same expression she had on that afternoon twenty years before. The only difference was that she was even more beautiful now, even more terrifying. Becky felt her soul melt within her body.

Agnes reached to take her by the hips, and Becky, in her terror, noticed the manicured nails pressing lightly into her flesh.

"All right, young lady. You're going to be spanked now till you think your bottom's on fire."

Agnes pulled her down across her thighs. The sight of the white curved body over her lap sent a rush of sweetness into her breast, and she believed that in some mystical way the past twenty years had destined her for this moment. She picked up the hairbrush, determined not to betray the long years of preparation.

She raised the brush and brought it down sharply onto the right cheek of Becky's bottom. The flat wood smacked resoundingly against the flesh, and Becky trembled fearfully, pressing more deeply into her lap, letting out just the slightest gasp. At the second smack, the gasp grew louder, and with the third it transformed itself into a shrill little yelp.

"You see now I'm not fooling with you, don't you, young lady?" Agnes asked sternly, noticing with satisfaction the rosy marks beginning to emerge.

Becky managed a weak, "Yes ma'am."

"Well, there's a good deal more to come," Agnes announced, raising the brush again and bringing it down now with full confidence.

Becky let out a genuine wail.

"Cry as much as you like," Agnes said, adding two more stinging whacks. "It won't change anything."

"Oh! Please, Mrs. Warner!" Becky moaned, her legs fluttering helplessly.

"No Becky," Agnes asserted, still spanking the quivering flesh. "You've earned this. Begging will do no good."

The sound of the brush against the reddening flesh continued until a full two dozen strokes had been delivered. Becky's entire bottom and the backs of her thighs began to glow with scarlet ovals. The cries accompanying the cracks of the brush grew ever more shrill as the spanking progressed, the final blows producing outright shrieks: "Oh! Oh, no! Oh! Please! Please! Please!" Even when the thwacks had stopped, Becky's body was still gripped by sobs, while her hips moved convulsively against Agnes's thighs. It took some minutes for these to subside, and for the body to go limp and press down into the lap.

"There, there," Agnes soothed, laying the brush aside and placing her palms flat on Becky's burning cheeks. "All over now."

"Oh, it hurt so much," Becky sobbed.

"Well, of course it hurt. You didn't expect to get spanked without its hurting, did you?"

"But, I didn't know."

"Now you do.

That's what you can anticipate when you go across my knee. Understand?"

"Yes ma'am," came the trembling reply.

"I'm sure lots of girls have got worse," Agnes trilled, running her hand down Becky's spine. "So, come on now, don't be a baby."

"I'll try," Becky answered, still sniffling.

Agnes continued to massage the young woman's back, while gradually the tremors quieted. She felt the full weight of Becky's body, relaxed now, sinking into her. The room was quiet, pervaded by peace.

Agnes was content to sit as long as Becky needed, and the latter showed no sign of wanting to raise herself. Having waited the long years and endured more pain than she could have imagined, she found it glorious to absorb the sense of having been corrected, the reality of submission to the woman she had admired more than anyone she had known, the truth of having, in some curious way, paid a long-standing debt. Now the relief was ecstatic. She had tried to imagine how it would be, had ached to drink in the reward that was now hers. Yet, her most intense reveries had not approached the actuality of what she was feeling. It had happened! That was the fact pounding in her brain. Agnes—Agnes Warner—Agnes who represented everything Becky wanted to be—had commanded her sternly, with no hint of play, with conviction that had to be genuine, to present herself for a bare-bottom punishment which surely rivalled anything Victorian schoolgirls had endured. She knew now exactly what was meant when she read the promise in the old books: "I'm going to wear you out, young lady!"—for Agnes had worn her out, in a fashion that must have won praise from any of her predecessors.

Becky was grateful, so glowingly, meltingly grateful, she could imagine nothing other than continuing to lie across her mentor's lap, her bottom still throbbing, while she watered the patchwork counterpane with her tears. After long minutes Agnes broke the silence, speaking in a conversational tone. "You know, if I had been a teacher back in the last century, I suppose I would have spanked dozens of girls just as I've spanked you now. I wonder if that would have made for a better life?"

Becky didn't know what to answer. In truth, the thought of Agnes's spanking anyone else filled her with agony. But that was a feeling she had to keep to herself.

"No matter," Agnes continued. "I doubt that one time is any better, or any worse, than another. Still, I'm glad you brought it up. It felt right, somehow, like something I was meant to do." She paused. "Does that sound crazy?"

Becky shook her head, and managed to murmur, "No. Oh, no."

53. A Tabloid Intrusion

An interesting light is thrown on the universality of the need for and benefits of corporal punishment by the reaction of undercover journalists attending my lessons. Over a two-week period in February 1994 journalists from two papers, *The Sunday Telegraph* and *The News of the World* independently sent reporters to attend lessons.

Mr. Nicholas Farrell of *The Sunday Telegraph*, known to me as "Fletcher", arrived attired in obedience to the letter of the dress code but not the spirit. He was wearing an unkempt suit with his hair unbrushed, his tie askew, and his eyes red and bleary with a self-admitted hangover. Instead of beginning with a spelling test as usual, I spent the first half an hour talking to him about his scruffiness and the muddle and confusion I could sense in his mind, and the implications thereof of his collaboration with the prevalent mores of the late twentieth century. Asked to comment on what I had said he (rather stupidly) wrote: "Maybe my scruffiness is a reaction against the late twentieth century".

"Oh no!" I reproved him, "your scruffiness is a reaction in obedience to the late twentieth century!" And so to the first punishment, given I believe for said scruffiness, a spanking over the desk. With a pupil unused to corporal punishment, I often administer a fairly gentle spanking, explaining in a soothing tone that I consider that the function of discipline is to look after people. that a spanking is a somewhat motherly punishment and that the pupil is to try to accept the punishment and feel the security and relaxation that results from so doing. With Mr. Farrell I sensed a great tension and wariness. He was as taut inside as a tiger about to spring. He continually requested that I should not hit him hard; this while the merest taps were rhythmically beating on his backside. I assured him that I would not hit him hard and that my word was to be trusted. I described to him the sense I had of the tense animal in him, and he pretended he had once been set on and punished suddenly at school. I say "pretended" with no real knowledge of whether he was lying, but given that his wariness was in fact because he was a reporter doing a rather underhand job of work (and I suspect feeling rather guilty about it, because he could sense my capacity to give attention and kindness to complete strangers), I think it is safe to assume a lack of veracity in his childhood reminiscences.

He did begin to believe me that I would not suddenly attack him with hard strokes, and as he did so, he began to relax. I experienced a vivid psychic sense of him, and described it to him thus: "I'm beginning to get a very strong feeling of being like a mother as I give this punishment. This spanking is having a strong effect on you. I can sense you feeling like a little baby, and I get an impression as though the spanking is wrapping you up in cotton wool."

He said nothing; no word of affirmation or denial. He remained prostrate over the desk, quiet, soft, relaxed, accepting, no longer tense or distrustful and instead sinking into a blissful acceptance of the gentle, motherly punishment.

Something of a similar nature happened to *The News of the World* undercover journalist. He introduced himself as Bill Cork, and he was extremely nervous. He said that he had never "done anything like this before" and feeling that there was something a little dubious about him despite his friendly manner, I repeated at least twice more the assertion that "he did understand I hoped, that there was absolutely no element of immodesty or impropriety in my lessons."

After entering the schoolroom, I told him that as he was so nervous, I was going to give him a spanking, what I call my "settling-in" punishment for nervous pupils. As he bent over the desk and I laid my hand on his back I felt a great wall of tension. I had already told him about how he was very tense and stressful and how corporal punishment acted to drive out physical tension. Although he too was nervous, no doubt for similar reasons to Mr. Farrell, he at least was brave enough not to call out. The spanking was both gentle and rhythmic and Mr. Cork suddenly decided to relax and accept the punishment. I felt a great wave of tension pass from his back and though my hand and up my arm. After this his back felt very soft and was no longer tense. At the end of the punishment, he admitted that it had been very relaxing, and although he probably did not realise this, his whole face has altered with the discharge of tension and was softer of expression.

Whatever one's views on the benefit of corporal punishment, it is surely of interest to note that two separate individuals behaving in the ungentleman-like manner of the modern mass media Mafia should respond so definitely and absolutely to a gentle smack. Let me close by saying that the little boys concerned were obviously not smacked as much as they deserved in childhood and it is a great shame that my kindness of heart prevented me from suspecting their perfidy and giving them the six of the best they deserved!

54. MODERN THOUGHTS ON SPANKING

HOW SHOULD THE spanking be carried out? With the hand, insists the writer Tony Duvert. "A bare hand and bare buttocks achieve perfection in this field." It is not usual to spank each buttock separately. It is not a question of beating one and then the other, you beat across both of them at once. The blows administered should compress and shake up both buttocks with firmness and speed, "with all that is beneath them and everything that imbues their fat and skin with this pleasant and fluid grain, this luminous perfection that has killed off all the painters who have contemplated it. In fact these smacks, slaps or shakings are concerned principally with the cleft, the division between the buttocks. And willy-nilly they come together like a seismic shock or the trembling of a jaw over the child's anus, which is a ring like the tyre on a little car, its suspension at that age being especially adaptable and labile. The entire nervous system will be stimulated by these stinging vibrations and the genital organs will be definitely aroused, sometimes even calmed." So, Duvert concludes, spanking is or should be a pleasure. It is close to sodomy. Only the axis of the blows is different... Which is to say that beating is not always as barbarous as people maintain and can even seem particularly cordial.

No, not at all, in any situation and on any pretext, should one spank children, replies Jacques Serguine, in Eloge de la fesseé (In Praise of Spanking). And why not? Well, in the first place there is no room. "Their bottoms, which are very attractive, are still so small, you see." In the second place, it hurts them. It has to be said that Serguine is a monomaniac about spanking. He too has evolved a delightful theory about it, which applies particularly to the woman he loves and who loves him. Of course he has not adopted this habit of spanking Order to punish her, and he objects strongly to the proverb which runs: "if if you don't know why she knows why." No, it's not to silence her, triumph over her or humiliate her, it's in order to love her more. This beating is not for restraint but for acquiescence. A beating, says Serguine, is only one of the gestures of love. For the derriere in general, and that of his wife in particular, dazzles him, amazes him. "It could be said that it leaves me thunderstruck, it's sparkling and soft, it unleashes my hunger and thirst, in fact it drives me into a rage. It turns me into a madman, a creature who has been turned inside out, like a rabbit being skinned, a cannibal." That is what he says. As for knowing whether he would agree to being beaten in his turn, Jacques Serguine notes somewhat soberly and without great enthusiasm: "If ever the woman I love decides to do so, well, why not?" In any case he doesn't believe that one should carry out a spanking just like that, on the spur of the moment, on an impulse. It should be done in accordance with extremely precise rules which he has drawn up in order to transform spanking into a work of art.

In the first place, when should you spank? The best thing is not to spank in a moment of anger, for spanking depends on feeling, not ill-feeling, and you should not spank in too irregular a fashion. So he decided to spank his wife every Friday. Friday, he says, is a good day.

What position should one adopt? Simple: the woman has only to turn over, or he can turn her over himself, like a warm pancake. He places her on her stomach across his knees. In this position her wonderfully spherical little derriere stands up in an unforgettable, harmonious and provocative fashion. As for her, she tries to get things on a more equal footing but in fact she is secretly delighted.

What about her knickers? For, according to Serguine, the woman one beats should be neither dressed nor standing, but neither should she be naked, that is totally naked. "It seems to me clear that the purpose and meaning of the spanking depend on the act of leaning over, bending down and on the act of undressing: I mean, to be even more precise, partially undressing the part involved in the spanking.' He is very demanding too about the fabric and the colour of those "catastrophic, confusing, overwhelming little knickers." He wants the fabric to be as thin as possible, but not transparent or barely so, as soft, plain and smooth as possible: that, he says, is what suits his meticulous madness. For in this way it imitates, or at least does not insult the velvety moistness of the skin. In any case, the most erotic colour, in smooth fabric at least, rather soft and silky, remains white.

How should one undress her? First of all by pulling down those tiny knickers, as though one is removing, with exquisite suffering, a layer of skin from one's own heart. Take care not to remove them completely, so that they can go on serving as a frame or a case for the derriere. Many other people have insisted on the importance of what surrounds the buttocks, whether it consists of stockings, leather thongs or the garland of thorns as in the case of Sade's Juliette. The surroundings of the buttocks supply them with a halo. "So," writes Serguine, "inserted between the halo and the other little crumpled rolled-up skirt, the dazzling and moist derriere, pale and radiant, seems to be offered in entirety, almost tense, at once innocent and provocative, weak and tender like children, and, like them also no doubt, unspeakably proud and perverse."

After the knickers have been taken down, how should the spanking be administered? As simply as possible, moving from one part to the other of this delightful derriere, from top to bottom, from left to right, cheek against cheek and so on. One then reaches, says Serguine, the very moment when the woman one is spanking begins to cry. These feminine tears are the irrefutable proof that the spanking is a success. There are others: the sound first of all. A woman's derrière is certainly not a drum, but the spanking should provoke certain sounds. She can respond to them by uttering a brief stifled cry. Then comes relaxation, abandonment, the moment when the woman accepts the spanking and loves it: her behind softens, and opens out too, very calm beneath the stinging rain of blows.

Finally, and above all, this graceful and disturbing bottom becomes scarlet, it assumes the velvety and burning hue of a light-coloured raspberry in the sunshine, which makes Serguine say that he can still feel this spanking in his hand. This is the moment when one gathers up the woman in one's arms, when quickly and carelessly one undresses her, when one throws her down anywhere flat on her back or on her stomach, when the man's sex can burrow right into those dunes of yielding and voracious flesh that the spanking has brought together.

There is one more resource, the hairbrush. Unlike Erskine Caldwell in *God's Little Acre*, Serguine regards its use, of Anglo-Saxon origin, apparently, as totally heretical, whether you use the handle or the bristles. For the hairbrush only retains the flagellant and repressive aspect of a spanking, depriving it thus of its carnal side. No, spanking is carried out with the hand, everyone agrees on this point (except in Singapore, where it is still used as punishment with the birch). Brisk or not, prolonged or short-lived, a spanking should be somewhere between a blow and a caress, one could allege that it begins and ends half-way between the two as though it began and developed on what medicine calls the threshold of exquisite pain.

55. AN AMERICAN LADY'S TESTAMENT

THE BEST PUNISHMENTS are those which fit the crime. In this case there is nothing better than the safe, but reliable old fashioned method of washing out of his mouth with a foul tasting bar of soap. I realise most of you have heard of this method, but have probably little experience with it either. Therefore, a few words of advice are in order. Have him kneel by a sink (the kitchen or bathroom sink will do fine) and stick his tongue out while you thoroughly lather up a bar of soap. Now, briskly rub the frothing bar of soap back and forth across his outstretched tongue for a few moments before telling him to open his mouth wide enough to place the bar firmly into his mouth. Have him wrap his lips around the bar of soap and hold it there for a few minutes before removing it and allowing him to rinse out his mouth. You may be sure this will not be an experience he wishes to repeat. The foul taste of the soap will serve as a constant reminder for him to watch his language.

A large measure of self discipline is essential in order for you to become a disciplinarian in your marriage. Being a good disciplinarian is not easy and can only be accomplished with your direct, active involvement in your husband's life. The importance of being consistent and the necessity of carrying through with a punishment can be very demanding at times and require great will power and energy to accomplish. The traits you will acquire as you learn how to be a disciplinarian will benefit you in every area of your life. The truth is that you will both gain from the experience of discipline.

Rules are important. They define the limits of behavior and provide the order and cohesion he needs in his life. The rules you set must be sensible, easily understood, and strictly enforced. The rules you wish to set must be spelled out and agreed upon before they are implemented, along with the consequences for violating them. Don't set any rules that you can't abide by yourself. You lead by example as well as strength and you must be fair to be credible. Domestic discipline is a two-way street.

Once agreed too, the establishment of behavioral goals along with the rules put in place to assure their attainment are spelled out, putting them in place requires both common sense and some serious thoughts about creating the right environment in your lives to assist you in attaining your goals.

Common sense is the wisdom called upon to develop and use discipline. It will assure you that your discipline will work and that it will always be tempered with love and understanding. Your maternal ancestors knew everything one could possibly know about the need to establish good behavior and the best ways to achieve it. They possessed a treasure trove of common sense that was developed over thousands of years and passed from one generation to the next without interruption until, sadly and mistakenly, being cast aside, with disastrous consequences, in the latter part of the Twentieth Century. Fortunately, the body of knowledge that common sense developed still exists and may be easily called upon by looking no further back than a generation or two.

Discipline cannot take place amidst chaos. It needs an environment consistent with its goals to work. That is why a structure must be built to allow its implementation and assure its success. Doing this requires taking a moment and stepping back to contemplate the past and the future. By taking that step, you can begin to see and evaluate where your lives have been and where you would like them to go. It will reveal obstacles placed in your path, by yourselves or others, that have blocked your progress through life in the past and allow you to overcome ones you have placed, as well as diminish the effects of those placed by others. By allowing yourselves this precious moment and honestly and openly discussing your dreams and aspirations during this pause, you gain not only tremendous insight, but an intimate understanding of each other you never before thought possible. This, in turn, will enable you to make adjustments in your life to establish and meet your goals in the future.

Don't move too fast. Work slowly and methodically. Both of you will need time to make adjustments. It took Bob and I years to grow together and develop the discipline that has delivered us so many benefits in our lives.

Discipline cannot exist in a home where only one party is willing to work at it. Even if your husband has asked you to be his disciplinarian, always keep in mind that no matter how much your husband may want you to discipline him, the reality of being required to obey your rules and suffer the consequences for failing to do so, will require a period of time for him to adjust. Surrendering a portion of his freedom, or more appropriately, the license to do as he pleases, will not be easy, even though he has agreed that it is essential and for his own benefit. It is important to remember, that he has spent much of his adult life doing what he wants to do, when he wants to do it.

In time, he will learn to surrender that license which was actually depriving him of true freedom, and allow discipline to take place and work as intended. Persistence and firm resolve on your part are required to see it through should he ever waver in his commitment. There will be times when he tries your patience and tests your resolve.

Beyond accepting obedience to your will, there are some other reasons for his resistance to your discipline that I will address.

Most men who seek discipline in their lives have done so since early in childhood. They have spent most of their lives thinking about what the realization of discipline might be like, without in many cases ever having experienced it. With the onset of puberty and the inevitable discovery of erotica, they begin to see their desire for discipline as a sexual one, which in turn leads them to develop powerful sexual fantasies about discipline. Disciplinary fantasies can be wonderful and lead to great foreplay. Foreplay can open a window to enable you to see deep inside your husband and can, like the lessons of life learned on the playground, be a great place to learn some important and practical lessons (like learning how to give a spanking) that can be applied later in life. Discipline as foreplay is not really discipline at all. It is just as the name implies, play. No matter how this play develops, and how elaborate it may become, all that transpires is for mutual enjoyment. No real control is ever surrendered and no real discipline ever takes place. While it may be exciting theater and great fun, it is a world apart from the reality and goals of genuine discipline.

Real discipline requires obedience to your authority and the acceptance of very real sanctions that are far from pleasurable to endure. Don't let the two become confused or they will undermine your efforts with your husband. The two types of discipline, fantasy and real, can both play important roles in your lives.

I have spent the past few pages sharing my views about bringing about discipline in your life and some of the difficulties you might encounter along the way with your husband. I haven't discussed the reasons why you might resist assuming the role of a disciplinarian in your marriage.

Your resistance is perfectly natural. For thousands of years the perceived role of women has been that of subservience to men. This is the first obstacle we face, and must reassess if we mistakenly hold that view. Most woman, myself included, were taught to believe men wanted women to be subservient to them. Most women tend to gravitate to this role during courtship and marriage despite the fact that we have served as authority figures for men throughout their childhoods and during their experiences with courtship. Women, by far, have the greatest role in raising and educating children in society. Women have also always held the reins of authority that governs courtship by establishing both the limits of opportunity and the rules of engagement. Well beyond these all important and traditional roles we have in society, we now engage and excel in every possible career including governing entire nations.

As women, our ability to lead and govern is unquestioned. We understand and know how to do it. We have thousands of years of experience and wisdom to lead us. Most men seek our authority and guidance, even those who are loath to admit it. Giving the man you love the benefit of your authority, leadership and guidance is something he will treasure. Authority is only alien to us when it comes to our husbands. Once you accept the fact that you are quite capable of exercising your authority, you now have to conquer other perceptions about how you see your husband and the worries you may have about how your position of authority will affect him.

All women like their men strong, courageous, protective, chivalrous and loving. A real man, in my mind, is all of these things and more. He is good-natured, kind, gentle, nurturing and at ease with who he is.

Men who need discipline in their lives are real men. They possess all the qualities we women admire and seek in our men. They come from all walks of life. Many enjoy positions of power and stature. What these men have that others lack is the courage to own up to their need for discipline and the strength to embrace it. You needn't worry that discipline will diminish your husband's self-esteem. If anything, it will surely elevate it. Your discipline will allow him to overcome the negative aspects of his behavior, teach him to be more focused and disciplined in all areas of his life, and provide him a warm nurturing place of peace and comfort in his life.

Another very good reason you may resist assuming the role of a disciplinarian with your husband is because you have been led to believe that corporal punishment (spanking) is a form of abuse. I believe that abuse involves one person ruthlessly imposing and inflicting their power over the weak and powerless in an attempt to degrade and debase. A spanking, given with love, is using your power to give power to the person you love. A spanking is an act and expression of love. That belief and knowledge is shared by anyone who has ever been spanked by a loving hand. It stings while being received and for a while in its aftermath, but when it is over, it leaves the clear and unmistakable feeling that the spanking was a powerful act of love given to prevent them from doing something that would harm them much more than the pain they felt while being punished. When you spank your husband, he knows that by being spanked, he can atone for his actions and will be redeemed by your chastisement. He will love you all the more in its aftermath. Spanking is a safe, simple and loving method of chastisement that clears the air, cleanses the soul, and eliminates the need for further retribution.

Finally, and perhaps the most troublesome barrier to discipline you and your husband will encounter as you bring discipline about in your lives, is the concept itself. You are likely to ask yourselves, how any concept so quaint, old-fashioned and uncomplicated can really work? How could anything so clear and simple, yet so far removed from modern beliefs ever be considered a serious option?

It is never easy to swim against the tide and that is precisely what you will be called upon to do by choosing the path of a disciplined life. The currents of the modern world are strong and running in the opposite direction of where you wish to go. We have been swimming against that tide for the greater part of our lives. It hasn't been easy and we have occasionally tired and succumbed to the strong currents trying to pull us off course. Our persistence is undiminished and our faith in the beliefs we share becomes more resolute each day as we see the rewards our discoveries have brought us.

56. AN EROTIC PUNISHMENT

"ARE YOU GOING to punish me, Josie? Are you going to smack my legs?'

Josephine nodded. She was tense. She didn't trust herself to speak.

"Sit up, then. '

Josephine sat up on the bed. Jackie lifted her knee, placed it on the bed beside her. She hiked her skirt up behind, up above her bottom. Deliberately she reached to unfasten her suspenders.

Josephine watched as she rolled down the top of her stocking to the knee. Her thigh was white, her skin smooth and unmarked. It seemed to fill the circle of lamplight. She offered Josephine her fair white thigh. Her knee touched Josephine's hip.

"I mark very well, I should say," Jackie said softly.

Josephine lifted her hand.

She looked at Jackie's legs parted before her, the neat, light coloured panties revealed beneath the gathered skirt, the fabric of them stretched at the crotch. There was a fringe of fine hair, red-gold, escaping from the hem around the mound of her pubis. Josephine could smell the odour of her sex. She fell back, dizzy, against the headboard. Her weals hurt.

"I can't!"

Jackie stroked her head. "Are we taking you too fast?"

"Yes.'

"Would you like me to strip? Shall I take all my clothes off?"

Josephine shook her head. Her neck muscles ached with tension.

She breathed deep, gulping air into her body.

She put her hand on Jackie's bottom.

Her voice trembled. "Come here over my knee," she said.

Jackie got up beside her, kneeling upright on the bed. Then she leaned forward, bending over on hands and knees, making herself a bridge across Josephine's thighs.

Her hair fell down around her head. She was dappled with freckles in the lamplight, all down her neck and shoulders, spilling down the back of her dress.

She lowered herself gently until she lay over Josephine's lap, stretched out across the bed. Her face was turned away. Josephine could see only the back of her head. She stroked her glorious wild red hair. Somehow that made it easier, not to see her face. Made it possible.

She pulled Jackie's dress up as far as it would go, halfway up her back.

"I'm going to take your knickers down now, Jacqueline," she said.

Did she sound stern?

Jackie did not move or speak.

Josephine took the elastic of Jackie's panties between finger and thumb of each hand. She stretched the waistband out and pulled it back and down.

The freckles ran on down her back, all the way to her bottom.

Josephine took a deep breath and lifted her hand and before she could change her mind, smacked her.

It sounded very loud. The soft flesh bounced beneath her hand.

Was that too hard?

She smacked her again, the other side.

Where the first smack had fallen, she could see a white print of her hand, with all the fingers clear. She lifted her hand and saw another one beneath it. The pale outlines were rapidly filling in a delicate shade of pink.

Again she smacked her, again.

Still she made no sound.

Josephine thought of Roy, when he had spanked her. She wished she knew how to do this, how hard, how fast, how many: how you could tell. She remembered feeling his hand moving around her bottom, never falling in the same place twice running. He had smacked her all over: on the swell of her buttocks, on both sides, above and below. He had smacked her thighs.

She smacked Jackie low down, where the bulge of her bottom curved in to the tops of her thighs.

Jackie gasped.

"Too hard?" murmured Josephine.

Jackie shook her head. Still she didn't look around.

Josephine smacked her again, in the same place the other side of the dark soft cleft.

Jackie's legs kicked and straightened.

Josephine smacked her again and again. She was falling into a rhythm now, slow and lazy. She was lifting her hand higher, bringing it down with more feeling. The white skin under her hand was a mass of indistinct blotches, pale pink at the edges rising towards red in the middle. Her hand was stinging.

Jackie lifted her head. She clung to the edge of the mattress. "Oh!" she cried. "Oh!" Her cries were cries of passion and relief. She arched her back. She ground her pelvis against Josephine's thigh. Josephine felt the hair rasping her skin, the moisture seeping through the hair.

She slipped her left arm around Jackie's waist, turning her bottom towards her as she smacked and smacked and smacked her. Jackie cried out, writhing on her lap.

Josephine planted her left hand firmly on Jackie's left buttock. The skin was hot to the touch.

Jackie spun around again, crouching astride Josephine's body, nuzzling between her thighs. Her red bottom bounced in Josephine's face. Josephine could see the marks of her fingers. She had done that. She had.

Josephine laid her cheek against Jackie's bottom. "Will you ever forgive me?" she asked.

"Never," said Jackie. ✻

The Time in Between

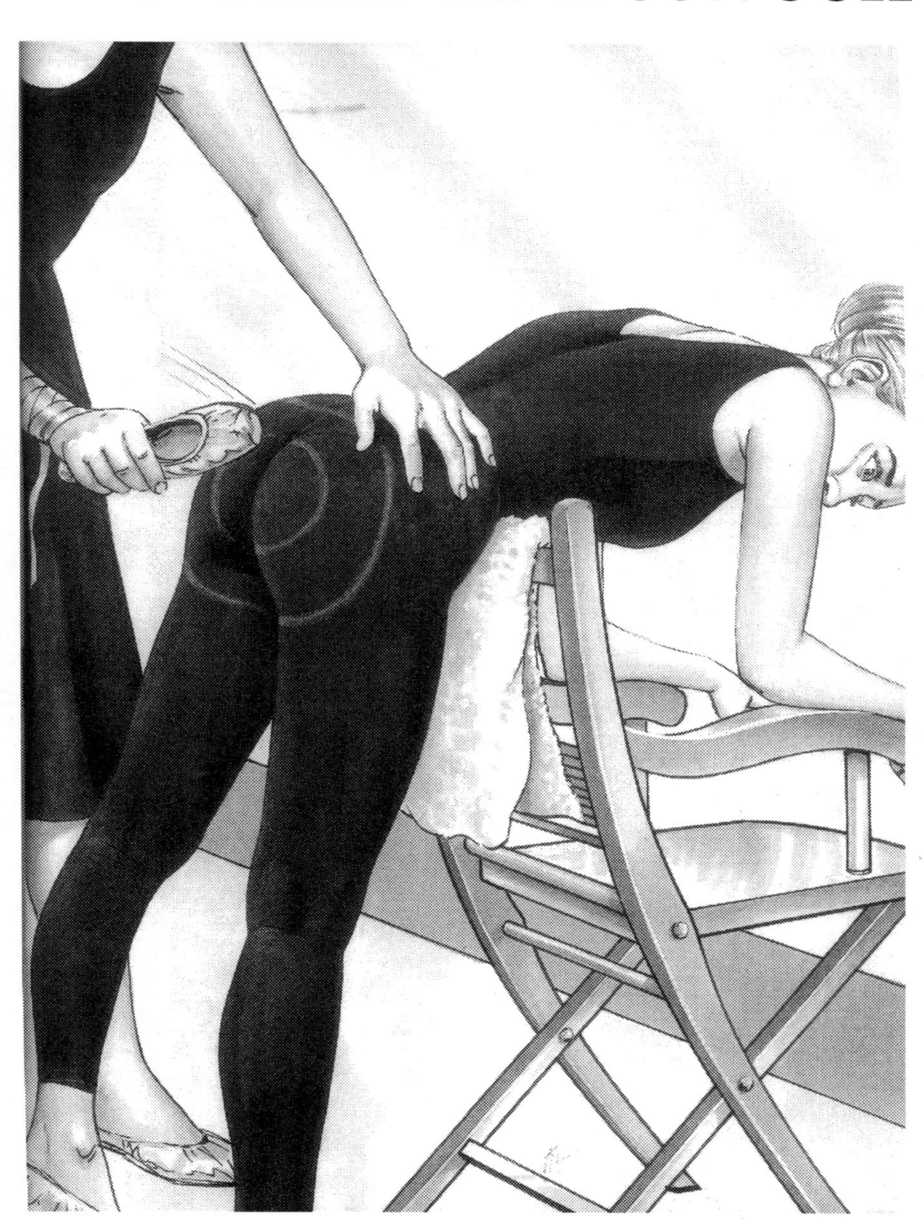

1. A PADDLING AT THE INN

HE WATCHED her long beautiful throat as she swallowed, and kissed her eyelids.

"Now listen to me, I want you to learn from this," he said. "Everyone here can see you, all your charms, you're aware of it. But I want you to be very aware of it. Behind you, the townspeople at the windows are admiring you as they did when I brought you through the town. This should make you proud of yourself, not vain, but proud, proud that you have pleased me, and caught their admiration."

"Yes, my Prince," she said when he paused.

"Now think, you are very naked and very helpless, and you are mine completely."

"Yes, my Prince," she cried softly.

"That is your life now, and you are to think of nothing else, and regret nothing else. I want that dignity peeled away from you as if it were so many skins of the onion. I don't mean that you should ever be graceless. I mean that you should surrender to me."

"Yes, my Prince," she said.

The Prince looked up at the Innkeeper who stood at the kitchen door with his wife and his daughter. They came to attention at once. But the Prince looked only at the daughter. She was a young woman, very pretty in her own way, though nothing compared to Beauty. She had black hair and round cheeks, and a very tiny waist, and she dressed as many peasant women did, in a low-cut ruffled shirtwaist, and a short broad skirt that revealed her smart little ankles. She had an innocent face. She was watching Beauty in wonder, her big brown eyes moving anxiously to the Prince and then shyly back to Beauty who knelt at the Prince's feet in the firelight. "Now, as I told you," the Prince said softly to Beauty, "all here admire you, and they enjoy you, the sight of you, your plump little rear, your lovely legs, those breasts which I cannot stop myself from kissing. But there is no one here, not the lowliest, who is not better than you, my Princess, if I command you to serve him." Beauty was frightened. She nodded quickly as she answered "Yes, my Prince," and then very impulsively she bent and kissed the Prince's boot, but then she appeared terrified.

"No, that is very good, my darling," the Prince, stroking her neck, reassured her. "That is very good. If I allow you one gesture to speak your heart unbidden it is that one. You may always show me respect of your own accord in that manner."

Again Beauty pressed her lips to the leather. But she was trembling.

"These townspeople hunger for you, hunger for more of your loveliness," the Prince continued. "And I think they deserve a little taste of it that will delight them."

Beauty kissed the Prince's boot again, and let her lips rest there.

"O, don't think I should really let them have their fill of your charms. O, no," the Prince said thoughtfully.

"But I should use this opportunity, both to reward their devoted attention and teach you that punishment will come whenever I desire to give it. You need not be disobedient to merit it. I will punish when it pleases me. Sometimes that will be the only reason for it."

Beauty couldn't keep herself from whimpering.

The Prince smiled and beckoned to the Innkeeper's daughter. But she was so frightened of him that she didn't come forward until her father pushed her.

"My dear," said the Prince gently. "In the kitchen, have you a flat wooden instrument, for shoveling the hot pans into the oven?"

There was a faint movement throughout the room as the soldiers glanced at one another. The

people outside were pressing closer to the windows. The young girl nodded and quickly returned with a wooden paddle, very flat and smooth from years of use, with a good handle.

"Excellent," said the Prince.

But Beauty was crying helplessly.

The Prince quickly ordered the Innkeeper's daughter to seat herself on the edge of the high hearth which was the height of a chair, and told Beauty, on her hands and knees, to go to her.

"My dear," he said to the Innkeeper's daughter, "these good people deserve a little spectacle. Their life is hard and barren. My men deserve it as well. And my Princess can well use the chastisement."

Beauty knelt crying before the girl who, seeing what she was to do, was fascinated.

"Up over her lap, Beauty," said the Prince, "hands behind your neck, and lift your lovely hair out of the way. At once!" he said, almost sharply.

Pricked by his voice, Beauty almost scurried to obey, and all those around her saw her tear-stained face.

"Keep your chin up like that, yes, lovely. Now, my dear," said the Prince looking at the girl who held Beauty over her lap and the wooden paddle in her other hand. "I want to see if you can wield that as hard as a man might wield it. Do you think you can do that?"

He could not keep from smiling at the girl's delight and desire to please. She nodded murmuring a respectful reply, and when he gave her the command, she brought the paddle down hard on Beauty's naked buttocks. Beauty couldn't keep still. She struggled to keep quiet, but she couldn't keep still, and finally even the whimpers and moans escaped her.

The tavern girl spanked her harder and harder, and the Prince enjoyed this, savoring it far more than the spanking he had given Beauty himself.

It was because he could see it much better, see Beauty's breasts heaving, and the tears spilling down her face, and her little buttocks straining, as if, without moving, Beauty might somehow escape or deflect the girl's hard blows.

Finally, when the buttocks were very red but not welted, he told the girl to stop. He could see his soldiers enthralled and all the townspeople as well, and then he snapped his fingers and told Beauty to come to him. "Now eat your suppers, all of you, talk amongst yourselves, do as you like," he said quickly.

For a moment no one obeyed him. Then the soldiers turned to one another, and those outside, seeing that Beauty was retired down to kneeling at the Prince's feet, her hair veiling her red face, her raw and stinging buttocks pressed to her ankles, were murmuring and talking at the windows.

The Prince gave Beauty another drink of wine. He was not sure he was entirely satisfied with her. He was thinking of many things. He called the Innkeeper's daughter to him and told her she had been very good, gave her a gold coin, and took the paddle from her. Finally it was time to go up. And driving Beauty before him, he gave her a few gentle but brisk spanks to hurry her up the stairs to the bedchamber.

2. The Discipline Shop

Madame Becker's Emporium was set three levels below the most fashionable part of Regent Street. An escalator took them smoothly down to the entrance, and conservatively-clad assistants bowed them inside.

There was a single vast, circular, carpeted showroom, with groups of chairs around elegant tables where visitors could sit in comfort while various items were fetched for their approval. Offices, cubicles and private rooms led off in all directions. It was warm, and well lit: the vastness of the showroom was broken up by glass display cases here and there, in each of which reposed a selection of items of discipline: six different punishment straps in buff leather with lacquered wooden handles, artfully coiled into a rosette and magically suspended as if in aspic from invisible wires; five so-called "permarods"—many-switched rods made, not of the traditional birch or willow, but of cunning composite materials, each actually a moulding of an original, natural twig but able to be reproduced ad infinitum, bound together prettily with ribbons of silk and velvet and posed as a "stand-of-arms"; and a dozen canes of green Japanese rattan elegantly displayed in a fan pattern on a bed of crumpled old-gold velvet with a scattering of dried rattan leaves. Lysis saw the discreetly-marked prices and gasped.

There were also various mannequins posed on stands: each of these modelled punishment clothing of one kind or another, and one was strapped well down on a whipping-block of rare hardwoods, beautifully carved and inlaid, furnished with gleaming brass fittings and a sliding drawer to contain the restraints when not in use, and supplied (as its label said) with appropriate snap-on cushioning in the purchaser's choice of washable fabrics. It was clearly something of a centrepiece, and was illuminated by carefully positioned spotlights on stands. The mannequin knelt across the block, its breeches pushed well down but its underwear primly in place and its shirt not yet turned back out of the way, strapped tightly into position at waist, knees and elbows with its blank, plastic stare well out of sight. A long and exceedingly bushy rod, made of real birch-twigs and dressed with black silk ribbon, stood nearby in a tall white-wood bucket (with no liquid in: Lysis peeped) and a yellow cane with a bound hessian grip lay quietly on a reproduction Sheraton table.

They were welcomed by the senior manageress, ushered to chairs, and offered refreshment. Lysis politely accepted a small *citron pressé* and the Demoiselle took a cup of black tea from a silver samovar.

"Show us some canes," said the Demoiselle, lighting a cheroot.

In the next half-hour Lysis learned a great deal about the cane. She discovered that the differences in the various grades of rattan contributed another parameter to those she already guessed: length and thickness. The denser (and dearer) grades of this invaluable Asian grass are greatly more punitive than the cheaper and more easily-grown kinds, being rather less flexible and with more mass for a given volume. The quality of cane purchased by the Home Office for judicial discipline was of a middling grade, and that purchased by most schools and reformatories cheaper still. "No doubt," sniffed the manageress, "there are budgetary requirements which oblige them to adopt such a purchasing policy."

"But such canes hurt less, do they not, for a given degree of force?" asked Lysis timidly. True to her sense of moderation, she did not wish to

begin at the severest level. "Might one of them not be better for a novice such as myself? Perhaps later on…"

"A charming and merciful approach, madam, which does you great credit and will also be appreciated by others!" With this heavy joke, the manageress clapped her hands and a selection of "lesser" (ordinary) canes was produced for her inspection.

"Take one, darling," urged her mentor, "and swish it about. They're all different, every one. See which one feels best in the hand."

Lysis stood up and did so, hearing the whish-whish-whish sound: she felt the elasticity, tried to estimate its bite. "I don't think I'm really able to judge," she said uncertainly, looking to the Demoiselle for advice.

The Demoiselle fixed the manageress with her eye. "Is that machine still in operation that I saw last time?" she asked.

"Certainly, *ma Demoiselle*," said the manageress smoothly. "I was about to suggest it. If both you ladies will follow me…"

"The machine" was in a side room and appeared to be a composite simulacrum of a pair of human hips, buttocks and thighs mounted on a box at waist-height. Furtively, Lysis touched it. It "gave" like (but otherwise did not resemble) human tissue.

"If you will just administer a single stroke, madam," said the manageress, going to a nearby console and flicking a key.

Lysis, holding her cane, advanced and took position. She aligned herself—mistakenly, as she was soon to discover—exactly at right angles to an imaginary line passing down the culprit's spine and emerging below the coccyx. She took aim. She drew back her arm. She let fly with all her might. There was a whine and a thick, smacking sound as the cane lashed across the artificial stern. She lowered the cane and looked to the others for comment.

The manageress was touching keys. "If you will glance at the wall display, madam…" she said. The display showed a representation, in colour, of the target as seen from directly astern at eye-level. The slightly curving line of Lysis's trial stroke showed up in red. But the thickness of the line and the saturation of the colour were visibly greater on the right buttock, and the stroke itself was too high. The overall line was good.

"You're standing too square-on, darling," said Delilah, leaving it to the shop-woman to explain the mechanics of caning, and the desirability of allowing, in one's stance, for the curvature, in flight and on impact, of a ordinarily flexible punishment cane of standard length. "The ideal, madam, assuming that the stroke is of reasonable force, is to take a position just where the far buttock becomes occluded by the near. Then you have only to align the cane on the near buttock at the correct height, and with good line, and all will be well. The tip will wrap around on impact so that both buttocks are struck with equal force at virtually the same instant."

"I always go by the sound," supplemented the Demoiselle.

As for height, the manageress said, the easiest way to observe these limits was to ensure that the culprit was bent at as near to an exact right-angle as could be contrived. ("Across a table, perhaps with a small cushion under the stomach, is an excellent position, madam, providing the subject remains still, of course!") Then all the caner had to do was to extend the line of the spine to an imaginary exit point—and aim a near-horizontal stroke a palm's-width below that point. "You will find, madam," she said, "that this corresponds to the fullest part of the derrière. Further strokes should be on or below that line."

"When in doubt, aim low," added the Demoiselle. "And keep your eye on the aiming point until at least one second after you've got home. Do you play golf?"

Lysis did not, but admitted to an understanding from the tennis court of the necessity of keeping the aiming eye fixed until well after impact.

The Manageress bowed in respectful acknowledgement of these well-known maxims. "Perhaps another trial stroke…"

Over the next ten minutes Lysis administered another eighteen strokes with a selection of canes. Her accuracy improved steadily, and even more rapidly with the last cane offered for trial. The final three cuts showed, on the display, as precise horizontal lines of equal colour saturation directly across the buttocks at their broadest part. Each was about half an inch apart—a perfect "group".

"Excellent, madam!" said the manageress.

"Well done, darling!" said the Demoiselle.

Lysis basked in this praise but was visibly out of breath.

"It's very tiring," she managed, smiling ruefully.

"That," said Delilah, "is because you gave that brute there"—here she pointed to the artificial bottom—"nineteen of the best at full stretch. If you cane so severely you'll seldom need so many strokes. But you don't have to cane so severely. You might use rather less force with scarcely diminished effect—and if you're going to give him more than twelve, you ought to."

"The intended recipient is a young gentleman, then?" asked the manageress with polite interest.

"He may become one, one day," smiled Lysis. "At the moment he is merely my pageboy."

(The observant reader will by now have noticed Anni's absence. Peace! We shall explain all in a moment.)

The cane, coiled into a circle, tied with ribbon, and packaged in an exactly circular container like a hat-box with a depth of no more than three inches, was put aside for later delivery. "Is there any further way we may be of service?" asked the manageress.

"Yes, she needs a tapette," said the Demoiselle. "A 'Tartar'."

"Which model, *ma Demoiselle*? I only ask because that company—and I agree they are the best—produces over forty different ones. Shall I show you their catalogue?"

"No, bring a selection."

This time choosing did not take so long. Lysis instantly "fell" for a tapette with a short ivory handle and a dark blade shaped like a rectangle twelve inches by four inches with rounded corners. It was made of a rubber and nylon composite, exquisitely encased in fine leather and cunningly constructed so that its thickness slightly decreased, across the full width of the blade, from handle to tip. This, as the manageress explained, was designed to neutralise the same problem of "tip acceleration" that required an efficient caning to be inflicted from slightly "round the corner". The upper end of the flexible blade travelled faster and further, in the final milliseconds, than the rest of the instrument, and reducing the thickness (and so the mass and therefore the kinetic energy) helped to compensate. Otherwise, Lysis was told, the result would be, as with the cane, an unequal application of force to the further buttock, and an "underdone" near buttock—unless this were manually compensated for by repeated modifications to the "point of aim" and the "angle of attack".

"You can always tell if you've done it properly because the whole bottom will be glowing evenly like a cherry after you've finished," said the Demoiselle, who favoured empirical methods, though she did not object to a scientific approach.

"Which is the best position for use?" asked Lysis, swishing the tapette through the air, hearing it hum, and marvelling at its perfection of balance. She longed to smack something with it, even the nearby dummy.

"Any position will serve, madam," said the manageress.

"Across your knees," said the Demoiselle. The manageress bowed to register respectful non-disagreement with this opinion.

"I'll take this one with me," said Lysis.

"Very good, madam. Shall I have it packaged?"

"No need!" said Lysis, and the Demoiselle laughed.

"Do I understand," she asked, as the manageress left to supervise the bill, "that your clumsy pageboy still remains unpunished for last night's affair?"

"He remains *unbeaten*," said Lysis, grimly. "Until I get home."

3. DISCIPLINE ON THE STAGE

MAN is discovered centre stage in armchair, relaxed, legs crossed. To his right: a Victorian chaise longue, upholstered in leather. He lights a cigarette. As he does so GIRL A enters right. She is dressed like a Victorian parlour maid—black dress, high button shoes, maid's cap. She carries a birch rod. MAN watches her as she crosses to the chaise longue and kneels on it, placing the birch rod near her feet. She bends forward, resting her head on her folded arms. She raises her skirt and tucks it above her waist. She is wearing Victorian drawers. Her rear faces the audience as she bends again. MAN exhales, still watching her. GIRL B is now lowered from the flies, slightly to the left of MAN. She is encased in a net of stout rope, which dangles five feet above stage level. She is wearing a bikini. Her wrists and ankles are tied, her mouth is gagged, and she is doubled up. MAN watches her descent with impassive interest. Rising, he taps the ash from his cigarette and addresses the audience.

MAN (easy, slow, conversational tone): Like most civilised people, I believe in democracy. I thought I'd better make that clear right from the beginning. I don't believe that any one person is essentially more important than any other. Or less. On the other hand, there are obviously differences between people. Some are taller or thinner or more redheaded than others. And some are what you might call more resonant.

He walks toward Girl B.

For example, Susan here has resonance. I call her Susan because that's the name of the character she is playing. Susan is a pert English girl of good background, who has been captured and trussed up by a tribe of savages in Sumatra. Indignities of many kinds—some nameless, others specific—are in store for her. Susan has resonance because many people respond to her. They love reading books about her or looking at pictures of her, or seeing films about her. From time to time she's trussed up by Martians or Vikings or Gauleiters. But she's always the same old Susan, always defenceless, always known to her admirers as a damsel in distress. And she strikes a chord. Can you hear it? (Pause.) It's a statistical fact that some of you can. That makes Susan a resounding person. Let's hope it comforts her in bondage—against which (GIRL B wriggles desperately) she struggles in vain.

He walks over to GIRL A.

This is Jean. Jean also has resonance. She is a parlour maid employed in a Scottish mansion during the middle years of the nineteenth century. The master of the house is an attractive widower, brushed with gray at the temples, and his regime is stern but just, like the glint in his ice-blue eyes. Jean has been caught stealing bottled plums, and now awaits chastisement at the hands of her master. She will now formally present herself.

GIRL A pulls down her drawers to mid-thigh.

She will now arch and offer.

GIRL A arches her back. Jean is now fully disclosed. From between her buttocks, the puckered rim of a virgin target tremulously peeps.

Like Susan, she is known in many disguises—as a wayward novice in an Irish cloister, or an indolent prefect at a strict finishing school. Many thousands of people respond to her plight, often quite vividly. Let us not blink at the facts. A high degree of resonance attaches to Jean. May it solace her in her humility, that lovely, well-built girl.

He takes up a position between the two girls.

Remember Lenin—the great Lenin—who said that the world was divided into the "who" and "whom"? He was talking about those who do, and those to whom it is done. Wouldn't you say that Susan and Jean, in their very different ways, were a classic pair of whom?

He turns and stubs out his cigarette. He then faces the audience again.

You'll have noticed I said they were different. But how do they differ? In my view very significantly.

He indicates GIRL B.

Have a good squint at Susan. This girl is where she is as a direct consequence of physical coercion. Brute force and nimble fingers have been at work. The principle of choice—the very heartland of liberty—has been rudely violated. It's an outrage to the human spirit.

He turns to GIRL A

Now let's take another look at Jean. She kneels

there—or squats there—in a posture that must be profoundly embarrassing. You might even call it humiliating. However, if the spirit moves her, she is at liberty to get up and go. Jean, the submissive household servant in temporary disgrace, is a free agent.

He picks up the birch rod and fingers it.

And she is free not only as a parlour maid but as a human being. The girl you are watching—the docile squatter—is Eleanor Brown. (Or whatever her real name*.) Born 1941, trained at RADA, professional debut with Oldham Rep—you can see the details in the programme. If Miss Brown, the employed female performer, decides now—tonight, this moment—to get up and leave the stage, there will be no reprisals. Neither I, nor the author, nor the director will hold it against her. She will return to the theatre tomorrow night with her professional reputation untarnished. Whatever happens, she is the master of her fate.

He turns toward GIRL B.

Susan, for all her resonance, is dependent on the will of others. (He shouts at the wings.) Take Susan away! Whereas Eleanor—aged 25, divorced with one daughter, favourite food lobster chop suey—remains her own mistress. She is free to stop blushing and go.

He moves closer to her.

Are you listening to me, Eleanor?

She does not move.

Eleanor—do you want to leave the stage?

She does not move.

For the last time, will you please make a sign if you wish to leave the stage?

She does not move. Pause.

As I was saying, I am a strict believer in democracy.

SLOW FADE TO BLACKOUT

4. Community Care

JANINE IS WAITING for me when I arrive at the office. String-thin in her navy-blue dress, the stockings thick and black, the heavy, low-heeled shoes gleaming as per regulation, and the tightly scraped-back hair making her look like a caricature of an old-time schoolmistress. The girl simply hasn't a clue—quite apart from those damned spectacles which she will wear. There's not a lot I've ever been able to do about Janine's ongoing sartorial self-destruct programme, so I simply smile sweetly as I sail in the door, parking my bag on the desk, and say:

"Morning, Jan. Had a nice weekend?"

"Thank you, ma'am, yes," says Janine, coming forward. She has her PDA already booted up, but I have not yet had my coffee. The wall spigot gurgles, then gushes black, faintly steaming liquid into my cup. I sip gently, turning away from the dispenser and sitting down at my desk. There are fresh sweet-peas in the vase—a pleasant sight and a delicious fragrance. Janine, of course—she has her good points.

"You have an easy schedule this morning, ma'am," she says, stabbing at the PDA screen with the stylus. "First—"

"Just a moment," I say, sipping once more at the coffee. Just right, for once. I take another mouthful—the last I'm likely to enjoy, or even notice, for Janine is beginning to look impatient, in her usual respectful way.

"Yes?"

"Nothing till twelve-forty-five," says Janine, consulting her PDA, "apart from two juveniles on Mother's Referral in Reception. Corporal Dean or I can deal with them if you like." She looks up at me expressionlessly.

"I'll look them over first," I say.

"The first formally booked-in contract punishment's the twelve-forty-five thing—a Workplace Referral." She stabs at her PDA screen. "Do you want to be briefed on that first or shall I continue?"

"Continue," I say, taking the last mouthful.

"This afternoon things are a little busier. At two-thirty you're at the Remedial Therapy Centre—"

"Which one?"

"Lawrence House. I'm not sure how many you've got—they had a disturbance over the weekend and the sentencing is still taking place.

"Then at four-thirty Mistress Ballard of Roscombe Park is booked in for private tuition. You remember? She's bringing both husbands with her."

"Both?"

"She's paying the extra," says Janine. "You did agree it at the time, ma'am, even though I…"

She's right: it's quiet for a Monday. Nothing—bar the kids—until just before lunchtime. Then an early-afternoon batch of canings at Lawrence House. They're fairly efficient there—not like some RT centres—and I might easily expect to be back at the Department in time for the free-lance work with Mistress Ballard. Most Ladies are ashamed to admit it if they haven't got what it takes in the discipline department (though many haven't, in my opinion, otherwise we'd get a lot less trade), and are willing to pay for discreet private lessons. Forty guineas per hour is my standard rate, though I know that Brenda MacMaurice over at Zone 14 charges fifty, and gets it. One of these days I'll put my own rates up.

Janine briefs me on the waiting juveniles, but I am only half paying attention. At around this time of the morning, if things are running to schedule, the Night Patrol returns—the girls on fire for their breakfasts—and then we might have something more interesting than a brace of unruly whippersnappers brought in by their mothers to have their seats warmed by the Big Bad Punishment Lady.

"Community Disciplinarian" is actually my proper title, but I—we—get called lots of other things. "The Bot Squad" is one of my secret favourites, though Janine says it's vulgar. In many ways we're almost exact opposites, she and I, which is the way things should be with Chief and Deputy. We complement each other—but in any case we're the only civilians in the place. The other girls all have ranks—they're seconded to us from the Police or Remedial Therapy Departments—but Janine and I are civil servants in the employ of the Community; and this is a Community establishment.

Janine puts the waiting-room up on the monitor. Two boys sit with their mothers, on opposite benches. Kids of about ten or eleven, neatly and conventionally dressed in dark brown shorts, white shirts, bow ties, short brown socks, and brown sandals. Neither of the mothers looks incapable, the way some undeniably are—the ones who bring in their offspring because they can't or won't do the job themselves. The main type of client—I assume that today's are typical—is the mother who drags in a naughty kid for topping-up, as it were; something a bit exemplary to underscore a particular offence or period of continuous bad behaviour. Well, that's one of the services we're here to provide.

Neither boy looks like he's going to give trouble. I delegate my powers whenever I can: it's good for morale. "You can do one, and Corporal Dean the other," I say to Janine, who brightens. "But I'll do the verbal." She nods and moves away, and a moment later I hear her talking to Tess on the phone. "She'll be there in half a minute," she says.

We go down to the lobby. Tess Dean is already there, smart and brisk in her dark-blue uniform, unbuttoning the wrists of her jacket. She is carrying two Number Six PTs ("Punishment Tapettes"—the rest of the world would call them paddles but for some reason the UK Ministry of Disciplinary Affairs has to be different). "Good morning, ma'am," she says, saluting. I say, Morning Tess, feeling fit? and then Janine opens the waiting-room door and we pass inside; first Tess Dean, then Janine, and finally, after a second or two, myself.

"Stand up!" This from Tess, in her best parade-ground manner. The brats leap to their feet—the mothers, naturally, remain seated.

Tess closes the door. I ask, sternly, "Which of you is——?" The boy nearest me—tall for his age, with black hair falling over his eyes and a flushed face—coughs and says, "Me, ma'am."

I turn to the other. "Then you are———?"

The blond boy with the thin, sulky face says: "Yes, ma'am." He glances uneasily past me—presumably at the brace of PTs in Corporal Dean's hand

I begin the peroration. It's standard, worked out over many such occasions until it covers all the bases. There's a variant I use when a culprit is on his (or her) Second Referral—then I take him (or her) into the Punishment Room and show him the frame, and the canes, straps and paddles lined up like soldiers in the implement closet. I draw attention to the four camera-lenses, there to record the event for archiving and possible public display if the offence has been particularly grave. I point out the padding on the walls, to absorb the sounds they are likely to make while "kissing the donkey". Then, when they're absolutely wilting, I take them back into the waiting-room and spank them instead—good and properly. It's very seldom kids are brought back a third time, but if they are... well, promises are made to be kept.

Both these two are first-timers; they shuffle their feet while I talk to them of their conduct, their attitude and of the trouble they are putting others to. The mothers look grim, and satisfied. One glances at her watch.

I look at the boys with a frown. Their expressions of alarm and woe are comical, but what must be done, must be done.

"You will now both be soundly smacked. Proceed!"

Janine steps forward and grabs the fair-haired boy firmly by the upper arm. Corporal Dean similarly takes the other. Each of the girls marches her client to a chair, and sits down: there is a standard procedure for this, as for all things. I wait only to see the unbuttoning begin—neither brat is making the least resistance and the blond one has already started to snivel—before I bestow my special smile (best described as "conspiratorial regret") upon the mothers, then leave. My status demands I depart if not personally engaged in punishment—it would undermine the authority of the actual punishers were I to remain.

Back upstairs in the office a minute or so later, I turn on the monitor. The double spanking is nearing its climax—both culprits are in full wriggle, with legs kicking and arms waving. The mother of the blond boy is stooping over him, speaking to the back of his neck while Tess's paddle addresses another part of him. Janine is thwacking away, coldly and accurately—her client is doing his best to lie still, but more often than not nature takes its course. The sounds from the room are growing shriller and shriller so I turn the volume down and go over to the coffee spigot. The next time I look it is over. Both culprits, eyes screwed up, mouths wide agape, heads thrown back (my staff have plainly done their usual sound job of work) are being buttoned up by their mothers in (for me) merciful silence.

I kill the display, and at the same moment the phone beeps.

It's Sergeant Myra Kelly reporting from the garage. The Night Patrol is back—with some trade. Two Yobs, two Sluts, out after curfew and caught in a stolen car. They've already been put in cells. Corporals Adamson and Piper are on their way up to report.

On cue, there is a tap on my door and Maxine and Karen come in, smiling and weary, still in their black night coveralls. I pour coffee for both of them and they flop into chairs to make their report—we're not needlessly formal here; that's not the way women work.

They'd had no trade, Karen reports, until 5 a. m., when in the course of a routine infra-red scan of a row of parked cars, Maxine picked up heat emanations from a four-seater. Karen had stopped the Department van a block further on, and they'd checked out the vehicle on the police database via secure microwave link. It had been reported stolen at 9. 00 p.m .the previous night. They'd walked back quietly, electric prods in hand, ready to bleep the fuzz if necessary.

Sure enough, there were two couples, one in the front seat, the other in the back. When Maxine had tapped on the window the kids had panicked and tried to drive away. The code for the Engine Authority Processor was of course already loaded into Karen's PDA, and as the car began to pull away she'd aimed the PDA at the rear numberplate and squirted, and a second later the engine died as the nullifying code entered the EAP and killed the spark. At the same time the doors locked. The kid brought the car to a halt—there being not much else he could Do—and then all four were taken into custody and put in the back of the van. You don't argue with a standard police-issue electric prod, and these four didn't.

Curfew breaking by juveniles—for they are all under 25—is well within the remit of this Department to punish, and we do it all the time. Car stealing aggravates the matter. Technically it's a felony, but under the Penal Reform Act of 1998 it's also one of a small class of offences which may be dealt with by us without the necessity of a hearing before the court. Three agreements have to be obtained before this can happen—from the Community Disciplinarian; from the Parent or Guardian, and from the culprit. Since the sentence of the court for this offence is very often corporal punishment plus a custodial sentence, most juvenile car thieves settle for what they often see at the time as the lesser of two evils

By this time Janine has returned and I ask her to begin this procedure. She sits down at her desktop terminal and starts to check out the IDs against the public database—it can take some time to pin down and contact every consenting person required. I give instructions for the prisoners to be given breakfast; if they want it.

It is now ten o'clock and, against initial prediction, the day is turning out to be busy after all. Time for coffee and a hot apple turnover from the vendomat. Janine takes her iced tea to her desk in order to continue the checking-out—she's already got the ID screens up and tiled; now she's hunting down the Parents or Guardians. I get on with some routine admin. work. The phone beeps twice during the next thirty minutes and I take both calls in order to avoid distracting Janine. The first is from Central Stores wanting to know if we need anything. We don't, but I have a pleasant ten-minute chat with Mavis O'Brien (the real reason she phoned, I think). The second is from the new Assistant Governor at Lawrence House, confirming the 2.30 appointment. It's a woman I don't know, called Margot Jaffee. Apparently Lawrence House has five of its inmates in cells. The Governor—Judith Mitcham, my predecessor in this job—has sentenced each of the rioting youths to eighteen strokes apiece. The frame has already been erected in the gymnasium, says the Jaffee woman. She sounds excited.

"Oh, and the Governor asks if you're all right for birch," she adds.

"They're to be birched?" I ask, in some surprise. Caning is more usual at RT centres.

"Mistress Mitcham thought it was appropriate," she says. "She assumes you have the twigs in store."

"Well, I haven't," I say, pretty sharply. "Judith must know we don't keep a lot of fresh birch in-house. I'll have to send down to Central Stores for some."

"Oh, we can do that," says Jaffee.

"Don't bother, I'll do it," I say, and hang up. I immediately punch in the code for Central Stores. While I wait for Mavis to answer I hear Janine saying "...It's much the best policy since it keeps your daughter's record sheet clean of endorsement."

Mavis answers, and I say: "I was a bit previous, Mave. Birches for five by two this afternoon. Can do?"

Mavis asks, what grade? and I tell her Grade Two—36-inches, nine switches per spray, total weight three and a half ounces. There's a moment while she checks her inventory and then she confirms. The birches will be with us before two o'clock, each a freshly-picked, properly sterilised rod trimmed and bound as per specification and supplied in individual clear-plastic bags. She's good at her job, Mavis. But then, so am I.

Janine says, into her phone: "Thank-you-so-much. Please stay by your terminal while I fax you the form for signature." She thumbs the touchscreen at the spot indicated and turns to me. "That's the lot," she says.

"All agree?"

"Yes."

"We'd better break it to them, then." I tell her of the Lawrence House requirement and what I've done about it. Then I go down to the cells."

"Yobs" and "Sluts" are not official terms, of course—they're Department argot for Bad Boys and Bad Girls. Yobs is "boys" backwards—young men whose social attitude is so backward that it constitutes an outrage crying out for correction. Sluts? Let's just say that one of the main things wrong with the old world order was the near-total debasement of young womanhood. They did it to themselves, no doubt about that, but the fashion and pop-music industries of the time actively collaborated. Well, that's all changed. The New World Order requires excellent behaviour and deportment at all times from its young men—and even better from its young ladies. Some idiot egalitarians claim this is unfair—they forget that most young ladies, if they put their minds to it, find good behaviour and serene deportment far easier of attainment (and maintenance) than young men.

The girl in Cell 4 is eighteen years old and dressed tartily in a brief lurex skirt and idiotic silver boots with preposterous heels. She wears no stockings—not even tights—and her hair is short and dyed a fluorescent orange. There is a huge silver earring in her left ear and her face is covered with paint. She has been crying, and the paint has run down her face.

I explain the situation: the felony of car theft; the misdemeanour of curfew-breaking; the choice that lies before her, of a court hearing tomorrow, or a thrashing within the next half-hour and a clean sheet afterwards. She weeps a little, swallows hard, and asks, what will the thrashing be like? How many strokes? What with? She spews all these questions out in a terrified rush. I tell her: it will hurt you and make you ashamed; you will receive one stroke for each year of your age, plus one; the implement will be a punishment strap of the standard weight and length for a girl of your age. I don't tell her it will be digitally recorded, or that she will be restrained across the frame. I don't specifically tell her it will be on her bare bottom, but I think she guesses anyway.

She agrees, weeping, and I give her the form to sign.

Then I say: "You will now be left alone for about twenty minutes. During that time you will remove all your clothes and jewellery. You will shower, and wash your face clean of that makeup. You will wash the dye out of your hair if you can. I advise you to make use of the toilet. You will put on the clothes which my staff will supply. You will then sit on your bed and wait until you are fetched. If you then cooperate, and take your punishment bravely, it will all be over very quickly.

"Any questions?"

"No, ma'am," says the girl, pale as a sheet.

I lock the door behind me and nod to the waiting corporal, who makes a mark on the clipboard. An orderly coming up behind with a large wheeled basket opens it and begins to sort through punishment uniforms.

I enter the second cell. The boy, age recorded as twenty, climbs slowly to his feet. He, too, looks ashamed and fearful. To him I say much the same. He asks no questions about what is going to happen. He has some sense after all. He signs without demur—having said barely a word—and I move to the next cell. Here the inhabitant—the second boy, of 21 years—is in blustery mood; even defiant. I do not rise to the sneers—I ignore them entirely—because I can see they are born of a desperate desire to retain his good opinion of himself until the last second. Courage? I prefer to think of it as a form of stupidity. In any case, he was the driver of the stolen car and must know he is due for a little extra.

"Twenty-four strokes with the cane," I announce. This is what we call a "solid" punishment and he blenches; then he recovers with another stream of near-abuse. I remind him that under the Act I am empowered to reduce the nominal award by up to fifty percent at my own discretion. Also—here I let my voice grow stony—I may increase it by the same proportion. The prospect of three dozen with the cane puts paid to my young man's bluster. He goes pale, and his knees give way so that he sits down hard on the cot. I tell him to be careful of his attitude and issue the instructions about stripping and showering. He nods, dumbly. I leave him deeply regretting his violent rudeness, and in terror of 36 strokes. In fact, I am perfectly sure that the nominated award of two dozen will be more than enough: I know my own skill.

The fourth prisoner and second girl, of 24 according to her sheet, is the worst—by which I mean toughest—of them all. With long, dark-red hair, black eyes and blood-red lips, she says nothing, but watches me with glittering eyes. I sense she is drawing in her reserves of courage and preparing herself to withstand the coming ordeal without "singing". I deliver the standard phrases, all the same, watching carefully for a reaction. There is none, just that snake-like unwinking stare. But she signs the form without a word, almost with contempt, a large, open, beflourished signature. She makes no response when I order her to strip, shower and change, and I wonder if she will prove to be one of the rare ones who have to be put by force into the required condition of cleanliness and clothing. Outside the cell, I tell the duty corporal of my suspicions and she undertakes to do whatever is necessary.

The cane for boys, the strap for girls—that's general practice, though circumstances vary. Corporals Dean and Donohue are laying out two of each on the side-table as I pass through the Punishment Room on my way back to my office. Rattan is no longer used for official canings. It's too erratic in growth, can't be produced locally and is very difficult to sterilise. The compound canes we now use are marvels of aerospace technology—each comprising a central core of one-eighth-inch epoxy dowel, wound tightly with flat elastic ribbon, enclosed in an impermeable sheath of very hard, black rubber, and bonded into a single ferrule under intense cold and high pressure. They can be manufactured to virtually any weight, diameter, length and Flex Factor, are whippy without being over-elastic, stiff without rigidity, and easy and quick to sterilise. They last for years, too—of our original "set" of 16 compound canes, only four have ever needed replacing, each time because of a fatigue fracture of the inner epoxy core. I too have been an afiçionada of good traditional rattan—I still use such canes for informal punishments where Department Rules need not apply—and to some extent I miss the whish! and crack! good rattan produces in action. Compound canes are virtually silent in descent—an almost imperceptible hum—and the sound they make on impact is more of a thwup. But they are deadly accurate in the right hands, and very effective in the purely physical sense.

Punishment Straps are manufactured by a version of the same process (the objection to leather, the traditional material, was on moral grounds). They are a laminate of two thin panels of epoxy fibre between three layers of vulcanised rubber, bonded together into a single flat sheet two-fifths of an inch thick, then sliced down the cross-section, like bacon, into strips, with widths varying from one-and-a-quarter to two-and-a-half inches. There are no tails. They are not floppy like traditional straps—held out at arm's length, a properly made compound strap (we call them swips, as a combination of "strap" and "whip" and also because of the noise it makes in action) will droop under gravity for about one-third of its length, like a dressage whip. Less stiff than a cane, it is nevertheless much stiffer than an old-fashioned tawse of the kind our grandmothers used, and therefore much easier to control. It can be aimed with precision, and the wraparound effect is much reduced. As a final touch, the bonding process is made more intense proportionally down the strap's length, so that the thickness of the weapon at the tip is rather less than at the handle. This increases the whip-like qualities, and also the physical effect. It is a very painful weapon—to my mind, every bit as excruciating as the cane, which is the more greatly feared.

We are now ready. I glance at the Punishment Room clock. Ten-fifty-one. Just myself, Tess Dean and Liz Donohue in the room—Janine is upstairs in my office, holding the fort (and watching on the monitor).

I say: "We'll start with——."

Tess and Liz are looking at me expectantly. All my girls are qualified to punish, of course, but they only do so at my discretion. Some Community Disciplinarians hog all the action to themselves and never let their staff polish their skills. Others are bone-idle, and delegate everything. The ideal, to my mind, lies between the two: I reserve the more serious punishments to my own right arm: this means the majority of canings and nearly all birchings; but when "lesser" implements are involved—the strap, the PT, spankings—I often let my assistants try their hand. I don't know how they're supposed to learn if they never get their chance.

Such a moment has now arrived, and we all know it.

Tess Dean is the best thrasher on the strength, save moi, but I may need her this afternoon, and besides, she's already had one turn this morning. Whereas Elizabeth Donohue is new—recently seconded from the police department—and has not yet used the "swip" in earnest. I smile at her and say: "You're on, Corporal Donohue. Nineteen of the best. Don't worry about the cameras, just do your job as you've been taught, and watch your timing. I'll count. Keep your eye on me in between strokes. Remember the hand-signals? Good. Fetch her in."

Half a minute later the girl from Cell 4 appears in the doorway, framed between my two girls. Her face is pale and clean—she has obediently scrubbed off every last trace of the filthy "make-up". Her hair is still lurid orange—presumably a fast dye—and damp; but the horrible earring is gone. She is wearing the regulation punishment smock of dark brown calico, knee-length, with short sleeves. No stockings or socks, just a pair of Turkish-style canvas slippers. Her wrists and forearms are already bound together with an elastic bandage. She eyes the room with wide eyes, then stares at me in appeal.

Sometimes I'm asked if I feel sorry for kids in this situation, especially when they look at me like Bambi eyeing the wolf. My answer is: of course: I'm human, too. But the Law must take its course; the only way I am legally able to show compassion is to make the punishment as efficient and quick as circumstances allow. There's no sense in adopting a "kind" persona—that would only confuse the culprit and possibly undermine the psychological effect of the punishment. A calm, neutral manner is always best: it steadies the nerves of all involved. Afterwards, of course, it's a different matter; then one can be as kind as one wishes (or as the late culprit deserves).

"Efficient and quick" means getting on with things, though without overt rush. I nod to the escort and the girl is marched to the frame. In confusion, she starts to bend across the padded bar but Corporal Donohue holds her upright while the kneeling Tess Dean wraps another elastic bandage around the knees, taking every other turn around the central post. She stands up, and then the girl is bent forwards. Tess goes to the front of the frame and secures the wrists to the ring, pulling the cord moderately tight. With a gasp the girl stoops even lower. She is now bent into a hairpin shape across the bar, her abdomen supported by thick plastic-coated padding, her thighs resting against the similarly cushioned centre post, her wrists fastened to the base. Tess takes off the brake lever and the entire apparatus rotates forward twelve degrees—there is another gasp at this point—until the imaginary line we call "Ground Zero" is uppermost. The girl's head and knees are now at the same level. Tess puts on the brake.

Corporal Donohue has already tied her hair back and removed her uniform jacket; she is holding the strap in both hands, flexing it thoughtfully, keeping well back out of the way. At my signal, Tess grasps the hem of the brown smock and lifts it all the way up the girl's back, where a press stud attaches it to a canvas yoke sewn into the shoulder-blades. Without haste, she inserts a thumb in each side of the waist-elastic of the brown calico pants, and draws this garment smoothly down as far as the knees (it can descend no further due to the ties). There is a muffled wail from ground level.

I touch the switch that activates the cameras, and glance at the repeating monitor, paging rapidly through all the views—left elevation, right elevation, top-down, and face close-up (from a lens mounted obliquely in the floor at the foot of the "donkey"). The titles come up—the culprit's name, the offence, the date, the time, the instrument, the number of strokes awarded, the name of the punishing officer, and—still blank—the number of strokes administered.

I speak: "You will receive nineteen strokes of the strap. They will be administered at approximately eight-second intervals. You may make as much noise as you wish, though if you are abusive you may receive extra punishment at my discretion." (Small chance in this case!) "The punishment will now begin. Corporal, do your duty!"

You've probably seen strappings on Channel 99. There's a right way and a wrong way: the right way is for the punishing officer to hold the strap at both ends, while standing one pace back from her "mark". She then takes a stride forwards with her left foot (right foot for southpaws), at the same time releasing the tip of the strap with her left hand and swinging it back and up with her right—an ascent of 35–40 degrees is considered ideal—then, as the weight comes on to the front foot, bringing the weapon round and through in a wide, slightly descending arc. If all has been calculated correctly—the positioning of the "mark" is of great importance—the last ten inches or so of the blade arrive simultaneously across the width of the cheeks with a sharp smack, printing, for an instant, a perfect, rectangular flush across the seat. This flush fades rapidly, but should still be evident when the second stroke arrives. Gradually it seems permanently painted, as it were; the target area—between Ground Zero and the upper thigh—becoming an even, and ever-deeper, shade of rose, then scarlet, and finally purple if it has been an unusually severe strapping.

Corporal Donohue lives well up to expectation. As is so often the case with girls in our Department, Liz is unusually tall, with a long reach and a lusty swing. And the eye of the excellent tennis-player I have heard her to be. The forearm that applies the "swip", again and again, with such accuracy, has no doubt volleyed many hopeful services away into unreachable corners. It is plain the instrument suits her—it is equally plain it does not suit the culprit, who, almost from the first, sets up a continuous, wailing screech. I glance at the monitor. The close-up shows a wide-open mouth, a waving tongue, and tight-shut eyes from which tears roll. I sigh—when she sees the recording she'll wish she'd made less fuss. But the judicial strap takes many bad girls by surprise.

It's not my practice to remit strokes unless circumstances are exceptional, and there is no justification for doing so on this occasion. I let it go through to the end. Then the knickers are drawn decently up to hide the scarlet bottom, the skirt unhooked and pulled down to conceal the knickers, the frame rotated back to the upright position, the wrists and knees unfastened, and—— stands in our midst, howling, her skirt clutched to her backside with both hands. I say: "The punishment is over" (as I'm legally obliged to do, though I don't think she hears me) and then she's bundled out of the door and back to her cell. She'll be taken home later with the others, so she has about half an hour to pull herself together.

I say: "You may as well carry on now you've got your eye in, Corporal Dean", and I give orders for the second girl, the bold, bad 24-year-old with gypsy looks and snake eyes, to be brought in. I say, casually, to Liz: "Twenty-five this time. Attitude problem, I'd say, so give it a bit extra. Just a bit."

"Yes, ma'am," says Liz, nostrils flaring.

But twenty minutes of waiting—and the recent sounds of distress, have done much to undermine ——'s silent arrogance. She looks scared as they bring her in: she has dressed, or been dressed, in the proper manner. She opens her mouth to speak; but although she's now apparently in the mood for conversation, I'm not. Within half a minute she's kissing the donkey like her predecessor, knickers round her knees, and the camera LEDs are red and glowing.

Although Liz Donohue obviously does her best to follow my unofficial instructions—the instrument swishes loudly in the descent and cracks wickedly on impact—this culprit makes a much more successful effort to hold herself in. She only starts to squeal about the fifteenth, and although by the twenty-fifth and last she is roaring as ear-splittingly as her forerunner, I never yet knew a female of any age who could take more than a score with the strap without "singing" at high volume. (Though I once knew a 17-year-old male get through 30 strokes in perfect silence, which only proves that he should have been caned instead—like everybody else, I have made mistakes from time to time.)

But now it's the turn of the boys. The straps are put away. The cane's turn has come.

I select the nearest of the two matt-black ferrules and swish it through the air. I take the tip in my left hand and test the flex. I swish it again. Then I lay it down and select the other. In fact, I could detect nothing wrong with the first cane but it's as well, now and again, to assume a mantle of perfectionism.

The first boy—the scared one—is brought in, wearing only his underpants, as per regulation for males. He blinks at the cane, and drops his gaze in obvious shame when he sees the three women waiting to chastise him. He makes no fuss, obediently walking forwards to the "donkey" and waiting submissively while Liz adjusts the height of the bar and Tess fastens his knees to the centrepost. Then he takes a deep breath and bends forward.

"Lower!" says Tess, in a sharp tone. He bends lower. "Lower!" she says again. "I can't!" he whispers, but all the same he manages that extra inch. His wrists are fastened to the ring and the cinch jerked tight.

Twenty years, twenty-one strokes. I say the necessary short phrases, and then Tess peels down the white underwear, exposing the slim, male hindquarters. They are pale and pink, like a little boy's. But not for long. I take aim, pause, and whip the cane straight into Ground Zero. Thwup. Liz blinks, the boy says: "Oooh!", and Tess says "One!". I prepare the second stroke. I administer it. Thwup. It makes a thick red stripe precisely one-inch below the first. Perfect aim. A squeal from the culprit, and Tess says "Two!" in a choking voice.

I steal a quick glance at her while I allow the prescribed seconds to tick by. She is staring at the target, rapt, eyes wide, a faint smile on her lips. During the strapping she was calm and collected. There is, I decide, more to learn about Tess Dean. Then it is time, and I step forward and whip the black cane across the crease between thigh and lower buttock. Thwup. This time the boy howls. Tess says "Three!", and...

And so it goes on. You must have been caned yourself at least once in your life, or seen somebody else caned, or watched judicial canings on Channel 99. You know how they are: the remorseless rhythm, the swishes and percussions, the steady accumulation of deep-red bars across the presented stern, the steadily increasing volume and pitch of the responses.

Mind you, I don't say that 21 strokes of the cane isn't a sharp punishment—it is. The cane is considered the severest of all instruments in physical effect. All the same one has a certain latitude. I am using about 70 percent of my strength on this occasion but might go up to 95 percent (though perfect control at this level of output is difficult to achieve) and of course the choice of cane is up to me, provided I remain within the legally defined "envelope". The cane is not judicially used on pre-pubescents, nor (usually) on girls, and there are strict rules—based on age, gravity of offence and medical assessment—governing the physical characteristic of the instrument and the maximum number of strokes that may be administered with it. But that still leaves room to manœuvre. Because of his obvious repentance, this boy is not getting it as badly as he might, though he's not to be blamed for failing to realise it. A "blackjack" is still more than anything he would have got at school; and when I finish his bottom is black, blue and scarlet and he's sobbing like an infant. That's as it should be.

As he's released and put back into a condition of decency, I talk to him quietly for a few seconds, commending his attitude, and telling him the marks will be gone inside a fortnight—as they will, if I'm any judge of bottoms. Then he's gone; and a minute later the last of the Night Patrol's "bag" is being rotated into position.

I'm well attuned to Culprit Attitude and it seems to me that despite this one's partial repentance some work remains to be done. He has four strokes more to come than his friend, but in this case I decide that this does not represent a sufficient differential. I have the choice of selecting a slightly heavier cane, or of using more strength. I choose the latter course.

This one does not only howl and sob—he pleads. It upsets everyone when a culprit begs to be let off: they must know it can't happen so why do they do it? It argues a fundamental misunderstanding of the nature of the proceedings; a persisting capacity for self-delusion. It's unintelligent, and craven. We expect howls. We are used to sobbing, and copious tears of repentance. We are not unfamiliar with (though we intensely dislike) involuntary loss of bladder control (and I have to say that is this respect girls are worse than boys). We take all of these phenomena in our stride—but, to a woman, we find abjectness creepy and unsympathetic. A blend of submissiveness and courage is the best way to gain our respect—and yes, I do mean "respect", since there can often develop a healer-healed relationship between punisher and culprit not at all unlike that between surgeon and patient; those times when we know beyond doubt that we are doing valuable, ethical work for the Community.

For now, I have to take it on trust. I cane the coward as hard as I think necessary: so, entirely because of his personality defects, he receives a punishment much more severe, though only slightly more protracted, than his predecessor's. He marks more easily, too; these welts will take three weeks to vanish, and for at least three days he's going to be in acute discomfort. That, too, is as it should be. But I have a feeling, all the same—call it my professional nose—that we're going to see this one back on the frame one of these days. What he really needs is a residential course, and maybe it would have been better if he'd taken the court hearing option after all... but one can't be right every time.

When I get back to the office it is twelve-fifteen and Janine is waiting with some impatience to brief me on the Workplace Referral who, she informs me, has already arrived and is waiting in reception. I examine the file while she talks. I have already mentioned that this is an unusual case: the culprit in question is neither male nor juvenile, but an unmarried woman of 35; a person of status in Society by virtue of gender and age-group. She has, apparently, been repeatedly lazy and slipshod in the discharge of her workplace duties, and has been referred to us for private correction by her Personnel Manageress.

Reading the file, and half-listening to Janine, something nags at my mind; then it clicks into place and I say: "Put her up on the monitor, will you, Jan?" A moment later I am looking at a plump blonde sitting quietly and composedly: she is smartly dressed in the ankle-length skirts of the Unmarried Female, and she wears expensive jewellery. Then something attracts her attention to the waiting-room camera—its LED perhaps—and she looks up. That's all I need. I ask Janine to kill the display and sit down at my desk.

"Let's have that file again," I say, and Janine slides it across. I study it with a fresh eye. Just as I thought!

"Babette," I say, half to myself.

"Who?"

"We used to call her Babette."

"Her name is Macaulay. Simona Macaulay, of..."

"I know" I explain, "'Babette' was our nickname for her."

"You know her?" asks Janine, surprised.

"You might say that. At my last place, when I was ACD, she used to put in an appearance about twice a year. Once it was a Mother's Referral. Twice it was a Workplace Referral, like today. One day Ariadne got suspicious. She checked her out. Her mother had been dead for twelve years and she lived on a private income."

Janine stares. "Then why—"

"Well, it's obvious, isn't it? She gets a charge out of being disciplined. But as there's no-one legally entitled to discipline her, she invents reasons and Referrals in order to collect a tanning from the Department. She must have moved to this district."

"Oh," says Janine, feebly. "I didn't know..."

"How could you? We assume that a lady of her status would only submit to judicial correction if the law compelled her. But some people are different."

"It's supposed to be a punishment!" says Janine.

"For most people, it is. For others, it's simply something they need. Or want. If it's a man, all he has to do is offend his wife or his Mistress, and over he goes. Same for female juveniles. But for adult females with no legal superior, it's very difficult indeed."

"I never heard of such a thing," says Janine.

"No? Well, you have now. Tell you what, just

call up the supposed Personnel Manageress at the company and find out her name."

Janine makes the call—it takes about a minute—then says, wonderingly: "The Personnel Manageress is Miss Simona Macaulay."

"What I expected."

"She's referred herself!"

"No reason why she shouldn't, in theory," I say, chuckling at human ingenuity. "And anyway, I'm not even sure it's illegal."

"Why do you call her 'Babette'?" asks Janine.

"Because what she likes, really likes, is to be treated as a little girl—a very little girl—and smacked over the knee. Very hard. And scolded at the same time, as if she was about seven years old. The last time Ariadne gave her about two hundred of the best. It took the best part of an hour and Ariadne couldn't use her hand for about a week afterwards."

"What are you going to do?"

"Me? I'm not going to do anything. I've got those birchings this afternoon, remember, and I don't want to tire myself. You can do it, if you like; or Corporal Donohue. No—I've a better idea. We'll let Myra Kelly have a go. She's built like a horse—she'll give Babette something to remember. Give her a call."

"I don't mind doing it," says Janine. "I need the experience. Though it's going to feel strange smacking a woman nearly ten years older than myself."

"It won't feel strange for long. Ariadne said the same thing, the first time, but afterwards she said that within a minute or so she really did feel as if she was spanking a seven-year-old—apart from the number of the smacks, of course. I think she quite enjoyed it."

"It's very unusual," muses Janine.

"Not as unusual as you think," I say.

Then the phone bleeps. It's Margot Jaffee at Lawrence House. This afternoon's birchings have been cancelled.

I ask why.

"German Measles," says Jaffee, cheerfully. "One of the culprits was diagnosed an hour ago. So we're all in quarantine for ten days."

"Has Judith let them off, then?" I ask incredulously.

"Oh, no! The remaining four are going to be caned instead. We're going to have a Madrigal."

"I see. Well, give Judith my regards and tell her I'm sorry not to be seeing her again this afternoon."

"I'll do that," says the Jaffee woman. Then: "Might I ask you something? It's only because I'm new here, and I don't like to… you know."

"Ask away," I say, shortly. It's hard not to feel disappointed at times like these.

"What exactly *is* a Madrigal? What happens?"

"Four trestles are arranged in a hollow square. One culprit is tied down across each trestle, heads inwards, backside out. You need four thrashers, one to each culprit."

"We've had nine volunteers from the staff," says Margot Jaffee.

"I bet you have," I say, drily. "Well, each of your girls will be issued with a standard compound cane, all your inmates will be marched in to form a larger square surrounding the trestles, and at the word of command the thrashers all thrash at once, at their own speed."

"But why is it called a Madrigal?" she asks.

"A Madrigal is an old-fashioned type of singing. Four-part harmony."

"Oh!" says Jaffee. Then: "What a witty expression!"

"Yes, isn't it?" I reply, and after a few more platitudes, ring off. By now I am in a foul temper—I'd been denying myself all morning, in expectation of the exercise to come… and now it isn't happening.

But I'm not the boss for nothing.

Five minutes later Babette and I are in the Punishment Room, she's face down across my lap, and I'm rolling back her skirts and petticoats.

"What a *bad*, *naughty*, *wicked* little girl!" I say reprovingly and tautologically. "Have you anything to say for yourself? I thought not. Well, I'm going to take your knickers down, right down to your *knees*, and I'm going to smack you very hard on your *bare bottom*. There! I hope you feel properly ashamed, you idle little minx! Now—head down and keep still!"

So Babette gets what she wants, and I get what I want, and the day hasn't been so bad after all.

It's a pleasant thing, to know you're serving the Community. *

REFERENCES

IN OLDEN TIMES

1. Lord Drialys: *The Beautiful Flagellants of New York* (1900)
2. Justin of Padua, writing in *Chronicon Ursitius Basiliensis* (13th century) and quoted in William M. Cooper's *A History of the Rod* (1885).
3. Antonia Forrest: *The Player's Boy*
4. Algernon Swinburne: *Laugh and Lie Down*
5. Aubrey Fowkes: *A Youth of Fourteen*

Poems:

Sir Ingoldsby's Penance (p. 4) from *The Ingoldsby Legends*
The Schoolmistress (p. 5) by William Shenstone

THE EIGHTEENTH CENTURY

1. *History of the Rod*
2. Crebillon LeFils: *A Lady of Quality* (Brandon House)
3. Ibid.
4. *History of the Rod*
5. From *Experiences of Flagellation*, privately printed 1885.
6. Nominally from Aubrey Beardsley's *Venus & Tannhauser*. In fact the quoted passage is a pastiche, added in the 1960s by John Glassco.

Poems:

The Birch Tree (p. 10). From "The Rod", a poem in three cantos, by Henry Layng, quoted in *A History of the Rod.*
Enigma (p. 11). Also possibly by Henry Layng, quoted in *A History of the Rod*
Another Birch Tree (p. 14). Written by "a youth of thirteen" and also quoted in *A History of the Rod*

THE NINETEENTH CENTURY

1. *Experiences of Flagellation*
2. Jacqueline Ophir: *The Fellowship of the Rod*
3. *Venus School-Mistress.* A collection of short stories, playlets, poems, letters and anecdotes on the subject of flagellation, dating from about 1790 in places and probably published for the first time in 1837 by George Cannon, who also wrote the Preface. The original edition was stolen from the British Museum in 1964.
4. Original source unknown.
5. Captain Marryat: *Percival Keene*
6. "Miss Coote's Confession", *The Pearl*, c. 1880
7. Wilhelm Reinhard: *Nell in Bridewell* (Lenchen in Zuchthause)
8. Testament by "Florrie", the most famous flagellomane patient of the British psychologist Henry Havelock Ellis.
9. *East Dene.*
10. Letter to *The Englishwoman's Domestic Magazine* (c. 1866)
11. Letter to *Society* (c. 1890)
12. A. de Grassal: *The Memoirs of Dolly Morton*
13. *The Romance of Chastisement*
14. Margaret Anson: *Personal Recollections of the Use of the Rod.*
15. The Whippingham Papers (Wordsworth)
16. Letter to *EDM.*
17. *Personal Recollections of the Use of the Rod*
18. *The Callipyges* (recently republished under the appalling title *The Cult of Pain*)
19. Louisa May Alcott: *Little Women*
20. Letter to *Town Talk*

21. *The Autobiography of Mark Twain*
22. Aubrey Fowkes: *More Butterfly Days*
23. Algernon Swinburne: *Lesbia Brandon*
24. *The Romance of Lust.*
25. Original source unknown
26. Letter to *EDM.*
27. Leonard Mosley: *Curzon.* A biography of the last Viceroy of India, famous for the well-known passage concerning the cruel governess Miss Paraman.
28. *Nell in Bridewell*
29. Leopold von Sacher-Masoch: *Venus in Furs*
30. St. George H. Stock: *The Romance of Chastisement.*
31. Letter to *EDM*
32. *The Beautiful Flagellants of New York*
33. Letter to *EDM*
34. Ibid.
35. The Beautiful Flagellants of New York
36. A. De Grassal: *"Frank" and I*
37. Letter to *EDM*
38. Edith Cadiveç: *Confessions and Experiences.* Frau Cadivec was a Viennese teacher convicted of child abuse in 1924. The two volumes of her autobiography were published in 1930 under a medical imprint.
39. Edith Cadivec: *Eros: The Meaning of My Life.* The writer of this passage is Frau Cadivec's friend and correspondent, Senta—.
40. Letter to *EDM.*
41. *The Petticoat Dominant.* An earlier (and lesser) work by the author of *Gynæcocracy*
42. See n. 39.
43. Letter to *Society*
44. *Gynæcocracy*
45. *"Frank" and I*
46. Frances Hodgson Burnett: *A Woman's Will.* Mrs Burnett was also the author of the children's classic *The Secret Garden.*
47. Aimée van Rod: *La Gouvernante.*
48. Letter to *Society*
49. Ibid.
50. Ibid.
51. *The Beautiful Flagellants of New York*

Poems:

Lydia's Woe (p. 22). An ode to Miss L—y W—n, on finding her in tears after a maternal whipping. Quoted in *A History of the Rod.*

Squire Hardman (pp. 23–73 passim). In the style of *The Rodiad* and attributed, like that poem, to George Colman the Younger. In fact poor Colman wrote neither poem. *Squire Hardman*, a monstrous and yet blackly humorous epic, is another example of the skills as a pasticheur of the Canadian John Glassco, and was probably written in the early 1960s.

A Polemic on the Birch (p. 24). A parody on Sappho's Ode, by Miss C—, a girl of eight years, quoted in *A History of the Rod.*

The Stepmother (p. 28). From *Madam Birchini's Dance.*

Betsy Fry (p. 34). From a longer poem called "The Terrors of the Rod", privately printed in 1815 by Francis Newberry, a friend of Dr., Johnson and Goldsmith's publisher. Quoted in *A History of the Rod.*

Miss Abrahams (p. 36). From *Venus School-Mistress.*

A Demon Schoolmaster (p. 40). All we could bear to reproduce from *The Rodiad*, an epic allegedly by George Colman the Younger but almost certainly by "Pisanus Fraxi", a mid-Victorian flagellomane publisher.

THE TWENTIETH CENTURY

1. Jacqueline Ophir: *The House in St. John's Wood*
2. D. H. Lawrence: *The Rainbow*
3. Clare Sheridan: *Nuda Veritas.*
4. Letter printed in *Monsieur Paulette* (Jacques D'Icy). French novels of the period (1900-1930) often included "readers' letters", partly to fill out the pages, but also because in France at the time there were no equivalents of *Town Talk* or *Bits of Fun* (or *London Life*) in which "fetishistic" subjects might be broached.
5. *Sweet Sixteen: A Romance of Family Discipline*
6. Jacques D'Icy: *Paulette Trahiée* (a. k. a *Paulette's Film*)
7. Elizabeth Starling: *Victoria Dunlap*
8. *Paulette Trahiée*
9. *Sweet Sixteen*
10. Theodora von Prittwitz: *Der Rude in Knabesheim*
11. Miles Underwood: *Harriet Marwood, Governess.* This famous novel (actually written by the prolific John Glassco), has had several incarnations and several titles, including *Under the Birch* and *The English Governess.*
12. Verily Anderson: *Daughters of Divinity.*
13. Marquise de Mannoury D'Ectot: *The Two Sisters.*